EVERYMAN, I will go with thee.

and be thy guide,

In thy most need to go by thy side

HERBERT OF CHERBURY

Edward Lord Herbert of Cherbury was born at Eyton-on-Severn in 1583. English Ambassador in Paris. Died in 1648.

THOMAS CAREW

Born c. 1594. Travelled on embassies to Italy and France. King's Server and Gentleman of the Privy Chamber. Died in 1640.

SIR JOHN SUCKLING

Born in 1609 at Whitton, Middlesex. Died by his own hand in Paris in 1642.

RICHARD LOVELACE

Born in 1618 at Woolwich, Kent. Imprisoned as a Royalist. Died in 1657.

Minor Poets of the Seventeenth Century

EDITED BY

R. G. HOWARTH, B.A., B.LITT., F.R.S.L.
Professor of English Literature in the University of Cape Town

DENT: LONDON
EVERYMAN'S LIBRARY
DUTTON: NEW YORK

No. 873   Hardback ISBN 0 460 00873 0
No. 1873   Paperback ISBN 0 460 01873 6

INTRODUCTION

I

THE poets of the seventeenth century, excluding Milton, may be broadly divided into three groups: those who cling to the ideals of a past age, those who are influenced by modern, revolutionary example, and those who look forward to the poetry of the future. They are the Spenserians, the followers of Jonson and Donne, and the "transitional" or early Augustan poets. Of the first class the chief representatives are Giles and Phineas Fletcher, William Browne, and George Wither. The second group may be subdivided into Cavalier lyrists and sacred poets, the former holding mainly from Jonson, the latter deriving from Donne. Herrick, Carew, Suckling, and Lovelace are the best-known Cavaliers, and George Herbert, Vaughan, Crashaw, and Traherne the leading divine poets. Among the first consistent users of the heroic couplet, the writers of "smooth" verse, Waller must be counted foremost, with Cowley, Denham, and D'Avenant as the other prominent members of his group. One class does not necessarily exclude another, but the divisions are at least historical, and form a better means of distinguishing the poets than by reckoning all, or almost all, as "Metaphysicals." The truth is that the term "metaphysical" does not sufficiently and finally characterize the poets of the time: the metaphysical style, established if not introduced by Donne, is more a potent influence, to which most in varying degrees succumb, than the entire guiding principle and source of their art.

Plainly, the distinctive character of the century in poetry must be looked for in the work of the second group, who are neither retrospective nor futurist. Here it is possible to see the religious poetry and the courtly poetry of love as merely two sides of the same poetical nature. For the two strains are not sharply divided: they intermingle, or alternately hold sway, in the same man and the same volume. One half of Donne's poetry is expression of the love of woman, the other of the love of God. Ben Jonson, whose best lyrics are of love, is also the author of a series of divine poems. Herrick,

Carew, Waller, Herbert of Cherbury, Habington, and John Hall again pay their dues to the two compelling powers. Then among the devotional poems of Crashaw, Vaughan, and Herbert are to be found lyrics of love. Yet there was more than mere interweaving. Love poetry and poetry of religion sprang often from a common basis of inspiration. Thus from The Song of Solomon is derived not only the imagery of one of Carew's most voluptuous poems, *The Complement*, but also that of one of Vaughan's most sublime religious lyrics, *The Night*. Donne's questings in love are powerfully illuminated by reference to the divine learning of his time. In the Platonism which runs through English poetry from Spenser to Henry More this harmonizing of apparently different elements, the reconciliation of religion and earthly love, is supremely accomplished.

This presents the reason for regarding the Cavaliers as the key to their age. Their poetry of religion ranges through all the possible moods without settling down to the glorification of some particular object; their poetry of love moves from cynicism and licentiousness at the one extreme to abstract devotion and worship of pure beauty at the other. They are characteristic, too, in that they reflect the Puritan movement, to which they were naturally hostile, no less than the temper of cultured society at Court. As direct products of social conditions they are the index to the outlook and aspirations of their time.

The circumstances under which poetry was composed necessarily gave it a complimentary turn. The Court, not the people, was the patron of literature. The drama had long rested on popular support, but in the reign of Charles I it followed the lead of poetry and began to look more to the Court for its inspiration and life, with the result that the people at last united to stamp it out. No such fate attended poetry, because, though frequently very gross, it had never provoked Puritan notice to quite the same degree. But the dependence upon the King, the nobles, and a small circle of educated and wealthy men made compliment a condition of existence. At no time in the whole history of English literature has verse been so deliberately and skilfully applied to occasional purposes. Births and marriages had to be celebrated, deaths to be mourned, according to well-defined conventions; extraordinary state or personal events were expected to be glorified. Here it was that the poet obtained his pecuniary reward, and

not from the sale of his published work. Elizabethan pre-
judice had made it difficult for a gentleman to publish, and a
taint still attached to professionalism in letters. Publication,
therefore, was almost always under cover of a fiction or with
an apology, the circulation and preservation of pieces being
usually accomplished by manuscript. The poems, sent in
compliment, or exchanged in rivalry, or written and passed
around merely for amusement, were collected on all sides into
commonplace books; and the remarkable numbers of these
private anthologies which still exist bear witness to the part
which poetry played in contemporary life.

This complimentary and by nature esoteric condition of
poetry exactly fitted the temper of a Carew, a Waller, a
Herrick. Poets like Waller and Carew are almost systematic
in celebration. To others the obligation gives a flavour of
reality, a valuable link with the life around them. Yet from
the inevitable prosaic or conventional restrictions of their
themes all can escape, in a manner that is often at once
ingenious and sublime.

II

Edward Lord Herbert of Cherbury, who was born in 1583
and died in 1648, is part Elizabethan, part Cavalier; and this
is suggestive of a complex and not wholly consistent nature.
Amongst his posthumously published verses are to be found
sonnets, madrigals, and satires which are distinctly in the
Elizabethan manner, mingled with philosophical inquiries,
meditations upon death, echo-poems, and lyrics of love which
bear the impress of a later generation. The loftiness and
rarity of his mind create a sheer intellectual poetry, which,
whilst it has affinities in art with that of Herrick and Carew,
in its essential content links backward with the *Amoretti* and
Four Hymns of Spenser and forward with much of the poetry
of Rossetti.

Herbert was early a student, but growing desirous of seeing
the world he set out for Paris in 1608, and until 1619, when he
was appointed ambassador there, spent much of his time
travelling, soldiering, and learning fashionable accomplish-
ments. Of his life until 1624 we possess an interesting if
not always accurate record in the *Autobiography*. He finally
returned to England in 1624, and was raised to the peerage;

after which his public career ended, and he devoted himself to philosophy, history, and poetry. In the Civil War troubles he sought the middle course, and spent his last years in illness and as a pensioner of the Parliament.

Until very recently Herbert's poetry remained almost unknown, but with fresh editions the claim was made for him that "in poetic feeling and art he outsoars his brother George." Comparison is difficult, and perhaps unnecessary, for at any rate he will never be received in popular estimation as a finer than the poet of *The Temple*. Yet the claim is not so arbitrary as a first reading of Lord Herbert's poems might seem to suggest. The comparative obscurity and roughness of his diction in some pieces, the difficulty of his syntax, are real obstacles to the understanding of a peculiarly interesting mind, from the workings of which spring his poems. Herbert is deeply conscious of the fallibility of the body and of the possibilities of knowledge through the soul:

> Our life is but a dark and stormy night,
> To which sense yields a weak and glimmering light.

Therefore, with a fine gesture, he is able to say to the emissaries of Death:

> Willing to you this carcase I submit,
> A gift so free I do not care for it.

As a human being the poet claims that he does not

> live and move
> By outward sense so much as faith and love,

which together will wing him to that place

> Where faithful loving souls with joys are crown'd.

Yet his power to see into the heart and composition of things, his continual probing into the mysteries of existence, is equally responsible for the conviction that death brings the soul "to its desired place"; that its character is "open and eternal peace," "freedom and rest."

Herbert's thinking on love is coloured by the same transcendental beliefs: beauty in its quintessence is imperishable; love that is spiritual is capable of eternal endurance:

> We will possess
> A love must live when we do die.

For exalted love

> Will to that union come, as but one voice
> Shall speak, one thought but think the other's will;

which must

> Transform and fix them to one star at last.

His preoccupation with these high and moving subjects prevents the too frequent resolution of Herbert's poetry into mere argumentation, into detached pieces of intellectual research. He feels his thought to a degree which only Donne could exceed, and it is this basis of deep feeling which imparts such sustained harmony and beauty of form to the finest of his poems. With a sure instinct did Tennyson choose one of Herbert's most beautiful metres for his not dissimilar thinking on love and death in *In Memoriam*.

Herbert, who turned away from sense, makes little of the sensuous appeal of poetry. Radiance, colour, and their absence, have more value for him than more intimate beauty and form. His poetry, indeed, depends so little upon the things of earth that we are apt to note their absence and to find the atmosphere a little too rarefied. Yet the strangeness of this ethereal region at times gives an indefinable thrill. We feel, in the *Ode upon a Question moved, Whether Love should continue for ever*, in the *Elegy over a Tomb*, or even in the powerful though rugged *To his Mistress for her true Picture*, that in common with the poet we are quaffing "large draughts of intellectual day."

The earthy, as opposed to the philosophical and noble-minded, is seen in the brilliantly polished verses of Herbert's friend Thomas Carew, who employed himself with terrestrial beauty and became "The Oracle of Love." Yet even in Carew, the typical courtier poet of the century, and, after the departure of Herrick to Devonshire in 1629, the leader of the Cavaliers, there is a strain of deeper feeling, the sense of hidden and eternal things which haunts other poets. Amid the elaborate and richly tinted mosaic of his poems this sober stone is easily overlooked. As he grows older, it actually commences to predominate in the general pattern.

From his poems, and from the fragments that we possess of his life, there is every indication that Carew was a selfish voluptuary:

> with delight
> I feast my Epicurean appetite
> With relishes so curious, as dispense
> The utmost pleasure to the ravish'd sense.

His friend Paman deplored his lack of "charity." And quite
candidly he admits insensibility:

> I, that ne'er more of private sorrow knew
> Than from my pen some froward mistress drew,
> And for the public woe had my dull sense
> So sear'd with ever-adverse influence,
> As the invader's sword might have, unfelt,
> Pierc'd my dead bosom. . . .

Carew certainly cost his old father Sir Matthew many a sigh
over his failure to settle into any profession. He spent the
years 1613 to 1616 as secretary to Sir Dudley Carleton at
Florence and The Hague, and in 1619 went abroad again in
the train of Lord Herbert of Cherbury. Finally, when at the
conclusion of his travels—and also, it seems, of the one love
affair which touched him at all nearly—he becomes server
to the King and a great wit of the Court, he finds his true
medium in dealing out with the one hand discreetly moral
compliments to chastity and the Queen, with the other riotous
"Persuasions to Love." But there is a growing alienation
of mind from the mere physical and lawless. Towards the
close of a life which was clouded and shortened by illness,
this better feeling comes out in his poetry; and the tradition
that the paraphrases of psalms which pass under his name
were made by him in his last illness has in it nothing
improbable. His

> lyric feet, that of the smooth soft way
> Of love and beauty only know the tread,

in 1632, somehow follow the path which leads in 1638 to a
sincere public avowal of changed endeavour and belief, when
of his unpurified Muse he says:

> Who knows but that her wand'ring eyes, that run
> Now hunting glow-worms, may adore the sun?
> A pure flame may, shot by Almighty Power
> Into my breast, the earthy flame devour;
> My eyes in penitential dew may steep
> That brine which they for sensual love did weep . . .
> Perhaps my restless soul, tir'd with pursuit
> Of mortal beauty, seeking without fruit
> Contentment there, which hath not, when enjoy'd,
> Quench'd all her thirst, nor satisfi'd, though cloy'd,
> Weary of her vain search below, above
> In the first fair may find th' immortal love.

This is indeed a confession from the author of *A Rapture* and

The Second Rapture, a remarkable alteration in the man who could write earlier, in a kind of savage cynicism:

> Give me a wench about thirteen,
> Already voted to the queen
> Of lust and lovers . . .
> . . . in whose sweet embraces I
> May melt myself to lust, and die.
> This is true bliss, and I confess
> There is no other happiness.

"Silence, and stealth of days" in illness may have helped the moral revolution. Even the choice of psalms is significant, and in one of them there is an indication of the poet's state of mind. The reference to health in the verse,

> Send me Thy saving health again,
> And with Thy Spirit those joys maintain,

does not appear in the original.

Yet it was not altogether the fear of death that made the difference in Carew. Some of his earlier compliments to chastity may have been sincere, and certain it is that we find the note of

> the rude male satisfi'd
> With one fair female by his side

recurring in later poems like *A Married Woman* and *Love's Force*. The conviction that marriage is human perfection returns upon him; and it may not be too fanciful to discern in the poem *To Celia, upon Love's Ubiquity* his own experience in sickness, the recurrence of his thoughts to the real Celia who was the central image in his heart, and to the events which led to his deposition from love.

Carew as a poet suffers from misunderstanding and superficial treatment. Enough has been said to show that, whatever the themes of his verses, he was not wholly "an elegant Court trifler," a mere glorifier of the trivial. Poetry to Carew was a serious occupation:

> his Muse was hard-bound, and th' issue of 's brain
> Was seldom brought forth but with trouble and pain,

in Suckling's words: yet in Carew there was not so much personal difficulty as literary pride:

> Repine not at the taper's thrifty waste,
> That sleeks thy terser poems; nor is haste
> Praise, but excuse.

Carew is a man of solid intellectual powers, a literary critic of remarkable penetration, a moral theorist occupied with the problem of the imposition of abstract sanctions and restraints upon human conduct:

> By what power was love confin'd
> To one object?

Finally he is an artist of a masculine strength and reach. In his poetry sound and structure combine with a beautiful concrete imagery to produce wonderful effects.

Essentially different is the attitude to his art of that happy-go-lucky Cavalier, "natural, easy" Sir John Suckling, who

> lov'd not the Muses so well as his sport;
> And priz'd black eyes, or a lucky hit
> At bowls, above all the trophies of wit.

Endowed with an ear for music and with a jesting spirit, he runs a jingle of ridicule through the more earnest and some-times solemnly ludicrous poetry of the time. Naturally he cannot contain himself enough to write the adulations and panegyrics which were customary. A disagreeable person in some respects he may have been, but he won the hearts of many, and was long remembered with Lovelace as a type of the Cavalier. He was born in 1609, and after returning in 1632 from travel, lived a life of dissipation and gallantry at Court. In the first Scottish war of 1639 he made an extra-vagant attempt to aid the King by leading into the field a hundred beautifully tailored horsemen, who were uncere-moniously put to rout, thereby earning their leader much ridicule. But this folly he redeemed by a more serious effort on behalf of the King in the Army Plot of 1641; on the failure of which he fled to France and died a suicide in the following year.

The Suckling we tend to remember is the gay libertine whose characteristic utterances are such as: "Never believe me if I love!" "I am confirm'd a woman can Love this, or that, or any other man," "There never yet was woman made, Nor shall, but to be curs'd," "The devil take her!" "Fie upon hearts that burn with mutual fire!" The Suckling we are apt to forget is the more thoughtful, if never profound, poet who could write such lines as these:

> I hold that perfect joy makes all our parts
> As joyful as our hearts.
> Our senses tell us, if we please not them,
> Our love is but a dotage or a dream;

the defender and praiser of womankind, as in *Detraction
Execrated, Non est Mortale quod Opto*, and *Love's Representation*.
His easy cynicism in matters of the heart is not all pose, but
it is occasionally broken down. There are, too, snatches of
beauty in his poetry that almost atone for the worst efforts
in mockery:

> No, no, fair heretic, it needs must be
> But an ill love in me . . .

As an offset to the more cynical poems, however, the delightful
Ballad upon a Wedding is not likely to be forgotten. There
is in fact beneath Suckling's careless and mocking exterior
much sound sense and true feeling, which occasionally he
makes no attempt to disguise. Besides this, most of his
poems give a pleasure which is due to the absence of com-
plexity, of needless obscurity; and the ability to laugh at
himself and the world constitutes one of his most refreshing
qualities.

The keen sense of humour possessed by Suckling, and
more or less defective in Herbert of Cherbury and Carew,
is altogether lacking in Richard Lovelace. Humour he has,
of a rough-and-ready schoolboy sort, but he seems never to
have realized what bathos lay in some of his lines. Here is
the cow which offered a "breakfast on her teat" to Aramantha:

> Out of the yeomanry o' th' herd,
> With grave aspect, and feet prepar'd,
> A rev'rend lady cow draws near,
> Bids Aramantha welcome here;
> And from her privy purse lets fall
> A pearl or two, which seem to call
> This adorn'd, adored fairy
> To the banquet of her dairy.

Lovelace has almost a flair for the unfit epithet, and takes
a childish pleasure in the recurrence of the same combination
of sounds:

> Unplanted had this plantain plant.

With solemn persistence, and with an entire want of self-
criticism, he produces reams of verse that is merely dull.
Slovenly in execution, weak in poetic sense, he often plods
a very wearisome way. Yet fine lines illumine the prevailing
greyness:

> . . . on the glow-worm's useless light
> Bestow the watching flames of night,
> Or give the rose's breath
> To executed death. . . .

The splendid and typical Cavalier lyrics, *To Lucasta, going to the Wars*, and *To Althea, from Prison*, do not stand alone. The same grace and quiet strength are evident in many a less finished poem. It is a mistake to regard such songs as strokes of luck. They are the crown of Lovelace's art, deliberately achieved.

Born in 1618, Lovelace became one of the chief ornaments of the Court, spoke and fought for the King, was for a time imprisoned, and fled abroad. After returning in 1647 he was again apprehended, and before his release in 1649 had prepared *Lucasta* for the press. Later he seems to have been hunted and in want, and, if contemporary accounts are to be trusted, he perished miserably, in 1657. His fate and Suckling's are not dissimilar. But in life he stood for ideals which Suckling only faintly represented. The chivalry of the Cavaliers embodied itself in Lovelace; so much so that a contemporary writer was led to compare him with the ever-memorable Sir Philip Sidney. In the spirit of his poetry, too, he approaches Sidney, whose *Arcadia* must have been one of his favourite books. Lovelace delights in weaving romances, sometimes banal, but often true to the tradition. A good instance is *Aramantha*, which is ostensibly "A Pastoral." Some lines penned by the poet on another subject are an apt description of himself and his art:

> . . . ravish'd with these noble dreams,
> And crowned with mine own soft beams,
> Enjoying of myself I lie.

More of a dreamer, a self-pleaser, than either Carew or Suckling, less entirely of this world, he has, too, a remarkable feeling for nature which they do not share. Again there is a romantic tinge in this feeling:

> . . . her dear lar . . .
> Whose roof enchanted she doth free
> From haunting gnat and goblin bee.

And many of Lovelace's poems deal in a fresh and charming manner, despite the importation of conceits, with nature subjects: *The Rose, The Grasshopper, The Falcon*; even *The Ant, The Snail, The Toad and the Spider, A Fly caught in a Cobweb*. If the manner of some of these poems is Horace's, the soft beauty and exquisite quiet music belong to Lovelace. Equally with repose and loveliness he sees conflict in nature —the duel of toad and spider, the battle of hawk and heron.

At times he evinces a closeness of observation that might have done credit to many a professed nature-poet. As an example of this power, and of his incomplete sophistication, compare his glad escape from town to country in *Aramantha* with Carew's highly artificial study of *The Spring*.

Virility is not to be denied to Lovelace as the possessor of these gentler qualities. His life shows that he could act as well as dream. But in essence his was a "mind innocent and quiet," which turbulent times deprived of the opportunity to flower in a congenial environment.

III

Restricted as the scope of Cavalier poetry may be, bound as it is to the Court, it is yet wonderfully varied. The sharp contrasts which are observable between the four poets chosen are indicative of this variety. Poetry, it is true, had many set forms and prescribed conventions. As an inheritance from the Elizabethan age, the age of the sonneteers, the adoption of a mistress who could be alternately hymned and hated was almost compulsory. Again, all poets but Donne, who was too original to be followed except weakly (and already at his death Carew was prophesying that

thy strict laws will be
Too hard for libertines in poetry),

drew from a common treasury of ideas and metaphors, classical in the main, which was the gift of the English Renaissance. Thus when a poet thought of love the unfailing symbol was Cupid; when he wished to evoke the conception of great wealth he recalled the Indies, Pactolus, and the Ganges; a beautiful aroma expressed itself for him as all the perfumes of Arabia: yet the variations on such essential commonplaces are infinite. A significant fact is that poetic talent in this age is not so much concentrated as diffused. Something like a hundred and twenty poets were writing between 1616 and 1660, and all of them at some moment capable of becoming fine poets. So a mere hack like Thomas Jordan could pen the superb plea for the goods of this life, "Let us drink and be merry, dance, joke and rejoice." A beautiful lyric, "When, dearest, I but think on thee," first printed as Suckling's, is that by which Owen Felltham may claim to be remembered. Richard Corbet, whose other verse is of mainly academic interest and contains little hint of poetry, gave us the ever-delightful "Farewell, rewards and fairies." Richard Flecknoe, held up to eternal ridicule in Dryden's satire, is the author of an impressive *Invocation of Silence*. Many a gem of poetry with which we would not willingly part—"Love will find out the way," "Down in a garden sat my dearest love," "Be she fair as lilies be,"—remains anonymous, and may have been the choice effort of some poet still unknown. Admittedly some of this scattering of the sparks of heavenly poesy in diverse directions arises from the common use of a magical metre which was the old ballad measure transmuted by cadence into something rare and strange:

> Thou sent to me a heart was crown'd,
>   I thought it had been thine;
> But when I saw it had a wound,
>   I knew the heart was mine.

Once it was shaped, poetry dwelt in it. Yet other more mysterious causes were present, things which had their roots in the life and changing temper of the nation. Like the Elizabethan, but with stronger currents and deeper undertones, and with a newly infused personal element, the age is one of splendid lyrical achievement.

The texts of the poets are from the early editions and numerous contemporary manuscripts. Professor G. C. Moore Smith's edition of Herbert of Cherbury and Mr. C. H. Wilkinson's edition of Lovelace have been of invaluable assistance. To Mr. P. J. Dobell, who kindly permitted me to collate the Wyburd and Cosens MSS., and to print poems of Carew's from the former, my thanks are due.

August 1931.   R. G. HOWARTH.

NOTE ON PRONUNCIATION

IN seventeenth-century verse lengthenings and shortenings of words are frequent. Words containing *r* or *l*, e.g. *fair*, *untorn*, *kindled*, *nobly*, sometimes gain a syllable. *Possession*, *motion*, *affection*, and the like are often expanded. Final *-ed* where written in full is sounded. Various elisions are employed, e.g. *th' art* (= *the art*, *thou art*), *th' express* (= *the express*, *they express*), *h'as* (=*he has*), *cull's* (=*cull us*, *cull his*), *y' are* (*you are*). A further difference from modern English is in the placing of the accent. *Aspèct*, *Jùly* are invariable; other words often take the stress required by the line.

CONTENTS

CONTENTS xxiii

CONTENTS

BIBLIOGRAPHIES

EDWARD LORD HERBERT OF CHERBURY (1583–1648)

De Veritate, 1624. *The Expedition to the Isle of Rhé*, 1630 (printed 1860). *The Life and Reign of King Henry VIII*, 1632–9 (printed 1649). *The Life of Edward, Lord Herbert of Cherbury, written by himself*, 1643–4 (printed 1764). *De Causis Errorum; Religio Laici*, 1645. *De Religione Gentilium*, ?1645 (printed 1663). *A Dialogue between a Tutor and a Pupil*, ?1645 (printed 1768). *Occasional Verses*, 1665.

Autobiography, edited by Sir Sidney Lee, 1886, 1907. *Poems*, edited by J. Churton Collins, 1881; edited by G. C. Moore Smith, 1923, 1968. See B. Willey, *Lord Herbert of Cherbury*, 1942.

THOMAS CAREW (1594 or 5–1640)

Cælum Britannicum: a Masque, 1634. *Poems*, 1640, 1642, 1651.

Poems and Masque, edited by W. C. Hazlitt, 1870; edited by J. W. Ebsworth, 1893; edited by A. Vincent, 1905; edited by R. Dunlap, 1949. See E. I. Selig, *The Flourishing Wreath: A Study of Thomas Carew's Poetry*, 1958.

SIR JOHN SUCKLING (1609–42)

An Account of Religion by Reason, 1637 (printed 1646). *Aglaura: a Tragedy*, 1638, 1646. *The Goblins: a Comedy*, 1639 (printed 1646). *The Discontented Colonel* (Brennoralt): *a Tragedy*, 1639, 1646. *The Sad One: a Tragedy*, ?1640 (printed 1659). *A Letter* [to Mr Henry Jermyn], 1641, 1646. *Fragmenta Aurea*, 1646, 1648, 1658, 1696. *Last Remains*, 1659, 1696.

Works, edited by A. Suckling, 1836; edited by W. C. Hazlitt, 1874, 1892; edited by A. H. Thompson, 1910.

RICHARD LOVELACE (1618–57)

The Scholars: a Comedy, ?1635 (never printed). *The Soldier: a Tragedy*, 1640 (never printed). *Lucasta*, 1649. *Lucasta: Posthume Poems*, 1659.

Poems, edited by Singer, 1817–18; edited by W. C. Hazlitt, 1897; Unit Library edition, 1906; edited by C. H. Wilkinson, 1925, 1930. See C. H. Hartmann, *The Cavalier Spirit and its Influence on the Life and Work of Richard Lovelace*, 1925.

EDWARD LORD HERBERT OF CHERBURY
(1583–1648)

TO HIS WATCH, WHEN HE COULD NOT SLEEP

UNCESSANT minutes, whilst you move you tell
    The time that tells our life, which, though it run
Never so fast or far, your new-begun
    Short steps shall overtake; for though life well

May 'scape his own account, it shall not yours: 5
    You are Death's auditors, that both divide
And sum whate'er that life inspir'd endures
    Past a beginning, and through you we bide

The doom of Fate, whose unrecall'd decree
    You date, bring, execute; making what 's new   10
(Ill and good) old; for as we die in you,
    You die in Time, Time in Eternity.

DITTY

DEEP sighs, records of my unpitied grief,
    Memorials of my true though hopeless love,
Keep time with my sad thoughts, till wish'd relief
    My long despairs for vain and causeless prove.

Yet if such hap never to you befall,   5
I give you leave, break time, break heart and all.

SONNET

LORD, thus I sin, repent, and sin again,
    As if repentance only were in me
Leave for new sin; thus do I entertain
    My short time and thy grace abusing thee

And thy long-suffering, which, though it be   5
Ne'er overcome by sin, yet were in vain
   If tempted oft: thus we our errors see
Before our punishment, and so remain
   Without excuse; and, Lord, in them 'tis true
Thy laws are just; but why dost thou distrain   10
   Aught else for life save life? That is thy due,
The rest thou mak'st us owe, and mayst to us
   As well forgive—but oh! my sins renew,
Whilst I do talk with my Creator thus.

A DESCRIPTION

I SING her worth and praises high,
Of whom a poet cannot lie.
The little world the great shall blaze[1]:
Sea, earth her body; heaven her face;
Her hair sunbeams, whose every part   5
Lightens, inflames each lover's heart,
That thus you prove the axiom[2] true,
Whilst the sun help'd nature in you.

Her front the white and azure sky,
In light and glory raised high;   10
Being o'ercast by a cloudy frown,
All hearts and eyes dejecteth down.

Her each brow a celestial bow,
Which through this sky her light doth show,
Which doubled, if it strange appear,   15
The sun's likewise is doubled there.

Her either cheek a blushing morn,
Which, on the wings of beauty borne,
Doth never set, but only fair
Shineth, exalted in her hair.   20

Within her mouth, heaven's heav'n, reside
Her words: the soul 's there glorifi'd.

Her nose th' equator of this globe,
Where nakedness, beauty's best robe,
Presents a form all hearts to win.   25

Last Nature made that dainty chin,
Which, that it might in every fashion

---

[1] Μικρόκοσμος μακρόκοσμος.
[2] *Sol et homo generant hominem.*

Answer the rest, a constellation,
Like to a desk, she there did place
To write the wonders of her face.   30
  In this celestial frontispiece,
Where happiness eternal lies,
First arranged stand three senses,
This heaven's intelligences,
Whose several motions, sweet combin'd,   35
Come from the first mover, her mind.
  The weight of this harmonic sphere
The Atlas of her neck doth bear,
Whose favours day to us imparts,
When frowns make night in lovers' hearts.   40
  Two foaming billows are her breasts,
That carry rais'd upon their crests
The Tyrian fish: more white 's their foam
Than that whence Venus once did come.
  Here take her by the hand, my Muse,   45
With that sweet foe to make my truce,
To compact manna best compar'd,
Whose dewy inside 's not full hard.
  Her waist 's an invers'd pyramis,
Upon whose cone love's trophy is.   50
  Her belly is that magazine
At whose peep Nature did resign
That precious mould by which alone
There can be framed such a one.
  At th' entrance of which hidden treasure,   55
Happy making above measure,
Two alabaster pillars stand,
To warn all passage from that land;
At foot whereof engraved is
The sad *Non ultra* of man's bliss.   60
  The back of this most precious frame
Holds up in majesty the same,
Where, to make music to all hearts,
Love bound the descant of her parts.
  Though all this Beauty's temple be,   65
There 's known within no deity
Save virtues shrin'd within her will.
As I began, so say I still,
I sing her worth and praises high,
Of whom a poet cannot lie.   70

TO HER FACE

FATAL aspect! that hast an influence
   More powerful far than those immortal fires
That but incline the will and move the sense,
   Which thou alone constrain'st, kindling desires
   Of such an holy force as more inspires   5
The soul with knowledge, than experience
Or revelation can do with all
Their borrow'd helps: sacred astonishment
Sits on thy brow, threat'ning a sudden fall
To all those thoughts that are not lowly sent,   10
In wonder and amaze; dazzling that eye
   Which on those mysteries doth rudely gaze,
Vow'd only unto Love's divinity:
   Sure Adam sinn'd not in that spotless face.

TO HER BODY

REGARDFUL presence! whose fix'd majesty
   Darts admiration on the gazing look
That brings it not: state sits enthron'd in thee,
   Divulging forth her laws in the fair book
   Of thy commandëments, which none mistook   5
That ever humbly came therein to see
Their own unworthiness. Oh! how can I
Enough admire that symmetry, express'd
In new proportions, which doth give the lie
To that arithmetic which hath profess'd   10
All numbers to be hers? Thy harmony
   Comes from the spheres, and there doth prove
Strange measures so well grac'd, as majesty
   Itself like thee would rest, like thee would move.

TO HER MIND

EXALTED mind! whose character doth bear
   The first idea of perfection, whence
Adam's came, and stands so, how canst appear
   In words, that only tell what here-

Tofore hath been? Thou need'st as deep a sense 5
As prophecy, since there's no difference
 In telling what thou art and what shall be.
Then pardon me that rapture do profess
 At thy outside, that want for what I see
Description, if here amaz'd I cease 10
 Thus——
Yet grant one question, and no more, crav'd under
 Thy gracious leave: How, if thou wouldst express
Thyself to us, thou shouldst be still a wonder?

SONNET

Thus ends my love, but this doth grieve me most,
 That so it ends; but that ends too; this yet,
Besides the wishes, hopes and time I lost,
 Troubles my mind awhile, that I am set
Free, worse than deni'd: I can neither boast 5
 Choice nor success, as my case is, nor get
Pardon from myself that I loved not
 A better mistress, or her worse; this debt
Only's her due still, that she be forgot
 Ere chang'd, lest I love none; this done, the taint 10
 Of foul inconstancy is clear'd at least
In me, there only rests but to unpaint
 Her form in my mind, that so dispossess'd,
It be a temple, but without a saint.

UPON COMBING HER HAIR

Breaking from under that thy cloudy veil,
 Open and shine yet more, shine out more clear,
 Thou glorious golden-beam-darting hair,
Even till my wonder-strucken senses fail.

Shoot out in light, and shine those rays on far, 5
 Thou much more fair than is the Queen of Love
 When she doth comb her in her sphere above,
And from a planet turns a blazing star.

Nay, thou art greater too, more destiny
    Depends on thee than on her influence,   10
    No hair thy fatal hand doth now dispense,
But to someone a thread of life must be.

While, gracious unto me, thou both dost sunder
    Those glories which, if they united were,
    Might have amazed sense, and show'st each hair,   15
Which if alone had been too great a wonder.

And now, spread in their goodly length, sh' appears
    No creature which the earth might call her own,
    But rather one that in her gliding down
Heav'n's beams did crown, to show us she was theirs.   20

And come from thence, how can they fear Time's rage,
    Which, in his power else on earth most strange,
    Such golden treasure doth to silver change,
By that improper alchemy of age?

But stay, methinks new beauties do arise,   25
    While she withdraws these glories which were spread.
    Wonder of beauties, set thy radiant head,
And strike out day from thy yet fairer eyes.

DITTY IN IMITATION OF THE SPANISH

Entre tanto que l'Avril

Now that the April of your youth adorns
    The garden of your face,
Now that for you each knowing lover mourns,
    And all seek to your grace,
Do not repay affection with scorns.   5

What though you may a matchless beauty vaunt,
    And that all hearts can move
By such a power as seemeth to enchant,
    Yet, without help of love,
Beauty no pleasure to itself can grant.   10

Then think each minute that you lose, a day;
 The longest youth is short,
The shortest age is long; Time flies away,
 And makes us but his sport,
And that which is not Youth's is Age's prey. 15

See but the bravest horse that prideth most,
 Though he escape the war,
Either from master to the man is lost,
 Or turn'd unto the car;
Or else must die with being ridden post. 20

Then lose not beauty, lovers, time, and all;
 Too late your fault you see,
When that in vain you would these days recall;
 Nor can you virtuous be,
When, without these, you have not wherewithal. 25

SATIRES

I

THE STATE PROGRESS OF ILL

I SAY, 'tis hard to write satires.   Though Ill
Great'ned in his long course, and swelling still,
Be now like to a deluge, yet, as Nile,
'Tis doubtful in his original; this while,
We may thus much on either part presume, 5
That what so universal are must come
From causes great and far.   Now in this state
Of things, what is least like Good men hate,
Since 'twill be the less sin.   I do see
Some ill requir'd, that one poison might free 10
The other; so States to their greatness find
No faults requir'd but their own, and bind
The rest.   And though this be mysterious, still,
Why should we not examine how this Ill
Did come at first, how 't keeps his greatness here, 15
When 'tis disguis'd, and when it doth appear?
This Ill, having some attributes of God—
As, to have made itself, and bear the rod
Of all our punishments, as it seems—, came
Into the world to rule it, and to tame 20

The pride of Goodness; and though his reign
Great in the hearts of men he doth maintain
By love, not right, he, yet the tyrant here
(Though it be him we love, and God we fear),
Pretence yet wants not that it was before   25
Some part of Godhead, as mercy, that store
For souls grown bankrupt their first stock of grace,
And that which the sinner of the last place
Shall number out, unless th' Highest will show
Some power not yet reveal'd to man below.   30

But that I may proceed, and so go on
To trace Ill in his first progression,
And through his secret'st ways, and where that he
Had left his nakedness as well as we,
And did appear himself: I note that in   35
The yet infant world how Mischief and Sin,[1]
His agents here on earth, and easy known,
Are now conceal'd intelligencers grown;
For since that as a guard th' Highest at once
Put Fear t' attend their private actions,   40
And Shame their public (other means being fail'd),
Mischief under doing of good was veil'd,
And Sin of pleasure; though in this disguise
They only hide themselves from mortal eyes.
Sins, those that both com- and o-mitted be,   45
Once hot and cold but in a third degree,
Are now such poisons, that though they may lurk
In secret parts awhile, yet they will work
Though after death; nor ever come alone,
But sudden-fruitful multiply ere done.   50
While in this monstrous birth, they only die
Whom we confess, those live which we deny.
Mischiefs, like fatal constellations,
Appear unto the ignorant at once
In glory and in hurt, while th' unseen part   55
Of the great cause may be perchance the art
Of th' Ill, and hiding it; which that I may
Ev'n in his first original display
And best example, sure amongst Kings he
Who first wanted succession, to be   60

[1] *Gradus mali sunt quo* $\begin{cases} peccamus\ nobis \\ nocemus\ aliis. \end{cases}$

A tyrant, was wise enough to have chose
An honest man for King, which should dispose
Those beasts which, being so tame, yet otherwise,
As it seems, could not herd; and with advice
Somewhat indifferent for both, he might   65
Yet have provided for their children's right,
If they grew wiser, not his own, that so
They might repent, yet under treason, who
Ne'er promis'd faith; though now we cannot spare
(And not be worse) Kings, on those terms they are,   70
No more than we could spare (and have been sav'd)
Original sin. So then those priests that rav'd
And prophesi'd, they did a kind of good
They knew not of by whom the choice first stood.

    Since, then, we may consider now, as fit,   75
State-government and all the arts of it,
That we may know them yet let us see how
They were deriv'd, done, and are maintain'd now,
That Princes may by this yet understand
Why we obey, as well as they command.   80

    State a proportion'd colour'd table is;
Nobility, the master-piece, in this
Serves to show distances, while being put
'Twixt sight and vastness they seem higher but
As they 're further off; yet, as those blue hills   85
Which th' utmost border of a region fills,
They are great and worse parts, while in the steep
Of this great prospective they seem to keep
Further absent from those below. Though this
Exalted spirit, that 's sure a free soul, is   90
A greater privilege than to be born
At Venice, although he seek not rule, doth scorn
Subjection but as he is flesh—and so
He is to dulness, shame, and many mo
Such properties—, knows (but the painter's art)   95
All in the frame is equal; that desert
Is a more living thing, and doth obey,
As he gives poor, for God's sake (though they
And Kings ask it not so); thinks honours are
Figures compos'd of lines irregular;   100
And, happy-high, knows no election
Raiseth man to true greatness but his own.
Meanwhile sugar'd divines, next place to this,

Tells us humility and patience is
The way to heaven, and that we must there   105
Look for our kingdom; that the great'st rule here
Is for to rule ourselves; and that they might
Say this the better, they to no place have right
B' inheritance, while whom Ambition sways,
Their office is to turn it other ways.   110
    Those yet whose harder minds Religion
Cannot invade, nor turn from thinking on
A present greatness, that combin'd curse of Law,
Of officers, and neighbours' spite doth draw
Within such whirlpools, that till they be drown'd   115
They ne'er get out, but only swim them round.
    Thus brief, since that the infinite of Ill
Is neither easy told nor safe, I will
But only note how free-born man, subdu'd
By his own choice, that was at first indu'd   120
With equal power over all, doth now submit
That infinite of number, spirit, wit,
To some eight monarchs.   Then why wonder men
Their rule of horses?
The world, as in the Ark of Noah, rests,   125
Compos'd as then: few men and many beasts.

August 1608.

   At Merlou in France.

II

Of Travellers: from Paris

Ben Jonson, travel is a second birth,
Unto the children of another earth:
Only, as our King Richard was, so they appear,
New-born to another world, with teeth and hair,
While got by English parents, carried in   5
Some womb of thirty ton, and lightly twin,
They are deliver'd at Calais or at Dieppe,
And strangely stand, go, feed themselves—nay, keep
Their own money straightways; but that is all,
For none can understand them when they call   10
For anything—no more than Badger,
That call'd the Queen Monsieur, laid a wager
With the King of his dogs, who understood
Them all alike: which, Badger thought, was good.

But that I may proceed: since their birth is 15
Only a kind of metempsychosis,
Such knowledge as their memory could give
They have for help, what time these souls do live
In English clothes (a body which again
They never rise unto); but as you see 20
When they come home, like children yet, that be
Of their own bringing up, all they learn is
Toys and the language; but, to attain this,
You must conceive they 're cozen'd, mock'd, and come
To Faubourg St. Germain, there take a room, 25
Lightly about th' ambassadors, and where,
Having no church, they come Sundays to hear;
An invitation, which they have most part,
If their outside but promise a desert,
To sit above the Secretary's place, 30
Although it be almost as rare a case
To see English well-cloth'd here, as with you
At London, Indians. But that your view
May comprehend at once them gone for Blois
Or Orleans, learn'd French, now no more boys 35
But perfect men at Paris, putting on
Some forc'd disguise or labour'd fashion
To appear strange at home besides their stay:
Laugh and look on with me, to see what they
Are now become (but that the poorer sort, 40
A subject not fit for my Muse nor sport,
May pass untouch'd); let 's but consider what
Elpus is now become, one young, handsome, and that
Was such a wit as very well with four
Of the six might have made one and no more, 45
Had he been at their *Valentine*, and could
Agree Tom Rus should use the stock, who would
Carefully in that, ev'n as 'twere his own,
Put out their jests; briefly, one that was grown
Ripe to another taste than that wherein 50
He is now seasoned and dri'd, as in
His face by this you see, which would perplex
A stranger to define his years or sex;
To which his wrinkles, when he speaks, doth give
That age his words should have, while he doth strive 55
As if such births had never come from brain,
To show he 's not deliver'd without pain,

Nor without after-throes. Sometimes, as grace
Did overflow in circles o'er his face,
Ev'n to the brim, which he thinks [. . . .] Sure,   60
If this posture do but so long endure
That it be fix'd by age, he 'll look as like
A speaking sign as our St. George to strike;
That, where he is, none but will hold their peace,
If th' have but th' least good manners, or confess,   65
If he should speak, he did presume too far
In speaking then, when others readier are.
Now, that he speaks are complimental speeches,
That never go off but below the breeches
Of him he doth salute, while he doth wring,   70
And with some loose French words which he doth string,
Windeth about the arms, the legs and sides,
Most serpent-like, of any man that bides
His indirect approach, which being done
Almost without an introduction,   75
If we have heard but any bragging French
Boast of the favour of some noble wench,
He 'll swear 'twas he did her graces possess,
And damn his own soul for the wickedness
Of other men, strangest of all in that.   80
But I am weary to describe you what
Ere this you can.   As for the little fry
That all along the street turn up the eye
At everything they meet, that have not yet
Seen that swoll'n vicious Queen, Margaret,   85
Who were a monster ev'n without her sin;
Nor the Italian comedies, wherein
Women play boys—I cease to write,
So end this satire, and bid thee good night.

September 1608.

"I MUST DEPART"

I MUST depart, but like to his last breath
    That leaves the seat of life, for liberty
I go, but dying, and in this our death,
    Where soul and soul is parted, it is I
        The deader part that fly away,   5
            While she, alas, in whom before
            I liv'd, dies her own death and more,
        I feeling mine too much and her own stay.

But since I must depart, and that our love,
  Springing at first but in an earthly mould, 10
Transplanted to our souls now doth remove
  Earthly effects, what time and distance would,
    Nothing now can our loves allay,
      Though as the better spirits will
      That both love us and know our ill, 15
    We do not either all the good we may.

Thus when our souls that must immortal be—
  For our loves cannot die, nor we (unless
We die not both together)—shall be free
  Unto their open and eternal peace, 20
    Sleep, Death's ambassador, and best
      Image, doth yours often so show,
      That I thereby must plainly know
    Death unto us must be freedom and rest.

May 1608.

MADRIGAL

How should I love my best?
What though my love unto that height be grown,
    That taking joy in you alone
      I utterly this world detest,
Should I not love it yet as th' only place 5
    Where Beauty hath his perfect grace,
        And is possess'd?

But I beauties despise,
You universal beauty seem to me,
    Giving and showing form and degree 10
      To all the rest in your fair eyes:
Yet should I not love them as parts whereon
    Your beauty, their perfection
        And top, doth rise?

But ev'n myself I hate, 15
So far my love is from the least delight
    That at my very self I spite,
      Senseless of any happy state:
Yet may I not with justest reason fear
    How, hating hers, I truly her 20
        Can celebrate?

Thus unresolved still,
Although world, life, nay, what is fair beside,
    I cannot for your sake abide,
       Methinks I love not to my fill;   25
Yet is a greater love you can devise,
    In loving you some other wise,
       Believe 't, I will.

ANOTHER

DEAR, when I did from you remove,
I left my joy but not my love—
    That never can depart:
It neither higher can ascend,
    Nor lower bend,   5
Fix'd in the centre of my heart
    As in his place,
And lodged so, how can it change,
    Or you grow strange?
Those are earth's properties, and base: 10
    Each-where, as the bodies divine,
    Heav'n's lights and you to me will shine.

TO HIS FRIEND, BEN JONSON, OF HIS HORACE MADE ENGLISH

'TWAS not enough, Ben Jonson, to be thought
Of English poets best, but to have brought
In greater state to their acquaintance one
So equal to himself and thee, that none
Might be thy second, while thy glory is   5
To be the Horace of our times and his.

EPITAPHIUM CAECILIAE BOULSTRED, QUAE POST LANGUESCENTEM MORBUM NON SINE INQUIETUDINE SPIRITUS ET CONSCIENTIAE OBIIT

METHINKS Death like one laughing lies,[1]
Showing his teeth, shutting his eyes,
Only thus to have found her here
He did with so much reason fear,
    And she despise.   5

[1] *Intelligitur de figura mortis praefigenda.*

For, barring all the gates of sin,
Death's open ways to enter in,
   She was with a strict siege beset,
   So what by force he could not get,
      By time to win.   10

This mighty warrior was deceived yet,
For what he mutine in her powers thought
   Was but their zeal,
And what by their excess might have been wrought
   Her fasts did heal.   15

Till that her noble soul, by these as wings
Transcending the low pitch of earthly things,
   As b'ing reliev'd by God and set at large,
   And grown by this worthy a higher charge,
Triumphing over Death, to Heaven fled,   20
And did not die, but left her body dead.

July 1609.

EPITAPHIUM GULIELMI HERBERT DE SWANSEA, QUE SINE PROLE OBIIT AUGUST. 1609

GREAT spirit, that in new ambition
   Stoop'd not below his merit,
But with his proper worth being carri'd on,
Stoop'd at no second place, till now in one
   He doth all place inherit: 5

Live endless here in such brave memory
   The best tongue cannot spot it,
While they which knew, or but have heard of thee,
Must never hope thy like again can be,
   Since thou hast not begot it.   10

IN A GLASS WINDOW, FOR INCONSTANCY

LOVE, of this clearest, frailest glass
Divide the properties, so as
In the division may appear
Clearness for me, frailty for her.

ELEGY FOR THE PRINCE

Must he be ever dead?   Cannot we add
Another life unto that Prince that had
Our souls laid up in him?   Could not our love,
Now when he left us, make that body move
After his death one age?   And keep unite   5
That frame wherein our souls did so delight?
For what are souls but love, since they do know
Only for it, and can no further go?
Sense is the soul of beasts, because none can
Proceed so far as t' understand like man: 10
And if souls be more where they love than where
They animate, why did it not appear
In keeping him alive?   Or how is fate
Equal to us, when one man's private hate
May ruin kingdoms, when he will expose   15
Himself to certain death, and yet all those
Not keep alive this Prince who now is gone,
Whose loves would give thousands of lives for one?
Do we then die in him, only as we
May in the world's harmonic body see   20
An universally diffused soul
Move in the parts which moves not in the whole?
So though we rest with him, we do appear
To live and stir a while, as if he were
Still quick'ning us.   Or do (perchance) we live   25
And know it not?   See we not Autumn give
Back to the earth again what it receiv'd
In th' early Spring?   And may not we, deceiv'd,
Think that those powers are dead, which do but sleep,
And the world's soul doth reunited keep?   30
And though this Autumn gave what never more
Any Spring can unto the world restore,
May we not be deceiv'd, and think we know
Ourselves for dead?   Because that we are so
Unto each other, when as yet we live   35
A life his love and memory doth give,
Who was our world's soul, and to whom we are
So reunite that in him we repair
All other our affections ill-bestow'd:
Since by this love we now have such abode   40
With him in Heaven as we had here before

He left us dead. Nor shall we question more,
Whether the soul of man be memory,
As Plato thought: we and posterity
Shall celebrate his name, and virtuous grow,   45
Only in memory that he was so;
And on those terms we may seem yet to live,
Because he lived once, though we shall strive
To sigh away this seeming life so fast,
As if with us 'twere not already past.   50
We then are dead, for what doth now remain
To please us more, or what can we call pain,
Now we have lost him? And what else doth make
Diff'rence in life and death, but to partake
Nor joy nor pain?   O death, couldst not fulfil   55
Thy rage against us no way but to kill
This Prince, in whom we liv'd, that so we all
Might perish by thy hand at once, and fall
Under his ruin? Thenceforth though we should
Do all the actions that the living would,   60
Yet we shall not remember that we live,
No more than when our mothers' womb did give
That life we felt not; or should we proceed
To such a wonder that the dead should breed,
It should be wrought to keep that memory,   65
Which, being his, can therefore never die.

November 9, 1612.

EPITAPH OF KING JAMES

HERE lies King James, who did so propagate
Unto the world that blest and quiet state
Wherein his subjects liv'd, he seem'd to give
That peace which Christ did leave, and so did live
As once that King and Shepherd of his Sheep,   5
That whom God saved here he seem'd to keep;
Till with that innocent and single heart,
With which he first was crown'd, he did depart
To better life. Great Britain, so lament,
That strangers more than thou may yet resent   10
The sad effects, and while they feel the harm
They must endure from the victorious arm
Of our King Charles, may they so long complain,
That tears in them force thee to weep again.

A VISION [1]

WITHIN an open curled sea of gold,[2]
   A bark of ivory [3] one day I saw,
   Which striking with his oars [4] did seem to draw
Tow'rds a fair coast [5] which I then did behold.

A lady held the stern, while her white hand,   5
   Whiter than either ivory or sail,[6]
   Over the surging waves did so prevail,
That she had now approached near the land.[7]

When suddenly, as if she fear'd some wrack
   (And yet the sky was fair, and air was clear,   10
   And neither rock [8] nor monster [9] did appear),
Doubting the point which spi'd, she turned back.

Then with a second course I saw her steer [10]
   As if she meant to reach some other bay,
   Where being approach'd she likewise turn'd away,   15
Though in the bark some waves now ent'red were.[11]

Thus varying oft her course, at last I found,
   While I in quest of the adventure go,
   The sail took down, and oars had ceas'd to row,[12]
And that the bark itself was run aground.   20

Wherewith earth's fairest creature [13] I behold,
   For which both bark and sea I gladly lost.[14]
   Let no philosopher of knowledge boast,
Unless that he my vision can unfold.

---

[1] A lady combing her hair.   [2] The hair.
[3] The comb.   [4] The teeth of the comb.
[5] Her side.   [6] The cuff or smock sleeve.
[7] Her shoulder.   [8] Wart.
[9] Lice.   [10] Combing in another place.
[11] Hairs in the comb.   [12] She had given over combing.
[13] Her face.   [14] Her hair put up, and comb cast away.

DITTY

Tears, flow no more; or if you needs must flow,
    Fall yet more slow,
    Do not the world invade;
From smaller springs than yours rivers have grown,
    And they again a sea have made,   5
Brackish like you, and which like you hath flown.

Ebb to my heart, and on the burning fires
    Of my desires
    O let your torrents fall;
From smaller heat than theirs such sparks arise   10
    As into flame converting all,
This world might be but my love's sacrifice.

Yet if the tempests of my sighs so blow,
    You both must flow
    And my desires still burn;   15
Since that in vain all help my love requires,
    Why may not yet their rages turn
To dry those tears, and to blow out those fires?

Italy, 1614.

DITTY TO THE TUNE OF *A CHE DEL QUANTO MIO* OF PESARINO

Where now shall these accents go,
    At which creatures silent grow,
    While woods and rocks do speak,
      And seem to break
Complaints too long for them to hear,   5
    Saying, I call in vain—*Echo*. All in vain—
    Where there is no relief?   *Echo*. Here is no relief.

Ah, why then should I fear
Unto her rocky heart to speak that grief,
    In whose laments these bear a part?   10
      Then, cruel heart,
      Do but some answer give,
I do but crave—Do you forbid to live, or bid to live?
Echo. Live.

DITTY

Can I then live to draw that breath
    Which must bid farewell to thee?
    Yet how should death not seize on me?
Since absence from the life I hold so dear must needs be death,
    While I do feel in parting   5
    Such a living dying,
  As in this my most fatal hour
    Grief such a life doth lend,
      As, quick'ned by his power,
    Even death cannot end.   10

"I AM THE FIRST THAT EVER LOV'D"

I am the first that ever lov'd:
    He yet that for the place contends
    Against true love so much offends,
That even this way it is prov'd.

For whose affection once is shown,   5
    No longer can the world beguile,
    Who see his penance all the while
He holds a torch to make her known.

You are the first were ever lov'd,
    And who may think this not so true,   10
    So little knows of love or you,
It need not otherwise be prov'd.

For though the more judicious eyes
    May know when diamonds are right,
    There is requir'd a greater light   15
Thiir estimate and worth to prize.

While they who most for beauty strives
    Can with no art so lovely grow
    As she who doth but only owe
So much as true affection gives.   20

Thus first of lovers I appear,
    For more appearance makes me none;
    And thus are you belov'd alone,
That are priz'd infinitely dear.

Yet as in our northern clime 25
  Rare fruits, though late, appear at last;
   As we may see, some years b'ing past,
Our orange-trees grow ripe with time;—

So think not strange, if love to break
  His wonted silence now make bold, 30
   For [when] a love is seven years old,
Is it not time to learn to speak?

Then gather in that which doth grow
  And ripen to that fairest hand;
   'Tis not enough that trees do stand, 35
If their fruit fall and perish too.

EPITAPH OF A STINKING POET

HERE stinks a poet, I confess,
Yet wanting breath stinks so much less.

A DITTY TO THE TUNE OF *COSE FERITE*

MADE BY LORENZO ALLEGRE TO ONE SLEEPING TO BE SUNG

   AH, wonder!
  So fair a heaven,
  So fair a heaven
And no star shining,
Ay me, and no star shining, 5
  'Tis past my divining.

   Yet stay!
May not perchance this be some rising morn,
  Which in the scorn
Of our world's light discloses 10
This air of violets, that sky of roses?

   'Tis so.
An oriental sphere
Doth open and appear,
  Ascending bright. 15
Then since thy hymn I chant,
Mayst thou new pleasures grant,
  Admired light.

EPITAPH ON SIR EDWARD SACKVILLE'S CHILD, WHO DIED IN HIS BIRTH

READER, here lies a child that never cri'd,
And therefore never di'd;
'Twas neither old nor young,
Born to this and the other world in one:
Let us then cease to moan,   5
Nothing that ever di'd hath liv'd so long.

KISSING

COME hither, womankind and all their worth,
Give me thy kisses as I call them forth.
Give me the billing kiss, that of the dove,
A kiss of love;
The melting kiss, a kiss that doth consume   5
To a perfume;
The extract kiss, of every sweet a part,
A kiss of art;
The kiss which ever stirs some new delight,
A kiss of might;   10
The twaching smacking kiss, and when you cease,
A kiss of peace;
The music kiss, crotchet-and-quaver time;
The kiss of rhyme;
The kiss of eloquence, which doth belong   15
Unto the tongue;
The kiss of all the sciences in one,
The kiss alone.
So, 'tis enough.

DITTY

IF you refuse me once, and think again
I will complain,
You are deceiv'd: love is no work of art,
It must be got and born,
Not made and worn,   5
Or such wherein you have no part.

Or do you think they more than once can die,
                    Whom you deny,
Who tell you of a thousand deaths a day,
                    Like the old poets feign,   10
                    And tell the pain
                    They met but in the common way?

Or do you think it is too soon to yield,
                    And quit the field?
You are deceiv'd, they yield who first entreat;   15
                    Once one may crave for love,
                    But more would prove
                    This heart too little, that too great.

Give me then so much love that we may burn
                    Past all return.   20
Who midst your beauty's flames and spirit lives,
                    So great a light must find
                    As to be blind
                    To all but what their fire gives.

Then give me so much love, as in one point   25
                    Fix'd and conjoint,
May make us equal in our flames arise,
                    As we shall never start
                    Until we dart
                    Lightning upon the envious eyes.   30

Then give me so much love that we may move
                    Like stars of love,
And glad and happy times to lovers bring;
                    While glorious in one sphere
                    We still appear,   35
                    And keep an everlasting Spring.

ELEGY OVER A TOMB

Must I then see, alas! eternal night
                    Sitting upon those fairest eyes,
And closing all those beams, which once did rise
                    So radiant and bright
That light and heat in them to us did prove   5
                    Knowledge and love?

Oh, if you did delight no more to stay
    Upon this low and earthly stage,
But rather chose an endless heritage,
    Tell us at least, we pray,   10
Where all the beauties that those ashes ow'd
    Are now bestow'd.

Doth the sun now his light with yours renew?
    Have waves the curling of your hair?
Did you restore unto the sky and air   15
    The red and white and blue?
Have you vouchsaf'd to flowers since your death
    That sweetest breath?

Had not heav'n's lights else in their houses slept,
    Or to some private life retir'd?   20
Must not the sky and air have else conspir'd,
    And in their regions wept?
Must not each flower else the earth could breed
    Have been a weed?

But thus enrich'd may we not yield some cause   25
    Why they themselves lament no more,
That must have chang'd the course they held before,
    And broke their proper laws,
Had not your beauties giv'n this second birth
    To heaven and earth?   30

Tell us (for oracles must still ascend
    For those that crave them at your tomb),
Tell us, where are those beauties now become,
    And what they now intend;
Tell us, alas, that cannot tell our grief,   35
    Or hope relief.

1617.

EPITAPH ON SIR FRANCIS VERE

READER,
    If thou appear
Before this tomb, attention give,
    And do not fear,
    Unless it be to live:
For dead is great Sir Francis Vere.   5

Of whom this might be said: should God ordain
  One to destroy all sinners whom that one
  Redeem'd not there, that so he might atone
His chosen flock, and take from earth that stain 10
  That spots it still, he worthy were alone
  To finish it, and have, when they were gone,
This world for him made Paradise again.

TO MISTRESS DIANA CECIL

DIANA CECIL, that rare beauty thou dost show
  Is not of milk or snow,
  Or such as pale and whitely things do owe,
But an illustrious oriental bright,
Like to the diamond's refracted light, 5
Or early morning breaking from the night.

Nor is thy hair and eyes made of that ruddy beam
  Or golden-sanded stream
  Which we find still the vulgar poets' theme,
But reverend black, and such as you would say 10
Light did but serve it, and did show the way
By which at first night did precede the day.

Nor is that symmetry of parts and form divine
  Made of one vulgar line,
  Or such as any know how to define, 15
But of proportions new, so well express'd,
That the perfections in each part confess'd
Are beauties to themselves and to the rest.

Wonder of all thy sex! let none henceforth inquire
  Why they so much admire, 20
  Since they that know thee best ascend no higher;
Only, be not with common praises woo'd,
Since admiration were no longer good,
When men might hope more than they understood.

TO HER EYES

  BLACK eyes, if you seem dark,
It is because your beams are deep,
  And with your soul united keep.
    Who could discern

Enough into them, there might learn 5
Whence they derive that mark,
And how their power is such
That all the wonders which proceed from thence,
Affecting more the mind than sense,
Are not so much 10
The works of light as influence.

As you then joined are
Unto the soul, so it again
By its connexion doth pertain
To that first cause, 15
Who, giving all their proper laws,
By you doth best declare
How he at first b'ing hid
Within the veil of an eternal night,
Did frame for us a second light, 20
And after bid
It serve for ordinary sight.

His image then you are.
If there be any yet who doubt
What power it is that doth look out 25
Through that your black,
He will not an example lack,
If he suppose that there
Were grey or hazel glass,
And that through them though sight or soul might shine,
He must yet at the last define 31
That beams which pass
Through black cannot but be divine.

TO HER HAIR

BLACK beamy hairs, which so seem to arise
From the extraction of those eyes,
That into you she destine-like doth spin
The beams she spares, what time her soul retires,
And by those hallow'd fires 5
Keeps house all night within;

Since from within her awful front you shine
As threads of life which she doth twine,
And thence ascending with your fatal rays,

Do crown those temples where love's wonders wrought 10
    We afterwards see brought
  To vulgar light and praise;

Lighten through all your regions, till we find
    The causes why we are grown blind,
That when we should your glories comprehend, 15
Our sight recoils and turneth back again,
    And doth, as 'twere in vain,
  Itself to you extend.

Is it because past black there is not found
    A fix'd or horizontal bound, 20
And so, as it doth terminate the white,
It may be said all colours to enfold,
    And in that kind to hold
  Somewhat of infinite?

Or is it that the centre of our sight 25
    Being veiled in its proper night
Discerns your blackness by some other sense
Than that by which it doth pi'd colours see,
    Which only therefore be
  Known by their difference? 30

Tell us, when on her front in curls you lie,
    So diap'red from that black eye
That your reflected forms may make us know
That shining light in darkness all would find,
    Were they not upward blind 35
  With the sunbeams below.

SONNET OF BLACK BEAUTY

Black beauty, which, above that common light,
  Whose power can no colours here renew
  But those which darkness can again subdue,
Dost still remain unvari'd to the sight,
  And like an object equal to the view,
                    5
Art neither chang'd with day, nor hid with night;
When all these colours which the world call bright,
  And which old poetry doth so pursue,

Are with the night so perished and gone
    That of their being there remains no mark,   10
Thou still abidest so entirely one,
    That we may know thy blackness is a spark
Of light inaccessible, and alone
    Our darkness which can make us think it dark.

ANOTHER SONNET TO BLACK ITSELF

THOU Black, wherein all colours are compos'd,
    And unto which they all at last return;
    Thou colour of the sun where it doth burn,
And shadow where it cools; in thee is clos'd
Whatever Nature can, or hath dispos'd   5
    In any other hue: from thee do rise
Those tempers and complexions which, disclos'd
    As parts of thee, do work as mysteries
Of that thy hidden power; when thou dost reign,
    The characters of fate shine in the skies,   10
And tell us what the Heavens do ordain:
    But when earth's common light shines to our eyes,
Thou so retir'st thyself that thy disdain
    All revelation unto man denies.

THE FIRST MEETING

As sometimes with a sable cloud
        We see the heavens bow'd,
        And dark'ning all the air
Until the lab'ring fires they do contain
        Break forth again,   5
    Ev'n so from under your black hair
    I saw such an unusual blaze
Light'ning and sparkling from your eyes,
        And with unused prodigies
    Forcing such [terrors and] amaze,   10
    That I did judge your empire here
    Was not of love alone, but fear.

But as all that is violent
    Doth by degrees relent,
So when that sweetest face,   15
Growing at last to be serene and clear,
    Did now appear
With all its wonted heav'nly grace,
    And your appeased eyes did send
A beam from them so soft and mild   20
    That former terrors were exiled,
And all that could amaze did end;
Darkness in me was chang'd to light,
Wonder to love, love to delight.

Nor here yet did your goodness cease   25
    My heart and eyes to bless,
For being past all hope
That I could now enjoy a better state,
    An orient gate
(As if the heav'ns themselves did ope)   30
    First form'd in thee, and then disclos'd
So gracious and sweet a smile,
    That my soul, ravished the while,
And wholly from itself unloos'd,
Seem'd hov'ring in your breath to rise,   35
To feel an air of Paradise.

Nor here yet did your favours end,
    For whilst I down did bend,
As one who now did miss
A soul, which, grown much happier than before, 40
    Would turn no more,
You did bestow on me a kiss,
    And in that kiss a soul infuse,
Which was so fashion'd by your mind,
    And which was so much more refin'd   45
Than that I formerly did use,
That if one soul found joys in thee,
The other fram'd them new in me.

But as those bodies which dispense
    Their beams, in parting hence   50
Those beams do re-collect,

Until they in themselves resumed have
      The forms they gave,
So when your gracious aspect
      From me was turned once away,   55
Neither could I thy soul retain,
      Nor you gave mine leave to remain,
To make with you a longer stay,
Or suffer'd aught else to appear
But your hair, night's hemisphere.   60

Only as we in loadstones find
      Virtue of such a kind
That what they once do give,
B'ing neither to be chang'd by any clime
      Or forc'd by time,   65
Doth ever in its subjects live,
      So though I be from you retir'd,
The power you gave yet still abides,
      And my soul ever so guides,
By your magnetic touch inspir'd,   70
That all it moves or is inclin'd
Comes from the motions of your mind

A MERRY RHYME SENT TO THE LADY WROTH UPON
    THE BIRTH OF MY LORD OF PEMBROKE'S CHILD,
    BORN IN THE SPRING

MADAM, though I am one of those
That every Spring use to compose—
That is, add feet unto round prose—,
Yet you a further art disclose,
And can, as everybody knows,   5
Add to those feet fine dainty toes.
Satires add nails, but they are shrews;
My Muse therefore no further goes,
But for her feet craves shoes and hose.
Let a fair season add a rose,   10
While thus attired we 'll oppose
The tragic buskins of our foes.
And herewith, madam, I will close,
And 'tis no matter how it shows:
All I care is, if the child grows.   15

THE THOUGHT

IF you do love as well as I,
Then every minute from your heart
   A thought doth part;
And winged with desire doth fly
Till it hath met in a straight line 5
   A thought of mine
So like to yours, we cannot know
Whether of both doth come, or go,
   Till we define
Which of us two that thought doth owe. 10

I say, then, that your thoughts which pass
Are not so much the thoughts you meant,
   As those I sent:
For as my image in a glass
Belongs not to the glass you see, 15
   But unto me,
So when your fancy is so clear
That you would think you saw me there,
   It needs must be
That it was I did first appear. 20

Likewise, when I send forth a thought,
My reason tells me 'tis the same
   Which from you came,
And which your beauteous image wrought.
Thus, while our thoughts by turns do lead, 25
   None can precede;
And thus, while in each other's mind
Such interchanged forms we find,
   Our loves may plead
To be of more than vulgar kind. 30

May you then often think on me,
And by that thinking know 'tis true
   I thought on you;
I in the same belief will be,
While by this mutual address 35
   We will possess

A love must live when we do die;
Which rare and secret property
   You will confess,
If you do love as well as I.   40

TO A LADY WHO DID SING EXCELLENTLY

WHEN our rude and unfashion'd words, that long
  A being in their elements enjoy'd,
   Senseless and void,
Come at last to be formed by thy tongue,
  And from thy breath receive that life and place,   5
   And perfect grace,
That now thy power diffus'd through all their parts
   Are able to remove
All the obstructions of the hardest hearts,
  And teach the most unwilling how to love;   10

When they again, exalted by thy voice,
  Tun'd by thy soul, dismiss'd into the air,
   To us repair,
A living, moving, and harmonious noise,
  Able to give the love they do create   15
   A second state,
And charm not only all his griefs away,
   And his defects restore,
But make him perfect, who, the poets say,
  Made all was ever yet made heretofore;   20

When again all these rare perfections meet,
  Composed in the circle of thy face,
   As in their place,
So to make up of all one perfect sweet;
  Who is not then so ravish'd with delight   25
   Ev'n of thy sight,
That he can be assur'd his sense is true,
   Or that he die, or live,
Or that he do enjoy himself, or you,
  Or only the delights which you did give?   30

1618.

MELANDER SUPPOS'D TO LOVE SUSAN, BUT DID LOVE ANN

WHO doth presume my mistress's name to scan,
Goes about more than any way he can,
Since all men think that it is Susan. *Echo.* Ann.

What sayst? Then tell who is as white as swan,
While others set by her are pale and wan; 5
Then, Echo, speak, is it not Susan? *Echo.* Ann.

Tell, Echo, yet, whose middle 's but a span,
Some being gross as bucket, round as pan;
Say, Echo, then, is it not Susan? *Echo.* Ann.

Say, is she not soft as meal without bran? 10
Though yet in great haste once from me she ran,
Must I not however love Susan? *Echo.* Ann.

ECHO TO A ROCK

THOU heaven-threat'ning rock, gentler than she!
    Since of my pain
  Thou still more sensible wilt be,
Only when thou giv'st leave but to complain—
                Echo. Complain. 5
But thou dost answer too, although in vain
  Thou answer'st when thou canst no pity show.
                Echo. Oh.
    What, canst thou speak, and pity too?
    Then yet a further favour do, 10
And tell if of my griefs I any end shall know.
                Echo. No.
Sure she will pity him that loves her so truly.
                Echo. You lie.
    Vile rock, thou now grow'st so unruly, 15
    That hadst thou life as thou hast voice,
    Thou shouldst die at my foot.
                Echo. Die at my foot.

Thou canst not make me do 't,
   Unless thou leave it to my choice,   **20**
   Who thy hard sentence shall fulfil,
When thou shalt say I die to please her only will.
          Echo. I will.
When she comes hither, then, I pray thee tell
Thou art my monument, and this my last farewell.   **25**
          Echo. Well.

ECHO IN A CHURCH

WHERE shall my troubled soul at large
          Discharge
The burden of her sins, oh where?
          Echo. Here.

   Whence comes this voice I hear?   **5**
   Who doth this grace afford?
   If it be thou, O Lord,
Say if thou hear my prayers when I call.
          Echo. All.
And wilt thou pity grant when I do cry?   **10**
          Echo. Ay

Then though I fall,
   Thy grace will my defects supply,
   But who will keep my soul from ill,
   Quench bad desires, reform my will?   **15**
          Echo. I will.

   Oh may that will and voice be blest,
Which yields such comforts unto one distress'd,
More blessed yet, wouldst thou thyself unmask,
Or tell, at least, who undertakes this task.   **20**
          Echo. Ask.

Then quickly speak,
Since now with crying I am grown so weak
I shall want force even to crave thy name;
O speak before I wholly weary am.   **25**
          Echo. I am.

TO HIS MISTRESS FOR HER TRUE PICTURE

DEATH, my life's mistress, and the sovereign queen
Of all that ever breath'd, though yet unseen,
My heart doth love you best; but I confess,
Your picture I beheld, which doth express
No such eye-taking beauty; you seem lean,   5
Unless you 're mended since. Sure he did mean
No honour to you that did draw you so:
Therefore I think it false: besides, I know
The picture Nature drew (which sure 's the best)
Doth figure you by sleep and sweetest rest: 10
Sleep, nurse of our life, care's best reposer,
Nature's high'st rapture, and the vision-giver;
Sleep, which when it doth seize us, souls go play,
And make man equal as he was first day.
Yet some will say, Can pictures have more life   15
Than the original? To end this strife,
Sweet mistress, come, and show yourself to me
In your true form, while then I think to see
Some beauty angelic that comes t' unlock
My body's prison, and from life unyoke   20
My well-divorced soul, and set it free
To liberty eternal. Thus you see
I find the painter's error, and protect
Your absent beauties ill-drawn by th' effect.
For grant it were your work, and not the grave's,   25
Draw love by madness then, tyrants by slaves,
Because they make men such. Dear mistress, then,
If you would not be seen by owl-ey'd men,
Appear at noon i' th' air, with so much light
The sun may be a moon, the day a night;   30
Clear to my soul, but dark'ning the weak sense
Of those the other world's Cimmeriens;
And in your fatal robe, embroidered
With star-characters, teaching me to read
The destiny of mortals, while your clear brow   35
Presents a majesty to instruct me how
To love or dread naught else. May your bright hair,
Which are the threads of life, fair crown'd appear
With that your crown of immortality;
In your right hand the keys of Heaven be;   40

In th' other those of the Infernal Pit,
Whence none retires, if once he enter it.
And here let me complain how few are those
Whose souls you shall from earth's vast dungeon loose
To endless happiness! few that attend   45
You, the true guide, unto their journey's end;
And if of old virtue's way narrow were,
'Tis rugged now, having no passenger.
Our life is but a dark and stormy night,
To which sense yields a weak and glimmering light,   50
While wand'ring man thinks he discerneth all
By that which makes him but mistake and fall.
He sees enough who doth his darkness see;
These are great lights, by which less dark'ned be.
Shine then sun-brighter through my sense's veil,   55
A day-star of the light doth never fail;
Show me that goodness which compounds the strife
'Twixt a long sickness and a weary life;
Set forth that justice which keeps all in awe,
Certain and equal more than any law;   60
Figure that happy and eternal rest,
Which till man do enjoy he is not blest.
Come and appear then, dear soul-ravisher,
Heaven's light-usher, man's deliverer,
And do not think, when I new beauties see,   65
They can withdraw my settled love from thee.
Flesh-beauty strikes me not at all: I know,
When thou dost leave them to the grave, they show
Worse than they now show thee: they shall not move
In me the least part of delight or love,   70
But as they teach your power.   Be she nut-brown,
The loveliest colour which the flesh doth crown,
I'll think her like a nut, a fair outside,
Within which worms and rottenness abide;
If fair, then like the worm itself to be;   75
If painted, like their slime and sluttery.
If any yet will think their beauties best,
And will against you, spite of all, contest,
Seize them with age: so in themselves they'll hate
What they scorn'd in your picture, and too late   80
See their fault and the painter's.   Yet if this,
Which their great'st plague and wrinkled torture is,
Please not, you may to the more wicked sort,

Or such as of your praises make a sport,
Denounce an open war, send chosen bands   85
O₁ worms, your soldiers, to their fairest hands,
And make them leprous-scabb'd; upon their face
Let those your pioneers, ring-worms, take their place,
And safely near with strong approaches got,
Entrench it round, while their teeth's rampire, rot   90
With other worms, may with a damp inbred
Stink to their senses, which they shall not dead:
And thus may all that ere they prided in
Confound them now.   As for the parts within,
Send gut-worms, which may undermine a way   95
Unto their vital parts, and so display
That your pale ensign on the walls; then let
Those worms, your veterans, which never yet
Did fail, enter pell-mell and ransack all,
Just as they see the well-rais'd building fall;   100
While they do this, your foragers command,
The caterpillars, to devour their land,
And with them wasps, your wing'd-worm-horsemen, bring,
To charge, in troop, those rebels with their sting:
All this, unless your beauty they confess.   105

    And now, sweet mistress, let m' a while digress,
T' admire these noble worms whom I invoke,
And not the Muses—You that eat through oak
And bark, will you spare paper and my verse,
Because your praises they do here rehearse?   110

    Brave legions then, sprung from the mighty race
Of man corrupted, and which hold the place
Of his undoubted issue; you that are
Brain-born, Minerva-like, and like her war,
Well-arm'd complete-mail jointed soldiers,   115
Whose force Herculean links in pieces tears;
To you the vengeance of all spill-blood falls,
Beast-eating men, men-eating cannibals.
Death-privileg'd, were you in sunder smit
You do not lose your life but double it;   120
Best-framed types of the immortal soul,
Which in yourselves and in each part are whole;
Last-living creatures, heirs of all the earth,
For when all men are dead, it is your birth:
c 873

When you die, your brave self-kill'd general   125
(For nothing else can kill him) doth end all.
What vermin-breeding body then thinks scorn
His flesh should be by your brave fury torn?

  Willing to you this carcase I submit,
A gift so free I do not care for it;   130
Which yet you shall not take until I see
My mistress first reveal herself to me.

  Meanwhile, great mistress whom my soul admires,
Grant me your true picture who it desires,
That he your matchless beauty might maintain   135
'Gainst all men that will quarrels entertain
For a flesh-mistress; the worst I can do
Is but to keep the way that leads to you,
And howsoever the event doth prove,
To have revenge below, reward above;   140
Hear, from my body's prison, this my call,
Who from my mouth-grate and eye-window bawl.

EPITAPH ON SIR PHILIP SIDNEY, LYING IN ST. PAUL'S WITHOUT A MONUMENT; TO BE FAST'NED UPON THE CHURCH DOOR

      READER,
      Within this church Sir Philip Sidney lies,
      Nor is it fit that I should more acquaint,
          Lest superstition rise
              And men adore,   5
      Soldiers their martyr, lovers their saint.

EPITAPH FOR HIMSELF

READER,

The monument which thou beholdest here
    Presents Edward, Lord Herbert to thy sight,
A man who was so free from either hope or fear
    To have or lose this ordinary light,   5
That when to elements his body turned were,
    He knew that as those elements would fight,
So his immortal soul should find above,
    With his Creator, peace, joy, truth and love.

SONNET

MADE UPON THE GROVES NEAR MERLOU CASTLE

You well-compacted groves, whose light and shade,
  Mix'd equally, produce nor heat nor cold,
  Either to burn the young or freeze the old,
But to one even temper being made,
Upon a green embroidering through each glade   5
  An airy silver and a sunny gold,
  So clothe the poorest that they do behold
Themselves in riches which can never fade;
  While the wind whistles, and the birds do sing,
While your twigs clip, and while the leaves do friss,   10
  While the fruit ripens which those trunks do bring,
  Senseless to all but love, do you not spring
Pleasure of such a kind as truly is
A self-renewing vegetable bliss?

TO THE C[OUNTESS] OF D[ORSET?]

Since in your face, as in a beauteous sphere,
Delight and state so sweetly mix'd appear
That love 's not light, nor gravity severe,
  All your attractive graces seem to draw
  A modest rigour keepeth so in awe,   5
  That in their turns each of them gives the law.

Therefore, though chaste and virtuous desire
Through that your native mildness may aspire,
Until a just regard it doth acquire,
  Yet if love thence a forward hope project,   10
  You can, by virtue of a sweet neglect,
  Convert it straight to reverend respect.

Thus, as in your rare temper, we may find
An excellence so perfect in each kind,
That a fair body hath a fairer mind;   15
  So all the beams you diversely do dart,
  As well on th' understanding as the heart,
  Of love and honour equal cause impart.

DITTY

Why dost thou hate return instead of love,
    And with such merciless despite
      My faith and hope requite?
    Oh! if th' affection cannot move,
    Learn innocence yet of the dove,   5
And thy disdain to juster bounds confine;
Or if t'wards man thou equally decline
    The rules of justice and of mercy too,
Thou mayst thy love to such a point refine,
    As it will kill more than thy hate can do.   10

Love, love, Melaina, then, though death ensue,
    Yet [if] it is a greater fate
      To die through love than hate,
    Rather a victory pursue,
    To beauty's lawful conquest due,   15
Than tyrant eyes envenom with disdain;
Or if thy power thou wouldst so maintain,
    As equally to be both lov'd and dread,
Let timely kisses call to life again
    Him whom thy eyes have planet-strucken dead.   20

Kiss, kiss, Melaina, then, and do not stay
    Until these sad effects appear
      Which now draw on so near,
    That didst thou longer help delay,
    My soul must fly so fast away,   25
As would at once both life and love divorce;
Or if I needs must die without remorse,
    Kiss and embalm me so with that sweet breath,
That while thou triumph'st o'er Love and his force,
    I may triumph yet over Fate and Death.   30

ELEGY FOR DOCTOR DONNE

What though the vulgar and received praise
With which each common poet strives to raise
His worthless patron seem to give the height
Of a true excellence, yet as the weight
Forc'd from his centre must again recoil,   5
So every praise, as if it took some foil

Only because it was not well employ'd,
Turns to those senseless principles and void,
Which, in some broken syllables being couch'd,
Cannot above an alphabet be vouch'd,   10
In which dissolved state they use to rest,
Until some other in new forms invest
Their easy matter, striving so to fix
Glory with words, and make the parts to mix.
    But since praise that wants truth, like words that want
Their proper meaning, doth itself recant,   16
Such terms, however elevate and high,
Are but like meteors, which the pregnant sky
Varies in divers figures, till at last
They either be by some dark cloud o'ercast,   20
Or, wanting inward sustenance, do devolve,
And into their first elements resolve.
    Praises, like garments, then, if loose and wide,
Are subject to fall off; if gay and pi'd,
Make men ridiculous: the just and grave   25
Are those alone which men may wear and have.
    How fitting were it then each had that part
Which is their due; and that no fraudulent art
Could so disguise the truth but they might own
Their rights, and by that property be known!   30
    For since praise is public inheritance,
If any intercommoner do chance
To give or take more praise than doth belong
Unto his part, he doth so great a wrong,
That all who claim an equal interest   35
May him implead until he do divest
His usurpations, and again restore
Unto the public what was theirs before.
    Praises should then, like definitions, be
Round, neat, convertible, such as agree   40
To persons so, that were their names conceal'd,
Must make them known as well as if reveal'd;
Such as contain the kind and difference,
And all the properties arising thence.
All praises else, or more or less than due,   45
Will prove or strongly false or weakly true.
    Having deliver'd now what praises are,
It rests that I should to the world declare
Thy praises, Donne, whom I so lov'd alive,

That with my witty Carew I should strive   50
To celebrate thee dead, did I not need
A language by itself, which should exceed
All those which are in use; for while I take
Those common words which men may even rake
From dunghill-wits, I find them so defil'd,   55
Slubber'd and false, as if they had exil'd
Truth and propriety, such as do tell
So little other things, they hardly spell
Their proper meaning, and therefore unfit
To blazon forth thy merits, or thy wit.   60
   Nor will it serve that thou didst so refine
Matter with words, that both did seem divine
When thy breath utter'd them, for thou b'ing gone,
They straight did follow thee: let therefore none
Hope to find out an idiom and sense   65
Equal to thee and to thy eminence,
Unless our gracious king give words their bound,
Call in false titles, which each-where are found,
In prose and verse, and as bad coin and light
Suppress them and their values, till the right   70
Take place and do appear, and then in lieu
Of those forg'd attributes stamp some anew,
Which, being current, and by all allow'd,
In epitaphs and tombs might be avow'd
More than their escutcheons.   Meanwhile, because 75
Nor praise is yet confined to its laws,
Nor railing wants his proper dialect,
Let thy detractors thy late life detect;
And though they term all thy heat frowardness,
Thy solitude self-pride, fasts niggardness,   80
And on this false supposal would infer
They teach not others right, themselves who err;
Yet as men to the adverse part do ply
Those crooked things which they would rectify,
So would, perchance, to loose and wanton man,   85
Such vice avail more than their virtues can.

THE BROWN BEAUTY

WHILE the two contraries of black and white
In the brown Phaië are so well unite
That they no longer now seem opposite,
  Who doubts but love hath this his colour chose,
  Since he therein doth both th' extremes compose,   5
  And as within their proper centre close?

Therefore, as it presents not to the view
That whitely raw and unconcocted hue,
Which beauty northern nations think the true;
  So neither hath it that adust aspect   10
  The Moor and Indian so much affect,
  That for it they all other do reject.

Thus, while the white well-shadow'd doth appear,
And black doth through his lustre grow so clear
That each in other equal part doth bear,   15
  All in so rare proportion is combin'd,
  That the fair temper which adorns her mind
  Is even to her outward form confin'd.

Phaië, your sex's honour, then so live,
That when the world shall with contention strive   20
To whom they would a chief perfection give,
  They might the controversy so decide,
  As, quitting all extremes on either side,
  You more than any may be dignifi'd.

AN ODE UPON A QUESTION MOVED, WHETHER LOVE SHOULD CONTINUE FOR EVER

HAVING interr'd her infant-birth,
  The wat'ry ground, that late did mourn,
  Was strew'd with flow'rs for the return
Of the wish'd bridegroom of the earth.

The well-accorded birds did sing   5
  Their hymns unto the pleasant time,
  And in a sweet consorted chime
Did welcome in the cheerful Spring;

To which soft whistles of the wind,
   And warbling murmurs of a brook,   10
   And vari'd notes of leaves that shook,
An harmony of parts did bind,

While, doubling joy unto each other,
   All in so rare concent was shown,
   No happiness that came alone,   15
Nor pleasure that was not another;

When with a love none can express,
   That mutually happy pair,
   Melander and Celinda fair,
The season with their loves did bless.   20

Walking thus towards a pleasant grove,
   Which did, it seem'd, in new delight
   The pleasures of the time unite,
To give a triumph to their love,

They stay'd at last, and on the grass   25
   Reposed so, as o'er his breast
   She bow'd her gracious head to rest,
Such a weight as no burden was.

While over either's compass'd waist
   Their folded arms were so compos'd,   30
   As if, in straitest bonds enclos'd,
They suffer'd for joys they did taste.

Long their fix'd eyes to heaven bent
   Unchanged, they did never move,
   As if so great and pure a love   35
No glass but it could represent.

When with a sweet though troubled look,
   She first brake silence, saying, "Dear friend,
   O that our love might take no end,
Or never had beginning took!   40

"I speak not this with a false heart—"
   Wherewith his hand she gently strain'd—
   "Or that would change a love maintain'd
With so much faith on either part.

"Nay, I protest, though Death with his   45
 Worst counsel should divide us here,
 His terrors could not make me fear
To come where your lov'd presence is.

"Only if love's fire with the breath
 Of life be kindled, I doubt   50
 With our last air 'twill be breath'd out,
And quenched with the cold of death.

"That if affection be a line
 Which is clos'd up in our last hour,
 Oh how 'twould grieve me any pow'r   55
Could force so dear a love as mine!"

She scarce had done, when his shut eyes
 An inward joy did represent,
 To hear Celinda thus intent
To a love he so much did prize.   60

Then with a look, it seem'd, deni'd
 All earthly pow'r but hers, yet so
 As if to her breath he did owe
This borrow'd life, he thus repli'd:

"O You wherein they say souls rest   65
 Till they descend pure heavenly fires,
 Shall lustful and corrupt desires
With your immortal seed be blest?

"And shall our love, so far beyond
 That low and dying appetite,
 And which so chaste desires unite,   70
Not hold in an eternal bond?

"Is it because we should decline,
 And wholly from our thoughts exclude
 Objects that may the sense delude,
And study only the divine?   75

"No, sure, for if none can ascend
 Ev'n to the visible degree
 Of things created, how should we
The invisible comprehend?   80

"Or rather since that Pow'r express'd
  His greatness in his works alone,
    B'ing here best in his creatures known,
Why is he not lov'd in them best?

"But is 't not true, which you pretend,   85
  That since our love and knowledge here
    Only as parts of life appear,
So they with it should take their end.

"Oh no, belov'd, I am most sure
  Those virtuous habits we acquire,   90
    As being with the soul entire,
Must with it evermore endure.

"For if where sins and vice reside
  We find so foul a guilt remain,
    As never dying in his stain   95
Still punish'd in the soul doth bide,

"Much more that true and real joy,
  Which in a virtuous love is found,
    Must be more solid in its ground
Than Fate or Death can e'er destroy.   100

"Else should our souls in vain elect,
  And vainer yet were Heaven's laws,
    When to an everlasting cause
They gave a perishing effect.

"Nor here on earth then, nor above,   105
  Our good affection can impair,
    For where God doth admit the fair,
Think you that he excludeth love?

"These eyes again, then, eyes shall see,
  And hands again these hands enfold,   110
    And all chaste pleasures can be told
Shall with us everlasting be.

"For if no use of sense remain,
  When bodies once this life forsake,
    Or they could no delight partake,   115
Why should they ever rise again?

"And if every imperfect mind
　　Make love the end of knowledge here,
　　How perfect will our love be, where
All imperfection is refin'd!　　　　　　　120

"Let then no doubt, Celinda, touch,
　　Much less your fairest mind invade;
　　Were not our souls immortal made,
Our equal loves can make them such.

"So when one wing can make no way,　　125
　　Two joined can themselves dilate,
　　So can two persons propagate,
When singly either would decay.

"So when from hence we shall be gone,
　　And be no more, nor you, nor I,　　　130
　　As one another's mystery,
Each shall be both, yet both but one."

This said, in her uplifted face,
　　Her eyes which did that beauty crown,
　　Were like two stars, that having fall'n down,　135
Look up again to find their place;

While such a moveless silent peace
　　Did seize on their becalmed sense,
　　One would have thought some Influence
Their ravish'd spirits did possess.　　　140

THE GREEN-SICKNESS BEAUTY

THOUGH the pale white within your cheeks compos'd,
　　And doubtful light unto your eye confin'd,
Though your short breath not from itself unloos'd,
　　And careless motions of your equal mind,
Argue your beauties are not all disclos'd;　　　5

Yet as a rising beam, when first 'tis shown,
　　Points fairer than when it ascends more red,
Or as a budding rose, when first 'tis blown,
　　Smells sweeter far than when it is more spread;
As all things best by principles are known;　　　10

So in your green and flourishing estate
  A beauty is discern'd, more worthy love
Than that which further doth itself dilate,
  And those degrees of variation prove,
Our vulgar wits so much do celebrate.   15

Thus, though your eyes dart not that piercing blaze
  Which doth in busy lovers' looks appear,
It is because you do not need to gaze
  On other object than your proper sphere,
Nor wander further than to run that maze.   20

So, if you want that blood which must succeed,
  And give at last a tincture to your skin,
It is because neither in outward deed
  Nor inward thought you yet admit that sin
For which your cheeks a guilty blush should need.   25

So, if your breath do not so freely flow,
  It is because you love not to consume
That vital treasure which you do bestow,
  As well to vegetate as to perfume
Your virgin leaves, as fast as they do grow.   30

Yet stay not here, love for his right will call,
  You were not born to serve your only will;
Nor can your beauty be perpetual:
  'Tis your perfection for to ripen still,
And to be gather'd rather than to fall.   35

THE GREEN-SICKNESS BEAUTY

From thy pale look while angry love doth seem
  With more imperiousness to give his law
Than where he blushingly doth beg esteem,
  We may observe pi'd beauty in such awe,
That the brav'st colour under her command,   5
  Affrighted, oft before you doth retire,
While, like a statue of yourself, you stand
  In such symmetric form as doth require
No lustre but his own.   As then in vain
  One should flesh-colouring to statues add,   10

So were it to your native white a stain,
    If it in other ornaments were clad
Than what your rich proportions do give,
    Which in a boundless fair being unconfin'd,
Exalted in your soul so seem to live   15
    That they become an emblem of your mind,
That so who to your orient white should join
    Those fading qualities most eyes adore,
Were but like one, who, gilding silver coin,
    Gave but occasion to suspect it more.   20

LA GIALLETTA GALLANTE,
OR THE SUN-BURN'D EXOTIC BEAUTY

CHILD of the sun, in whom his rays appear
Hatch'd to that lustre as doth make thee wear
Heav'n's livery in thy skin, what need'st thou fear
    The injury of air and change of clime,
    When thy exalted form is so sublime   5
    As to transcend all power of change or time?

How proud are they that in their hair but show
Some part of thee, thinking therein they owe
The greatest beauty Nature can bestow,
    When thou art so much fairer to the sight,   10
    As beams each-where diffused are more bright
    Than their deriv'd and secondary light!

But thou art cordial both to sight and taste,
While each rare fruit seems in his time to haste
To ripen in thee, till at length they waste   15
    Themselves to inward sweets, from whence again
    They, like elixirs, passing through each vein,
    An endless circulation do maintain.

How poor are they, then, whom if we but greet,
Think that raw juice which in their lips we meet   20
Enough to make us hold their kisses sweet,
    When that rich odour which in thee is smelt
    Can itself to a balmy liquor melt,
    And make it to our inward senses felt!

Leave then thy country soil and mother's home,   25
Wander a planet this way, till thou come
To give our lovers here their fatal doom;
   While if our beauties scorn to envy thine,
   It will be just they to a jaundice pine,
   And by thy gold show like some copper-mine.   30

PLATONIC LOVE

MADAM, your beauty and your lovely parts
Would scarce admit poetic praise and arts
As they are love's most sharp and piercing darts;
   Though, as again they only wound and kill
   The more deprav'd affections of our will,   5
   You claim a right to commendation still.

For as you can unto that height refine
All love's delights, as while they do incline
Unto no vice they so become divine,
   We may as well attain your excellence,   10
   As without help of any outward sense
   Would make us grow a pure intelligence.

And as a soul, thus being quite abstract,
Complies not properly with any act
Which from its better being may detract,   15
   So through the virtuous habits you infuse,
   It is enough that we may like and choose,
   Without presuming yet to take or use.

Thus angels in their starry orbs proceed
Unto affection, without other need
Than that they still on contemplation feed;   20
   Though, as they may unto this orb descend,
   You can, when you would so much lower bend,
   Give joys beyond what man can comprehend.

Do not refuse then, madam, to appear,   25
Since every radiant beam comes from your sphere
Can so much more than any else endear,
   As while through them we do discern each grace,
   The multiplied lights from every place
   Will turn, and circle, with their rays, your face.   30

PLATONIC LOVE

MADAM, believe 't, love is not such a toy
As it is sport but for the idle boy
   Or wanton youth, since it can entertain
   Our serious thoughts, and make us know how vain
All time is spent we do not thus employ.   5

For though strong passion oft on youth doth seize,
It is not yet affection, but disease
   Caus'd from repletion, which their blood doth vex,
   So that they love not woman but the sex,
And care no more than how themselves to please.   10

Whereas true lovers check that appetite
Which would presume further than to invite
   The soul unto that part it ought to take,
   When that from this address it would but make
Some introduction only to delight.   15

For while they from the outward sense transplant
The love grew there in earthly mould, and scant,
   To the soul's spacious and immortal field,
   They spring a love eternal, which will yield
All that a pure affection can grant.   20

Besides, what time or distance might effect
Is thus remov'd, while they themselves connect
   So far above all change as to exclude
   Not only all which might their sense delude,
But mind to any object else affect.   25

Nor will the proof of constancy be hard,
When they have plac'd upon their mind that guard,
   As no ignoble thought can enter there,
   And love doth such a virtue persevere,
And in itself so find a just reward.   30

And thus a love made from a worthy choice
Will to that union come, as but one voice
   Shall speak, one thought but think the other's will,
   And while, but frailty, they can know no ill,
Their souls more than their bodies must rejoice.   35

In which estate nothing can so fulfil
Those heights of pleasure which their souls instil
    Into each other, but that love thence draws
    New arguments of joy, while the same cause
That makes them happy makes them greater still.   40

So that, however multipli'd and vast
Their love increase, they will not think it past
    The bounds of growth till their exalted fire,
    B'ing equally enlarg'd with their desire,
Transform and fix them to one star at last.   45

Or when that otherwise they were inclin'd
Unto those public joys which are assign'd
    To blessed souls when they depart from hence,
    They would, besides what heaven doth dispense,
Have their contents they in each other find.   50

THE IDEA

MADE OF ALNWICK, IN HIS EXPEDITION TO SCOTLAND WITH THE ARMY, 1639

ALL beauties vulgar eyes on earth do see,
At best but some imperfect copies be
Of those the Heavens did at first decree.

For though th' ideas of each sev'ral kind,
Conceiv'd above by the Eternal Mind,   5
Are such as none can error in them find

(Since from his thoughts and presence he doth bear
And shut out all deformity so far
That the least beauty near him is a star);

As Nature yet from far th' ideas views,   10
And doth besides but vile materials choose,
We in her works observe no small abuse:

Some of her figures therefore, foil'd and blurr'd,
Show as if Heaven had no way concurr'd
In shapes so disproportion'd and absurd;   15

Which, being again vex'd with some hate and spite
That doth in them vengeance and rage excite,
Seem to be tortur'd and deformed quite.

While so being fix'd, they yet in them contain
Another sort of ugliness and stain, 20
B'ing with old wrinkles interlin'd again.

Lastly, as if Nature ev'n did not know
What colour every sev'ral part should owe,
They look as if their galls did overflow.

Fair is the mark of Good, and foul of Ill, 25
Although not so infallibly, but still
The proof depends most on the mind and will:

As Good yet rarely in the foul is met,
So 'twould as little by its union get
As a rich jewel that were poorly set; 30

For since Good first did at the fair begin,
Foul being but a punishment for sin,
Fair 's the true outside to the Good within.

In these the Supreme Pow'r then so doth guide
Nature's weak hand, as he doth add beside 35
All by which creatures can be dignifi'd;

While you in them see so exact a line,
That through each sev'ral part a glimpse doth shine
Of their original and form divine.

Therefore the characters of fair and good 40
Are so set forth and printed in their blood,
As each in other may be understood.

That beauty so accompani'd with grace,
And equally conspicuous in the face,
In a fair woman's outside takes the place. 45

Thus while in her all rare perfection meets,
Each as with joy its fellow beauty greets,
And varies so into a thousand sweets.

Or if some tempting thought do so assault
As doubtful she 'twixt two opinions halt, 50
A gentle blush corrects and mends the fault,

That so she still fairer and better grows,
Without that thus she more to passion owes
Than what fresh colour on her cheeks bestows.

To which again her lips such helps can add   55
As both will chase all grievous thoughts and sad,
And give what else can make her good or glad.

As statuaries yet, having fram'd in clay
An hollow image, afterwards convey
The molten metal through each several way;   60

But when it once unto its place hath pass'd,
And th' inward statua perfectly is cast,
Do throw away the outward clay at last:

So, when that form the Heav'ns at first decreed
Is finished within, souls do not need   65
Their bodies more, but would from them be freed.

For who still cover'd with their earth would lie?
Who would not shake their fetters off and fly,
And be, at least, next to a deity?

However then you be most lovely here,   70
Yet when you from all elements are clear,
You far more pure and glorious shall appear.

Thus from above I doubt not to behold
Your second self renew'd in your own mould,
And rising thence fairer than can be told.   75

From whence ascending to the elect and blest,
In your true joys you will not find it least
That I in heav'n shall know and love you best.

For while I do your coming there attend,
I shall much time on your idea spend,   80
And note how far all others you transcend.

And thus, though you more than an angel be,
Since being here to sin and mischief free,
You will have rais'd yourself to their degree,

That so victorious over Death and Fate,   85
And happy in your everlasting state,
You shall triumphant enter heaven gate.

Hasten not thither yet, for as you are
A beauty upon earth without compare,
You will show best still where you are most rare.   90

Live all out lives then: if the picture can
Here entertain a loving absent man,
Much more th' idea where you first began.

PLATONIC LOVE

DISCONSOLATE and sad,
So little hope of remedy I find,
That when my matchless mistress were inclined
    To pity me, 'twould scarcely make me glad,
The discomposing of so fair a mind   5
    B'ing that which would to my afflictions add.

For when she should repent
This act of charity had made her part
With such a precious jewel as her heart,
    Might she not grieve that ere she did relent?   10
And then were it [not] fit I felt the smart
    Until I grew the greater penitent?

Nor were 't a good excuse,
When she pleas'd to call for her heart again,
To tell her of my suffering and pain,   15
    Since that I should her clemency abuse,
While she did see what wrong she did sustain
    In giving what she justly might refuse.

Vex'd thus with me at last,
When from her kind restraint she now were gone,   20
And I left to the manacles alone,
    Should I not on another rock be cast,
Since they who have not yet content do moan
    Far less than they whose hope thereof is past?

Besides, I would deserve,   25
And not live poorly on the alms of love,
Or claim a favour did not singly move
    From my regard if she her joys reserve
Unto some other, she at length should prove,
    Rather than beg her pity I would starve.   30

Let her then be serene,
Alike exempt from pity and from hate;
Let her still keep her dignity and state;
　　Yet from her glories something I shall glean,
For when she doth them everywhere dilate,　　35
　　A beam or two to me must intervene.

　　And this shall me sustain,
For though due merit I cannot express,
Yet she shall know none ever lov'd for less
　　Or easier reward: let her remain
Still great and good, and from her happiness　　40
　　My chief contentment I will entertain.

"RESTRAINED HOPES, THOUGH YOU DARE NOT ASPIRE"

Restrained hopes, though you dare not aspire
To fly an even pitch with my desire,
　　Yet fall no lower, and at least take heed
　　That you no way unto despair proceed,
Since in what form soe'er you keep entire,　　5
　　I shall the less all other comforts need.

I know how much presumption did transcend,
When that affection could at most pretend
　　To be believ'd, would needs yet higher soar,
　　And love a beauty which I should adore,　　10
Though yet therein I had no other end
　　But to assure that none could love her more.

Only may she not think her beauty less
That on low objects it doth still express
　　An equal force, while it doth rule all hearts　　15
　　Alike in the remot'st as nearest parts,
Since if it did at any distance cease,
　　It wanted of that pow'r it should impart.

Small earthly lights but to some space extend,
And then unto the dim and dark do tend,　　20
　　And common heat doth at some length so stop,
　　That it cannot so much as warm one drop,
While light and heat that doth from heav'n descend
　　Warms the low valley more than mountain's top.

Nor do they always best of the heav'ns deserve   25
Who gaze on 't most, but they who do reserve
    Themselves to know it, since not all that will
    Climb up into a steeple or a hill
So well its pow'r and influence observe,
    As they who study and remark it still.   30

Would she then in full glory on me shine,
An image of that light which is divine,
    I then should see more clear, while she did draw
    Me upwards, and the vapours 'twixt us awe:
To open her eyes were to open mine,   35
    And teach me wonders which I never saw.

Nor would there thus be any cause to fear
That while her pow'r attractive drew me near,
    The odds betwixt us would the lesser show,
    Since the most common understandings know   40
That inequalities still most appear
    When brought together and composed so.

As there is nothing yet doth so excel
But there is found, if not its parallel,
    Yet something so conform, as though far least   45
    May yet obtain therein an interest,
Why may not faith and truth then join so well,
    As they may suit her rare perfections best?

Then hope, sustain thyself, though thou art hid
Thou livest still, and must till she forbid;   50
    For when she would my vows and love reject,
    They would a being in themselves project,
Since infinites as they yet never did
    Nor could conclude without some good effect.

A MEDITATION UPON HIS WAX CANDLE BURNING OUT

WHILE thy ambitious flame doth strive for height,
Yet burneth down, as clogged with the weight
    Of earthly parts to which thou art combin'd,
Thou still dost grow more short of thy desire,
And dost in vain unto that place aspire   5
    To which thy native powers seem inclin'd.

Yet when at last thou com'st to be dissolv'd,
And to thy proper principles resolv'd,
　　And all that made thee now is discompos'd,
Though thy terrestrial part in ashes lies,　　　　　10
Thy more sublime to higher regions flies,
　　The rest b'ing to the middle ways expos'd.

And while thou doest thyself each-where disperse,
Some parts of thee make up this universe,
　　Others a kind of dignity obtain,　　　　　　　15
Since thy pure wax, in its own flame consum'd,
Volumes of incense sends, in which perfum'd
　　Thy smoke mounts where thy fire could not attain.

Much more our souls then, when they go from hence,
And back unto the elements dispense　　　　　　20
　　All that built up our frail and earthly frame,
Shall through each pore and passage make their breach,
Till they with all their faculties do reach
　　Unto that place from whence at first they came.

Nor need they fear thus to be thought unkind　　25
To those poor carcases they leave behind,
　　Since, being in unequal parts commix'd,
Each in his element their place will get;
And who thought elements unhappy yet,
　　As long as they were in their stations fix'd?　　30

Or if they salli'd forth, is there not light
And heat in some, and spirit prone to fight?
　　Keep they not, in the earth and air, the field?
Besides, have they not pow'r to generate,
When, more than meteors, they stars create,[1]　　35
　　Which while they last scarce to the brightest yield?

That so in them we more than once may live,
While these materials which here did give
　　Our bodies essence, and are most of use,
Quick'ned again by the world's common soul,　　40
Which in itself and in each part is whole,
　　Can various forms in divers kinds produce.

If then, at worst, this our condition be,
When to themselves our elements are free,

　　　　　[1] In the constellation of Cassiopeia, 1572.

And each doth to its proper place revert,   45
What may we not hope from our part divine,
Which can this dross of elements refine,
   And them unto a better state assert?

Or if as cloy'd upon this earthly stage,
Which represents nothing but change or age,   50
   Our souls would all their burdens here divest,
They singly may that glorious state acquire,
Which fills alone their infinite desire
   To be of perfect happiness possess'd.

And therefore I, who do not live and move   55
By outward sense so much as faith and love,
   Which is not in inferior creatures found,
May unto some immortal state pretend,
Since by these wings I thither may ascend,
   Where faithful loving souls with joys are crown'd.   60

OCTOBER 14, 1644

ENRAGING griefs, though you most diverse be
In your first causes, you may yet agree
   To take an equal share within my heart,
   Since if each grief strive for the greatest part,
You needs must vex yourselves as well as me.   5

For your own sakes and mine then make an end,
In vain you do about a heart contend,
   Which, though it seem in greatness to dilate,
   Is but a tumour, which, in this its state,
The choicest remedies would but offend.   10

Then storm 't at once: I neither feel constraint,
Scorning your worst, nor suffer any taint,
   Dying by multitudes; though if you strive,
   I fear my heart may thus be kept alive,
Until it under its own burden faint.   15

What, is 't not done? Why then, my God, I find,
Would have me use you to reform my mind,
   Since through his help I may from you extract
   An essence pure, so spriteful and compact,
As it will be from grosser parts refin'd.   20

Which b'ing again converted by his grace
To godly sorrow, I may both efface
   Those sins first caus'd you, and together have
   Your pow'r to kill turn'd to a power to save,
And bring my soul to its desired place.   25

TO THE AUTHOR

[Prefixed to John Davies's *The Holy Rood, of Christ's Cross*, 1609.]

THINE art and subject both such worth contain,
That thou art best requited in thy pain.

ODE: OF OUR SENSE OF SIN

[Printed as Donne's in his *Poems*, 1635, but attributed to Herbert in a
manuscript of earlier date in the Bodleian Library.]

VENGEANCE will sit above our faults, but till
      She there doth sit,
We see her not, nor them.   Thus, blind, yet still
We lead her way; and thus, whilst we do ill,
      We suffer it.   5

Unhappy he whom youth makes not beware
      Of doing ill.
Enough we labour under age and care;
In number th' errors of the last place are
      The greatest still.   10

Yet we, that should the ill we new begin
      As soon repent,
(Strange thing!) perceive not; our faults ne'er are seen
But past us; neither felt, but only in
      Our punishment.   15

But we know ourselves least: mere outward shows
      Our minds so store,
That our souls no more than our eyes disclose
But form and colour.   Only he who knows
      Himself knows more.   20

INCONSTANCY

[From a manuscript in the Bodleian Library.]

INCONSTANCY's the greatest of sins,
It neither ends well nor begins;
All other faults we simply do:
This, 'tis the same fault and next too.

Inconstancy no sin will prove,
If we consider that we love
But the same beauty in another face,
Like the same body in another place.

SONNET

[From an autograph manuscript in the British Museum.]

INNUMERABLE beauties, thou white hair
Spread forth like to a region of the air,
  Curl'd like a sea, and like ethereal fire
  Dost from thy vital principles aspire
To be the highest element of fair;   5
  From thy proud heights thou so command'st desire,
That when it would presume, it grows despair,
  And from itself a vengeance doth require;
While absolute in that thy brave command,
  Knitting each hair into an awful frown   10
Like to an host of lightnings, thou dost stand
  To ruin all that fall not prostrate down,
  While to the humble like a beamy crown
Thou seemest, wreath'd by some immortal hand.

TO ONE BLACK AND NOT VERY HANDSOME, WHO EXPECTED COMMENDATION

[From the autograph manuscript.]

WHAT though your eyes be stars, your hair be night,
  And all that beauty which adorns your face
Yield in effect but such a sullen light
  It hardly serves for to set off that grace
  Which every shadow yieldeth in his place,   5
Yet more than any other you delight.

For since I love not with mine eyes but heart,
  Your red or white so little could incline,
Whether it came from nature or from art,
  I should not think it either yours or mine,   10
  As that which doth but with the skin confine,
And with the light that gave it first depart.

Let novices in love themselves address
  Unto those parts which superficial be:
Chloris, I must ingeniously confess,   15
  Nothing appears a real fair to me
  Which at the most but sometimes I do see,
But never can at any time possess.

Give me a beauty at such distance set,
  That all the senses which I would employ   20
Being within an even compass met,
  Each sense may there such equal share enjoy,
  That neither one the other shall destroy,
Or force it for to pay its fellow's debt.

So though with dovelike murmurs I did rest,   25
  Faster enchanted than with any spell,
Lying within your arms, upon your breast,
  Sipping a nectar kiss whose fragrant smell
  My tongue within your lips alone should tell,
I would not think my powers were oppress'd.   30

Then leave your simp'ring, Chloris, and make haste,
  Without delighting thus to hear me pray,
That all your sweets I may together taste.
  Should I too long on one perfection stay,
  I might be forc'd to linger on my way,   35
Or leave thee with the praise of being chaste.

A DIVINE LOVE

[Printed as Carew's in his *Poems*, 1642.]

WHY should dull Art, which is wise Nature's ape,
    If she produce a shape
So far beyond all patterns that of old
    Fell from her mould,

As thine, admir'd Lucinda, not bring forth   5
An equal wonder to express that worth
    In some new way, that hath
Like her great work no print of vulgar path?

Is it because the rapes of poetry,
    Rifling the spacious sky   10
Of all his fires, light, beauty, influence,
      Did those dispense
On aëry creations, that surpass'd
The real works of Nature, she at last,
    To prove their raptures vain,   15
Show'd such a light as poets could not feign?

Or is it 'cause the factious wits did vie,
    With vain idolatry,
Whose goddess was supreme, and so had hurl'd
      Schism through the world;   20
Whose priest sung sweetest lays; thou didst appear,
A glorious mystery, so dark, so clear,
    As Nature did intend
All should confess, but none might comprehend?

Perhaps all other beauties share a light   25
    Proportion'd to the sight
Of weak mortality, scatt'ring such loose fires
    As stir desires,
And from the brain distil salt amorous rheums,
Whilst thy immortal flame such dross consumes,   30
    And from the earthy mould
With purging fires severs the purer gold.

If so, then why in Fame's immortal scroll
    Do we their names enrol,
Whose easy hearts and wanton eyes did sweat   35
    With sensual heat?
If Petrarch's unarm'd bosom catch a wound
From a light glance, must Laura be renown'd?
    Or both a glory gain,
He from ill-govern'd love, she from disdain?   40

Shall he more fam'd in his great art become,
    For wilful martyrdom?
Shall she more title gain to chaste and fair,
    Through his despair?

Is Troy more noble 'cause to ashes turn'd   45
Than virgin cities that yet never burn'd?
      Is fire, when it consumes
Temples, more fire than when it melts perfumes?

'Cause Venus from the ocean took her form,
    Must love needs be a storm?   50
'Cause she her wanton shrines in islands rears,
    Through seas of tears,
O'er rocks and gulfs, with our own sighs for gale,
Must we to Cyprus or to Paphos sail?
      Can there no way be given   55
But a true hell that leads to her false heaven?

A TRANSLATION FROM SILIUS ITALICUS

[Included in *A Dialogue between a Tutor and a Pupil*, ?1645]

*Imilce, the wife of Hannibal, when her son Aspar was commanded
to be sacrificed, speaks thus :*

WHAT is this with blood to stain
The sacred temples?   'Tis, alas! the main
Cause of all sin, that men are ignorant
And do the knowledge of God's nature want.
Go, pray for what is just with frankincense,   5
And let the cruel rites of slaughter hence
Be banish'd; God is mild and near alli'd
To mortals, 'tis enough that we have dy'd
The altars with the blood of slaughter'd beasts.
Or if within the gods' most cruel breasts   10
This wickedness is fix'd, let me be slain
Who am the mother.   Why would you so fain
Deprive all Libya of this towardness?

THOMAS CAREW (?1595–?1639)

THE SPRING

Now that the Winter's gone, the earth hath lost
Her snow-white robes; and now no more the frost
Candies the grass, or casts an icy cream
Upon the silver lake or crystal stream:
But the warm sun thaws the benumbed earth,   5
And makes it tender; gives a sacred birth
To the dead swallow; wakes in hollow tree
The drowsy cuckoo and the humble-bee.
Now do a choir of chirping minstrels bring
In triumph to the world the youthful Spring: 10
The valleys, hills, and woods in rich array
Welcome the coming of the long'd-for May.
Now all things smile: only my love doth lour,
Nor hath the scalding noonday sun the power
To melt that marble ice which still doth hold   15
Her heart congeal'd, and makes her pity cold.
The ox, which lately did for shelter fly
Into the stall, doth now securely lie
In open fields; and love no more is made
By the fireside, but in the cooler shade   20
Amyntas now doth with his Chloris sleep
Under a sycamore, and all things keep
    Time with the season: only she doth carry
    June in her eyes, in her heart January.

TO A. L.
PERSUASIONS TO LOVE

THINK not, 'cause men flatt'ring say
Y' are fresh as April, sweet as May,
Bright as is the morning star,
That you are so; or, though you are,
Be not therefore proud, and deem   5
All men unworthy your esteem:

For, being so, you lose the pleasure
Of being fair, since that rich treasure
Of rare beauty and sweet feature
Was bestow'd on you by Nature　　　　　　　10
To be enjoy'd, and 'twere a sin
There to be scant, where she hath bin
So prodigal of her best graces:
Thus common beauties and mean faces
Shall have more pastime, and enjoy　　　　　15
The sport you lose by being coy.
Did the thing for which I sue
Only concern myself, not you;
Were men so fram'd as they alone
Reap'd all the pleasure, women none;　　　　20
Then had you reason to be scant:
But 'twere a madness not to grant
That which affords (if you consent)
To you, the giver, more content
Than me, the beggar.　 Oh, then be　　　　　25
Kind to yourself, if not to me.
Starve not yourself, because you may
Thereby make me pine away;
Nor let brittle beauty make
You your wiser thoughts forsake;　　　　　　30
For that lovely face will fail:
Beauty 's sweet, but beauty 's frail;
'Tis sooner past, 'tis sooner done,
Than Summer's rain, or Winter's sun;
Most fleeting, when it is most dear,　　　　　35
'Tis gone, while we but say 'tis here.
These curious locks, so aptly twin'd,
Whose every hair a soul doth bind,
Will change their auburn hue, and grow
White and cold as Winter's snow.　　　　　　40
That eye, which now is Cupid's nest,
Will prove his grave, and all the rest
Will follow; in the cheek, chin, nose,
Nor lily shall be found, nor rose.
And what will then become of all　　　　　　45
Those whom now you servants call?
Like swallows, when your Summer 's done,
They 'll fly, and seek some warmer sun.
Then wisely choose one to your friend

Whose love may, when your beauties end,   50
Remain still firm: be provident,
And think, before the Summer's spent,
Of following Winter; like the ant,
In plenty hoard for time of scant.
Cull out, amongst the multitude   55
Of lovers that seek to intrude
Into your favour, one that may
Love for an age, not for a day;
One that will quench your youthful fires,
And feed in age your hot desires.   60
For when the storms of time have mov'd
Waves on that cheek which was belov'd,
When a fair lady's face is pin'd,
And yellow spread where red once shin'd;
When beauty, youth, and all sweets leave her,   65
Love may return, but lover never:
And old folks say there are no pains
Like itch of love in aged veins.
O love me, then, and now begin it,
Let us not lose this present minute;   70
For time and age will work that wrack
Which time or age shall ne'er call back.
The snake each year fresh skin resumes,
And eagles change their aged plumes;
The faded rose each Spring receives   75
A fresh red tincture on her leaves:
But if your beauties once decay,
You never know a second May.
O then, be wise, and whilst your season
Affords you days for sport, do reason;   80
Spend not in vain your life's short hour,
But crop in time your beauty's flower,
Which will away, and doth together
Both bud and fade, both blow and wither.

LIPS AND EYES

In Celia's face a question did arise,
Which were more beautiful, her lips or eyes?
"We," said the eyes, "send forth those pointed darts
Which pierce the hardest adamantine hearts."

"From us," repli'd the lips, "proceed those blisses 5
Which lovers reap by kind words and sweet kisses."
Then wept the eyes, and from their springs did pour
Of liquid oriental pearl a shower;
Whereat the lips, mov'd with delight and pleasure,
Through a sweet smile unlock'd their pearly treasure 10
  And bade Love judge, whether did add more grace,
  Weeping or smiling pearls, to Celia's face.

A DIVINE MISTRESS

In Nature's pieces still I see
Some error that might mended be;
Something my wish could still remove,
Alter or add; but my fair love
Was fram'd by hands far more divine, 5
For she hath every beauteous line:
Yet I had been far happier,
Had Nature, that made me, made her.
Then likeness might (that love creates)
Have made her love what now she hates; 10
Yet, I confess, I cannot spare
From her just shape the smallest hair;
Nor need I beg from all the store
Of heaven for her one beauty more.
She hath too much divinity for me: 15
You gods, teach her some more humanity.

SONG

A BEAUTIFUL MISTRESS

If, when the sun at noon displays
            His brighter rays,
            Thou but appear,
He then, all pale with shame and fear,
            Quencheth his light, 5
Hides his dark brow, flies from thy sight,
            And grows more dim,
      Compar'd to thee, than stars to him.
If thou but show thy face again,
When darkness doth at midnight reign, 10

The darkness flies, and light is hurl'd
Round about the silent world:
So as alike thou driv'st away
Both light and darkness, night and day.

A CRUEL MISTRESS

WE read of kings and gods that kindly took
A pitcher fill'd with water from the brook;
But I have daily tend'red without thanks
Rivers of tears that overflow their banks.
A slaughter'd bull will appease angry Jove,   5
A horse the Sun, a lamb the God of Love;
But she disdains the spotless sacrifice
Of a pure heart, that at her altar lies.
Vesta is not displeas'd if her chaste urn
Do with repaired fuel ever burn;   10
But my saint frowns, though to her honour'd name
I consecrate a never-dying flame.
Th' Assyrian king did none i' th' furnace throw
But those that to his image did not bow;
With bended knees I daily worship her,   15
Yet she consumes her own idolater.
Of such a goddess no times leave record,
That burnt the temple where she was ador'd.

SONG

MURD'RING BEAUTY

I 'LL gaze no more on her bewitching face,
Since ruin harbours there in every place;
For my enchanted soul alike she drowns
With calms and tempests of her smiles and frowns.
I 'll love no more those cruel eyes of hers,   5
Which, pleas'd or anger'd, still are murderers:
For if she dart, like lightning, through the air
Her beams of wrath, she kills me with despair:
If she behold me with a pleasing eye,
I surfeit with excess of joy, and die.   10

MY MISTRESS COMMANDING ME TO RETURN
HER LETTERS

So grieves th' advent'rous merchant, when he throws
All the long-toil'd-for treasure his ship stows
Into the angry main, to save from wrack
Himself and men, as I grieve to give back
These letters: yet so powerful is your sway,   5
As if you bid me die, I must obey.
Go then, blest papers, you shall kiss those hands
That gave you freedom, but hold me in bands;
Which with a touch did give you life, but I,
Because I may not touch those hands, must die.   10
Methinks, as if they knew they should be sent
Home to their native soil from banishment,
I see them smile, like dying saints that know
They are to leave the earth, and tow'rd heaven go.
When you return, pray tell your sovereign   15
And mine, I gave you courteous entertain;
Each line receiv'd a tear, and then a kiss;
First bath'd in that, it 'scap'd unscorch'd from this:
I kiss'd it because your hand had been there;
But, 'cause it was not now, I shed a tear.   20
Tell her, no length of time, nor change of air,
No cruelty, disdain, absence, despair,
No, nor her steadfast constancy, can deter
My vassal heart from ever hon'ring her.
Though these be powerful arguments to prove   25
I love in vain, yet I must ever love.
Say, if she frown, when you that word rehearse,
Service in prose is oft call'd love in verse:
Then pray her, since I send back on my part
Her papers, she will send me back my heart.   30
If she refuse, warn her to come before
The God of Love, whom thus I will implore:
"Trav'lling thy country's road, great God, I spi'd
By chance this lady, and walk'd by her side
From place to place, fearing no violence,   35
For I was well arm'd, and had made defence
In former fights 'gainst fiercer foes than she
Did at our first encounter seem to be.
But, going farther, every step reveal'd

Some hidden weapon, till that time conceal'd.   40
Seeing those outward arms, I did begin
To fear some greater strength was lodg'd within;
Looking into her mind, I might survey
An host of beauties, that in ambush lay,
And won the day before they fought the field,   45
For I, unable to resist, did yield.
But the insulting tyrant so destroys
My conquer'd mind, my ease, my peace, my joys,
Breaks my sweet sleeps, invades my harmless rest,
Robs me of all the treasure of my breast,   50
Spares not my heart, nor yet a greater wrong,
For, having stol'n my heart, she binds my tongue.
But at the last her melting eyes unseal'd
My lips, enlarg'd my tongue: then I reveal'd
To her own ears the story of my harms,   55
Wrought by her virtues and her beauty's charms.
Now hear, just judge, an act of savageness;
When I complain, in hope to find redress,
She bends her angry brow, and from her eye
Shoots thousand darts.   I then well hop'd to die,   60
But in such sovereign balm Love dips his shot,
That, though they wound a heart, they kill it not.
She saw the blood gush forth from many a wound,
Yet fled, and left me bleeding on the ground,
Nor sought my cure, nor saw me since: 'tis true,   65
Absence and Time, two cunning leeches, drew
The flesh together; yet, sure, though the skin
Be clos'd without, the wound festers within.
Thus hath this cruel lady us'd a true
Servant and subject to herself and you;   70
Nor know I, great Love, if my life be lent
To show thy mercy or my punishment:
Since by the only magic of thy art
A lover still may live that wants his heart.
If this indictment fright her, so as she   75
Seem willing to return my heart to me,
But cannot find it (for perhaps it may,
'Mongst other trifling hearts, be out o' th' way);
If she repent, and would make me amends,
Bid her but send me hers, and we are friends."   80

SECRECY PROTESTED

FEAR not, dear love, that I 'll reveal
Those hours of pleasure we two steal;
No eye shall see, nor yet the sun
Descry, what thou and I have done.
No ear shall hear our love, but we   5
Silent as the night will be;
The God of Love himself (whose dart
Did first wound mine and then thy heart)
Shall never know that we can tell
What sweets in stol'n embraces dwell.   10
This only means may find it out:
If, when I die, physicians doubt
What caus'd my death, and there to view
Of all their judgments which was true,
Rip up my heart, oh then, I fear,   15
The world will see thy picture there.

A PRAYER TO THE WIND

Go, thou gentle whispering wind,
Bear this sigh, and if thou find
Where my cruel fair doth rest,
Cast it in her snowy breast,
So, inflam'd by my desire,   5
It may set her heart afire.
Those sweet kisses thou shalt gain
Will reward thee for thy pain;
Boldly light upon her lip,
There suck odours, and thence skip   10
To her bosom; lastly fall
Down, and wander over all.
Range about those ivory hills,
From whose every part distils
Amber dew; there spices grow,   15
There pure streams of nectar flow;
There perfume thyself, and bring
All those sweets upon thy wing.
As thou return'st, change by thy power
Every weed into a flower;   20

Turn each thistle to a vine,
Make the bramble eglantine;
For so rich a booty made,
Do but this, and I am paid.
Thou canst with thy powerful blast   25
Heat apace, and cool as fast;
Thou canst kindle hidden flame,
And again destroy the same:
Then, for pity, either stir
Up the fire of love in her,   30
That alike both flames may shine,
Or else quite extinguish mine.

SONG

MEDIOCRITY IN LOVE REJECTED

GIVE me more love, or more disdain;
  The torrid or the frozen zone
Bring equal ease unto my pain,
  The temperate affords me none:
Either extreme of love or hate   5
Is sweeter than a calm estate.

Give me a storm; if it be love,
  Like Danaë in that golden shower,
I swim in pleasure; if it prove
  Disdain, that torrent will devour   10
My vulture-hopes; and he 's possess'd
Of heaven, that 's but from hell releas'd.
    Then crown my joys, or cure my pain:
    Give me more love, or more disdain.

SONG

GOOD COUNSEL TO A YOUNG MAID

GAZE not on thy beauty's pride,
Tender maid, in the false tide
That from lovers' eyes doth slide.

Let thy faithful crystal show
How thy colours come and go: 5
Beauty takes a foil from woe.

Love, that in those smooth streams lies
Under pity's fair disguise,
Will thy melting heart surprise.

Nets of passion's finest thread,   10
Snaring poems, will be spread,
All to catch thy maidenhead.

Then beware! for those that cure
Love's disease, themselves endure
For reward a calenture.   15

Rather let the lover pine,
Than his pale cheek should assign
A perpetual blush to thine.

TO MY MISTRESS SITTING BY A RIVER'S SIDE

AN EDDY

MARK how yon eddy steals away
From the rude stream into the bay;
There lock'd up safe, she doth divorce
Her waters from the channel's course,
And scorns the torrent that did bring   5
Her headlong from her native spring.
Now doth she with her new love play,
Whilst he runs murmuring away.
Mark how she courts the banks, whilst they
As amorously their arms display,   10
T' embrace and clip her silver waves:
See how she strokes their sides, and craves
An entrance there, which they deny;
Whereat she frowns, threat'ning to fly
Home to her stream, and 'gins to swim   15
Backward, but from the channel's brim
Smiling returns into the creek,
With thousand dimples on her cheek.
   Be thou this eddy, and I 'll make
My breast thy shore, where thou shalt take   20
Secure repose, and never dream
Of the quite forsaken stream;

Let him to the wide ocean haste,
There lose his colour, name, and taste:
Thou shalt save all, and, safe from him,   25
Within these arms for ever swim.

SONG

CONQUEST BY FLIGHT

LADIES, fly from love's smooth tale,
Oaths steep'd in tears do oft prevail;
Grief is infectious, and the air
Inflam'd with sighs will blast the fair.
Then stop your ears when lovers cry,   5
Lest yourselves weep when no soft eye
Shall with a sorrowing tear repay
That pity which you cast away.

Young men, fly when beauty darts
Amorous glances at your hearts: 10
The fix'd mark gives the shooter aim,
And ladies' looks have power to maim;
Now 'twixt their lips, now in their eyes,
Wrapt in a smile or kiss, love lies:
Then fly betimes, for only they   15
Conquer love that run away.

SONG

TO MY INCONSTANT MISTRESS

WHEN thou, poor excommunicate
    From all the joys of love, shalt see
The full reward and glorious fate
    Which my strong faith shall purchase me,
    Then curse thine own inconstancy.   5

A fairer hand than thine shall cure
    That heart which thy false oaths did wound;
And to my soul a soul more pure
    Than thine shall by Love's hand be bound,
    And both with equal glory crown'd.   10

Then shalt thou weep, entreat, complain
   To Love, as I did once to thee;
When all thy tears shall be as vain
   As mine were then, for thou shalt be
   Damn'd for thy false apostacy.   15

SONG

PERSUASIONS TO ENJOY

If the quick spirits in your eye
Now languish, and anon must die;
If every sweet, and every grace
Must fly from that forsaken face:
   Then, Celia, let us reap our joys   5
   Ere Time such goodly fruit destroys.

Or if that golden fleece must grow
For ever free from aged snow;
If those bright suns must know no shade,
Nor your fresh beauties ever fade;   10
Then fear not, Celia, to bestow
What, still being gather'd, still must grow.
   Thus, either Time his sickle brings
   In vain, or else in vain his wings.

A DEPOSITION FROM LOVE

I was foretold your rebel sex
   Nor love nor pity knew;
And with what scorn you use to vex
   Poor hearts that humbly sue.
Yet I believ'd, to crown our pain,   5
   Could we the fortress win,
The happy lover sure should gain
   A paradise within:
I thought Love's plagues, like dragons, sate
Only to fright us at the gate.   10

But I did enter, and enjoy
   What happy lovers prove;
For I could kiss, and sport, and toy,
   And taste those sweets of love,

Which, had they but a lasting state,   15
   Or if in Celia's breast
The force of love might not abate,
   Jove were too mean a guest:
But now her breach of faith far more
Afflicts, than did her scorn before.   20

Hard fate! to have been once possess'd,
   As victor, of a heart,
Achiev'd with labour and unrest,
   And then forc'd to depart.
If the stout foe will not resign,   25
   When I besiege a town,
I lose but what was never mine;
   But he that is cast down
From enjoy'd beauty, feels a woe
Only deposed kings can know.   30

INGRATEFUL BEAUTY THREAT'NED

KNOW, Celia, since thou art so proud,
   'Twas I that gave thee thy renown;
Thou hadst in the forgotten crowd
   Of common beauties liv'd unknown,
Had not my verse exhal'd thy name,   5
And with it imp'd the wings of Fame.

That killing power is none of thine:
   I gave it to thy voice and eyes;
Thy sweets, thy graces, all are mine;
   Thou art my star, shin'st in my skies:
Then dart not from thy borrow'd sphere   10
Lightning on him that fix'd thee there.

Tempt me with such affrights no more,
   Lest what I made I uncreate;
Let fools thy mystic forms adore,
   I 'll know thee in thy mortal state.   15
Wise poets that wrapp'd Truth in tales
Knew her themselves through all her veils.

DISDAIN RETURNED

He that loves a rosy cheek,
　　Or a coral lip admires,
Or from star-like eyes doth seek
　　Fuel to maintain his fires;
As old Time makes these decay,　　　　　5
So his flames must waste away.

But a smooth and steadfast mind,
　　Gentle thoughts and calm desires,
Hearts with equal love combin'd,
　　Kindle never-dying fires.　　　　　　10
Where these are not, I despise
Lovely cheeks, or lips, or eyes.

No tears, Celia, now shall win
　　My resolv'd heart to return;
I have search'd thy soul within,　　　　15
　　And find naught but pride and scorn:
I have learn'd thy arts, and now
Can disdain as much as thou.
　　Some power, in my revenge, convey
　　That love to her I cast away.　　　　20

A LOOKING-GLASS

That flatt'ring glass, whose smooth face wears
Your shadow, which a sun appears,
Was once a river of my tears.

About your cold heart they did make
A circle, where the briny lake　　　　　5
Congeal'd into a crystal cake.

Gaze no more on that killing eye,
For fear the native cruelty
Doom you, as it doth all, to die:

For fear lest the fair object move　　　10
Your froward heart to fall in love:
Then you yourself my rival prove.

Look rather on my pale cheeks pin'd,
There view your beauties, there you 'll find
A fair face, but a cruel mind.   15

Be not for ever frozen, coy!
One beam of love will soon destroy
And melt that ice to floods of joy.

AN ELEGY ON THE LADY PEN[ISTON],

SENT TO MY MISTRESS OUT OF FRANCE

Let him who from his tyrant mistress did
This day receive his cruel doom, forbid
His eyes to weep that loss, and let him here
Open those flood-gates to bedew this bier;
So shall those drops, which else would be but brine,   5
Be turn'd to manna, falling on her shrine.
Let him who, banish'd far from her dear sight
Whom his soul loves, doth in that absence write
Or lines of passion or some powerful charms,
To vent his own grief or unlock her arms,   10
Take off his pen, and in sad verse bemoan
This general sorrow, and forget his own.
So may those verses live, which else must die;
For though the Muses give eternity
When they embalm with verse, yet she could give   15
Life unto that Muse by which others live.
Oh, pardon me, fair soul, that boldly have
Dropp'd though but one tear on thy silent grave,
And writ on that earth, which such honour had,
To clothe that flesh wherein thyself was clad.   20
And pardon me, sweet saint whom I adore,
That I this tribute pay out of the store
Of lines and tears that 's only due to thee.
Oh, do not think it new idolatry;
Though you are only sovereign of this land,   25
Yet universal losses may command
A subsidy from every private eye,
And press each pen to write; so to supply
And feed the common grief. If this excuse
Prevail not, take these tears to your own use,   30
As shed for you: for when I saw her die,
I then did think on your mortality.

For since nor virtue, will, nor beauty, could
Preserve from Death's hand this their heavenly mould,
Where they were framed all, and where they dwelt,   35
I then knew you must die too, and did melt
Into these tears; but, thinking on that day,
And when the gods resolv'd to take away
A saint from us, I that did know what dearth
There was of such good souls upon the earth,   40
Began to fear lest Death, their officer,
Might have mistook, and taken thee for her:
So hadst thou robb'd us of that happiness
Which she in heaven, and I in thee possess.
But what can heaven to her glory add?   45
The praises she hath dead, living she had;
To say she's now an angel is no more
Praise than she had, for she was one before.
Which of the saints can show more votaries
Than she had here? Even those that did despise   50
The angels, and may her now she is one,
Did, whilst she liv'd, with pure devotion
Adore and worship her: her virtues had
All honour here, for this world was too bad
To hate or envy her; these cannot rise   55
So high as to repine at deities:
But now she's 'mongst her fellow-saints, they may
Be good enough to envy her: this way
There's loss i' th' change 'twixt heaven and earth, if she
Should leave her servants here below, to be   60
Hated of her competitors above.
But sure her matchless goodness needs must move
Those blest souls to admire her excellence;
By this means only can her journey hence
To heaven prove gain, if, as she was but here   65
Worshipp'd by men, she be by angels there.
But I must weep no more over this urn,
My tears to their own channel must return;
And having ended these sad obsequies,
My Muse must back to her old exercise,   70
To tell the story of my martyrdom.
But oh, thou idol of my soul, become
Once pitiful, that she may change her style,
Dry up her blubber'd eyes, and learn to smile.
Rest then, blest soul, for as ghosts fly away   75

When the shrill cock proclaims the infant day,
So must I hence, for lo! I see from far
The minions of the Muses coming are,
Each of them bringing to thy sacred hearse
In either eye a tear, each hand a verse.   80

TO MY MISTRESS IN ABSENCE

THOUGH I must live here, and by force
Of your command suffer divorce;
Though I am parted, yet my mind,
That 's more myself, still stays behind.
I breathe in you, you keep my heart,   5
'Twas but a carcase that did part.
Then though our bodies are disjoin'd,
As things that are to place confin'd,
Yet let our boundless spirits meet,
And in love's sphere each other greet;   10
There let us work a mystic wreath,
Unknown unto the world beneath;
There let our clasp'd loves sweetly twin,
There let our secret thoughts unseen
Like nets be weav'd and intertwin'd,   15
Wherewith we 'll catch each other's mind.
There whilst our souls do sit and kiss,
Tasting a sweet and subtle bliss
(Such as gross lovers cannot know,
Whose hands and lips meet here below),   20
Let us look down, and mark what pain
Our absent bodies here sustain,
And smile to see how far away
The one doth from the other stray;
Yet burn and languish with desire   25
To join, and quench their mutual fire;
There let us joy to see from far
Our emulous flames at loving war,
Whilst both with equal lustre shine,
Mine bright as yours, yours bright as mine.   30
There seated in those heavenly bowers,
We 'll cheat the lag and ling'ring hours,
Making our bitter absence sweet,
Till souls and bodies both may meet.

TO HER IN ABSENCE

A SHIP

Toss'd in a troubled sea of griefs, I float
Far from the shore, in a storm-beaten boat;
Where my sad thoughts do, like the compass, show
The several points from which cross-winds do blow.
My heart doth, like the needle, touch'd with love,   5
Still fix'd on you, point which way I would move;
You are the bright pole-star, which, in the dark
Of this long absence, guides my wand'ring bark;
Love is the pilot: but, o'ercome with fear
Of your displeasure, dares not homewards steer.   10
My fearful hope hangs on my trembling sail,
Nothing is wanting but a gentle gale,
Which pleasant breath must blow from your sweet lip:
Bid it but move, and quick as thought this ship
Into your arms, which are my port, will fly,   15
Where it for ever shall at anchor lie.

SONG

ETERNITY OF LOVE PROTESTED

How ill doth he deserve a lover's name
      Whose pale weak flame
      Cannot retain
His heat, in spite of absence or disdain;
But doth at once, like paper set on fire,   5
      Burn and expire!
True love can never change his seat,
Nor did he ever love that could retreat.

That noble flame, which my breast keeps alive,
      Shall still survive   10
      When my soul 's fled;
Nor shall my love die, when my body 's dead;
That shall wait on me to the lower shade,
      And never fade:
My very ashes in their urn   15
Shall like a hallow'd lamp for ever burn.

UPON SOME ALTERATIONS IN MY MISTRESS, AFTER MY DEPARTURE INTO FRANCE

O GENTLE love, do not forsake the guide
Of my frail bark, on which the swelling tide
    Of ruthless pride
Doth beat, and threaten wrack from every side.
Gulfs of disdain do gape to overwhelm   5
This boat, nigh sunk with grief, whilst at the helm
    Despair commands;
And, round about, the shifting sands
Of faithless love and false inconstancy,
    With rocks of cruelty,   10
Stop up my passage to the neighbour lands.

My sighs have rais'd those winds, whose fury bears
My sails o'erboard, and in their place spreads fears;
    And from my tears
This sea is sprung, where naught but death appears.   15
A misty cloud of anger hides the light
Of my fair star; and everywhere black night
    Usurps the place
Of those bright rays which once did grace
My forth-bound ship: but when it could no more   20
    Behold the vanish'd shore,
In the deep flood she drown'd her beamy face.

GOOD COUNSEL TO A YOUNG MAID

WHEN you the sunburnt pilgrim see,
    Fainting with thirst, haste to the springs,
Mark how at first with bended knee
    He courts the crystal nymphs, and flings
His body to the earth, where he   5
Prostrate adores the flowing deity.

But when his sweaty face is drench'd
    In her cool waves, when from her sweet
Bosom his burning thirst is quench'd,
    Then mark how with disdainful feet   10
He kicks her banks, and from the place
That thus refresh'd him, moves with sullen pace.

So shalt thou be despis'd, fair maid,
  When by the sated lover tasted;
What first he did with tears invade   15
  Shall afterwards with scorn be wasted:
When all thy virgin-springs grow dry,
When no streams shall be left but in thine eye.

CELIA BLEEDING, TO THE SURGEON

FOND man, that canst believe her blood
  Will from those purple channels flow;
Or that the pure untainted flood
  Can any foul distemper know;
Or that thy weak steel can incise   5
  The crystal case wherein it lies:

Know, her quick blood, proud of his seat,
  Runs dancing through her azure veins;
Whose harmony no cold nor heat
  Disturbs, whose hue no tincture stains: 10
And the hard rock wherein it dwells
The keenest darts of love repels.

But thou repli'st, "Behold, she bleeds!"
  Fool! thou 'rt deceiv'd, and dost not know
The mystic knot whence this proceeds,   15
  How lovers in each other grow:
Thou struck'st her arm, but 'twas my heart
Shed all the blood, felt all the smart.

TO T. H., A LADY RESEMBLING MY MISTRESS

FAIR copy of my Celia's face,
Twin of my soul, thy perfect grace
Claims in my love an equal place.

Disdain not a divided heart,
Though all be hers, you shall have part: 5
Love is not ti'd to rules of art.

For as my soul first to her flew,
Yet stay'd with me, so now 'tis true
It dwells with her, though fled to you.

Then entertain this wand'ring guest,   10
And if not love, allow it rest:
It left not, but mistook, the nest.

Nor think my love, or your fair eyes,
Cheaper, 'cause from the sympathies
You hold with her these flames arise.   15

To lead or brass, or some such bad
Metal, a prince's stamp may add
That value which it never had;

But to the pure refined ore
The stamp of kings imparts no more   20
Worth than the metal held before.

Only the image gives the rate
To subjects; in a foreign state
'Tis priz'd as much for its own weight.

So though all other hearts resign   25
To your pure worth, yet you have mine
Only because you are her coin.

TO SAXHAM

THOUGH frost and snow lock'd from mine eyes
That beauty which without door lies,
Thy gardens, orchards, walks, that so
I might not all thy pleasures know,
Yet, Saxham, thou within thy gate   5
Art of thyself so delicate,
So full of native sweets, that bless
Thy roof with inward happiness,
As neither from nor to thy store
Winter takes aught, or Spring adds more.   10
The cold and frozen air had starv'd
Much poor, if not by thee preserv'd,
Whose prayers have made thy table blest
With plenty, far above the rest.
The season hardly did afford   15
Coarse cates unto thy neighbours' board,

Yet thou hadst dainties, as the sky
Had only been thy volary;
Or else the birds, fearing the snow
Might to another Deluge grow,   20
The pheasant, partridge, and the lark
Flew to thy house, as to the Ark.
The willing ox of himself came
Home to the slaughter, with the lamb,
And every beast did thither bring   25
Himself, to be an offering.
The scaly herd more pleasure took,
Bath'd in thy dish, than in the brook;
Water, earth, air, did all conspire
To pay their tributes to thy fire,   30
Whose cherishing flames themselves divide
Through every room, where they deride
The night and cold abroad; whilst they,
Like suns within, keep endless day.
Those cheerful beams send forth their light   35
To all that wander in the night,
And seem to beckon from aloof
The weary pilgrim to thy roof;
Where if, refresh'd, he will away,
He 's fairly welcome; or if stay,   40
Far more; which he shall hearty find
Both from the master and the hind:
The stranger's welcome each man there
Stamp'd on his cheerful brow doth wear.
Nor doth this welcome or his cheer   45
Grow less 'cause he stays longer here:
There 's none observes, much less repines,
How often this man sups or dines.
Thou hast no porter at the door
T' examine or keep back the poor;   50
Nor locks nor bolts: thy gates have bin
Made only to let strangers in;
Untaught to shut, they do not fear
To stand wide open all the year,
Careless who enters, for they know   55
Thou never didst deserve a foe:
And as for thieves, thy bounty 's such,
They cannot steal, thou giv'st so much.

UPON A RIBBAND

This silken wreath, which circles in mine arm,
Is but an emblem of that mystic charm
Wherewith the magic of your beauties binds
My captive soul, and round about it winds
Fetters of lasting love. This hath entwin'd   5
My flesh alone; that hath impal'd my mind.
Time may wear out these soft weak bands, but those
Strong chains of brass Fate shall not discompose.
This holy relic may preserve my wrist,
But my whole frame doth by that power subsist: 10
To that my prayers and sacrifice, to this
I only pay a superstitious kiss.
This but the idol, that 's the deity;
Religion there is due; here, ceremony.
That I receive by faith, this but in trust;   15
Here I may tender duty: there, I must.
This order as a layman I may bear,
But I become Love's priest when that I wear.
This moves like air; that as the centre stands;
That knot your virtue tied; this but your hands.   20
That, Nature fram'd; but this was made by Art;
This makes my arm your prisoner; that, my heart.

TO THE KING, AT HIS ENTRANCE INTO SAXHAM,

BY MASTER JOHN CROFTS

Sir,
Ere you pass this threshold, stay,
And give your creature leave to pay
Those pious rites, which unto you,
As to our household gods, are due.
Instead of sacrifice, each breast   5
Is like a flaming altar drest
With zealous fires, which from pure hearts
Love mix'd with loyalty imparts.
Incense nor gold have we, yet bring
As rich and sweet an offering;   10
And such as doth both these express,
Which is our humble thankfulness;

By which is paid the all we owe
To gods above, or men below.
The slaughter'd beast, whose flesh should feed   15
The hungry flames, we for pure need
Dress for your supper; and the gore
Which should be dash'd on every door,
We change into the lusty blood
Of youthful vines, of which a flood   20
Shall sprightly run through all your veins,
First to your health, then your fair train's.
We shall want nothing but good fare,
To show your welcome and our care;
Such rarities, that come from far,   25
From poor men's houses banish'd are:
Yet we 'll express in homely cheer
How glad we are to see you here.
We 'll have whate'er the season yields,
Out of the neighbouring woods and fields;   30
For all the dainties of your board
Will only be what those afford;
And, having supp'd, we may perchance
Present you with a country dance.
Thus much your servants, that bear sway   35
Here in your absence, bade me say,
And beg, besides, you 'ld hither bring
Only the mercy of a king,
And not the greatness: since they have
A thousand faults must pardon crave,   40
But nothing that is fit to wait
Upon the glory of your state.
Yet your gracious favour will,
They hope, as heretofore, shine still
On their endeavours, for they swore,   45
Should Jove descend, they could no more.

UPON THE SICKNESS OF E[LIZABETH] S[HELDON]

Must she then languish, and we sorrow thus,
And no kind god help her, nor pity us?
Is justice fled from heaven? can that permit
A foul deformed ravisher to sit
Upon her virgin cheek, and pull from thence   5

The rose-buds in their maiden excellence?
To spread cold paleness on her lips, and chase
The frighted rubies from their native place?
To lick up with his searching flames a flood
Of dissolv'd coral, flowing in her blood;   10
And with the damps of his infectious breath
Print on her brow moist characters of death?
Must the clear light, 'gainst course of nature, cease
In her fair eyes, and yet the flames increase?
Must fevers shake this goodly tree, and all   15
That ripened fruit from the fair branches fall,
Which princes have desir'd to taste?   Must she,
Who hath preserv'd her spotless chastity
From all solicitation, now at last
By agues and diseases be embrac'd?   20
Forbid it, holy Dian! else who shall
Pay vows, or let one grain of incense fall
On thy neglected altars, if thou bless
No better this thy zealous votaress?
Haste then, O maiden goddess, to her aid;   25
Let on thy quiver her pale cheek be laid,
And rock her fainting body in thine arms;
Then let the God of Music with still charms
Her restless eyes in peaceful slumbers close,
And with soft strains sweeten her calm repose.   30
Cupid, descend! and whilst Apollo sings,
Fanning the cool air with thy panting wings
Ever supply her with refreshing wind;
Let thy fair mother with her tresses bind
Her labouring temples, with whose balmy sweat   35
She shall perfume her hairy coronet,
Whose precious drops shall upon every fold
Hang like rich pearls about a wreath of gold;
Her looser locks, as they unbraided lie,
Shall spread themselves into a canopy;   40
Under whose shadow let her rest secure
From chilling cold or burning calenture:
Unless she freeze with ice of chaste desires,
Or holy Hymen kindle nuptial fires:
And when at last Death comes to pierce her heart,   45
Convey into his hand thy golden dart.

A NEW-YEAR'S SACRIFICE

TO LUCINDA

THOSE that can give, open their hands this day;
Those that cannot, yet hold them up to pray,
That health may crown the seasons of this year,
And mirth dance round the circle; that no tear,
Unless of joy, may with its briny dew　　　　　5
Discolour on your cheek the rosy hue;
That no access of years presume to abate
Your beauty's ever-flourishing estate.
Such cheap and vulgar wishes I could lay
As trivial off'rings at your feet this day;　　　10
But that it were apostacy in me
To send a prayer to any deity
But your divine self, who have power to give
Those blessings unto others, such as live
Like me, by the sole influence of your eyes,　　15
Whose fair aspects govern our destinies.
　　Such incense, vows, and holy rites as were
To the involved serpent of the year
Paid by Egyptian priests, lay I before
Lucinda's sacred shrine, whilst I adore　　　20
Her beauteous eyes, and her pure altars dress
With gums and spice of humble thankfulness.
　　So may my goddess from her heaven inspire
My frozen bosom with a Delphic fire;
And then the world shall, by that glorious flame,　25
Behold the blaze of thy immortal name.

SONG

TO ONE WHO, WHEN I PRAIS'D MY MISTRESS' BEAUTY, SAID I WAS BLIND

WONDER not, though I am blind,
　　　　For you must be
Dark in your eyes or in your mind,
　　　　If, when you see
Her face, you prove not blind like me.　　　5
If the powerful beams that fly
　　　　From her eye,

And those amorous sweets that lie
Scatter'd in each neighbouring part,
Find a passage to your heart;   10
Then you 'll confess your mortal sight
Too weak for such a glorious light:
For if her graces you discover,
You grow, like me, a dazzl'd lover:
But if those beauties you not spy,   15
Then are you blinder far than I.

SONG

TO MY MISTRESS, I BURNING IN LOVE

I BURN, and cruel you in vain
Hope to quench me with disdain;
If from your eyes those sparkles came
That have kindled all this flame,
What boots it me, though now you shroud   5
Those fierce comets in a cloud?
Since all the flames that I have felt
Could your snow yet never melt:
Nor can your snow, though you should take
Alps into your bosom, slake   10
The heat of my enamour'd heart.
But, with wonder, learn Love's art:
No seas of ice can cool desire,
Equal flames must quench Love's fire.
Then think not that my heat can die,   15
Till you burn, as well as I.

SONG

TO HER AGAIN, SHE BURNING IN A FEVER

Now she burns, as well as I,
Yet my heat can never die;
She burns that never knew desire,
She that was ice, she now is fire.
She whose cold heart chaste thoughts did arm   5
So as Love's flames could never warm
The frozen bosom where it dwelt,
She burns, and all her beauties melt.

She burns, and cries, "Love's fires are mild;
Fevers are God's, and he's a child."   10
Love, let her know the difference
'Twixt the heat of soul and sense:
Touch her with thy flames divine,
So shalt thou quench her fire, and mine.

UPON THE KING'S SICKNESS

SICKNESS, the minister of Death, doth lay
So strong a siege against our brittle clay,
As, whilst it doth our weak forts singly win,
It hopes at length to take all mankind in.
First, it begins upon the womb to wait,   5
And doth the unborn child there uncreate;
Then rocks the cradle where the infant lies,
Where, ere it fully be alive, it dies.
It never leaves fond youth, until it have
Found or an early or a later grave.   10
By thousand subtle sleights from heedless man
It cuts the short allowance of a span;
And where both sober life and art combine
To keep it out, age makes them both resign.
Thus, by degrees, it only gain'd of late   15
The weak, the aged, or intemperate.
But now the tyrant hath found out a way
By which the sober, strong, and young decay;
Ent'ring his royal limbs that is our head,
Through us, his mystic limbs, the pain is spread;   20
That man that doth not feel his part hath none
In any part of his dominion;
If he hold land, that earth is forfeited,
And he unfit on any ground to tread.
This grief is felt at Court, where it doth move 25
Through every joint, like the true soul of love.
All those fair stars that do attend on him,
Whence they deriv'd their light, wax pale and dim.
That ruddy morning beam of majesty,
Which should the sun's eclipsed light supply,   30
Is overcast with mists, and in the lieu
Of cheerful rays sends us down drops of dew.

That curious form, made of an earth refin'd,
At whose blest birth the gentle planets shin'd
With fair aspects, and sent a glorious flame   35
To animate so beautiful a frame,
That darling of the gods and men doth wear
A cloud on 's brow, and in his eye a tear.
And all the rest, save when his dread command
Doth bid them move, like lifeless statues stand.   40
So full a grief, so generally worn,
Shows a good king is sick, and good men mourn.

SONG

TO A LADY NOT YET ENJOY'D BY HER HUSBAND

COME, Celia, fix thine eyes on mine,
    And through those crystals our souls flitting
Shall a pure wreath of eye-beams twine,
    Our loving hearts together knitting.
Let eaglets the bright sun survey,   5
Though the blind mole discern not day.

When clear Aurora leaves her mate,
    The light of her grey eyes despising,
Yet all the world doth celebrate
    With sacrifice her fair uprising.   10
Let eaglets the bright sun survey,
Though the blind mole discern not day.

A dragon kept the golden fruit,
    Yet he those dainties never tasted;
As others pin'd in the pursuit,   15
    So he himself with plenty wasted.
Let eaglets the bright sun survey,
Though the blind mole discern not day.

SONG

THE WILLING PRISONER TO HIS MISTRESS

LET fools great Cupid's yoke disdain,
    Loving their own wild freedom better;
Whilst, proud of my triumphant chain,
    I sit, and court my beauteous fetter.

Her murd'ring glances, snaring hairs,   5
    And her bewitching smiles so please me,
As he brings ruin, that repairs
    The sweet afflictions that disease me.

Hide not those panting balls of snow
    With envious veils from my beholding;   10
Unlock those lips, their pearly row
    In a sweet smile of love unfolding.

And let those eyes, whose motion wheels
    The restless fate of every lover,
Survey the pains my sick heart feels,   15
    And wounds themselves have made discover.

A FLY THAT FLEW INTO MY MISTRESS HER EYE

WHEN this fly liv'd, she us'd to play
In the sunshine all the day;
Till, coming near my Celia's sight,
She found a new and unknown light,
So full of glory as it made   5
The noonday sun a gloomy shade.
Then this amorous fly became
My rival, and did court my flame;
She did from hand to bosom skip,
And from her breath, her cheek, and lip,   10
Suck'd all the incense and the spice,
And grew a bird of paradise.
At last into her eye she flew,
There scorch'd in flames and drown'd in dew,
Like Phaëton from the sun's sphere,   15
She fell, and with her dropp'd a tear,
Of which a pearl was straight compos'd,
Wherein her ashes lie enclos'd.
Thus she receiv'd from Celia's eye
Funeral, flame, tomb, obsequy.   20

SONG

CELIA SINGING

HARK how my Celia, with the choice
Music of her hand and voice,
Stills the loud wind, and makes the wild
Incensed boar and panther mild.
Mark how those statues like men move,   5
While men with wonder statues prove.
This stiff rock bends to worship her,
That idol turns idolater.
  Now see how all the new-inspir'd
Images with love are fir'd;   10
Hark how the tender marble groans,
And all the late-transformed stones
Court the fair nymph, with many a tear,
Which she, more stony than they were,
Beholds with unrelenting mind;   15
Whilst they, amaz'd to see combin'd
Such matchless beauty with disdain,
Are all turn'd into stones again.

SONG

CELIA SINGING

You that think Love can convey
    No other way
But through the eyes into the heart
    His fatal dart,
Close up those casements, and but hear   5
    This siren sing;
    And on the wing
Of her sweet voice it shall appear
That Love can enter at the ear.

Then unveil your eyes: behold   10
    The curious mould
Where that voice dwells; and, as we know
    When the cocks crow
[And Sol is mounted on his throne]

We freely may　　　　15
Gaze on the day,
So may you, when the music 's done,
Awake and see the rising sun.

SONG

TO ONE THAT DESIRED TO KNOW MY MISTRESS

SEEK not to know my love, for she
Hath vow'd her constant faith to me;
Her mild aspects are mine, and thou
Shalt only find a stormy brow:
For if her beauty stir desire　　　　5
In me, her kisses quench the fire.
Or I can to love's fountain go,
Or dwell upon her hills of snow;
But when thou burn'st, she shall not spare
One gentle breath to cool the air;　　　　10
Thou shalt not climb those Alps, nor spy
Where the sweet springs of Venus lie.
Search hidden Nature and there find
A treasure to enrich thy mind;
Discover arts not yet reveal'd,　　　　15
But let my mistress live conceal'd:
Though men by knowledge wiser grow,
Yet here 'tis wisdom not to know.

IN THE PERSON OF A LADY TO HER INCONSTANT SERVANT

WHEN on the altar of my hand,
　Bedew'd with many a kiss and tear,
Thy now revolted heart did stand
　An humble martyr, thou didst swear
　Thus (and the God of Love did hear):　　　　5
"By those bright glances of thine eye,
Unless thou pity me, I die."

When first those perjur'd lips of thine,
　Bepal'd with blasting sighs, did seal
Their violated faith on mine,　　　　10

From the soft bosom that did heal
  Thee, thou my melting heart didst steal:
My soul, inflam'd with thy false breath,
Poison'd with kisses, suck'd in death.

Yet I nor hand nor lip will move,   15
  Revenge or mercy to procure
From the offended God of Love:
  My curse is fatal, and my pure
  Love shall beyond thy scorn endure.
If I implore the gods, they 'll find   20
Thee too ingrateful, me too kind.

TRUCE IN LOVE ENTREATED

No more, blind god! for see, my heart
  Is made thy quiver, where remains
No void place for another dart;
  And, alas! that conquest gains
Small praise, that only brings away   5
A tame and unresisting prey.

Behold a nobler foe, all arm'd,
  Defies thy weak artillery,
That hath thy bow and quiver charm'd,
  A rebel beauty, conquering thee: 10
If thou dar'st equal combat try,
Wound her, for 'tis for her I die.

TO MY RIVAL

HENCE, vain intruder, haste away!
Wash not with thy unhallow'd brine
The footsteps of my Celia's shrine;
Nor on her purer altars lay
Thy empty words, accents that may   5
  Some looser dame to love incline:
  She must have offerings more divine;
Such pearly drops as youthful May
Scatters before the rising day;
  Such smooth soft language, as each line   10

Might stroke an angry god, or stay
   Jove's thunder, make the hearers pine
With envy: do this, thou shalt be
Servant to her, rival with me.

BOLDNESS IN LOVE

MARK how the bashful morn in vain
   Courts the amorous marigold,
With sighing blasts and weeping rain,
   Yet she refuses to unfold.
But when the planet of the day   5
Approacheth with his powerful ray,
Then she spreads, then she receives
His warmer beams into her virgin leaves.

So shalt thou thrive in love, fond boy;
   If thy tears and sighs discover   10
Thy grief, thou never shalt enjoy
   The just reward of a bold lover.
But when with moving accents thou
Shalt constant faith and service vow,
Thy Celia shall receive those charms   15
With open ears, and with unfolded arms.

A PASTORAL DIALOGUE

CELIA. CLEON

As Celia rested in the shade
   With Cleon by her side,
The swain thus courted the young maid,
   And thus the nymph repli'd.

Cleon. Sweet! let thy captive fetters wear   5
   Made of thine arms and hands;
Till such as thraldom scorn, or fear,
   Envy those happy bands.

Celia. Then thus my willing arms I wind
   About thee, and am so   10
Thy pris'ner, for myself I bind,
   Until I let thee go.

Cleon. Happy that slave whom the fair foe
     Ties in so soft a chain.
Celia. Far happier I, but that I know   15
     Thou wilt break loose again.

Cleon. By thy immortal beauties, never!
  Celia. Frail as thy love 's thine oath.
Cleon. Though beauty fade, my love lasts ever.
  Celia. Time will destroy them both.   20

Cleon. I dote not on thy snow-white skin.
  Celia. What then? *Cleon.* Thy purer mind.
Celia. It lov'd too soon. *Cleon.* Thou hadst not bin
     So fair, if not so kind.

Celia. Oh strange vain fancy! *Cleon.* But yet true.   25
  Celia. Prove it! *Cleon.* Then make a braid
     Of those loose flames that circle you,
     My suns, and yet your shade.

Celia. 'Tis done. *Cl.* Now give it me. *Cel.* Thus thou
     Shalt thine own error find;   30
     If these were beauties, I am now
     Less fair, because more kind.

Cleon. You shall confess you err: that hair,
     Shall it not change the hue,
     Or leave the golden mountain bare?   35
Celia. Ay me! it is too true.

Cleon. But this small wreath shall ever stay
     In its first native prime,
     And smiling when the rest decay,
     The triumphs sing of time.   40

Celia. Then let me cut from thy fair grove
     One branch, and let that be
     An emblem of eternal love,
     For such is mine to thee.

Cleon. Thus are we both redeem'd from time.   45
     I by thy grace. *Celia.* And I
     Shall live in thy immortal rhyme,
     Until the Muses die.

Cleon. By heaven! *Celia.* Swear not! if I must weep,
        Jove shall not smile at me;   50
This kiss, my heart, and thy faith keep.
Cleon. This breathes my soul to thee.

      Then forth the thicket Thyrsis rush'd,
        Where he saw all their play;
      The swain stood still, and smil'd, and blush'd: 55
        The nymph fled fast away.

GRIEF ENGROSS'D

WHEREFORE do thy sad numbers flow
        So full of woe?
Why dost thou melt in such soft strains,
        Whilst she disdains?
      If she must still deny,   5
        Weep not, but die;
      And in thy funeral fire
      Shall all her fame expire.
Thus both shall perish, and as thou on thy hearse
Shall want her tears, so she shall want thy verse.   10
      Repine not then at thy blest state:
      Thou art above thy fate;
      But my fair Celia will not give
      Love enough to make me live;
      Nor yet dart from her eye   15
      Scorn enough to make me die.
Then let me weep alone, till her kind breath
Or blow my tears away or speak my death.

A PASTORAL DIALOGUE

SHEPHERD. NYMPH. CHORUS

Shepherd. This mossy bank they press'd. *Nymph.* That
        aged oak
      Did canopy the happy pair
      All night from the damp air.

Chorus.   Here let us sit, and sing the words they spoke,
      Till the day breaking, their embraces broke.   5

Shepherd. See, love, the blushes of the morn appear,
　　　　And now she hangs her pearly store,
　　　　Robb'd from the Eastern shore,
　　　I' th' cowslip's bell and roses rare:
　　　Sweet, I must stay no longer here.　　　　10

Nymph.　Those streaks of doubtful light usher not day,
　　　　But show my sun must set; no morn
　　　　Shall shine till thou return:
　　　The yellow planets and the grey
　　　Dawn shall attend thee on thy way.　　　15

Shepherd. If thine eyes gild my paths they may forbear
　　　　Their useless shine. *Nymph.* My tears will quite
　　　　Extinguish their faint light.

Shepherd. Those drops will make their beams more clear,
　　　Love's flames will shine in every tear.　　　20

Chorus.　They kiss'd and wept, and from their lips and eyes,
　　　　In a mix'd dew of briny sweet
　　　　Their joys and sorrows meet.
　　　But she cries out. *Nymph.* Shepherd, arise!
　　　The sun betrays us else to spies.　　　25

Shepherd. The winged hours fly fast whilst we embrace,
　　　　But when we want their help to meet,
　　　　They move with leaden feet.
Nymph.　Then let us pinion Time, and chase
　　　The day for ever from this place.　　　30

Shepherd. Hark! *Nymph.* Ay me, stay! *Shepherd.* For
　　　　ever! *Nymph.* No, arise!
　　　We must be gone. *Shepherd.* My nest of spice!
Nymph.　My soul! *Shepherd.* My paradise!

Chorus.　Neither could say farewell, but through their eyes
　　　Grief interrupted speech with tears' supplies.　　　35

RED AND WHITE ROSES

READ in these roses the sad story
Of my hard fate and your own glory.
　In the white you may discover
　The paleness of a fainting lover;

E ℰ73

In the red the flames still feeding 5
On my heart, with fresh wounds bleeding.
The white will tell you how I languish,
And the red express my anguish;
The white my innocence displaying,
The red my martyrdom betraying. 10
The frowns that on your brow resided
Have those roses thus divided.
Oh let your smiles but clear the weather,
And then they both shall grow together.

TO MY COUSIN C[AREW] R[ALEGH] MARRYING MY LADY A[SHLEY]

HAPPY youth! that shalt possess
Such a spring-tide of delight,
As the sated appetite
Shall, enjoying such excess,
Wish the flood of pleasure less; 5
When the hymeneal rite
Is perform'd, invoke the night,
That it may in shadows dress
Thy too real happiness:
Else (as Semele) the bright 10
Deity, in her full might,
May thy feeble soul oppress.
Strong perfumes and glaring light
Oft destroy both smell and sight.

A LOVER, UPON AN ACCIDENT NECESSITATING HIS DEPARTURE, CONSULTS WITH REASON

Lover

WEEP not, nor backward turn your beams,
Fond eyes! Sad sighs, lock in your breath,
Lest on this wind, or in those streams,
My griev'd soul fly or sail to death.
Fortune destroys me if I stay, 5
Love kills me if I go away:
Since Love and Fortune both are blind,
Come, Reason, and resolve my doubtful mind.

Reason

Fly! and blind Fortune be thy guide,
　　And 'gainst the blinder god rebel.   10
Thy lovesick heart shall not reside
　　Where scorn and self-will'd error dwell;
Where entrance unto Truth is barr'd,
Where Love and Faith find no reward:
For my just hand may sometime move   15
The wheel of Fortune, not the sphere of Love.

PARTING, CELIA WEEPS

Weep not, my dear, for I shall go
Loaden enough with mine own woe;
Add not thy heaviness to mine;
Since fate our pleasures must disjoin,
Why should our sorrows meet?   If I   5
Must go, and lose thy company,
I wish not theirs: it shall relieve
My grief, to think thou dost not grieve.
Yet grieve, and weep, that I may bear
Every sigh and every tear   10
Away with me; so shall thy breast
And eyes, discharg'd, enjoy their rest;
And it will glad my heart to see
Thou wert thus loth to part with me.

A RAPTURE

I will enjoy thee now, my Celia, come,
And fly with me to Love's Elysium.
The giant, Honour, that keeps cowards out,
Is but a masquer, and the servile rout
Of baser subjects only bend in vain   5
To the vast idol; whilst the nobler train
Of valiant lovers daily sail between
The huge Colosse's legs, and pass unseen
Unto the blissful shore.   Be bold and wise,
And we shall enter: the grim Swiss denies   10
Only to tame fools a passage, that not know
He is but form, and only frights in show

The duller eyes that look from far; draw near,
And thou shalt scorn what we were wont to fear.
We shall see how the stalking pageant goes   15
With borrow'd legs, a heavy load to those
That made and bear him: not, as we once thought,
The seed of gods, but a weak model wrought
By greedy men, that seek to enclose the common,
And within private arms impale free woman.   20
   Come, then, and mounted on the wings of Love
We 'll cut the flitting air, and soar above
The monster's head, and in the noblest seats
Of those blest shades quench and renew our heats.
There shall the Queens of Love and Innocence,   25
Beauty and Nature, banish all offence
From our close ivy-twines; there I 'll behold
Thy bared snow and thy unbraided gold;
There my enfranchis'd hand on every side
Shall o'er thy naked polish'd ivory slide.   30
No curtain there, though of transparent lawn,
Shall be before thy virgin-treasure drawn;
But the rich mine, to the enquiring eye
Expos'd, shall ready still for mintage lie,
And we will coin young Cupids.   There a bed   35
Of roses and fresh myrtles shall be spread
Under the cooler shade of cypress groves;
Our pillows of the down of Venus' doves,
Whereon our panting limbs we 'll gently lay,
In the faint respites of our active play: 40
That so our slumbers may in dreams have leisure
To tell the nimble fancy our past pleasure,
And so our souls that cannot be embrac'd
Shall the embraces of our bodies taste.
Meanwhile the bubbling stream shall court the shore,   45
Th' enamour'd chirping wood-choir shall adore
In varied tunes the Deity of Love;
The gentle blasts of western winds shall move
The trembling leaves, and through their close boughs breathe
Still music, whilst we rest ourselves beneath   50
Their dancing shade; till a soft murmur, sent
From souls entranc'd in amorous languishment,
Rouse us, and shoot into our veins fresh fire,
Till we in their sweet ecstasy expire.
   Then, as the empty bee, that lately bore   55

Into the common treasure all her store,
Flies 'bout the painted field with nimble wing,
Deflow'ring the fresh virgins of the Spring,
So will I rifle all the sweets that dwell
In my delicious paradise, and swell   60
My bag with honey, drawn forth by the power
Of fervent kisses from each spicy flower.
I 'll seize the rose-buds in their perfum'd bed,
The violet knots, like curious mazes spread
O'er all the garden, taste the rip'ned cherry,   65
The warm firm apple, tipp'd with coral berry;
Then will I visit with a wand'ring kiss
The vale of lilies, and the bower of bliss;
And where the beauteous region doth divide
Into two milky ways, my lips shall slide   70
Down those smooth alleys, wearing as I go
A tract for lovers on the printed snow;
Thence climbing o'er the swelling Apennine,
Retire into thy grove of eglantine,
Where I will all those ravish'd sweets distil   75
Through Love's alembic, and with chemic skill
From the mix'd mass one sovereign balm derive,
Then bring that great elixir to thy hive.
   Now in more subtle wreaths I will entwine
My sinewy thighs, my legs and arms with thine;   80
Thou like a sea of milk shalt lie display'd,
Whilst I the smooth calm ocean invade
With such a tempest, as when Jove of old
Fell down on Danaë in a storm of gold;
Yet my tall pine shall in the Cyprian strait   85
Ride safe at anchor, and unlade her freight:
My rudder with thy bold hand, like a tri'd
And skilful pilot, thou shalt steer, and guide
My bark into love's channel, where it shall
Dance, as the bounding waves do rise or fall.   90
Then shall thy circling arms embrace and clip
My willing body, and thy balmy lip
Bathe me in juice of kisses, whose perfume
Like a religious incense shall consume,
And send up holy vapours to those pow'rs   95
That bless our loves and crown our sportful hours,
That with such halcyon calmness fix our souls
In steadfast peace, as no affright controls.

There no rude sounds shake us with sudden starts;
No jealous ears, when we unrip our hearts,   100
Suck our discourse in; no observing spies
This blush, that glance traduce; no envious eyes
Watch our close meetings; nor are we betray'd
To rivals by the bribed chambermaid.
No wedlock bonds unwreathe our twisted loves;   105
We seek no midnight arbour, no dark groves
To hide our kisses: there the hated name
Of husband, wife, lust, modest, chaste or shame,
Are vain and empty words, whose very sound
Was never heard in the Elysian ground.   110
All things are lawful there that may delight
Nature or unrestrained appetite;
Like and enjoy, to will and act is one:
We only sin when Love's rites are not done.
    The Roman Lucrece there reads the divine   115
Lectures of love's great master, Aretine,
And knows as well as Lais how to move
Her pliant body in the act of love.
To quench the burning ravisher, she hurls
Her limbs into a thousand winding curls,   120
And studies artful postures, such as be
Carv'd on the bark of every neighbouring tree
By learned hands, that so adorn'd the rind
Of those fair plants, which, as they lay entwin'd,
Have fann'd their glowing fires.   The Grecian dame,   125
That in her endless web toil'd for a name
As fruitless as her work, doth there display
Herself before the youth of Ithaca,
And th' amorous sport of gamesome nights prefer
Before dull dreams of the lost traveller.   130
Daphne hath broke her bark, and that swift foot
Which th' angry gods had fast'ned with a root
To the fix'd earth, doth now unfetter'd run
To meet th' embraces of the youthful Sun.
She hangs upon him like his Delphic lyre;   135
Her kisses blow the old, and breathe new fire;
Full of her god, she sings inspired lays,
Sweet odes of love, such as deserve the bays,
Which she herself was.   Next her, Laura lies
In Petrarch's learned arms, drying those eyes   140
That did in such sweet smooth-pac'd numbers flow,

As made the world enamour'd of his woe.
These, and ten thousand beauties more, that di'd
Slave to the tyrant, now enlarg'd deride
His cancell'd laws, and for their time mis-spent   145
Pay into Love's exchequer double rent.
  Come then, my Celia, we 'll no more forbear
To taste our joys, struck with a panic fear,
But will depose from his imperious sway
This proud usurper, and walk free as they,   150
With necks unyok'd; nor is it just that he
Should fetter your soft sex with chastity,
Which Nature made unapt for abstinence;
When yet this false impostor can dispense
With human justice and with sacred right,   155
And, maugre both their laws, command me fight
With rivals or with emulous loves that dare
Equal with thine their mistress' eyes or hair.
If thou complain of wrong, and call my sword
To carve out thy revenge, upon that word   160
He bids me fight and kill; or else he brands
With marks of infamy my coward hands.
And yet religion bids from bloodshed fly,
And damns me for that act.   Then tell me why
  This goblin Honour, which the world adores,   165
  Should make men atheists, and not women whores.

EPITAPH ON THE LADY MARY VILLIERS

    THE Lady Mary Villiers lies
    Under this stone; with weeping eyes
    The parents that first gave her birth,
    And their sad friends, laid her in earth.
    If any of them, Reader, were   5
    Known unto thee, shed a tear;
    Or if thyself possess a gem
    As dear to thee, as this to them,
    Though a stranger to this place,
    Bewail in theirs thine own hard case: 10
    For thou, perhaps, at thy return
    Mayest find thy darling in an urn.

ANOTHER

The purest soul that e'er was sent
Into a clayey tenement
Inform'd this dust; but the weak mould
Could the great guest no longer hold:
The substance was too pure, the flame　　5
Too glorious that thither came;
Ten thousand Cupids brought along
A grace on each wing, that did throng
For place there, till they all oppress'd
The seat in which they sought to rest:　　10
So the fair model broke, for want
Of room to lodge th' inhabitant.

ANOTHER

This little vault, this narrow room,
Of love and beauty is the tomb;
The dawning beam that gan to clear
Our clouded sky lies dark'ned here,
For ever set to us, by death　　5
Sent to inflame the world beneath.
'Twas but a bud, yet did contain
More sweetness than shall spring again;
A budding star, that might have grown
Into a sun when it had blown.　　10
This hopeful beauty did create
New life in Love's declining state;
But now his empire ends, and we
From fire and wounding darts are free;
His brand, his bow, let no man fear:　　15
The flames, the arrows, all lie here.

EPITAPH ON THE LADY S[ALTER],

WIFE TO SIR W[ILLIAM] S[ALTER]

The harmony of colours, features, grace,
Resulting airs (the magic of a face)
Of musical sweet tunes, all which combin'd
To crown one sovereign beauty, lies confin'd

To this dark vault. She was a cabinet 5
Where all the choicest stones of price were set:
Whose native colours purest lustre lent
Her eye, cheek, lip, a dazzling ornament;
Whose rare and hidden virtues did express
Her inward beauties, and mind's fairer dress. 10
The constant diamond, the wise chrysolite,
The devout sapphire, em'rald apt to write
Records of memory, cheerful agate, grave
And serious onyx, topaz that doth save
The brain's calm temper, witty amethyst, 15
This precious quarry, or what else the list
On Aaron's ephod planted had, she wore:
One only pearl was wanting to her store,
Which in her Saviour's book she found express'd:
To purchase that, she sold Death all the rest. 20

MARIA WENTWORTH,

THOMAE COMITIS CLEVELAND FILIA PRAEMORTUA PRIMA VIR-
GINEAM ANIMAM EXHALAVIT: ANNO DOMINI [1632]. AETATIS
SUAE [18]

AND here the precious dust is laid,
Whose purely temper'd clay was made
So fine, that it the guest betray'd.

Else the soul grew so fast within
It broke the outward shell of sin, 5
And so was hatch'd a cherubin.

In heighth it soar'd to God above;
In depth it did to knowledge move,
And spread in breadth to general love.

Before, a pious duty shin'd 10
To parents; courtesy behind;
On either side, an equal mind.

Good to the poor, to kindred dear,
To servants kind, to friendship clear:
To nothing but herself severe. 15

So, though a virgin, yet a bride
To every grace, she justifi'd
A chaste polygamy, and di'd.

Learn from hence, Reader, what small trust
We owe this world, where virtue must,   20
Frail as our flesh, crumble to dust.

ON THE DUKE OF BUCKINGHAM

BEATISSIMIS MANIBUS CHARISSIMI VIRI ILLUSTRISSIMA CONJUNX
SIC PARENTAVIT

WHEN in the brazen leaves of Fame
The life, the death of Buckingham
Shall be recorded, if Truth's hand
Incise the story of our land,
Posterity shall see a fair   5
Structure, by the studious care
Of two kings rais'd, that no less
Their wisdom than their power express.
By blinded zeal (whose doubtful light
Made murder's scarlet robe seem white;   10
Whose vain-deluding phantasms charm'd
A clouded sullen soul, and arm'd
A desperate hand, thirsty of blood,)
Torn from the fair earth where it stood,
So the majestic fabric fell.   15
His actions let our annals tell;
We write no chronicle; this pile
Wears only sorrow's face and style,
Which even the envy that did wait
Upon his flourishing estate,   20
Turn'd to soft pity of his death,
Now pays his hearse: but that cheap breath
Shall not blow here, nor th' unpure brine
Puddle those streams that bathe this shrine.
    These are the pious obsequies   25
Dropp'd from his chaste wife's pregnant eyes
In frequent show'rs, and were alone
By her congealing sighs made stone,
On which the carver did bestow
These forms and characters of woe: 30
So he the fashion only lent,
Whilst she wept all this monument.

ANOTHER

SISTE, HOSPES, SIVE INDIGENA, SIVE ADVENA, VICISSITUDINIS
RERUM MEMOR, PAUCA PELLEGE

READER, when these dumb stones have told
In borrow'd speech what guest they hold,
Thou shalt confess the vain pursuit
Of human glory yields no fruit
But an untimely grave. If Fate   5
Could constant happiness create,
Her ministers, Fortune and Worth,
Had here that miracle brought forth:
They fix'd this child of Honour where
No room was left for hope or fear,   10
Of more or less; so high, so great
His growth was, yet so safe his seat:
Safe in the circle of his friends,
Safe in his loyal heart, and ends;
Safe in his native valiant spirit,   15
By favour safe, and safe by merit;
Safe by the stamp of Nature, which
Did strength with shape and grace enrich;
Safe in the cheerful courtesies
Of flowing gestures, speech, and eyes;   20
Safe in his bounties, which were more
Proportion'd to his mind than store:
Yet, though for virtue he becomes
Involv'd himself in borrow'd sums,
Safe in his care, he leaves betray'd   25
No friend engag'd, no debt unpaid.
    But though the stars conspire to shower
Upon one head th' united power
Of all their graces, if their dire
Aspects must other breasts inspire   30
With vicious thoughts, a murderer's knife
May cut, as here, their darling's life.
Who can be happy then, if Nature must,
To make one happy man, make all men just?

FOUR SONGS BY WAY OF CHORUS TO A PLAY,

AT AN ENTERTAINMENT OF THE KING AND QUEEN BY MY LORD CHAMBERLAIN

I. OF JEALOUSY. DIALOGUE

Question. FROM whence was first this fury hurl'd,
This Jealousy, into the world?
Came she from hell? *Answer.* No, there doth reign
Eternal Hatred, with Disdain;
But she the daughter is of Love,   5
Sister of Beauty. *Question.* Then above
She must derive from the third sphere
Her heavenly offspring. *Answer.* Neither there,
From those immortal flames, could she
Draw her cold frozen pedigree.   10
Question. If nor from heaven nor hell, where then
Had she her birth? *Answer.* I' th' hearts of men.
Beauty and Fear did her create,
Younger than Love, elder than Hate,
Sister to both; by Beauty's side   15
To Love, by Fear to Hate, alli'd.
Despair her issue is, whose race
Of fruitful mischiefs drowns the space
Of the wide earth in a swoln flood
Of wrath, revenge, spite, rage, and blood.   20
Question. Oh, how can such a spurious line
Proceed from parents so divine?
Answer. As streams which from their crystal spring
Do sweet and clear their waters bring,
Yet, mingling with the brackish main,   25
Nor taste nor colour they retain.
Question. Yet rivers 'twixt their own banks flow
Still fresh; can Jealousy do so?
Answer. Yes, whilst she keeps the steadfast ground
Of Hope and Fear her equal bound.   30
Hope, sprung from favour, worth, or chance,
Towards the fair object doth advance;
Whilst Fear, as watchful sentinel,
Doth the invading foe repel:
And Jealousy, thus mix'd, doth prove   35
The season and the salt of Love.

But when Fear takes a larger scope,
Stifling the child of Reason, Hope,
Then, sitting on th' usurped throne,
She like a tyrant rules alone: 40
As the wild ocean unconfin'd,
And raging as the northern wind.

II. FEMININE HONOUR

In what esteem did the gods hold
    Fair Innocence and the chaste bed,
When scandall'd Virtue might be bold
    Bare-foot upon sharp coulters, spread
O'er burning coals, to march; yet feel   5
Nor scorching fire nor piercing steel!

Why, when the hard-edg'd iron did turn
    Soft as a bed of roses blown,
When cruel flames forgot to burn
    Their chaste pure limbs, should man alone   10
'Gainst female innocence conspire,
Harder than steel, fiercer than fire?

Oh, hapless sex! Unequal sway
    Of partial honour! Who may know
Rebels from subjects that obey,   15
    When malice can on vestals throw
Disgrace, and fame fix high repute
On the close shameless prostitute?

Vain Honour! thou art but disguise,
    A cheating voice, a juggling art;   20
No judge of Virtue, whose pure eyes
    Court her own image in the heart,
More pleas'd with her true figure there
Than her false echo in the ear.

III. SEPARATION OF LOVERS

Stop the chafed boar, or play
    With the lion's paw, yet fear
    From the lover's side to tear
Th' idol of his soul away.

Though love enter by the sight   5
  To the heart, it doth not fly
  From the mind, when from the eye
The fair objects take their flight.

But since want provokes desire,
  When we lose what we before   10
  Have enjoy'd, as we want more,
So is love more set on fire.

Love doth with an hungry eye
  Glut on beauty; and you may
  Safer snatch the tiger's prey,   15
Than his vital food deny.

Yet though absence for a space
  Sharpen the keen appetite,
  Long continuance doth quite
All love's characters efface: 20

For the sense not fed denies
  Nourishment unto the mind,
  Which with expectation pin'd,
Love of a consumption dies.

IV. INCOMMUNICABILITY OF LOVE

Question.   By what power was love confin'd
        To one object?   Who can bind,
  Or fix a limit to the free-born mind?

Answer.   Nature: for as bodies may
        Move at once but in one way,   5
  So nor can minds to more than one love stray.

Question.   Yet I feel a double smart,
        Love's twinn'd flame, his forked dart.
Answer.   Then hath wild lust, not love, possess'd thy heart.

Question.   Whence springs love?   *Answer.* From beauty.
        Question. Why   10
        Should th' effect not multiply
  As fast i' th' heart, as doth the cause i' th' eye?

Answer.   When two beauties equal are,
        Sense preferring neither fair,
  Desire stands still, distracted 'twixt the pair.   15

So in equal distance lay
Two fair lambs in the wolf's way:
The hungry beast will starve ere choose his prey.

But where one is chief, the rest
Cease, and that 's alone possess'd,   20
Without a rival, monarch of the breast.

SONGS IN THE PLAY

A LOVER, IN THE DISGUISE OF AN AMAZON, IS DEARLY BELOVED OF HIS MISTRESS

Cease, thou afflicted soul, to mourn,
Whose love and faith are paid with scorn;
For I am starv'd that feel the blisses
Of dear embraces, smiles, and kisses
From my soul's idol, yet complain   5
Of equal love more than disdain.

Cease, beauty's exile, to lament
The frozen shades of banishment;
For I in that fair bosom dwell
That is my paradise and hell: 10
Banish'd at home, at once at ease
In the safe port and toss'd on seas.

Cease in cold jealous fears to pine,
Sad wretch, whom rivals undermine;
For though I hold lock'd in mine arms   15
My life's sole joy, a traitor's charms
Prevail: whilst I may only blame
Myself, that mine own rival am.

ANOTHER

A LADY, RESCUED FROM DEATH BY A KNIGHT, WHO IN THE INSTANT LEAVES HER, COMPLAINS THUS:

Oh, whither is my fair sun fled,
Bearing his light, not heat, away?
If thou repose in the moist bed
Of the Sea-Queen, bring back the day
To our dark clime, and thou shalt lie   5
Bath'd in the sea flows from mine eye.

Upon what whirlwind didst thou ride
   Hence, yet remain fix'd in my heart,
From me and to me fled and ti'd?
   Dark riddles of the amorous art!   10
Love lent thee wings to fly, so he
Unfeather'd now must rest with me.

Help, help, brave youth! I burn, I bleed!
   The cruel god with bow and brand
Pursues the life thy valour freed;   15
   Disarm him with thy conquering hand;
And that thou mayest the wild boy tame,
Give me his dart, keep thou his flame.

TO BEN JONSON

UPON OCCASION OF HIS ODE OF DEFIANCE ANNEX'D TO HIS PLAY OF "THE NEW INN"

'Tis true, dear Ben, thy just chastising hand
Hath fix'd upon the sotted age a brand,
To their swoln pride and empty scribbling due;
It can nor judge nor write: and yet 'tis true
Thy comic Muse, from the exalted line   5
Touch'd by thy *Alchemist*, doth since decline
From that her zenith, and foretells a red
And blushing evening, when she goes to bed;
Yet such as shall outshine the glimmering light
With which all stars shall gild the following night.   10
Nor think it much, since all thy eaglets may
Endure the sunny trial, if we say
This hath the stronger wing, or that doth shine
Trick'd up in fairer plumes, since all are thine.
Who hath his flock of cackling geese compar'd   15
With thy tun'd choir of swans? or else who dar'd
To call thy births deform'd? But if thou bind
By city-custom or by gavelkind¹
In equal shares thy love on all thy race,
We may distinguish of their sex and place;   20
Though one hand form them, and though one brain strike
Souls into all, they are not all alike.

Why should the follies, then, of this dull age
Draw from thy pen such an immodest rage,
As seems to blast thy (else-immortal) bays,   25
When thine own tongue proclaims thy itch of praise?
Such thirst will argue drouth. No, let be hurl'd
Upon thy works by the detracting world
What malice can suggest: let the rout say,
The running sands that, ere thou make a play,   30
Count the slow minutes, might a Goodwin frame,
To swallow when th' hast done thy shipwrack'd name.
Let them the dear expense of oil upbraid,
Suck'd by thy watchful lamp, that hath betray'd
To theft the blood of martyr'd authors, spilt   35
Into thy ink, whilst thou growest pale with guilt.
Repine not at the taper's thrifty waste,
That sleeks thy terser poems; nor is haste
Praise, but excuse; and if thou overcome
A knotty writer, bring the booty home;   40
Nor think it theft, if the rich spoils so torn
From conquer'd authors be as trophies worn.
Let others glut on the extorted praise
Of vulgar breath; trust thou to after days:
Thy labour'd works shall live, when Time devours   45
Th' abortive offspring of their hasty hours.
Thou art not of their rank, the quarrel lies
Within thine own verge: then let this suffice,
The wiser world doth greater thee confess
Than all men else, than thyself only less.   50

AN HYMENEAL DIALOGUE

BRIDE AND GROOM

Groom. Tell me, my love, since Hymen ti'd
      The holy knot, hast thou not felt
   A new-infused spirit slide
      Into thy breast, whilst thine did melt?

Bride. First tell me, sweet, whose words were those?   5
      For though your voice the air did break,
   Yet did my soul the sense compose,
      And through your lips my heart did speak.

Groom.　Then I perceive, when from the flame
　　　　Of love my scorch'd soul did retire,　　　10
　　　　Your frozen heart in her place came,
　　　　And sweetly melted in that fire.

Bride.　'Tis true, for when that mutual change
　　　　Of souls was made, with equal gain,
　　　　I straight might feel diffus'd a strange　　　15
　　　　But gentle heat through every vein.

Chorus.　O blest disunion! that doth so
　　　　Our bodies from our souls divide,
　　　　As two do one, and one four grow,
　　　　Each by contraction multipli'd.　　　20

Bride.　Thy bosom then I 'll make my nest,
　　　　Since there my willing soul doth perch.
Groom.　And for my heart, in thy chaste breast,
　　　　I 'll make an everlasting search.

Chorus.　O blest disunion! that doth so
　　　　Our bodies from our souls divide,　　　25
　　　　As two do one, and one four grow,
　　　　Each by contraction multipli'd.

OBSEQUIES TO THE LADY ANNE HAY

I HEARD the virgins sigh, I saw the sleek
And polish'd courtier channel his fresh cheek
With real tears; the new-betrothed maid
Smil'd not that day; the graver Senate laid
Their business by: of all the courtly throng　　　5
Grief seal'd the heart, and silence bound the tongue.
I, that ne'er more of private sorrow knew
Than from my pen some froward mistress drew,
And for the public woe had my dull sense
So sear'd with ever-adverse influence,　　　10
As the invader's sword might have, unfelt,
Pierc'd my dead bosom, yet began to melt:
Grief's strong instinct did to my blood suggest
In the unknown loss peculiar interest.
But when I heard the noble Carlisle's gem,　　　15
The fairest branch of Denny's ancient stem,

Was from that casket stol'n, from this trunk torn,
I found just cause why they, why I, should mourn.
   But who shall guide my artless pen to draw
Those blooming beauties, which I never saw?   20
How shall posterity believe my story,
If I her crowded graces, and the glory
Due to her riper virtues, shall relate
Without the knowledge of her mortal state?
Shall I (as once Apelles) here a feature,   25
There steal a grace, and rifling so whole Nature
Of all the sweets a learned eye can see,
Figure one Venus, and say, Such was she?
Shall l her legend fill with what of old
Hath of the worthies of her sex been told;   30
And what all pens and times to all dispense,
Restrain to her, by a prophetic sense?
Or shall I, to the moral and divine
Exactest laws, shape, by an even line,
A life so straight, as it should shame the square   35
Left in the rules of Catherine or Clare,
And call it hers? say, So did she begin,
And, had she liv'd, such had her progress been?
These are dull ways, by which base pens for hire
Daub glorious vice, and from Apollo's choir   40
Steal holy ditties, which profanely they
Upon the hearse of every strumpet lay.
   We will not bathe thy corpse with a forc'd tear,
Nor shall thy train borrow the blacks they wear;
Such vulgar spice and gums embalm not thee,   45
Thou art the theme of truth, not poetry.
Thou shalt endure a trial by thy peers:
Virgins of equal birth, of equal years,
Whose virtues held with thine an emulous strife,
Shall draw thy picture, and record thy life.   50
One shall ensphere thine eyes; another shall
Impearl thy teeth; a third, thy white and small
Hand shall besnow; a fourth, incarnadine
Thy rosy cheek: until each beauteous line,
Drawn by her hand in whom that part excels,   55
Meet in one centre, where all beauty dwells.
Others, in task, shall thy choice virtues share,
Some shall their birth, some their ripe growth declare;
Though niggard Time left much unhatch'd by deeds,

They shall relate how thou hadst all the seeds 60
Of every virtue, which, in the pursuit
Of time, must have brought forth admired fruit.
Thus shalt thou, from the mouth of envy, raise
A glorious journal of thy thrifty days:
Like a bright star shot from his sphere, whose race 65
In a continu'd line of flames we trace.
This, if survey'd, shall to thy view impart
How little more than late thou wert, thou art.
This shall gain credit with succeeding times,
When, nor by bribed pens, nor partial rhymes 70
Of engag'd kindred, but the sacred truth
Is stori'd by the partners of thy youth:
Their breath shall saint thee, and be this thy pride,
Thus even by rivals to be deifi'd.

TO THE COUNTESS OF ANGLESEY, UPON THE IMMODERATELY - BY - HER - LAMENTED DEATH OF HER HUSBAND

MADAM, men say you keep with dropping eyes
Your sorrows fresh, wat'ring the rose that lies
Fall'n from your cheeks upon your dear lord's hearse.
Alas! those odours now no more can pierce
His cold pale nostril, nor the crimson dye 5
Present a graceful blush to his dark eye.
Think you that flood of pearly moisture hath
The virtue fabled of old Æson's bath?
You may your beauties and your youth consume
Over his urn, and with your sighs perfume 10
The solitary vault, which, as you groan,
In hollow echoes shall repeat your moan;
There you may wither, and an Autumn bring
Upon yourself, but not call back his Spring.
Forbear your fruitless grief, then, and let those 15
Whose love was doubted gain belief with shows
To their suspected faith. You, whose whole life
In every act crown'd you a constant wife,
May spare the practice of that vulgar trade,
Which superstitious custom only made. 20
Rather, a widow now, of wisdom prove
The pattern, as, a wife, you were of love.

Yet since you surfeit on your grief, 'tis fit
I tell the world upon what cates you sit
Glutting your sorrows; and at once include   25
His story, your excuse, my gratitude.
You that behold how yond' sad lady blends
Those ashes with her tears, lest, as she spends
Her tributary sighs, the frequent gust
Might scatter up and down the noble dust,   30
Know, when that heap of atoms was with blood
Kneaded to solid flesh, and firmly stood
On stately pillars, the rare form might move
The froward Juno's or chaste Cynthia's love.
In motion, active grace, in rest, a calm   35
Attractive sweetness, brought both wound and balm
To every heart.   He was compos'd of all
The wishes of ripe virgins, when they call
For Hymen's rites, and in their fancies wed
A shape of studi'd beauties to their bed.   40
Within this curious palace dwelt a soul
Gave lustre to each part, and to the whole:
This dress'd his face in courteous smiles, and so
From comely gestures sweeter manners flow;
This courage join'd to strength; so the hand, bent,   45
Was valour's, open'd, bounty's instrument,
Which did the scale and sword of Justice hold,
Knew how to brandish steel and scatter gold.
This taught him not to engage his modest tongue
In suits of private gain, though public wrong;   50
Nor misemploy (as is the great man's use,)
His credit with his master to traduce,
Deprave, malign, and ruin innocence,
In proud revenge of some misjudg'd offence:
But all his actions had the noble end   55
T' advance desert, or grace some worthy friend.
He chose not in the active stream to swim,
Nor hunted honour, which yet hunted him;
But like a quiet eddy, that hath found
Some hollow creek, there turns his waters round,   60
And in continual circles dances free
From the impetuous torrent; so did he
Give others leave to turn the wheel of State,
(Whose restless motion spins the subjects' fate,)
Whilst he, retir'd from the tumultuous noise   65

Of Court, and suitors' press, apart enjoys
Freedom and mirth, himself, his time, and friends,
And with sweet relish tastes each hour he spends.
    I could remember how his noble heart
First kindled at your beauties; with what art   70
He chas'd his game through all opposing fears,
When I his sighs to you, and back your tears
Convey'd to him; how loyal then, and how
Constant he prov'd since to his marriage-vow;
So as his wand'ring eyes never drew in   75
One lustful thought to tempt his soul to sin:
But that I fear such mention rather may
Kindle new grief, than blow the old away.
    Then let him rest, join'd to great Buckingham,
And with his brother's mingle his bright flame.   80
Look up, and meet their beams, and you from thence
May chance derive a cheerful influence.
Seek him no more in dust, but call agen
Your scatter'd beauties home; and so the pen
Which now I take from this sad elegy,   85
Shall sing the trophies of your conquering eye.

AN ELEGY UPON THE DEATH OF DOCTOR DONNE, DEAN OF PAUL'S

CAN we not force from widow'd poetry,
Now thou art dead, great Donne, one elegy
To crown thy hearse?   Why yet dare we not trust,
Though with unkneaded dough-bak'd prose, thy dust,
Such as the unscissor'd churchman, from the flower   5
Of fading rhetoric, short-liv'd as his hour,
Dry as the sand that measures it, should lay
Upon thy ashes on the funeral day?
Have we no voice, no tune?   Didst thou dispense
Through all our language both the words and sense?   10
'Tis a sad truth.   The pulpit may her plain
And sober Christian precepts still retain;
Doctrines it may, and wholesome uses, frame,
Grave homilies and lectures; but the flame
Of thy brave soul, that shot such heat and light   15
As burnt our earth, and made our darkness bright,
Committed holy rapes upon our will,

Did through the eye the melting heart distil,
And the deep knowledge of dark truths so teach,
As sense might judge what fancy could not reach, 20
Must be desir'd for ever. So the fire
That fills with spirit and heat the Delphic choir,
Which, kindled first by thy Promethean breath,
Glow'd here awhile, lies quench'd now in thy death.
The Muses' garden, with pedantic weeds 25
O'erspread, was purg'd by thee; the lazy seeds
Of servile imitation thrown away,
And fresh invention planted; thou didst pay
The debts of our penurious bankrupt age;
Licentious thefts, that make poetic rage 30
A mimic fury, when our souls must be
Possess'd, or with Anacreon's ecstasy,
Or Pindar's, not their own; the subtle cheat
Of sly exchanges, and the juggling feat
Of two-edg'd words, or whatsoever wrong 35
By ours was done the Greek or Latin tongue,
Thou hast redeem'd, and open'd us a mine
Of rich and pregnant fancy; drawn a line
Of masculine expression, which had good
Old Orpheus seen, or all the ancient brood 40
Our superstitious fools admire, and hold
Their lead more precious than thy burnish'd gold,
Thou hadst been their exchequer, and no more
They each in other's dust had rak'd for ore.
Thou shalt yield no precedence, but of time, 45
And the blind fate of language whose tun'd chime
More charms the outward sense: yet thou mayst claim
From so great disadvantage greater fame,
Since to the awe of thy imperious wit
Our stubborn language bends, made only fit 50
With her tough thick-ribb'd hoops to gird about
Thy giant fancy, which had prov'd too stout
For their soft melting phrases. As in time
They had the start, so did they cull the prime
Buds of invention many a hundred year, 55
And left the rifled fields, besides the fear
To touch their harvest; yet from those bare lands
Of what is purely thine, thy only hands
(And that thy smallest work,) have gleaned more
Than all those times and tongues could reap before. 60

But thou art gone, and thy strict laws will be
Too hard for libertines in poetry.
They will repeal the goodly exil'd train
Of gods and goddesses, which in thy just reign
Were banish'd nobler poems; now, with these,   65
The silenc'd tales o' th' *Metamorphoses*
Shall stuff their lines, and swell the windy page,
Till verse, refin'd by thee, in this last age
Turn ballad-rhyme, or those old idols be
Ador'd again with new apostacy.   70
    O pardon me, that break with untun'd verse
The reverend silence that attends thy hearse,
Whose awful solemn murmurs were to thee,
More than these faint lines, a loud elegy,
That did proclaim in a dumb eloquence   75
The death of all the arts: whose influence,
Grown feeble, in these panting numbers lies
Gasping short-winded accents, and so dies.
So doth the swiftly-turning wheel not stand
In th' instant we withdraw the moving hand,   8c
But some small time maintain a faint weak course,
By virtue of the first impulsive force:
And so, whilst I cast on thy funeral pile
Thy crown of bays, oh let it crack awhile,
And spit disdain, till the devouring flashes   85
Suck all the moisture up, then turn to ashes.
    I will not draw thee envy, to engross
All thy perfections, or weep all our loss;
Those are too numerous for an elegy,
And this too great to be express'd by me.   90
Though every pen should share a distinct part,
Yet art thou theme enough to tire all art;
Let others carve the rest; it shall suffice
I on thy tomb this epitaph incise:

Here lies a king, that rul'd as he thought fit   95
The universal monarchy of wit;
Here lie two flamens, and both those the best:
Apollo's first, at last the true God's priest.

IN ANSWER OF AN ELEGIACAL LETTER UPON THE DEATH OF THE KING OF SWEDEN

FROM AURELIAN TOWNSHEND, INVITING ME TO WRITE ON THAT SUBJECT

WHY dost thou sound, my dear Aurelian,
In so shrill accents from thy Barbican
A loud alarum to my drowsy eyes,
Bidding them wake in tears and elegies
For mighty Sweden's fall?   Alas! how may   5
My lyric feet, that of the smooth soft way
Of love and beauty only know the tread,
In dancing paces celebrate the dead
Victorious king, or his majestic hearse
Profane with th' humble touch of their low verse?   10
Virgil, nor Lucan, no, nor Tasso, more
Than both, not Donne, worth all that went before,
With the united labour of their wit,
Could a just poem to this subject fit.
His actions were too mighty to be rais'd   15
Higher by verse: let him in prose be prais'd,
In modest faithful story, which his deeds
Shall turn to poems.   When the next age reads
Of Frankfort, Leipzig, Wurzburg, of the Rhine,
The Lech, the Danube, Tilly, Wallenstein,   20
Bavaria, Pappenheim, Lutzen-field, where he
Gain'd after death a posthume victory,
They 'll think his acts things rather feign'd than done,
Like our romances of The Knight o' th' Sun.
Leave we him, then, to the grave chronicler,   25
Who, though to annals he cannot refer
His too-brief story, yet his journals may
Stand by the Cæsars' years, and, every day
Cut into minutes, each shall more contain
Of great designment than an emperor's reign.   30
And, since 'twas but his churchyard, let him have
For his own ashes now no narrower grave
Than the whole German continent's vast womb,
Whilst all her cities do but make his tomb.
Let us to supreme Providence commit   35
The fate of monarchs, which first thought it fit

To rend the empire from the Austrian grasp,
And next from Sweden's, even when he did clasp
Within his dying arms the sovereignty
Of all those provinces, that men might see   40
The Divine wisdom would not leave that land
Subject to any one king's sole command.
Then let the Germans fear if Cæsar shall,
Or the United Princes, rise and fall;
But let us, that in myrtle bowers sit   45
Under secure shades, use the benefit
Of peace and plenty, which the blessed hand
Of our good king gives this obdurate land;
Let us of revels sing, and let thy breath,
(Which fill'd Fame's trumpet with Gustavus' death, 50
Blowing his name to heaven), gently inspire
Thy past'ral pipe, till all our swains admire
Thy song and subject, whilst they both comprise
The beauties of the SHEPHERD'S PARADISE.
For who like thee (whose loose discourse is far   55
More neat and polish'd than our poems are,
Whose very gait 's more graceful than our dance)
In sweetly-flowing numbers may advance
The glorious night when, not to act foul rapes
Like birds or beasts, but in their angel-shapes,   60
A troop of deities came down to guide
Our steerless barks in passion's swelling tide
By virtue's card, and brought us from above
A pattern of their own celestial love?
Nor lay it in dark sullen precepts drown'd,   65
But with rich fancy and clear action crown'd,
Through a mysterious fable (that was drawn,
Like a transparent veil of purest lawn,
Before their dazzling beauties) the divine
Venus did with her heavenly Cupid shine.   70
The story's curious web, the masculine style,
The subtle sense, did Time and Sleep beguile;
Pinion'd and charm'd they stood to gaze upon
Th' angelic forms, gestures and motion;
To hear those ravishing sounds that did dispense   75
Knowledge and pleasure to the soul and sense.
It fill'd us with amazement to behold
Love made all spirit; his corporeal mould,
Dissected into atoms, melt away

To empty air, and from the gross allay 80
Of mixtures and compounding accidents
Refin'd to immaterial elements.
But when the Queen of Beauty did inspire
The air with perfumes, and our hearts with fire,
Breathing from her celestial organ sweet 85
Harmonious notes, our souls fell at her feet,
And did with humble reverend duty more
Her rare perfections than high state adore.
These harmless pastimes let my Townshend sing
To rural tunes; not that thy Muse wants wing 90
To soar a loftier pitch, for she hath made
A noble flight, and plac'd th' heroic shade
Above the reach of our faint flagging rhyme;
But these are subjects proper to our clime,
Tourneys, masques, theatres, better become 95
Our halcyon days.   What though the German drum
Bellow for freedom and revenge, the noise
Concerns not us, nor should divert our joys;
Nor ought the thunder of their carabins
Drown the sweet airs of our tun'd violins. 100
Believe me, friend, if their prevailing powers
Gain them a calm security like ours,
They 'll hang their arms up on the olive bough,
And dance and revel then, as we do now.

UPON MASTER W[ALTER] MONTAGUE
HIS RETURN FROM TRAVEL

LEAD the black bull to slaughter, with the boar
And lamb, then purple with their mingled gore
The ocean's curled brow, that so we may
The sea-gods for their careful waftage pay:
Send grateful incense up in pious smoke 5
To those mild spirits, that cast a curbing yoke
Upon the stubborn winds, that calmly blew
To the wish'd shore our long'd-for Montague.
Then, whilst the aromatic odours burn
In honour of their darling's safe return, 10
The Muses' choir shall thus with voice and hand
Bless the fair gale that drove his ship to land:

Sweetly breathing vernal air,
That with kind warmth dost repair
Winter's ruins; from whose breast 15
All the gums and spice of th' East
Borrow their perfumes; whose eye
Gilds the morn and clears the sky;
Whose dishevell'd tresses shed
Pearls upon the violet bed; 20
On whose brow, with calm smiles dress'd,
The halcyon sits and builds her nest:
Beauty, youth, and endless Spring
Dwell upon thy rosy wing.
Thou, if stormy Boreas throws 25
Down whole forests when he blows,
With a pregnant flowery birth
Canst refresh the teeming earth;
If he nip the early bud,
If he blast what's fair or good, 30
If he scatter our choice flowers,
If he shake our hills or bowers,
If his rude breath threaten us—
Thou canst stroke great Æolus,
And from him the grace obtain 35
To bind him in an iron chain.

Thus, whilst you deal your body 'mongst your friends,
And fill their circling arms, my glad soul sends
This her embrace: thus we of Delphos greet;
As laymen clasp their hands, we join our feet. 40

TO MASTER W. MONTAGUE

Sir, I arrest you at your country's suit,
Who, as a debt to her, requires the fruit
Of that rich stock which she by Nature's hand
Gave you in trust, to th' use of this whole land.
Next, she indicts you of a felony, 5
For stealing what was her propriety,
Yourself, from hence: so seeking to convey
The public treasure of the State away.
More, y' are accus'd of ostracism, the fate
Impos'd of old by the Athenian state 10

On eminent virtue; but that curse which they
Cast on their men, you on your country lay;
For, thus divided from your noble parts,
This kingdom lives in exile, and all hearts
That relish worth or honour, being rent   15
From your perfections, suffer banishment.
These are your public injuries; but I
Have a just private quarrel to defy,
And call you coward, thus to run away
When you had pierc'd my heart, not daring stay   20
Till I redeem'd my honour; but I swear
By Celia's eyes, by the same force to tear
Your heart from you, or not to end this strife
Till I or find revenge or lose my life.
But as in single fights it oft hath been   25
In that unequal equal trial seen,
That he who had receiv'd the wrong at first
Came from the combat oft too with the worst;
So, if you foil me when we meet, I 'll then
Give you fair leave to wound me so agen.   30

ON THE MARRIAGE OF T[HOMAS] K[ILLIGREW] AND C[ECILIA] C[ROFTS]: THE MORNING STORMY

Such should this day be, so the sun should hide
His bashful face, and let the conquering bride
Without a rival shine, whilst he forbears
To mingle his unequal beams with hers;
Or if sometimes he glance his squinting eye   5
Between the parting clouds, 'tis but to spy,
Not emulate her glories, so comes dress'd
In veils, but as a masquer to the feast.
Thus heaven should lour, such stormy gusts should blow,
Not to denounce ungentle fates, but show   10
The cheerful bridegroom to the clouds and wind
Hath all his tears and all his sighs assign'd.
Let tempests struggle in the air, but rest
Eternal calms within thy peaceful breast,
Thrice-happy youth! but ever sacrifice   15
To that fair hand that dri'd thy blubb'red eyes,
That crown'd thy head with roses, and turn'd all
The plagues of love into a cordial,

When first it join'd her virgin snow to thine;
Which when to-day the priest shall recombine,   20
From the mysterious holy touch such charms
Will flow, as shall unlock her wreathed arms,
And open a free passage to that fruit
Which thou hast toil'd for with a long pursuit.
But ere thou feed, that thou mayst better taste   25
Thy present joys, think on thy torments past;
Think on the mercy freed thee; think upon
Her virtues, graces, beauties, one by one:
So shalt thou relish all, enjoy the whole
Delights of her fair body and pure soul.   30
Then boldly to the fight of love proceed,
'Tis mercy not to pity, though she bleed.
We'll strew no nuts, but change that ancient form,
For till to-morrow we'll prorogue this storm,
Which shall confound with its loud whistling noise   35
Her pleasing shrieks, and fan thy panting joys.

FOR A PICTURE WHERE A QUEEN LAMENTS OVER THE TOMB OF A SLAIN KNIGHT

BRAVE youth, to whom Fate in one hour
Gave death and conquest, by whose power
Those chains about my heart are wound,
With which the foe my kingdom bound:
Freed and captiv'd by thee, I bring   5
For either act an offering:
For victory, this wreath of bay;
In sign of thraldom, down I lay
Sceptre and crown. Take from my sight
Those royal robes; since Fortune's spite   10
Forbids me live thy virtue's prize,
I'll die thy valour's sacrifice.

TO A LADY THAT DESIRED I WOULD LOVE HER

Now you have freely given me leave to love,
          What will you do?
Shall I your mirth or passion move
          When I begin to woo?
Will you torment, or scorn, or love me too?   5

Each petty beauty can disdain, and I,
      Spite of your hate,
Without your leave can see, and die.
      Dispense a nobler fate!
'Tis easy to destroy: you may create.   10

Then give me leave to love, and love me too:
      Not with design
To raise, as Love's curst rebels do,
      When puling poets whine,
Fame to their beauty from their blubb'red eyne.   15

Grief is a puddle, and reflects not clear
      Your beauty's rays;
Joys are pure streams; your eyes appear
      Sullen in sadder lays:
In cheerful numbers they shine bright with praise,   20

Which shall not mention, to express you fair,
      Wounds, flames, and darts,
Storms in your brow, nets in your hair,
      Suborning all your parts,
Or to betray or torture captive hearts.   25

I 'll make your eyes like morning suns appear,
      As mild and fair;
Your brow as crystal smooth and clear;
      And your dishevell'd hair
Shall flow like a calm region of the air.   30

Rich Nature's store, which is the poet's treasure,
      I 'll spend to dress
Your beauties, if your mine of pleasure
      In equal thankfulness
You but unlock, so we each other bless.   35

UPON MY LORD CHIEF JUSTICE HIS ELECTION OF MY LADY A[NNE] W[ENTWORTH] FOR HIS MISTRESS

      HEAR this, and tremble, all
      Usurping Beauties that create
      A government tyrannical
        In Love's free state!

Justice hath to the sword of your edg'd eyes   5
His equal balance join'd; his sage head lies
In Love's soft lap, which must be just and wise.

   Hark how the stern Law breathes
  Forth amorous sighs, and now prepares
   No fetters but of silken wreaths   10
    And braided hairs;
His dreadful rods and axes are exil'd,
Whilst he sits crown'd with roses: Love hath fil'd
His native roughness; Justice is grown mild.

   The Golden Age returns!   15
  Love's bow and quiver useless lie,
   His shaft, his brand, nor wounds nor burns,
    And cruelty
Is sunk to hell; the fair shall all be kind;
Who loves shall be belov'd, the froward mind   20
To a deformed shape shall be confin'd.

   Astræa hath possess'd
  An earthly seat, and now remains
   In Finch's heart, but Wentworth's breast
    That guest contains;   25
With her she dwells, yet hath not left the skies,
Nor lost her sphere: for, new-enthron'd, she cries,
I know no Heaven but fair Wentworth's eyes!

TO A. D. UNREASONABLE DISTRUSTFUL
OF HER OWN BEAUTY

FAIR Doris, break thy glass, it hath perplex'd
With a dark comment Beauty's clearest text;
It hath not told thy face's story true,
But brought false copies to thy jealous view.
No colour, feature, lovely air or grace,   5
That ever yet adorn'd a beauteous face,
But thou mayst read in thine; or justly doubt
Thy glass hath been suborn'd to leave it out.
But if it offer to thy nice survey
A spot, a stain, a blemish, or decay,   10
It not belongs to thee: the treacherous light

Or faithless stone abuse thy credulous sight.
Perhaps the magic of thy face hath wrought
Upon th' enchanted crystal, and so brought
Fantastic shadows to delude thine eyes   15
With airy repercussive sorceries;
Or else th' enamour'd image pines away
For love of the fair object, and so may
Wax pale and wan, and though the substance grow
Lively and fresh, that may consume with woe.   20
Give then no faith to the false specular stone,
But let thy beauties by th' effects be known.
Look, sweetest Doris, on my lovesick heart,
In that true mirror see how fair thou art!
There, by Love's never-erring pencil drawn,   25
Shalt thou behold thy face, like th' early dawn,
Shoot through the shady covert of thy hair,
Enamelling and perfuming the calm air
With pearls and roses, till thy suns display
Their lids and let out the imprison'd day;   30
Whilst Delphic priests, enlight'ned by their theme,
In amorous numbers count thy golden beam,
And from Love's altars clouds of sighs arise
In smoking incense, to adore thine eyes.
If, then, love flow from beauty, as th' effect, 35
How canst thou the resistless cause suspect?
Who would not brand that fool, that should contend
There were no fire, where smoke and flames ascend?
Distrust is worse than scorn: not to believe
My harms, is greater wrong than not to grieve.   40
What cure can for my fest'ring sore be found,
Whilst thou believ'st thy beauty cannot wound?
Such humble thoughts more cruel tyrants prove
Than all the pride that e'er usurp'd in love,
For beauty's herald here denounceth war,   45
There her false spies betray me to a snare.
If fire disguis'd in balls of snow were hurl'd,
It unsuspected might consume the world;
Where our prevention ends, danger begins,
So wolves in sheeps', lions in asses' skins,   50
Might far more mischief work, because less fear'd:
Those the whole flock, these might kill all the herd.
Appear then as thou art, break through this cloud,
Confess thy beauty, though thou thence grow proud;

Be fair, though scornful; rather let me find   55
Thee cruel, than thus mild and more unkind:
Thy cruelty doth only me defy,
But these dull thoughts thee to thyself deny.
Whether thou mean to barter, or bestow
Thyself, 'tis fit thou thine own value know.   60
I will not cheat thee of thyself, nor pay
Less for thee than th' art worth; thou shalt not say
That is but brittle glass, which I have found
By strict enquiry a firm diamond.
I 'll trade with no such Indian fool as sells   65
Gold, pearls, and precious stones, for beads and bells;
Nor will I take a present from your hand,
Which you or prize not, or not understand.
It not endears your bounty that I do
Esteem your gift, unless you do so too: 70
You undervalue me, when you bestow
On me what you nor care for, nor yet know.
No, lovely Doris, change thy thoughts, and be
In love first with thyself, and then with me.
You are afflicted that you are not fair,   75
And I as much tormented that you are.
What I admire you scorn, what I love, hate;
Through different faiths, both share an equal fate:
Fast to the truth, which you renounce, I stick;
I die a martyr, you an heretic.   80

TO MY FRIEND G[ILBERT] N[EVILLE?],

FROM WREST

I BREATHE, sweet Ghib, the temperate air of Wrest,
Where I no more, with raging storms oppress'd,
Wear the cold nights out by the banks of Tweed,
On the bleak mountains, where fierce tempests breed,
And everlasting Winter dwells; where mild   5
Favonius, and the vernal winds exil'd,
Did never spread their wings; but the wild North
Brings sterile fern, thistles, and brambles forth.
Here, steep'd in balmy dew, the pregnant earth
Sends from her teeming womb a flow'ry birth;   10
And, cherish'd with the warm sun's quick'ning heat,

Her porous bosom doth rich odours sweat;
Whose perfumes through the ambient air diffuse
Such native aromatics, as we use
No foreign gums, nor essence fetch'd from far,   15
No volatile spirits, nor compounds that are
Adulterate, but at Nature's cheap expense
With far more genuine sweets refresh the sense.
Such pure and uncompounded beauties bless
This mansion with an useful comeliness,   20
Devoid of art, for here the architect
Did not with curious skill a pile erect
Of carved marble, touch, or porphyry,
But built a house for hospitality;
No sumptuous chimney-piece of shining stone   25
Invites the stranger's eye to gaze upon,
And coldly entertains his sight, but clear
And cheerful flames cherish and warm him here;
No Doric or Corinthian pillars grace
With imagery this structure's naked face.   30
The lord and lady of this place delight
Rather to be in act, than seem in sight.
Instead of statues to adorn their wall,
They throng with living men their merry hall,
Where, at large tables fill'd with wholesome meats,   35
The servant, tenant, and kind neighbour eats.
Some of that rank, spun of a finer thread,
Are with the women, steward, and chaplain fed
With daintier cates; others of better note,
Whom wealth, parts, office, or the herald's coat   40
Have sever'd from the common, freely sit
At the lord's table, whose spread sides admit
A large access of friends to fill those seats
Of his capacious circle, fill'd with meats
Of choicest relish, till his oaken back   45
Under the load of pil'd up dishes crack.
Nor think, because our pyramids and high
Exalted turrets threaten not the sky,
That therefore Wrest of narrowness complains,
Or strait'ned walls; for she more numerous trains   50
Of noble guests daily receives, and those
Can with far more conveniency dispose,
Than prouder piles, where the vain builder spent
More cost in outward gay embellishment

Than real use; which was the sole design   55
Of our contriver, who made things not fine,
But fit for service. Amalthea's horn
Of plenty is not in effigy worn
Without the gate, but she within the door
Empties her free and unexhausted store.   60
Nor, crown'd with wheaten wreaths, doth Ceres stand
In stone, with a crook'd sickle in her hand;
Nor on a marble tun, his face besmear'd
With grapes, is curl'd unscissor'd Bacchus rear'd
We offer not in emblems to the eyes,   65
But to the taste, those useful deities;
We press the juicy god and quaff his blood,
And grind the yellow goddess into food.
Yet we decline not all the work of Art,
But where more bounteous Nature bears a part,   70
And guides her handmaid, if she but dispense
Fit matter, she with care and diligence
Employs her skill; for where the neighbour source
Pours forth her waters, she directs their course,
And entertains the flowing streams in deep   75
And spacious channels, where they slowly creep
In snaky windings, as the shelving ground
Leads them in circles, till they twice surround
This island mansion, which, i' th' centre plac'd,
Is with a double crystal heaven embrac'd;   80
In which our watery constellations float,
Our fishes, swans, our waterman and boat,
Envi'd by those above, which wish to slake
Their star-burnt limbs in our refreshing lake;
But they stick fast, nail'd to the barren sphere,   85
Whilst our increase in fertile waters here
Disport, and wander freely where they please
Within the circuit of our narrow seas.
  With various trees we fringe the water's brink,
Whose thirsty roots the soaking moisture drink;   90
And whose extended boughs in equal ranks
Yield fruit, and shade, and beauty to the banks.
On this side young Vertumnus sits, and courts
His ruddy-cheek'd Pomona; Zephyr sports
On th' other with lov'd Flora, yielding there   95
Sweets for the smell, sweets for the palate here.
But did you taste the high and mighty drink

Which from that fountain flows, you 'ld clearly think
The God of Wine did his plump clusters bring
And crush the Falerne grape into our spring;   100
Or else, disguis'd in watery robes, did swim
To Ceres' bed, and make her big of him,
Begetting so himself on her: for know,
Our vintage here in March doth nothing owe
To theirs in Autumn, but our fire boils here   105
As lusty liquor as the sun makes there.
   Thus I enjoy myself, and taste the fruit
Of this blest peace; whilst, toil'd in the pursuit
Of bucks and stags, th' emblem of war, you strive
To keep the memory of our arms alive.   110

A NEW-YEAR'S GIFT

TO THE KING

Look back, old Janus, and survey,
From Time's birth till this new-born day,
All the successful season bound
With laurel wreaths, and trophies crown'd;
Turn o'er the annals past, and where   5
Happy auspicious days appear,
Mark'd with the whiter stone, that cast
On the dark brow of th' ages past
A dazzling lustre, let them shine
In this succeeding circle's twine,   10
Till it be round with glories spread,
Then with it crown our Charles his head,
That we th' ensuing year may call
One great continu'd festival.
Fresh joys, in vari'd forms, apply   15
To each distinct captivity.
Season his cares by day with nights
Crown'd with all conjugal delights;
May the choice beauties that inflame
His royal breast be still the same,   20
And he still think them such, since more
Thou canst not give from Nature's store.
Then as a father let him be
With numerous issue blest, and see

The fair and godlike offspring grown 25
From budding stars to suns full-blown.
Circle with peaceful olive boughs
And conquering bays his regal brows;
Let his strong virtues overcome
And bring him bloodless trophies home; 30
Strew all the pavements where he treads
With loyal hearts or rebels' heads:
    But, Bifront, open thou no more
    In his blest reign the temple door.

TO THE QUEEN

THOU great Commandress, that dost move
Thy sceptre o'er the crown of Love,
And through his empire, with the awe
Of thy chaste beams, dost give the law;
From his profaner altars we 5
Turn to adore thy deity:
He only can wild lust provoke,
Thou those impurer flames canst choke;
And where he scatters looser fires,
Thou turn'st them into chaste desires. 10
His kingdom knows no rule but this:
Whatever pleaseth lawful is;
Thy sacred lore shows us the path
Of modesty and constant faith,
Which makes the rude male satisfi'd 15
With one fair female by his side;
Doth either sex to each unite,
And form Love's pure hermaphrodite.
To this thy faith, behold the wild
Satyr already reconcil'd, 20
Who from the influence of thine eye
Hath suck'd the deep divinity.
O free them then, that they may teach
The centaur and the horse-man preach
To beasts and birds, sweetly to rest 25
Each in his proper lair and nest;
They shall convey it to the flood,
Till there thy law be understood:
    So shalt thou with thy pregnant fire
    The water, earth, and air inspire. 30

TO THE NEW YEAR,

FOR THE COUNTESS OF CARLISLE

GIVE Lucinda pearl nor stone,
Lend them light who else have none:
Let her beauties shine alone.

Gums nor spice bring from the East,
For the phœnix in her breast   5
Builds his funeral pile and nest.

No tire thou canst invent
Shall to grace her form be sent:
She adorns all ornament.

Give her nothing: but restore   10
Those sweet smiles which heretofore
In her cheerful eyes she wore.

Drive those envious clouds away,
Veils that have o'ercast my day,
And eclips'd her brighter ray.   15

Let the royal Goth mow down
This year's harvest with his own
Sword, and spare Lucinda's frown.

Janus, if when next I trace
Those sweet lines, I in her face   20
Read the charter of my grace,

Then from bright Apollo's tree
Such a garland wreath'd shall be,
As shall crown both her and thee.

TO MY HONOURED FRIEND MASTER THOMAS MAY

UPON HIS COMEDY, "THE HEIR"

"THE HEIR" being born, was in his tender age
Rock'd in the cradle of a private stage,
Where, lifted up by many a willing hand,
The child did from the first day fairly stand;
Since, having gather'd strength, he dares prefer   5
His steps into the public theatre,

The world: where he despairs not but to find
A doom from men more able, not less kind.
    I but his usher am, yet if my word
May pass, I dare be bound he will afford   10
Things must deserve a welcome, if well known,
Such as best writers would have wish'd their own.
    You shall observe his words in order meet,
And softly stealing on with equal feet,
Slide into even numbers with such grace   15
As each word had been moulded for that place.
    You shall perceive an amorous passion spun
Into so smooth a web, as had the Sun,
When he pursu'd the swiftly flying maid,
Courted her in such language, she had stay'd;   20
A love so well express'd must be the same
The author felt himself from his fair flame.
    The whole plot doth alike itself disclose
Through the five acts, as doth a lock that goes
With letters, for, till every one be known,   25
The lock 's as fast as if you had found none;
And where his sportive Muse doth draw a thread
Of mirth, chaste matrons may not blush to read.
    Thus have I thought it fitter to reveal
My want of art, dear friend, than to conceal   30
My love.   It did appear I did not mean
So to commend thy well-wrought comic scene,
As men might judge my aim rather to be
To gain praise to myself, than give it thee:
Though I can give thee none but what thou hast 35
Deserv'd, and what must my faint breath outlast
    Yet was this garment (though I skilless be
To take thy measure,) only made for thee,
And if it prove too scant, 'tis 'cause the stuff
Nature allow'd me was not large enough   40

TO MY WORTHY FRIEND MASTER GEORGE SANDYS,

ON HIS TRANSLATION OF THE PSALMS

I PRESS not to the choir, nor dare I greet
The holy place with my unhallow'd feet;
My unwash'd Muse pollutes not things divine,
Nor mingles her profaner notes with thine;

Here humbly at the porch she list'ning stays,   5
And with glad ears sucks in thy sacred lays.
So devout penitents of old were wont,
Some without door and some beneath the font,
To stand and hear the Church's liturgies,
Yet not assist the solemn exercise.   10
Sufficeth her that she a lay-place gain,
To trim thy vestments, or but bear thy train;
Though nor in tune nor wing she reach thy lark,
Her lyric feet may dance before the Ark.
Who knows but that her wand'ring eyes, that run   15
Now hunting glow-worms, may adore the sun?
A pure flame may, shot by Almighty Power
Into my breast, the earthy flame devour;
My eyes in penitential dew may steep
That brine which they for sensual love did weep: 20
So, though 'gainst Nature's course, fire may be quench'd
With fire, and water be with water drench'd.
Perhaps my restless soul, tir'd with pursuit
Of mortal beauty, seeking without fruit
Contentment there, which hath not, when enjoy'd,   25
Quench'd all her thirst, nor satisfi'd, though cloy'd,
Weary of her vain search below, above
In the first fair may find th' immortal love.
Prompted by thy example then, no more
In moulds of clay will I my God adore;   30
But tear those idols from my heart, and write
What His blest Sp'rit, not fond love, shall indite.
Then I no more shall court the verdant bay,
But the dry leafless trunk on Golgotha,
And rather strive to gain from thence one thorn,   35
Than all the flourishing wreaths by laureates worn.

TO MY MUCH HONOURED FRIEND HENRY LORD CAREY OF LEPPINGTON,

UPON HIS TRANSLATION OF MALVEZZI

My Lord,
    In every trivial work 'tis known,
Translators must be masters of their own
And of their author's language, but your task
A greater latitude of skill did ask;

For your Malvezzi first requir'd a man 5
To teach him speak vulgar Italian;
His matter's so sublime, so new his phrase,
So far above the style of Bembo's days,
Old Varchi's rules, or what the Crusca yet
For current Tuscan mintage will admit, 10
As I believe your Marquess by a good
Part of his natives' hardly understood.
You must expect no happier fate; 'tis true
He is of noble birth, of nobler you:
So nor your thoughts nor words fit common ears; 15
He writes, and you translate, both to your peers.

TO MY WORTHY FRIEND MASTER D'AVENANT,

UPON HIS EXCELLENT PLAY, "THE JUST ITALIAN"

I 'LL not mis-spend in praise the narrow room
I borrow in this leaf; the garlands bloom
From thine own seeds, that crown each glorious page
Of thy triumphant work; the sullen age
Requires a satire. What star guides the soul 5
Of these our froward times, that dare control,
Yet dare not learn to judge? When didst thou fly
From hence, clear candid Ingenuity?
I have beheld when, perch'd on the smooth brow
Of a fair modest troop, thou didst allow 10
Applause to slighter works; but then the weak
Spectator gave the knowing leave to speak.
Now noise prevails, and he is tax'd for drouth
Of wit, that with the cry spends not his mouth.
Yet ask him reason why he did not like, 15
Him, why he did, their ignorance will strike
Thy soul with scorn and pity. Mark the places
Provoke their smiles, frowns, or distorted faces;
When they admire, nod, shake the head: they 'll be
A scene of mirth, a double comedy. 20
But thy strong fancies (raptures of the brain,
Dress'd in poetic flames) they entertain
As a bold impious reach; for they 'll still slight
All that exceeds Red Bull and Cockpit flight.
These are the men in crowded heaps that throng 25
To that adulterate stage, where not a tongue

Of th' untun'd kennel can a line repeat
Of serious sense, but like lips meet like meat:
Whilst the true brood of actors, that alone
Keep natural unstrain'd action in her throne,   30
Behold their benches bare, though they rehearse
The terser Beaumont's or great Jonson's verse.
Repine not thou, then, since this churlish fate
Rules not the stage alone; perhaps the State
Hath felt this rancour, where men great and good   35
Have by the rabble been misunderstood.
So was thy play, whose clear yet lofty strain
Wise men, that govern Fate, shall entertain.

TO THE READER OF MASTER WILLIAM D'AVENANT'S PLAY, ["THE WITS"]

It hath been said of old that plays are feasts,
Poets the cooks, and the spectators guests,
The actors waiters: from this simile
Some have deriv'd an unsafe liberty
To use their judgments as their tastes, which choose   5
Without control this dish, and that refuse.
But wit allows not this large privilege:
Either you must confess or feel its edge.
Nor shall you make a current inference,
If you transfer your reason to your sense: 10
Things are distinct, and must the same appear
To every piercing eye or well-tun'd ear.
Though sweets with yours, sharps best with my taste meet,
Both must agree this meat 's or sharp or sweet;
But if I scent a stench or a perfume,   15
Whilst you smell naught at all, I may presume
You have that sense imperfect: so you may
Affect a sad, merry, or humorous play,
If, though the kind distaste or please, the good
And bad be by your judgment understood.   20
But if, as in this play, where with delight
I feast my Epicurean appetite
With relishes so curious, as dispense
The utmost pleasure to the ravish'd sense,
You should profess that you can nothing meet   25
That hits your taste either with sharp or sweet,

But cry out, "'Tis insipid!" your bold tongue
May do its master, not the author, wrong;
For men of better palate will by it
Take the just elevation of your wit.　　　　30

TO WILL. D'AVENANT, MY FRIEND,

[UPON HIS POEM, "MADAGASCAR"]

WHEN I behold, by warrant from thy pen,
A prince rigging our fleets, arming our men,
Conducting to remotest shores our force,
(Without a Dido to retard his course),
And thence repelling in successful fight　　　　5
Th' usurping foe, whose strength was all his right,
By two brave heroes (whom we justly may
By Homer's Ajax or Achilles lay):
I doubt the author of the Tale of Troy,
With him that makes his fugitive enjoy　　　　10
The Carthage Queen, and think thy poem may
Impose upon posterity, as they
Have done on us.　What though romances lie
Thus blended with more faithful history;
We of th' adult'rate mixture not complain,　　　　15
But thence more characters of virtue gain;
More pregnant patterns of transcendent worth
Than barren and insipid Truth brings forth:
So oft the bastard nobler fortune meets
Than the dull issue of the lawful sheets.　　　　20

THE COMPARISON

DEAREST, thy tresses are not threads of gold,
Thy eyes of diamonds, nor do I hold
Thy lips for rubies, thy fair cheeks to be
Fresh roses, or thy teeth of ivory;
Thy skin that doth thy dainty body sheathe　　　　5
Not alabaster is, nor dost thou breathe
Arabian odours; those the earth brings forth,
Compar'd with which would but impair thy worth.
Such may be others' mistresses, but mine
Holds nothing earthly, but is all divine.　　　　10

Thy tresses are those rays that do arise
Not from one sun, but two: such are thy eyes;
Thy lips congealed nectar are, and such
As, but a deity, there 's none dare touch.
The perfect crimson that thy cheek doth clothe   15
(But only that it far exceeds them both,)
Aurora's blush resembles, or that red
That Iris struts in when her mantle 's spread.
Thy teeth in white do Leda's swan exceed;
Thy skin 's a heavenly and immortal weed;   20
And when thou breath'st, the winds are ready straight
To filch it from thee, and do therefore wait
Close at thy lips, and snatching it from thence,
Bear it to heaven, where 'tis Jove's frankincense.
Fair goddess, since thy feature makes thee one,   25
Yet be not such for these respects alone;
But as you are divine in outward view,
So be within as fair, as good, as true.

THE SPARK

[Also attributed to Walter or Walton Poole, and, as "The Guiltless
Inconstant," to Suckling.]

My first love, whom all beauties did adorn,
Firing my heart suppress'd it with her scorn;
Since like to tinder in my breast it lies,
By every sparkle made a sacrifice.
Each wanton eye now kindles my desire,   5
And that is free to all which was entire:
Desiring more, by the desire I lost,
As those that in consumptions hunger most,
And now my wand'ring thoughts are not confin'd
Unto one woman but to womankind;   10
This for her shape I love, that for her face,
This for her gesture or some other grace,
And, where I none of these do use to find,
I choose her by the kernel not the rind;
And so I hope, since my first hopes are gone,   15
To find in many what I lost in one,
And, like to merchants after some great loss,
Trade by retail that cannot now in gross.
The fault is hers that made me go astray,
He needs must wander that has lost his way.   20

Guiltless I am, she did this change provoke
And made that charcoal which to her was oak.
And, as a looking-glass from the aspect,
Whilst it is whole, doth but one face reflect,
But, being crack'd or broken, there are shown   25
Many half-faces, which at first were one,
So love unto my heart did first prefer
Her image, and there planted none but her,
But since 'twas broke and martyr'd by her scorn
Many less faces in her place are born.   30

THE COMPLEMENT

O MY dearest, I shall grieve thee,
When I swear (yet, sweet, believe me)
By thine eyes, the tempting book
On which even crabbed old men look,
I swear to thee, (though none abhor them,)   5
Yet I do not love thee for them.

I do not love thee for that fair
Rich fan of thy most curious hair;
Though the wires thereof be drawn
Finer than the threads of lawn,   10
And are softer than the leaves
On which the subtle spinner weaves.

I do not love thee for those flowers
Growing on thy cheeks (Love's bowers);
Though such cunning them hath spread,   15
None can part their white and red;
Love's golden arrows thence are shot,
Yet for them I love thee not.

I do not love thee for those soft
Red coral lips I 've kiss'd so oft;   20
Nor teeth of pearl, the double guard
To speech, whence music still is heard;
Though from those lips a kiss being taken
Might tyrants melt, and death awaken.

I do not love thee, O my fairest!   25
For that richest, for that rarest
Silver pillar which stands under
Thy round head, that globe of wonder;

Though that neck be whiter far
Than towers of polish'd ivory are.   30

I do not love thee for those mountains
Hill'd with snow, whence milky fountains
(Sugar'd sweets, as syrup'd berries)
Must one day run through pipes of cherries:
O how much those breasts do move me!   35
Yet for them I do not love thee.

I do not love thee for that belly,
Sleek as satin, soft as jelly;
Though within that crystal mound
Heaps of treasure might be found,   40
So rich, that for the least of them
A king might leave his diadem.

I do not love thee for those thighs,
Whose alabaster rocks do rise
So high and even, that they stand   45
Like sea-marks to some happy land:
Happy are those eyes have seen them,
More happy they that sail between them.

I love thee not for thy moist palm,
Though the dew thereof be balm;   50
Nor for thy pretty leg and foot,
Although it be the precious root
On which this goodly cedar grows:
Sweet, I love thee not for those.

Nor for thy wit, though pure and quick,   55
Whose substance no arithmetic
Can number down; nor for those charms
Mask'd in thy embracing arms;
Though in them one night to lie,
Dearest, I would gladly die.   60

I love not for those eyes, nor hair,
Nor cheeks, nor lips, nor teeth so rare;
Nor for thy speech, thy neck, nor breast,
Nor for thy belly, nor the rest;
Nor for thy hand nor foot so small: 65
But, wouldst thou know, dear sweet, for all.

ON SIGHT OF A GENTLEWOMAN'S FACE
IN THE WATER

STAND still, you floods! do not deface
   That image which you bear:
So votaries from every place
   To you shall altars rear.

No winds but lovers' sighs blow here,   5
   To trouble these glad streams,
On which no star from any sphere
   Did ever dart such beams.

To crystal then in haste congeal,
   Lest you should lose your bliss;   10
And to my cruel fair reveal
   How cold, how hard she is!

But if the envious nymphs shall fear
   Their beauties will be scorn'd,
And hire the ruder winds to tear   15
   That face which you adorn'd,

Then rage and foam amain, that we
   Their malice may despise;
When from your froth we soon shall see
   A second Venus rise.   20

A SONG

ASK me no more where Jove bestows,
When June is past, the fading rose;
For in your beauty's orient deep
These flowers, as in their causes, sleep.

Ask me no more whither doth stray   5
The golden atoms of the day;
For in pure love heaven did prepare
Those powders to enrich your hair.

Ask me no more whither doth haste
The nightingale, when May is past;   10
For in your sweet dividing throat
She winters, and keeps warm her note.

Ask me no more where those stars light,
That downwards fall in dead of night;
For in your eyes they sit, and there   15
Fixed become as in their sphere.

Ask me no more if east or west
The phœnix builds her spicy nest;
For unto you at last she flies,
And in your fragrant bosom dies.   20

THE SECOND RAPTURE

No, worldling, no, 'tis not thy gold,
Which thou dost use but to behold;
Nor fortune, honour, nor long life,
Children, or friends, nor a good wife,
That makes thee happy: these things be   5
But shadows of felicity.
Give me a wench about thirteen,
Already voted to the queen
Of lust and lovers; whose soft hair,
Fann'd with the breath of gentle air,   10
O'erspreads her shoulders like a tent,
And is her veil and ornament;
Whose tender touch will make the blood
Wild in the aged and the good;
Whose kisses, fast'ned to the mouth   15
Of threescore years and longer slouth,
Renew the age; and whose bright eye
Obscures those lesser lights of sky;
Whose snowy breasts (if we may call
That snow, that never melts at all)   20
Makes Jove invent a new disguise,
In spite of Juno's jealousies;
Whose every part doth re-invite
The old decayed appetite;
And in whose sweet embraces I   25
May melt myself to lust, and die.
        This is true bliss, and I confess
        There is no other happiness.

THE TINDER

Of what mould did Nature frame me?
Or was it her intent to shame me,
That no woman can come near me,
Fair, but her I court to hear me?
Sure that mistress to whose beauty   5
First I paid a lover's duty,
Burnt in rage my heart to tinder,
That nor prayers nor tears can hinder,
But wherever I do turn me,
Every spark let fall doth burn me.   10
Women, since you thus inflame me,
Flint and steel I 'll ever name ye.

A SONG

In her fair cheeks two pits do lie,
To bury those slain by her eye;
So, spite of death, this comforts me,
That fairly buried I shall be,
My grave with rose and lily spread;   5
O 'tis a life to be so dead!
　　Come then, and kill me with thy eye,
　　For if thou let me live, I die.

When I behold those lips again,
Reviving what those eyes have slain,   10
With kisses sweet, whose balsam pure
Love's wounds, as soon as made, can cure,
Methinks 'tis sickness to be sound,
And there 's no health to such a wound.
　　Come then, and kill me with thy eye,   15
　　For if thou let me live, I die.

When in her chaste breast I behold
Those downy mounts of snow ne'er cold;
And those blest hearts her beauty kills
Reviv'd by climbing those fair hills,   20
Methinks there 's life in such a death,
And so t' expire inspires new breath.
　　Come then, and kill me with thy eye,
　　For if thou let me live, I die.

Nymph, since no death is deadly, where   25
Such choice of antidotes are near,
And your keen eyes but kill in vain
Those that are sound, as soon as slain;
That I no longer dead survive,
Your way 's to bury me alive   30
In Cupid's cave, where happy I
May dying live, and living die.
    Come then, and kill me with thy eye,
    For if thou let me live, I die.

TO THE PAINTER

FOND man, that hop'st to catch that face
With those false colours, whose short grace
Serves but to show the lookers-on
The faults of thy presumption;
Or, at the least, to let us see   5
That is divine, but yet not she:
Say you could imitate the rays
Of those eyes that outshine the day's,
Or counterfeit in red and white
That most uncounterfeited light   10
Of her complexion; yet canst thou,
Great master though thou be, tell how
To paint a virtue?   Then desist,
This fair your artifice hath miss'd.
You should have mark'd how she begins   15
To grow in virtue, not in sins;
Instead of that same rosy dye,
You should have drawn out modesty,
Whose beauty sits enthroned there,
And learn to look and blush at her.   20
Or can you colour just the same,
When virtue blushes or when shame?
When sickness, and when innocence,
Shows pale or white unto the sense?
Can such coarse varnish e'er be said   25
To imitate her white and red?
This may do well elsewhere, in Spain,
Among those faces dy'd in grain;

So you may thrive, and what you do
Prove the best picture of the two.   30
Besides, if all I hear be true,
'Tis taken ill by some that you
Should be so insolently vain,
As to contrive all that rich gain
Into one tablet, which alone   35
May teach us superstition,
Instructing our amazed eyes
To admire and worship imag'ries,
Such as quickly might outshine
Some new saint, were 't allow'd a shrine,   40
And turn each wand'ring looker-on
Into a new Pygmalion.
Yet your art cannot equalize
This picture in her lover's eyes;
His eyes the pencils are which limn   45
Her truly, as hers copy him;
His heart the tablet which alone
Is for that portrait the tru'st stone.
If you would a truer see,
Mark it in their posterity: 50
And you shall read it truly there,
When the glad world shall see their heir.

LOVE'S COURTSHIP

Kiss, lovely Celia, and be kind,
Let my desires freedom find,
          Sit thee down,
And we will make the gods confess
Mortals enjoy some happiness.   5

Mars would disdain his mistress' charms
If he beheld thee in my arms,
          And descend,
Thee his mortal queen to make
Or live as mortal for thy sake.   10

Venus must lose her title now,
And leave to brag of Cupid's bow—
          Silly queen!
She hath but one, but I can spy
Ten thousand Cupids in thy eye.   15

Nor may the sun behold our bliss,
For sure thy eyes do dazzle his;
   If thou fear
That he 'll betray thee with his light,
Let me eclipse thee from his sight!   20

And while I shade thee from his eye,
Oh let me hear thee gently cry,
   Celia yields!
Maids often lose their maidenhead,
Ere they set foot in nuptial bed.   25

ON A DAMASK ROSE STICKING UPON A LADY'S BREAST

LET pride grow big, my rose, and let the clear
And damask colour of thy leaves appear;
Let scent and looks be sweet and bless that hand
That did transplant thee to that sacred land.
O happy thou that in that garden rests,   5
That paradise between that lady's breasts!
There 's an eternal Spring; there shalt thou lie
Betwixt two lily mounts, and never die.
There shalt thou spring amongst the fertile valleys,
By buds like thee that grow in midst of alleys.   10
There none dare pluck thee, for that place is such,
That, but a good divine, there 's none dare touch.
If any but approach, straight doth arise
A blushing lightning flash and blasts his eyes.
There, 'stead of rain, shall living fountains flow,   15
For wind, her fragrant breath for ever blow:
Nor now, as erst, one sun shall on thee shine,
But those two glorious suns, her eyes divine.
O then, what monarch would not think 't a grace
To leave his regal throne to have thy place?   20
Myself, to gain thy blessed seat, do vow,
Would be transform'd into a rose as thou.

THE PROTESTATION

A SONNET

No more shall meads be deck'd with flowers,
Nor sweetness dwell in rosy bowers,
Nor greenest buds on branches spring,
Nor warbling birds delight to sing,

Nor April violets paint the grove, 5
If I forsake my Celia's love.

The fish shall in the ocean burn,
And fountains sweet shall bitter turn;
The humble oak no flood shall know,
When floods shall highest hills o'erflow; 10
Black Lethe shall oblivion leave,
If e'er my Celia I deceive.

Love shall his bow and shaft lay by,
And Venus' doves want wings to fly;
The sun refuse to show his light, 15
And day shall then be turn'd to night,
And in that night no star appear,
If once I leave my Celia dear.

Love shall no more inhabit earth,
Nor lovers more shall love for worth, 20
Nor joy above in heaven dwell,
Nor pain torment poor souls in hell;
Grim death no more shall horrid prove,
If e'er I leave bright Celia's love.

THE TOOTHACHE CURED BY A KISS

FATE's now grown merciful to men,
    Turning disease to bliss;
For had not kind rheum vex'd me then,
    I might not Celia kiss.
Physicians, you are now my scorn, 5
    For I have found a way
To cure diseases, when forlorn
    By your dull art, which may
Patch up a body for a time,
    But can restore to health 10
No more than chemists can sublime
    True gold, the Indies' wealth.
That angel sure, that us'd to move
    The pool men so admir'd,
Hath to her lip, the seat of love, 15
    As to his heaven, retir'd.

TO HIS JEALOUS MISTRESS

ADMIT, thou darling of mine eyes,
　I have some idol lately fram'd,
That under such a false disguise
　Our true loves might the less be fam'd:
Canst thou, that knowest my heart, suppose　5
I 'll fall from thee, and worship those?

Remember, dear, how loth and slow
　I was to cast a look or smile,
Or one love-line to misbestow,
　Till thou hadst chang'd both face and style:　10
And art thou grown afraid to see
That mask put on thou mad'st for me?

I dare not call those childish fears,
　Coming from love, much less from thee;
But wash away, with frequent tears,　15
　This counterfeit idolatry:
And henceforth kneel at ne'er a shrine,
To blind the world, but only thine.

THE DART

[Also attributed to William Strode]

OFT when I look I may descry
A little face peep through that eye;
Sure, that 's the boy, which wisely chose
His throne among such beams as those,
Which, if his quiver chance to fall,　5
May serve for darts to kill withal.

THE MISTAKE

[Also attributed to Henry Blount]

WHEN on fair Celia I did spy
　A wounded heart of stone,
The wound had almost made me cry,
　Sure this heart was my own!

But when I saw it was enthron'd　5
　In her celestial breast,
O then I it no longer own'd,
　For mine was ne'er so blest.

Yet if in highest heavens do shine
　　Each constant martyr's heart,　　　　　　10
Then she may well give rest to mine,
　　That for her sake doth smart;

Where, seated in so high a bliss,
　　Though wounded, it shall live;
Death enters not in Paradise,　　　　　　　15
　　The place free life doth give.

Or if the place less sacred were,
　　Did but her saving eye
Bathe my sick heart in one kind tear,
　　Then should I never die.　　　　　　　　20

Slight balms may heal a slighter sore,
　　No medicine less divine
Can ever hope for to restore
　　A wounded heart like mine.

ON MISTRESS N[EVILLE]
TO THE GREEN SICKNESS

STAY, coward blood, and do not yield
To thy pale sister beauty's field,
Who, there displaying round her white
Ensigns, hath usurp'd thy right,
Invading thy peculiar throne,　　　　　　　5
The lip, where thou shouldst rule alone;
And on the cheek, where Nature's care
Allotted each an equal share,
Her spreading lily only grows,
Whose milky deluge drowns thy rose.　　　10
　　Quit not the field, faint blood, nor rush
In the short sally of a blush
Upon thy sister foe, but strive
To keep an endless war alive:
Though peace do petty states maintain,　　15
Here war alone makes beauty reign.

UPON A MOLE IN CELIA'S BOSOM

THAT lovely spot which thou dost see
In Celia's bosom was a bee,
Who built her amorous spicy nest
I' th' Hyblas of her either breast.

But from close ivory hives she flew 5
To suck the aromatic dew
Which from the neighbour vale distils,
Which parts those two twin-sister hills.
There feasting on ambrosial meat,
A rolling file of balmy sweat 10
(As in soft murmurs before death
Swan-like she sung) chok'd up her breath:
So she in water did expire,
More precious than the phœnix' fire.

Yet still her shadow there remains 15
Confin'd to those Elysian plains,
With this strict law, that who shall lay
His bold lips on that milky way,
The sweet and smart from thence shall bring
Of the bee's honey and her sting. 20

AN HYMENEAL SONG, ON THE NUPTIALS OF
THE LADY ANNE WENTWORTH AND
THE LORD LOVELACE

BREAK not the slumbers of the bride,
But let the sun in triumph ride,
　　Scattering his beamy light;
When she awakes, he shall resign
His rays, and she alone shall shine 5
　　In glory all the night.

For she, till day return, must keep
An amorous vigil, and not steep
Her fair eyes in the dew of sleep.

Yet gently whisper, as she lies, 10
And say her lord waits her uprise,
　　The priests at the altar stay;
With flow'ry wreaths the virgin crew
Attend, while some with roses strew,
　　And myrtles trim, the way. 15

Now to the temple and the priest
See her convey'd, thence to the feast;
Then back to bed, though not to rest:

For now, to crown his faith and truth,
We must admit the noble youth   20
    To revel in Love's sphere;
To rule, as chief Intelligence,
That orb, and happy time dispense
    To wretched lovers here.

For there exalted far above   25
All hope, fear, change, are they to move
The wheel that spins the fates of Love.

They know no night, nor glaring noon,
Measure no hours of sun or moon,
    Nor mark Time's restless glass;   30
Their kisses measure as they flow
Minutes, and their embraces show
    The hours as they pass.

Their motions the year's circle make,
And we from their conjunctions take   35
Rules to make Love an almanac.

A MARRIED WOMAN

When I shall marry, if I do not find
A wife thus moulded, I 'll create this mind:
Nor from her noble birth nor ample dower,
Beauty, or wit, shall she derive a power
To prejudice my right; but if she be   5
A subject born, she shall be so to me:
As to the soul the flesh, as appetite
To reason is, which shall our wills unite
In habits so confirm'd, as no rough sway
Shall once appear, if she but learn t' obey.   10
For in habitual virtues sense is wrought
To that calm temper, as the body 's thought
To have nor blood nor gall, if wild and rude
Passions of lust and anger are subdu'd;
When 'tis the fair obedience to the soul   15
Doth in the birth those swelling acts control.
If I in murder steep my furious rage,
Or with adult'ry my hot lust assuage,

Will it suffice to say my sense, the beast,
Provok'd me to 't? Could I my soul divest,   20
My plea were good. Lions and bulls commit
Both freely, but man must in judgment sit,
And tame this beast; for Adam was not free
When in excuse he said, Eve gave it me;
Had he not eaten, she perhaps had been   25
Unpunish'd: his consent made hers a sin.

LOVE'S FORCE

IN the first ruder age, when Love was wild,
Not yet by laws reclaim'd, not reconcil'd
To order, nor by Reason mann'd, but flew
Full-summ'd by Nature, on the instant view
Upon the wings of Appetite, at all   5
The eye could fair, or sense delightful call;
Election was not yet: but as their cheap
Food from the oak, or the next acorn-heap,
As water from the nearest spring or brook,
So men their undistinguish'd females took   10
By chance, not choice. But soon the heavenly spark
That in man's bosom lurk'd broke through this dark
Confusion: then the noblest breast first felt
Itself for its own proper object melt.

A FANCY

MARK how this polish'd Eastern sheet
Doth with our Northern tincture meet,
For though the paper seem to sink,
Yet it receives and bears the ink;
And on her smooth soft brow these spots   5
Seem rather ornaments than blots;
Like those you ladies use to place
Mysteriously about your face,
Not only to set off and break
Shadows and eye-beams, but to speak   10
To the skill'd lover, and relate
Unheard his sad or happy fate.
Nor do their characters delight
As careless works of black and white;
But 'cause you underneath may find   15
A sense that can inform the mind,

Divine or moral rules impart,
   Or raptures of poetic art:
So what at first was only fit
To fold up silks may wrap up wit.   20

TO HIS MISTRESS

GRIEVE not, my Celia, but with haste
   Obey the fury of thy fate;
'Tis some perfection to waste
   Discreetly out our wretched state:
To be obedient in this sense   5
Will prove thy virtue, though offence.

Who knows but destiny may relent?
   For many miracles have bin:
Thou proving thus obedient
   To all the griefs she plung'd thee in;   10
And then the certainty she meant
Reverted is by accident.

But yet, I must confess, 'tis much,
   When we remember what hath bin:
Thus parting, never more to touch,   15
   To let eternal absence in:
Though never was our pleasure yet
So pure, but chance distracted it.

What, shall we then submit to fate,
   And die to one another's love?   20
No, Celia, no, my soul doth hate
   Those lovers that inconstant prove.
Fate may be cruel, but if you decline,
The crime is yours, and all the glory mine.

Fate and the planets sometimes bodies part,   25
But canker'd nature only alters th' heart.

IN PRAISE OF HIS MISTRESS

You that will a wonder know,
   Go with me;
Two suns in a heaven of snow
   Both burning be:

All they fire, that but eye them,   5
Yet the snow 's unmelted by them.

Leaves of crimson tulips met
  Guide the way
Where two pearly rows be set,
  As white as day: 10
When they part themselves asunder,
She breathes oracles of wonder.

Hills of milk with azure mix'd
  Swell beneath,
Waving sweetly, yet still fix'd,   15
  While she doth breathe:
From those hills descends a valley,
Where all fall, that dare to dally.

As fair pillars under stand
  Statues two;   20
Whiter than the silver swan
  That swims in Po:
If at any time they move her,
Every step begets a lover.

All this but the casket is,   25
  Which contains
Such a jewel, as the miss
  Breeds endless pains;
That 's her mind, and they that know it
May admire, but cannot show it.   30

TO CELIA, UPON LOVE'S UBIQUITY

As one that strives, being sick, and sick to death,
By changing places to preserve a breath,
A tedious restless breath, removes, and tries
A thousand rooms, a thousand policies,
To cozen pain, when he thinks to find ease,   5
At last he finds all change but his disease;
So, like a ball with fire and powder fill'd,
I restless am, yet live, each minute kill'd,

And with that moving torture must retain,
With change of all things else, a constant pain.   10
Say I stay with you, presence is to me
Naught but a light to show my misery;
And partings are as racks to plague love on,
The further stretch'd, the more affliction.
Go I to Holland, France, or furthest Ind,   15
I change but only countries, not my mind;
And though I pass through air and water free,
Despair and hopeless fate still follow me.
Whilst in the bosom of the waves I reel.
My heart I 'll liken to the tottering keel,   20
The sea to my own troubled fate, the wind
To your disdain, sent from a soul unkind.
But when I lift my sad looks to the skies,
Then shall I think I see my Celia's eyes;
And when a cloud or storm appears between,   25
I shall remember what her frowns have been.
Thus, whatsoever course my Fates allow,
All things but make me mind my business, you.
The good things that I meet, I think streams be
From you, the fountain; but when bad I see,   30
How vile and cursed is that thing, think I,
That to such goodness is so contrary!
My whole life is 'bout you, the centre star,
But a perpetual motion circular.
I am the dial's hand, still walking round,   35
You are the compass: and I never sound
Beyond your circle, neither can I show
Aught but what first expressed is in you:
That, wheresoever my tears do cause me move,
My fate still keeps me bounded with your love;   40
Which, ere it die, or be extinct in me,
Time shall stand still, and moist waves flaming be.
Yet, being gone, think not on me: I am
A thing too wretched for thy thoughts to name:
But when I die, and wish all comforts given,   45
I 'll think on you, and by you think on heaven.

TO MISTRESS KATHERINE NEVILLE, ON HER GREEN SICKNESS

[Printed in *Musarum Deliciæ*, 1655; attributed to Carew in manuscripts.]

WHITE Innocence, that now lies spread
Forsaken on thy widow'd bed,
Cold and alone, if fear, love, hate,
Or shame recall thy crimson mate
From his dark mazes to reside 5
With thee his chaste and maiden bride;
That he may never backward flow,
Congeal him in thy virgin snow.
But if his own heat, with thy pair
Of neighbouring suns and flaming hair, 10
Thaw him into a new divorce;
Lest to the heart he take his course,
Oh lodge me there, where I'll defeat
All future hope of his retreat,
And force the fugitive to seek 15
A constant station in thy cheek.
    So each shall have his proper place,
    I in your heart, he in your face.

MR. CAREW TO HIS FRIEND

[From manuscripts in the Bodleian Library and the British Museum; also attributed to William Strode.]

LIKE to the hand that hath been us'd to play
One lesson long still runs the selfsame way,
And waits not what the hearers bid it strike,
But doth presume by custom this will like:
So run my thoughts, which are so perfect grown, 5
So well acquainted with my passion,
That now they dare prevent me with their haste,
And ere I think to sigh, my sigh is past:
It's past and flown to you, for you alone
Are all the object that I think upon: 10
And did you not supply my soul with thought,
For want of action it to none were brought.
What though our absent arms may not enfold

Real embraces, yet we firmly hold
Each other in possession; thus we see   15
The lord enjoys his land, where'er he be.
If kings possess'd no more than where they sate,
What were they greater than a mean estate?
This makes me firmly yours, you firmly mine,
That something more than bodies us combine.   20

TO HIS MISTRESS RETIRING IN AFFECTION

[From manuscripts in the British Museum.]

FLY not from him whose silent misery
Breathes many an unwitness'd sigh to thee,
Who, having felt thy scorn, yet constant is,
And whom thou hast thyself call'd only his.
   When first mine eyes threw flames, whose spirit mov'd thee,
   Hadst thou not look'd again I had not lov'd thee.   6

Nature did ne'er two different things unite
With peace, which are by nature opposite.
If thou force Nature, and be backward gone,
O, blame not me, that strive to draw thee on: 10
   But if my constant love shall fail to move thee,
   Then know my reason hates thee, though I love thee.

EXCUSE OF ABSENCE

[From the Cosens MS. and manuscripts in the Bodleian Library and the
British Museum.]

You will ask, perhaps, wherefore I stay,
Loving so much, so long away—
O do not think 'twas I did part,
It was my body, not my heart;
For, like a compass, on your love   5
One foot is fix'd, and cannot move:
Th' other may follow the blind guide
Of giddy Fortune, but not slide
   Beyond your service, nor dare venter
   To wander far from you, the centre.   10

A LADY'S PRAYER TO CUPID

[From the same manuscripts.]

SINCE I must needs into thy school return,
Be pitiful, O Love, and do not burn
Me with desire of cold and frozen age,
Nor let me follow a fond boy or page.
But, gentle Cupid, give me, if you can,   5
One to my love whom I may call a man;
Of person comely, and of face as sweet,
Let him be sober, secret, and discreet,
    Well practis'd in Love's school: let him within
    Wear all his beard, and none upon his chin.   10

TO A STRUMPET

[From manuscripts in the British Museum and the Bodleian Library.
Also claimed by Henry Bold.]

HAIL, thou true model of a cursed whore,
Damn'd by creation ever to live poor,
Though cloth'd in Indian silks, or what may be
Bestow'd in riot on thy venery!
Thou eldest daughter to the Prince of Night,   5
That canst outlie thy father at first sight,
Outscoff an Ishmaelite, and attempt more
Than all our wicked age hath done before;
Nay, when the Devil leaves thou canst begin,
And teach both him and us new ways to sin,   10
Making us to conclude that all vile crimes
Are but thy pieces copi'd by thy times.
Sure thou wast born a whore even from the womb
Of some rank bawd, unsavoury as a tomb,
Who, carted from all parishes, did sell   15
Forbidden fruits in the highway to hell.
There didst thou taste all nations that would crown
Thee with light feathers or a silken gown.
But oh, thou beastly surfeit, may they have
Thee in esteem as the insatiate grave,   20
Spew thee out of the Strand, and make thee fain
To shelter in the suburbs of Chick-lane:

G 873

There mayst thou serve with butchers upon straw,
And still be plagu'd with beadles and the law;
Ne'er mayst thou gain a ninepence to set up   25
With half an ounce, two bottles and a cup;
Mayst thou each day upon thy bared feet
Trudge for thy bread and drink to Turnbull Street,
Creep to Knockvergus, and there learn the thrift
Of raking dunghills, or some poorer shift.   30
Wither'd with age, and with diseases cross'd,
The Patient Gristle of thy nose being lost,
May both the hospitals grudge and repine
To give thee one poor plaster to thy groin:
And let no man ever bemoan thy case,   35
That once did know thee in the state of grace.

THE DEPARTURE

[Attributed to T. C. in Thomas Jordan's *Claraphil and Clarinda : In a Forest of Fancies*, ? 1650.]

By all thy glories willingly I go,
Yet could have wish'd thee constant in thy love;
But, since thou needs must prove
Uncertain, as is thy beauty,
Or as the glass that shows it thee,   5
My hopes thus soon to overthrow
Shows thee more fickle; but my flames by this
Are easier quench'd than his
Whom flattering smiles betray:
'Tis tyrannous delay   10
Breeds all this harm,
And makes that fire consume that should but warm.

Till Time destroys the blossoms of thy youth
Thou art our idol, worshipp'd at that rate;
But who can tell thy fate,   15
Or say that when thy beauty 's gone
Thy lover's torch will still burn on?
I could have serv'd thee with such truth
Devoutest pilgrims to their saints do owe
Departed long ago,   20
And at thy ebbing tide
Have us'd thee as a bride:
Who 's only true
'Cause you are fair, he loves himself, not you.

THE PROLOGUE TO A PLAY PRESENTED BEFORE THE KING AND QUEEN, AT AN ENTERTAINMENT OF THEM BY THE LORD CHAMBERLAIN, AT WHITE-HALL

[From the Wyburd MS.]

SIR,
Since you have been pleas'd this night to unbend
Your serious thoughts, and with your person lend
Your palace out, and so are hither come
A stranger, in your own house not at home:
Divesting state, as if you meant alone   5
To make your servant's loyal heart your throne:
Oh, see how wide these valves themselves display
To entertain his royal guests! survey
What arcs triumphal, statues, altars, shrines,
Inscrib'd to your great names, he these assigns: 10
So from that stock of zeal, his coarse cates may
Borrow some relish, though but thinly they
Cover'd his narrow table: so may these
Succeeding trifles by that title please.
Else, gracious Madam, must the influence   15
Of your fair eyes propitious beams dispense,
To crown such pastimes as he could provide
To oil the lazy minutes as they slide.
For well he knows upon your smile depends
This night success; since that alone commends   20
All his endeavours, gives the music praise,
Painters and us, and gilds your poet's bays.

THE EPILOGUE TO THE SAME PLAY

HUNGER is sharp, the sated stomach dull;
Feeding delights 'twixt emptiness and full:
The pleasure lies not in the end, but streams
That flow betwixt two opposite extremes.
So doth the flux from hot to cold combine   5
An equal temper; such is noble wine,
'Twixt fulsome must and vinegar too tart.
Pleasure 's the scratching betwixt itch and smart,
It is a shifting Tartar, that still flies
From place to place: if it stand still, it dies.   10

After much rest, labour delights; when pain
Succeeds long travail, rest grows sweet again.
Pain is the base on which his nimble feet
Move in continual change from sour to sweet.
   This the contriver of your sports to-night   15
Hath well observ'd, and so, to fix delight
In a perpetual circle, hath appli'd
The choicest objects that care could provide
To every sense. Only himself hath felt
The load of this great honour, and doth melt   20
All into humble thanks, and at your feet
Of both your Majesties prostrates the sweet
Perfume of grateful service, which he swears
He will extend to such a length of years
As fits not us to tell, but doth belong   25
To a far abler pen and nobler tongue.
   Our task ends here: if we have hit the laws
Of true delight, his glad heart joys: yet, 'cause
You cannot to succeeding pleasures climb,
Till you grow weary of the instant time,   30
He was content this last piece should grow sour
Only to sweeten the ensuing hour.
But if the cook, musician, player, poet,
Painter, and all, have fail'd, he 'll make them know it,
    That have abus'd him: yet must grieve at this, 35
    He should do penance, when the sin was his.

PARAPHRASES OF PSALMS

[From the Wyburd MS. and manuscripts in the Bodleian Library and the British Museum.]

PSALM I

1. HAPPY the man that doth not walk
    In wicked counsels, nor hath lent
His glad ear to the railing talk
    Of scorners, nor his prompt steps bent
    To wicked paths, where sinners went.   5

2. But, to those safer tracts confin'd,
    Which God's law-giving finger made,
Never withdraws his weari'd mind

From practice of that holy trade,
By noonday's sun or midnight's shade.   10

3. Like the fair plant whom neighbouring floods
Refresh, whose leaf feels no decays;
That not alone with flattering buds,
But early fruits, his Lord's hope pays:
So shall he thrive in all his ways.   15

4. But the loose sinner shall not share
So fix'd a state; like the light dust
That up and down the empty air
The wild wind drives with various gust,
So shall cross-fortunes toss the unjust.   20

5. Therefore, at the last Judgment-day,
The trembling sinful soul shall hide
His confus'd face, nor shall he stay
Where the elected troops abide,
But shall be chas'd far from their side.   25

6. For the clear paths of righteous men
To the all-seeing Lord are known;
But the dark maze and dismal den,
Where sinners wander up and down,
Shall by his hand be overthrown.   30

Psalm 2

1, 2, 3. Why rage the heathen? wherefore swell
The people with vain thoughts? why meet
Their kings in counsel to rebel
'Gainst God and Christ, trampling His sweet
But broken bonds under their feet?   5

4, 5, 6. Alas! the glorious God that hath
His throne in heaven, derides the unsound
Plots of weak mortals: in His wrath
Thus shall He speak: "Myself have crown'd
The monarch of my holy ground."   10

7, 8. I will declare what God hath told:
"Thou art My Son; this happy day
Did Thy incarnate birth unfold:
Ask, and the heathen shall obey,
With the remotest earth, Thy sway."   15

9, 10, 11. Thy rod of iron shall, if kings rise
  Against Thee, bruise them into dust,
Like pots of clay: therefore be wise,
  Ye Princes, and learn judgments just;
  Serve God with fear; tremble, yet trust.   20

12. Kiss and do homage to the Son,
  Lest His displeasure ruin bring:
For if that fire be but begun,
  Then happy those that themselves fling
  Under the shelter of His wing.   25

PSALM 51

1. GOOD God, unlock thy magazines
  Of mercy, and forgive my sins.

2. Oh, wash and purify the foul
  Pollution of my sin-stain'd soul.

3. For I confess my faults, that lie   5
  In horrid shapes before mine eye.

4. Against Thee only and alone,
  In Thy sight, was this evil done,
That all men might Thy justice see
  When Thou art judg'd for judging me.   10

5. Even from my birth I did begin
  With mother's milk to suck in sin.

6. But Thou lov'st truth, and shalt impart
  Thy secret wisdom to my heart.

7. Thou shalt with hyssop purge me, so   15
  Shall I seem white as Alpine snow.

8. Thou shalt send joyful news, and then
  My broken bones grow firm again.

9. Let not Thine eyes my sins survey;
  But cast those cancell'd debts away.   20

10. Oh, make my cleans'd heart a pure cell,
  Where a renewed spirit may dwell.

11. Cast me not from Thy sight, nor chase
    Away from me Thy spirit of grace.

12. Send me Thy saving health again,   25
    And with Thy Spirit those joys maintain.

13. Then will I teach Thy ways, and draw
    Converted sinners to Thy law.

14, 15. Oh God, my God of health, unseal
    My blood-shut lips, and I 'll reveal   30
    What mercies in Thy justice dwell,
    And with loud voice Thy praises tell.

16, 17. Could sacrifice have purg'd my vice,
    Lord, I had brought Thee sacrifice;
    But though burnt offerings are refus'd,   35
    Thou shalt accept the heart that 's bruis'd:
    The humbled soul, the spirit oppress'd,
    Lord, such oblations please Thee best.

18. Bless Sion, Lord! repair with pity
    The ruins of Thy Holy City.   40

19. Then will we holy vows present Thee,
    And peace-offerings that content Thee;
    And then Thine Altars shall be press'd
    With many a sacrificed beast.

PSALM 91

1, 2, 3. MAKE the great God thy fort, and dwell
    In Him by faith and do not care
    (So shaded) for the power of hell,
    Or for the cunning fowler's snare,
    Or poison of the infected air.   5

4, 5. His plumes shall make a downy bed,
    Where thou shalt rest: He shall display
    His wings of truth over thy head,
    Which, like a shield, shall drive away
    The fears of night, the darts of day.   10

6, 7. The winged plague that flies by night,
       The murdering sword that kills by day,
   Shall not thy peaceful sleeps affright,
       Though on thy right and left hand they
       A thousand and ten thousand slay.   15

8, 9, 10. Yet shall thine eyes behold the fall
       Of sinners; but, because thine heart
   Dwells with the Lord, not one of all
       Those ills, nor yet the plague and dart,
       Shall dare approach near where thou art.   20

11, 12, 13. His angels shall direct thy legs,
       And guard them in the stony street:
   On lions' whelps and adders' eggs
       Thy steps shall march; and if thou meet
       With dragons, they shall kiss thy feet.   25

14, 15, 16. When thou art troubled, He shall hear,
       And help thee, for thy love embrac'd
   And knew His name; therefore He 'll rear
       Thy honours high, and, when thou hast
       Enjoy'd them long, save thee at last.   30

PSALM 104

1. My soul the great God's praises sings,
   Circled round with glory's wings;

2. Cloth'd with light, o'er whom the sky
   Hangs like a starry canopy;

3. Who dwells upon the gliding streams,   5
   Enamell'd with His golden beams:
   Enthron'd in clouds, as in a chair,
   He rides in triumph through the air.

4. The winds and flaming element
   Are on His great ambassage sent.   10

5. The fabric of the earth shall stand
   For aye, built by His powerful hand.

6, 7, 8, 9. The floods, that with their wat'ry robe
   Once cover'd all this earthy globe,

Soon as Thy thund'ring voice was heard, 15
Fled fast, and straight the hills appear'd;
The humble valleys saw the sun,
Whilst the affrighted waters run
Into their channels, and no more
Shall drown the earth, or pass the shore. 20

10. Amongst those vales the cool springs flow,
And wash the mountains' feet below.

11. Thither for drink the whole herd strays;
There the wild ass his thirst allays;

12. And on the boughs that shade the spring 25
The feather'd choir shall sit and sing.

13, 14, 15. When on her womb the dew is shed,
The pregnant earth is brought to bed,
And, with a fruitful birth increas'd,
Yields herbs and grass for man and beast: 30
Heart-strengthening bread, care-drowning wine,
And oil that makes the sleek face shine.

16. On Lebanon His cedars stand,
Trees full of sap, works of His hand.

17. In them the birds their cabins dight: 35
The fir-tree is the stork's delight.

18. The wild goat on the hills, in cells
Of rocks the hermit coney, dwells.

19. The moon observes her course; the sun
Knows when his weary race is done. 40

20. And when the night her dark veil spreads,
The wilder beasts forsake their sheds:

21. The hungry lions hunt for blood,
And roaring beg from God their food.

22, 23. The sun returns: those beasts of prey 45
Fly to their dens, and from the day;
And whilst they in dark caverns lurk,
Man till the evening goes to work.

24. How full of creatures is the earth,
To which Thy wisdom gave their birth! 50

25. And those that in the wide sea breed,
    The bounds of number far exceed.

26. There the huge whale with finny feet
    Dance underneath the sailing fleet.

27, 28, 29, 30. All these expect their nourishment   55
    From Thee, and gather what is sent.
    Be Thy hand open, they are fed,
    Be Thy face hid, astonished;
    If Thou withdraw their soul, they must
    Return unto their former dust: 60
    If Thou send back Thy breath, the face
    Of th' earth is spread with a new race.

31. God's glory shall for ever stay;
    He shall with joy His works survey.

32, 33. The steadfast earth shall shake, if He   65
    Look down, and if the mountains be
    Touch'd, they shall smoke; yet still my verse
    Shall, whilst I live, His praise rehearse.

34. In Him with joy my thoughts shall meet;
    He makes my meditations sweet.   70

35. The sinner shall appear no more:
    Then, O my soul, the Lord adore!

PSALM 113

1, 2, 3. YE children of the Lord, that wait
    Upon His will, sing hymns divine,
    From henceforth to time's endless date,
    To His name, prais'd from the first shine
    Of the earth's sun, till it decline.   5

4, 5, 6. The hosts of heaven or earth have none
    May to His height of glory rise;
    For who like Him hath fix'd His throne
    So high, yet bends down to the skies,
    And lower earth, His humble eyes?   10

7, 8, 9. The poor from loathed dust He draws,
  And makes them regal state invest
  'Mongst kings, that gives His people laws:
  He makes the barren mother rest
  Under her roof with children blest.   15

PSALM 114

1, 2. WHEN the seed of Jacob fled
  From the cruel Pharaoh's land,
  Judah was in safety led
  By the Lord, whose powerful hand
  Guided all the Hebrew band.   5

3, 4. This the sea saw, and dismay'd
  Flies, swift Jordan backward makes;
  Mountains skip like rams afraid;
  And the lower hillocks shakes,
  Like a tender lamb that quakes.   10

5, 6. What, O sea, hath thee dismay'd?
  Why did Jordan backward make?
  Mountains, why, like rams afraid,
  Skipt you? wherefore did ye shake,
  Hillocks, like the lambs that quake? 15

7, 8. Tremble, O thou steadfast earth,
  At the presence of the Lord!
  That makes rocks give rivers birth,
  And by virtue of whose word
  Flints shall flowing springs afford. 20

PSALM 119

ALEPH. *Beati immaculati*

1. BLEST is he that spotless stands
  In the way of God's commands.

2. Blessed he that keeps His word:
  Whose entire heart seeks the Lord;

3. For the man that walketh in   5
  His just paths commits no sin.

4. By Thy strict commands we are
Bound to keep Thy laws with care.

5. O that my steps might not slide
From Thy statutes' perfect guide.   10

6. So shall I decline Thy wrath,
Treading Thy commanded path;

7. Having learn'd Thy righteous ways,
With true heart I 'll sing Thy praise.

8. In Thy statutes I 'll persever: 15
Then forsake me not for ever!

BETH.   *In quo corriget?*

9. How shall youth, but by the level
Of Thy word, be kept from evil?

10. Let my soul, that seeks the way
Of Thy truth, not go astray.   20

11. Where, lest my frail feet might slide,
In my heart Thy words I hide.

12. Blest be Thou, O Lord!   O show
How I may Thy statutes know.

13. I have publish'd the divine   25
Judgments of Thy mouth with mine;

14. Which have fill'd my soul with pleasure
More than all the heaps of treasure.

15. They shall all the subject prove
Of my talk and of my love.   30

16. Those my darlings no time shall
From my memory let fall.

GIMEL.   *Retribue servo tuo*

17. Let Thy grace, O Lord, preserve me,
That I may but live to serve Thee.

18. Open my dark eyes, that I   35
May Thy wondrous laws descry.

19. Let Thy glorious light appear:
    I am but a pilgrim here.

20. Yet the zeal of their desire
    Hath even set my heart on fire.   40

21. Thy fierce rod and curse o'ertaketh
    Him that proudly Thee forsaketh.

22. I have kept Thy laws, O God:
    Turn from me Thy curse and rod!

23. Though combined princes rail'd,   45
    Yet thy servant hath not fail'd

24. In their study to abide;
    For they are my joy, my guide.

DALETH.   *Adhæsit pavimento*

25. For Thy word's sake, give new birth
    To my soul that cleaves to earth.   50

26. Thou hast heard my tongue untwine
    All my ways: Lord, teach me Thine!

27. Make me know them, that I may
    All Thy wondrous works display.

28. Thou hast said the word: then bring   55
    Ease to my soul languishing.

29. Plant in me Thy laws' true love,
    And the veil of lies remove.

30. I have chosen truth to lie
    The fix'd object of mine eye.   60

31. On Thy word my faith I grounded,
    Let me not then be confounded.

32. When my soul from bonds is freed,
    I shall run Thy ways with speed.

HE.   *Legem pone*

33. Teach me, Lord, Thy ways, and I   65
    From that road will never fly.

34. Give me knowledge, that I may
    With my heart Thy laws obey.

35. Unto that path my steps move,
    For I there have fix'd my love.   70

36. Fill my heart with those pure fires,
    Not with covetous desires.

37. To vain sights, Lord, let me be
    Blind, but Thy ways let me see.

38. Make Thy promise firm to me,   75
    That with fear have served Thee.

39. 'Cause Thy judgments ever were
    Sweet, divert the shame I fear.

40. Let not him, in justice, perish,
    That desires Thy laws to cherish.   80

VAU.   *Et veniat super me*

41. Let Thy loving mercies cure me,
    As Thy promises assure me;

42. So shall the blasphemer see
    I not vainly trust in Thee;

43. Take not quite the words away   85
    Of Thy truth, that are my stay:

44. Then I 'll keep Thy laws, even till
    Winged time itself stand still.

45. And, whilst I pursue Thy search,
    With secure steps will I march.   90

46. Unashamed I 'll record,
    Even before great kings, Thy word.

47. That shall be my joy, for there
    My thoughts ever fixed were;

48. With bent mind and stretch'd-out hands   95
    I will seek Thy lov'd commands.

ZAINE.   *Memor esto verbi tui.*

49. Think upon Thy promise made,
    For in that my trust is laid;

50. That, my comfort in distress:
    That hath brought my life redress.   100

51. Though the proud hath scorn'd me, they
    Made me not forsake Thy way;

52. Thy eternal judgments brought
    Joy to my rememb'ring thought;

53. With great sorrow I am taken,   105
    When I see Thy laws forsaken:

54. Which have made me songs of mirth,
    In this pilgrimage of earth.

55. Which I mindful was to keep,
    When I had forgot to sleep: 110

56. Thy commands I did embrace,
    Therefore I obtain'd Thy grace.

HETH. *Portio mea, Domine.*

57. Thou, O Lord, art my reward:
    To Thy laws my thoughts are squar'd;

58. With an humble heart I crave,   115
    Thou wilt promis'd mercy have.

59. I have mark'd my steps, and now
    To Thy ways my feet I bow.

60. Nor have I the time delay'd,
    But with haste this journey made,   120

61. Where, though bands of sinners lay
    Snaring nets, I keep my way.

62. I myself at midnight raise,
    Singing Thy just judgments' praise.

63. I converse with those that bear   125
    To Thy laws obedient fear.

64. Teach me them, Lord, by that grace
    Which hath fill'd the world's wide space.

[Cætera desunt.]

PSALM 137

1. SITTING by the streams that glide
    Down by Babel's tow'ring wall,
  With our tears we fill'd the tide,
    Whilst our mindful thoughts recall
    Thee, O Sion, and thy fall.   5

2. Our neglected harps unstrung,
    Not acquainted with the hand
  Of the skilful tuner, hung
    On the willow-trees that stand
    Planted in the neighbour land.   10

3. Yet the spiteful foe commands
    Songs of mirth, and bids us lay
  To dumb harps our captive hands;
    And, to scoff our sorrows, say,
    "Sing us some sweet Hebrew lay!"   15

4. But say we, "Our holy strain
    Is too pure for heathen land;
  Nor may we God's hymns profane,
    Or move either voice or hand
    To delight a savage band."   20

5. Holy Salem, if thy love
    Fall from my forgetful heart,
  May the skill by which I move
    Strings of music tun'd with art,
    From my wither'd hand depart.   25

6. May my speechless tongue give sound
    To no accents, but remain
  To my prison-roof fast bound,
    If my sad soul entertain
    Mirth, till thou rejoice again.   30

7. In that day remember, Lord!
    Edom's breed, that in our groans
  They triumph; with fire and sword
    Burn their city, hew their bones,
    And make all one heap of stones.   35

8. Cruel Babel! thou shalt feel
    The revenger of our groans,
When the happy victor's steel,
    As thine ours, shall hew thy bones,
    And make thee one heap of stones.   40

9. Men shall bless the hand that tears
    From the mothers' soft embraces
Sucking infants, and besmears
    With their brains the rugged faces
    Of the rocks and stony places.   45

SIR JOHN SUCKLING (1609-42)

ON NEW-YEAR'S DAY, 1640

TO THE KING

AWAKE, great sir, the sun shines here,
Gives all your subjects a New-Year;
Only we stay till you appear,
For thus by us your power is understood,
He may make fair days, you must make them good.   5
      Awake, awake,
        And take
   Such presents as poor men can make;
     They can add little unto bliss
       Who cannot wish.   10

May no ill vapour cloud the sky,
Bold storms invade the sovereignty,
But gales of joy, so fresh, so high,
That you may think Heav'n sent to try this year
What sail, or burthen, a king's mind could bear.   15
      Awake, awake, etc.

May all the discords in your state
(Like those in music we create)
Be govern'd at so wise a rate,
That what would of itself sound harsh, or fright,   20
May be so temper'd that it may delight.
      Awake, awake, etc.

What conquerors from battles find,
Or lovers when their doves are kind,
   Take up henceforth our master's mind,   25
Make such strange rapes upon the place, 't may be
No longer joy there, but an ecstasy.
      Awake, awake, etc.

May every pleasure and delight
That has or does your sense invite,
Double this year, save those o' th' night: 30
For such a marriage-bed must know no more
Than repetition of what was before.
                    Awake, awake,
                        And take   35
Such presents as poor men can make;
They can add little unto bliss
                Who cannot wish.

LOVING AND BELOVED

THERE never yet was honest man
        That ever drove the trade of love;
It is impossible, nor can
        Integrity our ends promove;
For kings and lovers are alike in this,   5
That their chief art in reign dissembling is.

Here we are lov'd, and there we love;
        Good nature now and passion strive
Which of the two should be above,
        And laws unto the other give.   10
So we false fire with art sometimes discover,
And the true fire with the same art do cover.

What rack can fancy find so high?
        Here we must court, and here engage,
Though in the other place we die.   15
        Oh, 'tis torture all, and cozenage!
And which the harder is I cannot tell,
To hide true love, or make false love look well.

Since it is thus, God of Desire,
        Give me my honesty again,
And take thy brands back, and thy fire;   20
        I am weary of the state I 'm in:
Since (if the very best should now befall)
Love's triumph must be Honour's funeral.

"IF, WHEN DON CUPID'S DART"

IF, when Don Cupid's dart
Doth wound a heart,
　　We hide our grief
　　And shun relief,
The smart increaseth on that score;　　　5
For wounds unsearch'd but rankle more.

Then if we whine, look pale,
And tell our tale,
　　Men are in pain
　　For us again;　　　10
So neither speaking doth become
The lover's state, nor being dumb.

When this I do descry,
Then thus think I:
　　Love is the fart　　　15
　　Of every heart;
It pains a man when 'tis kept close,
And others doth offend when 'tis let loose.

A SESSIONS OF THE POETS

A SESSIONS was held the other day,
And Apollo himself was at it, they say,
The laurel that had been so long reserv'd
Was now to be given to him best deserv'd.
　　　　　　　　And　　5

Therefore the wits of the town came thither,
'Twas strange to see how they flock'd together,
Each strongly confident of his own way,
Thought to gain the laurel away that day.

There was Selden, and he sate hard by the chair;　　10
Wenman not far off, which was very fair;
Sandys with Townshend, for they kept no order;
Digby and Shillingsworth a little further.
　　　　　　　　And

There was Lucan's translator too, and he　　15
That makes God speak so big in 's poetry;
Selwin and Waller, and Bartlets both the brothers;
Jack Vaughan and Porter, and divers others.

The first that broke silence was good old Ben,
Prepar'd before with canary wine,   20
And he told them plainly he deserv'd the bays,
For his were call'd works, where others' were but plays.
                                                      And

Bid them remember how he had purg'd the stage
Of errors that had lasted many an age;   25
And he hopes they did not think *The Silent Woman*,
The Fox and *The Alchemist*, outdone by no man.

Apollo stopp'd him there, and bade him not go on,
'Twas merit, he said, and not presumption,
Must carry 't; at which Ben turned about,   30
And in great choler offer'd to go out.
                                                      But

Those that were there thought it not fit
To discontent so ancient a wit;
And therefore Apollo call'd him back agen,
And made him mine host of his own New Inn.   35

Tom Carew was next, but he had fault
That would not well stand with a laureat;
His Muse was hard-bound, and th' issue of 's brain
Was seldom brought forth but with trouble and pain.   4c
                                                      And

All that were present there did agree,
A laureate Muse should be easy and free,
Yet sure 'twas not that, but 'twas thought that His Grace
Consider'd he was well he had a cup-bearer's place.   45

Will D'Avenant, asham'd of a foolish mischance
That he had got lately travelling in France,
Modestly hop'd the handsomeness of 's Muse
Might any deformity about him excuse.
                                                   And 50

Surely the company would have been content,
If they could have found any precedent;
But in all their records either in verse or prose,
There was not one laureate without a nose.

To Will Bartlet sure all the wits meant well,   55
But first they would see how his snow would sell:
Will smil'd and swore in their judgments they went less,
That concluded of merit upon success.

Suddenly taking his place agen,
He gave way to Selwin, who straight stepp'd in,   60
But, alas! he had been so lately a wit,
That Apollo hardly knew him yet.

Toby Matthews (pox on him, how came he there?)
Was whispering nothing in somebody's ear;
When he had the honour to be nam'd in court,   65
But, sir, you may thank my Lady Carlisle for 't:

For had not her care furnish'd you out
With something of handsome, without all doubt
You and your sorry Lady-Muse had been
In the number of those that were not let in.   70

In haste from the Court two or three came in,
And they brought letters, forsooth, from the Queen;
'Twas discreetly done, too, for if th' had come
Without them, th' had scarce been let into the room.

This made a dispute, for 'twas plain to be seen   75
Each man had a mind to gratify the Queen;
But Apollo himself could not think it fit:
There was difference, he said, betwixt fooling and wit.

Suckling next was call'd, but did not appear,
But straight one whisper'd Apollo i' th' ear,   80
That of all men living he car'd not for 't,
He lov'd not the Muses so well as his sport;

And priz'd black eyes, or a lucky hit
At bowls, above all the trophies of wit;
But Apollo was angry, and publicly said,   85
'Twere fit that a fine were set upon 's head.

Wat Montague now stood forth to his trial,
And did not so much as suspect a denial;
But witty Apollo ask'd him first of all,
If he understood his own pastoral.   90

For, if he could do it, 'twould plainly appear
He understood more than any man there,
And did merit the bays above all the rest;
But the Monsieur was modest, and silence confess'd.

During these troubles, in the crowd was hid   95
One that Apollo soon miss'd, little Cid;
And having spi'd him call'd him out of the throng,
And advis'd him in his ear not to write so strong.

Then Murray was summon'd, but 'twas urg'd that he
Was chief already of another company.   100

Hales set by himself most gravely did smile
To see them about nothing keep such a coil;
Apollo had spi'd him, but knowing his mind
Pass'd by, and call'd Falkland that sate just behind.
                                                      But 105
He was of late so gone with divinity,
That he had almost forgot his poetry;
Though to say the truth (and Apollo did know it)
He might have been both his priest and his poet.

At length who but an Alderman did appear,   110
At which Will D'Avenant began to swear;
But wiser Apollo bade him draw nigher,
And when he was mounted a little higher,

He openly declar'd that it was the best sign
Of good store of wit to have good store of coin;   115
And without a syllable more or less said,
He put the laurel on the Alderman's head.

At this all the wits were in such a maze
That for a good while they did nothing but gaze
One upon another: not a man in the place   120
But had discontent writ in great in his face.

Only the small poets clear'd up again,
Out of hope, as 'twas thought, of borrowing;
But sure they were out, for he forfeits his crown,
When he lends any poets about the town.   125

LOVE'S WORLD

In each man's heart that doth begin
To love, there 's ever fram'd within
A little world, for so I found,
When first my passion reason drown'd.

Instead of earth unto this frame,   *Earth.* 5
I had a faith was still the same;
For to be right it doth behoove
It be as that, fix'd and not move;

Yet as the earth may sometimes shake
(For winds shut up will cause a quake),   10
So, often jealousy and fear,
Stol'n into mine, cause tremblings there.

My Flora was my sun, for as   *Sun.*
One sun, so but one Flora was:
All other faces borrow'd hence   15
Their light and grace, as stars do thence.

My hopes I call my moon, for they,   *Moon.*
Inconstant still, were at no stay;
But as my sun inclin'd to me,
Or more or less were sure to be: 20

Sometimes it would be full, and then
Oh, too too soon decrease again;
Eclips'd sometimes, that 'twould so fall
There would appear no hope at all.

My thoughts, 'cause infinite they be,   *Stars.* 25
Must be those many stars we see;
Of which some wand'red at their will,   *Fixed*
But most on her were fixed still.   *Planets.*

My burning flame and hot desire   *Element*
Must be the element of fire,   *of fire.* 30
Which hath as yet so secret been,
That it as that was never seen:

No kitchen fire nor eating flame,
But innocent, hot but in name;
A fire that 's starv'd when fed, and gone   35
When too much fuel is laid on.

But as it plainly doth appear
That fire subsists by being near
The moon's bright orb, so I believe
Ours doth, for hope keeps love alive.   40

My fancy was the air, most free   *Air.*
And full of mutability,

Big with chimeras, vapours here
Innumerable hatch'd as there.

The sea 's my mind, which calm would be, *Sea.* 45
Were it from winds (my passions) free;
But out, alas! no sea I find
Is troubled like a lover's mind.

Within it rocks and shallows be,
Despair and fond credulity. 50

But in this world it were good reason
We did distinguish time and season;
Her presence then did make the day,
And night shall come when she 's away.

Long absence in far-distant place 55
Creates the Winter; and the space *Winter.*
She tarri'd with me, well I might
Call it my Summer of delight. *Summer.*

Diversity of weather came
From what she did, and thence had name; 60
Sometimes sh' would smile—that made it fair;
And when she laugh'd, the sun shin'd clear.

Sometimes sh' would frown, and sometimes weep,
So clouds and rain their turns do keep;
Sometimes again sh' would be all ice, 65
Extremely cold, extremely nice.

But soft, my Muse, the world is wide,
And all at once was not descri'd:
It may fall out some honest lover
The rest hereafter will discover. 70

SONG

WHY so pale and wan, fond lover?
    Prithee, why so pale?
Will, when looking well can't move her,
      Looking ill prevail?
      Prithee, why so pale? 5

Why so dull and mute, young sinner?
        Prithee, why so mute?
Will, when speaking well can't win her,
        Saying nothing do 't?
        Prithee, why so mute?   10

Quit, quit, for shame; this will not move,
        This cannot take her;
If of herself she will not love,
        Nothing can make her:
        The devil take her!   15

SONNETS

I

Dost see how unregarded now
        That piece of beauty passes?
There was a time when I did vow
        To that alone;
        But mark the fate of faces;   5
The red and white works now no more on me,
Than if it could not charm, or I not see.

And yet the face continues good,
        And I have still desires,
And still the selfsame flesh and blood,   10
        As apt to melt,
        And suffer from those fires;
Oh, some kind power unriddle where it lies,
Whether my heart be faulty, or her eyes.

She every day her man does kill,   15
        And I as often die;
Neither her power, then, nor my will
        Can question'd be,
        What is the mystery?
Sure beauties' empires, like to greater states, 20
Have certain periods set, and hidden fates.

II

OF thee, kind boy, I ask no red and white,
    To make up my delight;
      No odd becoming graces,
Black eyes, or little know-not-whats, in faces;
Make me but mad enough, give me good store   5
Of love for her I court:
      I ask no more,
'Tis love in love that makes the sport.

There 's no such thing as that we beauty call,
    It is mere cozenage all;   10
      For though some long ago
Lik'd certain colours mingled so and so,
That doth not tie me now from choosing new:
If I a fancy take
      To black and blue,   15
That fancy doth it beauty make.

'Tis not the meat, but 'tis the appetite
    Makes eating a delight,
      And if I like one dish
More than another, that a pheasant is;   20
What in our watches, that in us is found;
So to the height and nick
      We up be wound,
No matter by what hand or trick.

III

O for some honest lover's ghost,
      Some kind unbodi'd post
      Sent from the shades below!
      I strangely long to know
Whether the nobler chaplets wear,   5
Those that their mistress' scorn did bear,
      Or those that were us'd kindly.

For whatsoe'er they tell us here
      To make those sufferings dear,
      'Twill there I fear be found,   10
      That to the being crown'd

T' have lov'd alone will not suffice,
Unless we also have been wise,
    And have our loves enjoy'd.

What posture can we think him in,   15
    That here unlov'd agen
    Departs, and 's thither gone,
    Where each sits by his own?
Or how can that Elysium be,
Where I my mistress still must see   20
    Circled in others' arms?

For there the judges all are just,
    And Sophonisba must
    Be his whom she held dear,
    Not his who lov'd her here: 25
The sweet Philoclea, since she di'd,
Lies by her Pirocles his side,
    Not by Amphialus.

Some bays, perchance, or myrtle bough,
    For difference crowns the brow   30
    Of those kind souls that were
    The noble martyrs here;
And if that be the only odds
(As who can tell?), ye kinder gods,
    Give me the woman here.   35

TO HIS MUCH HONOURED THE LORD LEPPINGTON, UPON HIS TRANSLATION OF MALVEZZI HIS "ROMULUS" AND "TARQUIN"

It is so rare and new a thing to see
Aught that belongs to young nobility
In print, but their own clothes, that we must praise
You as we would do those first show the ways
To arts or to new worlds.   You have begun;   5
Taught travell'd youth what 'tis it should have done:
For 't has indeed too strong a custom bin
To carry out more wit than we bring in.
You have done otherwise, brought home, my Lord,
The choicest things fam'd countries do afford: 10

Malvezzi by your means is English grown,
And speaks our tongue as well now as his own.
Malvezzi, he whom 'tis as hard to praise
To merit, as to imitate his ways.
He does not show us Rome great suddenly,   15
As if the Empire were a tympany,
But gives it natural growth, tells how and why
The little body grew so large and high;
Describes each thing so lively, that we are
Concern'd ourselves before we are aware: 20
And at the wars they and their neighbours wag'd,
Each man is present still, and still engag'd.
Like a good prospective he strangely brings
Things distant to us; and in these two kings
We see what made greatness; and what 't has been   25
Made that greatness contemptible again.
And all this not tediously deriv'd,
But like to worlds in little maps contriv'd.
'Tis he that doth the Roman dame restore,
Makes Lucrece chaster for her being whore;   30
Gives her a kind revenge for Tarquin's sin;
For ravish'd first, she ravisheth again.
She says such fine things after 't, that we must
In spite of virtue thank foul rape and lust,
Since 'twas the cause no woman would have had,   35
Though she 's of Lucrece' side, Tarquin less bad.
    But stay; like one that thinks to bring his friend
A mile or two, and sees the journey's end,
I straggle on too far; long graces do
But keep good stomachs off, that would fall to.   40

AGAINST FRUITION

STAY here, fond youth, and ask no more; be wise:
Knowing too much long since lost paradise.
The virtuous joys thou hast, thou wouldst should still
Last in their pride; and wouldst not take it ill,
If rudely from sweet dreams (and for a toy)   5
Thou wert wak'd? he wakes himself, that does enjoy.

Fruition adds no new wealth, but destroys,
And while it pleaseth much the palate, cloys;

Who thinks he shall be happier for that,
As reasonably might hope he might grow fat   10
By eating to a surfeit; this once past,
What relishes? even kisses lose their taste.

Urge not 'tis necessary: alas! we know
The homeliest thing which mankind does is so;
The world is of a vast extent, we see,   15
And must be peopled; children there must be;
So must bread too; but since they are enough
Born to the drudgery, what need we plough?

Women enjoy'd (whate'er before th' have been)
Are like romances read, or sights once seen;
Fruition 's dull, and spoils the play much more   20
Than if one read or knew the plot before;
'Tis expectation makes a blessing dear,
Heaven were not heaven, if we knew what it were.

And as in prospects we are there pleas'd most,   25
Where something keeps the eye from being lost,
And leaves us room to guess; so here restraint
Holds up delight, that with excess would faint.
They who know all the wealth they have are poor;
He 's only rich that cannot tell his store.   30

"THERE NEVER YET WAS WOMAN MADE"

THERE never yet was woman made,
    Nor shall, but to be curs'd;
And oh, that I, fond I, should first,
    Of any lover,
This truth at my own charge to other fools discover!   5

You that have promis'd to yourselves
    Propriety in love,
Know, women's hearts like straw do move;
    And what we call
Their sympathy, is but love to jet in general.   10

All mankind are alike to them;
　　　And though we iron find
That never with a loadstone join'd,
　　　　'Tis not the iron's fault,
It is because the loadstone yet was never brought.　15

If, where a gentle bee hath fall'n,
　　　And labour'd to his power,
A new succeeds not to that flower,
　　　　But passes by,
'Tis to be thought, the gallant elsewhere loads his thigh.　20

For still the flowers ready stand:
　　　One buzzes round about,
One lights, and tastes, gets in, gets out;
　　　　All all ways use them,
Till all their sweets are gone, and all again refuse them.　25

SONG

No, no, fair heretic, it needs must be
　　　But an ill love in me,
　　　And worse for thee:
For were it in my power
To love thee now this hour　　　　　　　5
　　　More than I did the last,
　　'Twould then so fall
　　I might not love at all:
Love that can flow, and can admit increase,
Admits as well an ebb, and may grow less.　　10

True love is still the same: the torrid zones,
　　　And those more frigid ones,
　　　It must not know;
For love grown cold or hot
Is lust or friendship, not　　　　　　　15
　　　The thing we have,
For that 's a flame would die,
　　Held down or up too high.
Then think I love more than I can express,
And would love more, could I but love thee less.　　20

TO MY FRIEND WILL D'AVENANT, UPON HIS POEM OF "MADAGASCAR"

WHAT mighty princes poets are! those things
The great ones stick at, and our very kings
Lay down, they venture on; and with great ease
Discover, conquer, what and where they please.
Some phlegmatic sea-captain would have stay'd   5
For money now, or victuals; not have weigh'd
Anchor without 'em; thou, Will, dost not stay
So much as for a wind, but go'st away,
Land'st, view'st the country; fight'st, put'st all to rout,
Before another could be putting out!   10
And now the news in town is, D'Av'nant 's come
From Madagascar, fraught with laurel home;
And welcome, Will, for the first time; but prithee,
In thy next voyage bring the gold too with thee.

TO MY FRIEND WILL D'AVENANT, ON HIS OTHER POEMS

THOU hast redeem'd us, Will, and future times
Shall not account unto the age's crimes
Dearth of pure wit. Since the great lord of it,
Donne, parted hence, no man has ever writ
So near him, in 's own way: I would commend   5
Particulars; but then, how should I end
Without a volume? Ev'ry line of thine
Would ask (to praise it right) twenty of mine.

"LOVE, REASON, HATE"

LOVE, Reason, Hate, did once bespeak
Three mates to play at barley-break:
Love Folly took; and Reason, Fancy;
And Hate consorts with Pride; so dance they:
Love coupled last, and so it fell,   5
That Love and Folly were in hell.

They break, and Love would Reason meet,
But Hate was nimbler on her feet;

Fancy looks for Pride, and thither
Hies, and they two hug together: 10
Yet this new coupling still doth tell
That Love and Folly were in hell.

The rest do break again, and Pride
Hath now got Reason on her side;
Hate and Fancy meet, and stand   15
Untouch'd by Love in Folly's hand;
Folly was dull, but Love ran well:
So Love and Folly were in hell.

SONG

I PRITHEE spare me, gentle boy,
Press me no more for that slight toy,
That foolish trifle of an heart;
I swear it will not do its part,   4
Though thou dost thine, employ'st thy power and art.

For through long custom it has known
The little secrets, and is grown
Sullen and wise, will have its will,
And, like old hawks, pursues that still
That makes least sport, flies only where 't can kill.   10

Some youth that has not made his story,
Will think, perchance, the pain 's the glory,
And mannerly sit out love's feast:
I shall be carving of the best,
Rudely call for the last course 'fore the rest.   15

And, oh, when once that course is past,
How short a time the feast doth last!
Men rise away, and scarce say grace,
Or civilly once thank the face
That did invite, but seek another place.   20

UPON MY LADY CARLISLE'S WALKING IN HAMPTON COURT GARDEN

Dialogue

T[HOMAS] C[AREW].   J[OHN] S[UCKLING]

Tom. DIDST thou not find the place inspir'd,
And flowers, as if they had desir'd
No other sun, start from their beds,
And for a sight steal out their heads?
Heard'st thou not music when she talk'd?   5
And didst not find that as she walk'd
She threw rare perfumes all about,
Such as bean-blossoms newly out,
Or chafed spices give?——

J. S. I must confess those perfumes, Tom,   10
I did not smell; nor found that from
Her passing by aught sprung up new:
The flow'rs had all their birth from you;
For I pass'd o'er the selfsame walk,
And did not find one single stalk   15
Of any thing that was to bring
This unknown after-after-Spring.

Tom. Dull and insensible, couldst see
A thing so near a deity
Move up and down, and feel no change?   20

J. S. None and so great were alike strange.
I had my thoughts, but not your way;
All are not born, sir, to the bay;
Alas! Tom, I am flesh and blood,
And was consulting how I could   25
In spite of masks and hoods descry
The parts deni'd unto the eye:
I was undoing all she wore;
And had she walk'd but one turn more,
Eve in her first state had not been   30
More naked, or more plainly seen.

Tom. 'Twas well for thee she left the place;
There is great danger in that face;

But hadst thou view'd her leg and thigh,
And upon that discovery   35
Search'd after parts that are more dear
(As fancy seldom stops so near),
No time or age had ever seen
So lost a thing as thou hadst been.

TO MR. D'AVENANT FOR ABSENCE

WONDER not, if I stay not here:
Hurt lovers, like to wounded deer,
Must shift the place; for standing still
Leaves too much time to know our ill:
Where there is a traitor eye,   5
That lets in from th' enemy
All that may supplant an heart,
'Tis time the chief should use some art:
Who parts the object from the sense,
Wisely cuts off intelligence.   10
Oh, how quickly men must die,
Should they stand all love's battery!
Persinda's eyes great mischief do:
So do, we know, the cannon too;
But men are safe at distance still: 15
Where they reach not, they cannot kill.
Love is a fit, and soon is past;
Ill diet only makes it last:
Who is still looking, gazing ever,
Drinks wine i' th' very height o' th' fever.   20

AGAINST ABSENCE

MY whining lover, what needs all
These vows of life monastical,
Despairs, retirements, jealousies,
And subtle sealing up of eyes?
Come, come, be wise; return again;   5
A finger burnt 's as great a pain;
And the same physic, selfsame art
Cures that, would cure a flaming heart,
Wouldst thou, whilst yet the fire is in,
But hold it to the fire again.   10

If you, dear sir, the plague have got,
What matter is 't whether or not
They let you in the same house lie,
Or carry you abroad to die?
He whom the plague or love once takes,   15
Every room a pest-house makes.
Absence were good if 'twere but sense
That only holds th' intelligence.
Pure love alone no hurt would do;
But love is love and magic too: 20
Brings a mistress a thousand miles,
And the sleight of looks beguiles,
Makes her entertain thee there,
And the same time your rival here;
And (oh the devil!) that she should   25
Say finer things now than she would;
So nobly fancy doth supply
What the dull sense lets fall and die.
Beauty, like man's old enemy, 's known
To tempt him most when he 's alone: 30
The air of some wild o'ergrown wood
Or pathless grove is the boy's food.
Return then back, and feed thine eye,
Feed all thy senses, and feast high:
Spare diet is the cause love lasts,   35
For surfeits sooner kill than fasts.

A SUPPLEMENT OF AN IMPERFECT COPY OF VERSES OF MR. WILL. SHAKESPEARE'S, BY THE AUTHOR

ONE of her hands one of her cheeks lay under,
    Cozening the pillow of a lawful kiss,
Which therefore swell'd, and seem'd to part asunder,
    As angry to be robb'd of such a bliss:
        The one look'd pale, and for revenge did long,   5
        While t' other blush'd, 'cause it had done the wrong.

Out of the bed the other fair hand was
    On a green satin quilt, whose perfect white
Look'd like a daisy in a field of grass,[1]
    And show'd like unmelt snow unto the sight: 10

[1] Thus far Shakespeare.

There lay this pretty perdue, safe to keep
The rest o' th' body that lay fast asleep.

Her eyes (and therefore it was night), close laid,
  Strove to imprison beauty till the morn;
But yet the doors were of such fine stuff made,   15
    That it broke through, and show'd itself in scorn,
      Throwing a kind of light about the place,
      Which turn'd to smiles still as 't came near her face.

Her beams, which some dull men call'd hair, divided,
  Part with her cheeks, part with her lips did sport;   20
But these, as rude, her breath put by still; some
    Wiselier downwards sought, but falling short,
      Curl'd back in rings, and seem'd to turn agen
      To bite the part so unkindly held them in.

"THAT NONE BEGUILED BE"

THAT none beguiled be by Time's quick flowing,
Lovers have in their hearts a clock still going;
      For though Time be nimble, his motions
          Are quicker
          And thicker   5
      Where Love hath his notions.

Hope is the mainspring on which moves Desire,
And these do the less wheels, Fear, Joy, inspire;
      The balance is Thought, evermore
          Clicking   10
          And striking,
      And ne'er giving o'er.

Occasion 's the hand which still 's moving round,
Till by it the critical hour may be found,
      And when that falls out, it will strike   15
          Kisses,
          Strange blisses,
      And what you best like.

"'TIS NOW, SINCE I SATE DOWN BEFORE"

'TIS now, since I sate down before
    That foolish fort, a heart,
(Time strangely spent) a year and more,
    And still I did my part:

Made my approaches, from her hand   5
    Unto her lip did rise,
And did already understand
    The language of her eyes;

Proceeded on with no less art—
    My tongue was engineer: 10
I thought to undermine the heart
    By whispering in the ear.

When this did nothing, I brought down
    Great cannon-oaths, and shot
A thousand thousand to the town;   15
    And still it yielded not.

I then resolv'd to starve the place
    By cutting off all kisses,
Praising and gazing on her face,
    And all such little blisses.   20

To draw her out, and from her strength,
    I drew all batteries in;
And brought myself to lie at length,
    As if no siege had been.

When I had done what man could do,   25
    And thought the place mine own,
The enemy lay quiet too,
    And smil'd at all was done.

I sent to know from whence and where
    These hopes and this relief: 30
A spy inform'd, Honour was there,
    And did command in chief.

March, march, quoth I, the word straight give,
    Let 's lose no time, but leave her;
That giant upon air will live,   35
    And hold it out for ever.

To such a place our camp remove,
    As will no siege abide:
I hate a fool that starves her love,
    Only to feed her pride.   40

UPON MY LORD BROGHILL'S WEDDING

Dialogue

S[UCKLING].   B[OND?]

S.   IN bed, dull man,
        When Love and Hymen's revels are begun,
        And the church ceremonies past and done!
B.   Why, who 's gone mad to-day?
S.   Dull heretic, thou wouldst say,   5
        He that is gone to heaven 's gone astray;
            Broghill our gallant friend
        Is gone to church, as martyrs to the fire:
            Who marry, differ but i' th' end,
                Since both do take   10
        The hardest way to what they most desire.
        Nor stay'd he till the formal priest had done,
        But ere that part was finish'd, his begun:
            Which did reveal
        The haste and eagerness men have to seal,   15
            That long to tell the money.
        A sprig of willow in his hat he wore
        (The loser's badge and liv'ry heretofore),
        But now so order'd that it might be taken,
        By lookers-on, forsaking as forsaken;   20
            And now and then
        A careless smile broke forth, which spoke his mind,
        And seem'd to say she might have been more kind.
            When this, dear Jack, I saw,
                              Thought I,   25
            How weak is lovers' law!
        The bonds made there (like gipsies' knots) with ease
        Are fast and loose, as they that hold them please.
[B.] But was the fair nymph's praise or power less
        That led him captive now to happiness,   30
        'Cause she did not a foreign aid despise,
        But enter'd breaches made by others' eyes?

[S.]   The gods forbid!
There must be some to shoot and batter down,
Others to force and to take in the town.   35
              To hawks, good Jack, and hearts
                        There may
        Be sev'ral ways and arts:
One watches them perchance, and makes them tame;
Another, when they 're ready, shows them game.   40

AN EPISTLE

Sir,
        Whether these lines do find you out,
        Putting or clearing of a doubt;
        Whether predestination,
        Or reconciling three in one,
        Or the unriddling how men die,   5
        And live at once eternally,
        Now take you up, know 'tis decreed
        You straight bestride the college steed,
        Leave Socinus and the schoolmen
        (Which Jack Bond swears do but fool men),   10
        And come to town: 'tis fit you show
        Yourself abroad, that men may know
        (Whate'er some learned men have guess'd)
        That oracles are not yet ceas'd.
        There you shall find the wit and wine   15
        Flowing alike, and both divine;
        Dishes, with names not known in books,
        And less amongst the college-cooks,
        With sauce so pregnant that you need
        Not stay till hunger bids you feed.   20
        The sweat of learned Jonson's brain,
        And gentle Shakespeare's eas'er strain,
        A hackney-coach conveys you to,
        In spite of all that rain can do;
        And for your eighteenpence you sit   25
        The lord and judge of all fresh wit.
        News in one day as much w' have here,
        As serves all Windsor for a year,
        And which the carrier brings to you,
        After 't has here been found not true.   30

* H 873

Then think what company 's design'd
To meet you here, men so refin'd,
Their very common talk at board
Makes wise or mad a young court-lord,
And makes him capable to be   35
Umpire in 's father's company:
Where no disputes, nor forc'd defence
Of a man's person for his sense
Take up the time: all strive to be
Masters of truth, as victory;   40
And where you come, I 'd boldly swear
A synod might as eas'ly err.

AGAINST FRUITION

FIE upon hearts that burn with mutual fire!
I hate two minds that breathe but one desire.
Were I to curse th' unhallow'd sort of men,
I 'd wish them to love, and be lov'd again.
Love 's a camelion, that lives on mere air,   5
And surfeits when it comes to grosser fare:
'Tis petty jealousies, and little fears,
Hopes join'd with doubts, and joys with April tears,
That crowns our love with pleasures: these are gone
When once we come to full fruition,   10
Like waking in a morning, when all night
Our fancy hath been fed with true delight.
Oh, what a stroke 'twould be! sure I should die,
Should I but hear my mistress once say ay.
That monster expectation feeds too high   15
For any woman e'er to satisfy;
And no brave spirit ever car'd for that
Which in down beds with ease he could come at.
She 's but an honest whore that yields, although
She be as cold as ice, as pure as snow: 20
He that enjoys her hath no more to say
But "Keep us fasting, if you 'll have us pray."
Then, fairest mistress, hold the power you have,
By still denying what we still do crave;
In keeping us in hopes strange things to see,   25
That never were, nor are, nor e'er shall be.

A BALLAD UPON A WEDDING

I TELL thee, Dick, where I have been;
Where I the rarest things have seen,
    Oh, things without compare!
Such sights again cannot be found
In any place on English ground,   5
    Be it at wake or fair.

At Charing Cross, hard by the way
Where we, thou know'st, do sell our hay,
    There is a house with stairs;
And there did I see coming down   10
Such folk as are not in our town,
    Vorty at least, in pairs.

Amongst the rest, one pest'lent fine
(His beard no bigger though than thine)
    Walk'd on before the rest: 15
Our landlord looks like nothing to him;
The King (God bless him!), 'twould undo him,
    Should he go still so dress'd.

At course-a-park, without all doubt,
He should have first been taken out   20
    By all the maids i' th' town,
Though lusty Roger there had been,
Or little George upon the Green,
    Or Vincent of the Crown.

But wot you what? the youth was going   25
To make an end of all his wooing;
    The parson for him stay'd:
Yet by his leave, for all his haste,
He did not so much wish all past,
    Perchance, as did the maid.   30

The maid—and thereby hangs a tale;
For such a maid no Whitsun-ale
    Could ever yet produce:
No grape that 's kindly ripe could be
So round, so plump, so soft as she,   35
    Nor half so full of juice.

Her finger was so small, the ring
Would not stay on which they did bring,
    It was too wide a peck;
And to say truth (for out it must)   40
It look'd like the great collar (just)
    About our young colt's neck.

Her feet beneath her petticoat
Like little mice stole in and out,
    As if they fear'd the light;   45
But oh! she dances such a way,
No sun upon an Easter day
    Is half so fine a sight.

He would have kiss'd her once or twice,
But she would not, she was so nice,   50
    She would not do 't in sight;
And then she look'd as who should say,
I will do what I list to-day,
    And you shall do 't at night.

Her cheeks so rare a white was on,   55
No daisy makes comparison,
    (Who sees them is undone);
For streaks of red were mingled there,
Such as are on a Kather'ne pear
    (The side that 's next the sun).   60

Her lips were red, and one was thin
Compar'd to that was next her chin—
    Some bee had stung it newly;
But, Dick, her eyes so guard her face,
I durst no more upon them gaze   65
    Than on the sun in July.

Her mouth so small, when she does speak,
Thou 'dst swear her teeth her words did break,
    That they might passage get;
But she so handled still the matter,   70
They came as good as ours, or better,
    And are not spent a whit.

If wishing should be any sin,
The parson himself had guilty bin,

She look'd that day so purely;   75
And did the youth so oft the feat
At night, as some did in conceit,
It would have spoil'd him surely.

Passion o' me! how I run on!
There 's that that would be thought upon,   80
I trow, besides the bride:
The business of the kitchen 's great,
For it is fit that men should eat;
Nor was it there deni'd.

Just in the nick the cook knock'd thrice,   85
And all the waiters in a trice
His summons did obey;
Each serving-man, with dish in hand,
March'd boldly up, like our train'd band,
Presented, and away.   90

When all the meat was on the table,
What man of knife or teeth was able
To stay to be entreated?
And this the very reason was
Before the parson could say grace   95
The company was seated.

Now hats fly off, and youths carouse;
Healths first go round, and then the house,
The bride's came thick and thick;
And when 'twas nam'd another's health,   100
Perhaps he made it hers by stealth:
(And who could help it, Dick?)

O' th' sudden up they rise and dance;
Then sit again, and sigh, and glance;
Then dance again and kiss: 105
Thus several ways the time did pass,
Whilst ev'ry woman wish'd her place,
And ev'ry man wish'd his.

By this time all were stol'n aside
To counsel and undress the bride;   110

But that he must not know:
But yet 'twas thought he guess'd her mind,
And did not mean to stay behind
    Above an hour or so.

When in he came, Dick, there she lay   115
Like new-fall'n snow melting away,
    ('Twas time, I trow, to part);
Kisses were now the only stay,
Which soon she gave, as who would say,
    God b' w' y', with all my heart.   120

But, just as Heav'ns would have, to cross it,
In came the bridesmaids with the posset:
    The bridegroom eat in spite;
For had he left the women to 't,
It would have cost two hours to do 't,   125
    Which were too much that night.

At length the candle 's out, and now
All that they had not done they do:
    What that is, who can tell?
But I believe it was no more   130
Than thou and I have done before
    With Bridget and with Nell.

"MY DEAREST RIVAL, LEST OUR LOVE"

My dearest rival, lest our love
Should with eccentric motion move,
Before it learn to go astray,
We 'll teach and set it in a way,
And such directions give unto 't,   5
That it shall never wander foot.
Know first then, we will serve as true
For one poor smile, as we would do,
If we had what our higher flame
Or our vainer wish could frame.   10
Impossible shall be our hope;
And love shall only have his scope
To join with fancy now and then,
And think what reason would condemn:

And on these grounds we 'll love as true,   15
As if they were most sure t' ensue:
And chastely for these things we 'll stay,
As if to-morrow were the day.
Meantime we two will teach our hearts
In love's burdens bear their parts: 20
Thou first shall sigh, and say she 's fair;
And I 'll still answer, past compare.
Thou shalt set out each part o' th' face,
While I extol each little grace;
Thou shalt be ravish'd at her wit,   25
And I, that she so governs it;
Thou shalt like well that hand, that eye,
That lip, that look, that majesty,
And in good language them adore;
While I want words and do it more.   30
Yea, we will sit and sigh a while,
And with soft thoughts some time beguile;
But straight again break out, and praise
All we had done before, new-ways.
Thus will we do till paler death   35
Come with a warrant for our breath,
And then, whose fate shall be to die
First of us two, by legacy
Shall all his store bequeath, and give
His love to him that shall survive;   40
For no one stock can ever serve
To love so much as she 'll deserve.

SONG

HONEST lover whosoever,
If in all thy love there ever
Was one wav'ring thought, if thy **flame**
Were not still even, still the same:
    Know this,   5
   Thou lov'st amiss;
    And to love true,
Thou must begin again, and love anew.

If, when she appears i' th' room,
Thou dost not quake, and art struck **dumb**,   10

And in striving this to cover,
Dost not speak thy words twice over:
   Know this, etc.

If fondly thou dost not mistake,
And all defects for graces take,   15
Persuad'st thyself that jests are broken,
When she hath little or nothing spoken:
   Know this, etc.

If, when thou appear'st to be within,
Thou lett'st not men ask and ask again;   20
And when thou answer'st, if it be,
To what was ask'd thee, properly:
   Know this, etc.

If, when thy stomach calls to eat,
Thou cutt'st not fingers 'stead of meat,   25
And with much gazing on her face
Dost not rise hungry from the place:
   Know this, etc.

If by this thou dost discover
That thou art no perfect lover,   30
And desiring to love true,
Thou dost begin to love anew:
   Know this,
     Thou lov'st amiss;
   And to love true,   35
Thou must begin again, and love anew.

UPON TWO SISTERS

BELIEVE 't, young man, I can as eas'ly tell
How many yards and inches 'tis to hell,
Unriddle all predestination,
Or the nice points we now dispute upon.
Had the three goddesses been just as fair,   5
[.   .   .   .   .]
It had not been so easily decided,
And sure the apple must have been divided:
It must, it must; he's impudent, dares say
Which is the handsomer till one's away.   10

And it was necessary it should be so:
Wise Nature did foresee it, and did know,
When she had fram'd the eldest, that each heart
Must at the first sight feel the blind god's dart:
And sure as can be, had she made but one,   15
No plague had been more sure destruction;
For we had lik'd, lov'd, burnt to ashes too,
In half the time that we are choosing now:
Variety and equal objects make
The busy eye still doubtful which to take,   20
This lip, this hand, this foot, this eye, this face,
The other's body, gesture, or her grace;
And whilst we thus dispute which of the two,
We unresolv'd go out, and nothing do.
He sure is happiest that has hopes of either;   25
Next him is he that sees them both together.

TO HIS RIVAL

Now we have taught our love to know
That it must creep where 't cannot go,
And be for once content to live,
Since here it cannot have to thrive;
It will not be amiss t' enquire   5
What fuel should maintain this fire:
For fires do either flame too high,
Or, where they cannot flame, they die.
First then (my half but better heart)
Know this must wholly be her part;   10
(For thou and I, like clocks, are wound
Up to the height, and must move round):
She then, by still denying what
We fondly crave, shall such a rate
Set on each trifle, that a kiss   15
Shall come to be the utmost bliss.
Where sparks and fire do meet with tinder,
Those sparks more fire will still engender:
To make this good, no debt shall be
From service or fidelity;   20
For she shall ever pay that score,
By only bidding us do more:
So (though she still a niggard be)

In gracing, where none 's due, she 's free.
The favours she shall cast on us,   25
(Lest we should grow presumptuous)
Shall not with too much love be shown,
Nor yet the common way still done;
But ev'ry smile and little glance
Shall look half lent, and half by chance: 30
The ribbon, fan, or muff that she
Would should be kept by thee or me,
Should not be giv'n before too many,
But neither thrown to 's, when there 's any;
So that herself should doubtful be   35
Whether 'twere fortune flung 't, or she.
She shall not like the thing we do
Sometimes, and yet shall like it too;
Nor any notice take at all
Of what, we gone, she would extol.   40
Love she shall feed, but fear to nourish;
For where fear is, love cannot flourish;
Yet live it must, nay must and shall,
While Desdemona is at all:
But when she 's gone, then love shall die,   45
And in her grave buried lie.

FAREWELL TO LOVE

WELL-SHADOW'D landskip, fare ye well:
How I have lov'd you none can tell,
   At least, so well
  As he that now hates more
  Than e'er he lov'd before.   5

But, my dear nothings, take your leave:
No longer must you me deceive,
   Since I perceive
  All the deceit, and know
  Whence the mistake did grow.   10

As he whose quicker eye doth trace
A false star shot to a mark'd place,
   Does run apace,
  And thinking it to catch,
  A jelly up does snatch: 15

So our dull souls, tasting delight
Far off, by sense and appetite,
   Think that is right
   And real good; when yet
   'Tis but the counterfeit.   20

Oh, how I glory now, that I
Have made this new discovery!
   Each wanton eye
   Inflam'd before: no more
   Will I increase that score.   25

If I gaze now, 'tis but to see
What manner of death's-head 'twill be,
   When it is free
   From that fresh upper skin,
   The gazer's joy and sin.   30

The gum and glist'ning which with art
And studi'd method in each part
   Hangs down the hair, 't
   Looks (just) as if that day
   Snails there had crawl'd the hay.   35

The locks that curl'd o'er each ear be,
Hang like two master-worms to me,
   That (as we see)
   Have tasted to the rest
   Two holes, where they like 't best.   40

A quick corse, methinks, I spy
In ev'ry woman; and mine eye,
   At passing by,
   Checks, and is troubled, just
   As if it rose from dust.   45

They mortify, not heighten me;
These of my sins the glasses be:
   And here I see
   How I have lov'd before.
   And so I love no more.   50

THE INVOCATION

Ye juster powers of Love and Fate,
　Give me the reason why
　　　A lover cross'd,
　　　And all hopes lost,
　May not have leave to die.　　　　　　　　5

It is but just, and Love needs must
Confess it is his part,
　　　When she doth spy
　　　One wounded lie,
　To pierce the other's heart.　　　　　　　10

But yet if he so cruel be
To have one breast to hate,
　　　If I must live,
　　　And thus survive,
　How far more cruel 's Fate?　　　　　　　15

In this same state I find too late
I am; and here 's the grief:
　　　Cupid can cure,
　　　Death heal, I 'm sure,
　Yet neither sends relief.　　　　　　　　20

To live or die, beg only I:
Just powers, some end me give;
　　　And traitor-like
　　　Thus force me not
　Without a heart to live.　　　　　　　　25

"OUT UPON IT!"

Out upon it! I have lov'd
　Three whole days together;
And am like to love three more,
　If it prove fair weather.

Time shall moult away his wings,　　　　　5
　Ere he shall discover
In the whole wide world again
　Such a constant lover.

But the spite on 't is, no praise
    Is due at all to me: 10
Love with me had made no stays,
    Had it any been but she.

Had it any been but she,
    And that very face,
There had been at least ere this 15
    A dozen dozen in her place.

THE ANSWER

SIR TOBY MATTHEWS

Say, but did you love so long?
    In troth, I needs must blame you:
Passion did your judgment wrong,
    Or want of reason shame you.

Truth, Time's fair and witty daughter, 5
    Shortly shall discover
Y' are a subject fit for laughter,
    And more fool than lover.

But I grant you merit praise
    For your constant folly: 10
Since you doted three whole days,
    Were you not melancholy?

She to whom you prov'd so true,
    And that very very face,
Puts each minute such as you 15
    A dozen dozen to disgrace.

LOVE TURN'D TO HATRED

I will not love one minute more, I swear,
No, not a minute; not a sigh or tear
Thou gett'st from me, or one kind look agen,
Though thou shouldst court me to 't and wouldst begin.
I will not think of thee but as men do 5
Of debts and sins, and then I 'll curse thee too:

For thy sake woman shall be now to me
Less welcome than at midnight ghosts shall be:
I 'll hate so perfectly, that it shall be
Treason to love that man that loves a she;   10
Nay, I will hate the very good, I swear,
That 's in thy sex, because it doth lie there;
Their very virtue, grace, discourse and wit,
And all for thee—what, wilt thou love me yet?

THE CARELESS LOVER

NEVER believe me if I love,
Or know what 'tis, or mean to prove;
And yet in faith I lie, I do,
And she 's extremely handsome too:
      She 's fair, she 's wondrous fair,   5
      But I care not who know it.
      Ere I 'll die for love, I 'll fairly forgo it.

This heat of hope, or cold of fear,
My foolish heart could never bear:
One sigh imprison'd ruins more   10
Than earthquakes have done heretofore.
      She 's fair, etc.

When I am hungry, I do eat,
And cut no fingers 'stead of meat;
Nor with much gazing on her face,   15
Do e'er rise hungry from the place.
      She 's fair, etc.

A gentle round fill'd to the brink
To this and t' other friend I drink;
And when 'tis nam'd another's health,   20
I never make it hers by stealth.
      She 's fair, etc.

Blackfriars to me, and old Whitehall,
Is even as much as is the fall
Of fountains on a pathless grove,   25
And nourishes as much my love.
      She 's fair, etc.

I visit, talk, do business, play,
And for a need laugh out a day:
Who does not thus in Cupid's school,   30
He makes not love, but plays the fool.
    She 's fair, she 's wondrous fair,
    But I care not who know it,
    Ere I 'll die for love, I 'll fairly forgo it.

LOVE AND DEBT ALIKE TROUBLESOME

THIS one request I make to him that sits the clouds above,
That I were freely out of debt, as I am out of love.
Then for to dance, to drink and sing, I should be very willing,
I should not owe one lass a kiss, nor ne'er a knave a shilling.
'Tis only being in love and debt that breaks us of our rest;   5
And he that is quite out of both, of all the world is blest:
He sees the Golden Age, wherein all things were free and common;
He eats, he drinks, he takes his rest, he fears no man nor woman.
Though Crœsus compassed great wealth, yet he still craved more,
He was as needy a beggar still as goes from door to door.   10
Though Ovid were a merry man, love ever kept him sad;
He was as far from happiness as one that is stark mad.
Our merchant he in goods is rich, and full of gold and treasure;
But when he thinks upon his debts, that thought destroys his
    pleasure.
Our courtier thinks that he 's preferr'd, whom every man envies;
When love so rumbles in his pate, no sleep comes in his eyes. 16
Our gallant's case is worst of all, he lies so just betwixt them;
For he 's in love and he 's in debt, and knows not which most
    vex him.
But he that can eat beef, and feed on bread which is so brown,
May satisfy his appetite, and owe no man a crown;   20
And he that is content with lasses clothed in plain woollen,
May cool his heat in every place: he need not to be sullen,
Nor sigh for love of lady fair; for this each wise man knows—
As good stuff under flannel lies, as under silken clothes.

SONG

    I PRITHEE send me back my heart,
      Since I cannot have thine:
    For if from yours you will not part,
      Why then shouldst thou have mine?

Yet now I think on 't, let it lie: 5
   To find it were in vain,
For th' hast a thief in either eye
   Would steal it back again.

Why should two hearts in one breast lie,
   And yet not lodge together?   10
O love, where is thy sympathy,
   If thus our breasts thou sever?

But love is such a mystery,
   I cannot find it out:
For when I think I 'm best resolv'd,   15
   I then am in most doubt.

Then farewell care, and farewell woe,
   I will no longer pine:
For I 'll believe I have her heart
   As much as she hath mine.   20

TO A LADY THAT FORBADE TO LOVE BEFORE COMPANY

WHAT! no more favours?   Not a ribband more,
Not fan nor muff to hold as heretofore?
Must all the little blisses then be left,
And what was once love's gift become our theft?
May we not look ourselves into a trance,   5
Teach our souls parley at our eyes, not glance,
Not touch the hand, not by soft wringing there
Whisper a love that only yes can hear?
Not free a sigh, a sigh that 's there for you?
Dear, must I love you, and not love you too?   10
Be wise, nice fair; for sooner shall they trace
The feather'd choristers from place to place,
By prints they make in th' air, and sooner say
By what right line the last star made his way
That fled from heaven to earth, than guess to know 15
How our loves first did spring, or how they grow.
Love is all spirit: fairies sooner may
Be taken tardy, when they night-tricks play,
Than we.   We are too dull and lumpish rather:
Would they could find us both in bed together!   20

LOVE'S REPRESENTATION

LEANING her head upon my breast,
There on love's bed she lay to rest;
My panting heart rock'd her asleep,
My heedful eyes the watch did keep;
Then love by me being harbour'd there,   5
(No hope to be his harbinger,)
Desire his rival kept the door;
For this of him I begg'd no more,
But that, our mistress to entertain,
Some pretty fancy he would frame,   10
And represent it in a dream,
Of which myself should give the theme.
Then first these thoughts I bid him show,
Which only he and I did know,
Array'd in duty and respect,   15
And not in fancies that reflect;
Then those of value next present,
Approv'd by all the world's consent;
But to distinguish mine asunder,
Apparell'd they must be in wonder.   20
Such a device then I would have,
As service, not reward, should crave,
Attir'd in spotless innocence,
Not self-respect, nor no pretence:
Then such a faith I would have shown,   25
As heretofore was never known,
Cloth'd with a constant clear intent,
Professing always as it meant:
And if love no such garments have,
My mind a wardrobe is so brave,   30
That there sufficient he may see
To clothe Impossibility.
Then beamy fetters he shall find,
By admiration subtly twin'd,
That will keep fast the wanton'st thought   35
That e'er imagination wrought:
There he shall find of joy a chain,
Fram'd by despair, of her disdain,
So curiously that it can't tie
The smallest hopes that thoughts now spy.   40

There acts as glorious as the sun
Are by her veneration spun,
In one of which I would have brought
A pure, unspotted, abstract thought,
Considering her as she is good,   45
Not in her frame of flesh and blood.
These atoms then, all in her sight,
I bade him join, that so he might
Discern between true love's creation,
And that love's form that 's now in fashion.   50
Love, granting unto my request,
Began to labour in my breast;
But with the motion he did make,
It heav'd so high that she did wake,
Blush'd at the favour she had done,   55
Then smil'd, and then away did run.

SONG

The crafty boy that had full oft assay'd
To pierce my stubborn and resisting breast,
But still the bluntness of his darts betray'd,
Resolv'd at last of setting up his rest,
    Either my wild unruly heart to tame,   5
    Or quit his godhead, and his bow disclaim.

So all his lovely looks, his pleasing fires;
All his sweet motions, all his taking smiles;
All that awakes, all that inflames desires,
All that sweetly commands, all that beguiles,   10
    He does into one pair of eyes convey,
    And there begs leave that he himself may stay.

And there he brings me, where his ambush lay,
Secure and careless, to a stranger land;
And, never warning me (which was foul play,)   15
Does make me close by all this beauty stand:
    Where, first struck dead, I did at last recover,
    To know that I might only live to love her.

So I 'll be sworn I do, and do confess
The blind lad's power, whilst he inhabits there;   20

But I 'll be even with him ne'ertheless,
If e'er I chance to meet with him elsewhere.
  If other eyes invite the boy to tarry,
  I 'll fly to hers as to a sanctuary.

UPON THE BLACK SPOTS WORN BY MY LADY D. E.

MADAM,
I know your heart cannot so guilty be,
That you should wear those spots for vanity;
Or, as your beauty's trophies, put on one
For every murther which your eyes have done:
No, they 're your mourning-weeds for hearts forlorn,   5
Which, though you must not love, you could not scorn;
To whom since cruel honour doth deny
Those joys could only cure their misery,
Yet you this noble way to grace them found,
Whilst thus your grief their martyrdom hath crown'd,   10
Of which take heed you prove not prodigal;
For if to every common funeral
By your eyes martyr'd, such grace were allow'd,
Your face would wear not patches, but a cloud.

TO MISTRESS CICELY CROFTS

[Also attributed to Sir Robert Aytoun.]

O THAT I were all soul, that I might prove
        For you as fit a love
As you are for an angel; for, I know,
None but pure spirits are fit loves for you.

You are all ethereal; there 's in you no dross,   5
        Nor any part that 's gross:
Your coarsest part is like a curious lawn,
The vestal relics for a covering drawn.

Your other parts, part of the purest fire
        That e'er Heaven did inspire,   10
Makes every thought that is refin'd by it,
A quintessence of goodness and of wit.

Thus have your raptures reach'd to that degree
        In Love's philosophy,
That you can figure to yourself a fire   15
Void of all heat, a love without desire.

Nor in Divinity do you go less:
            You think, and you profess,
That souls may have a plenitude of joy,
Although their bodies meet not to employ.   20

But I must needs confess, I do not find
            The motions of my mind
So purifi'd as yet, but at the best
My body claims in them an interest.

I hold that perfect joy makes all our parts   25
            As joyful as our hearts.
Our senses tell us, if we please not them,
Our love is but a dotage or a dream.

How shall we then agree? you may descend,
            But will not, to my end;   30
I fain would tune my fancy to your key,
But cannot reach to that obstructed way.

There rests but this, that whilst we sorrow here,
            Our bodies may draw near:
And when no more their joys they can extend,   35
Then let our souls begin where they did end.

PROFFER'D LOVE REJECTED

It is not four years ago,
    I offer'd forty crowns
To lie with her a night or so:
    She answer'd me in frowns.

Not two years since, she meeting me   5
    Did whisper in my ear,
That she would at my service be,
    If I contented were.

I told her I was cold as snow,
    And had no great desire;   10
But should be well content to go
    To twenty, but no higher.

Some three months since, or thereabout,
    She that so coy had been
Bethought herself and found me out,   15
    And was content to sin.

I smil'd at that, and told her I
    Did think it something late,
And that I'd not repentance buy
    At above half the rate.   20

This present morning early she
    Forsooth came to my bed,
And *gratis* there she offer'd me
    Her high-priz'd maidenhead.

I told her that I thought it then   25
    Far dearer than I did,
When I at first the forty crowns
    For one night's lodging bid.

DISDAIN

A quoy servent tant d'artifices

To what end serve the promises
    And oaths lost in the air,
Since all your proffer'd services
    To me but tortures are?

Another now enjoys my love,   5
    Set you your heart at rest:
Think not me from my faith to move,
    Because you faith protest.

The man that doth possess my heart
    Has twice as much perfection,   10
And does excel you in desert,
    As much as in affection.

I cannot break so sweet a bond,
    Unless I prove untrue:
Nor can I ever be so fond,   15
    To prove untrue for you.

Your attempts are but in vain
(To tell you is a favour):
For things that may be rack your brain;
Then lose not thus your labour.   20

LUTEA ALLISON

Si sola es, nulla es

THOUGH you Diana-like have liv'd still chaste,
Yet must you not, fair, die a maid at last:
The roses on your cheeks were never made
To bless the eye alone, and so to fade;
Nor had the cherries on your lips their being   5
To please no other sense than that of seeing:
You were not made to look on, though that be
A bliss too great for poor mortality:
In that alone those rarer parts you have,
To better uses sure wise Nature gave   10
Than that you put them to; to love, to wed,
For Hymen's rites and for the marriage-bed
You were ordain'd, and not to lie alone;
One is no number, till that two be one.
To keep a maidenhead but till fifteen   15
Is worse than murder, and a greater sin
Than to have lost it in the lawful sheets
With one that should want skill to reap those sweets:
But not to lose 't at all—by Venus, this,
And by her son, inexpiable is;   20
And should each female guilty be o' th' crime,
The world would have its end before its time.

PERJURY EXCUSED

ALAS, it is too late! I can no more
Love now than I have lov'd before:
My Flora, 'tis my fate, not I;
And what you call contempt is destiny.
I am no monster, sure: I cannot show   5
Two hearts; one I already owe;
And I have bound myself with oaths, and vow'd
Oft'ner, I fear, than Heaven hath e'er allow'd,

That faces now should work no more on me,
Than if they could not charm, or I not see. 10
And shall I break them? shall I think you can
Love, if I could, so foul a perjur'd man?
Oh no, 'tis equally impossible that I
Should love again, or you love perjury.

A SONG

HAST thou seen the down in the air,
  When wanton blasts have toss'd it?
Or the ship on the sea,
  When ruder waves have cross'd it?
Hast thou mark'd the crocodile's weeping, 5
  Or the fox's sleeping?
Or hast view'd the peacock in his pride,
  Or the dove by his bride,
  When he courts for his lechery?
O, so fickle, O, so vain, O, so false, so false is she! 10

UPON T[OM] C[AREW?] HAVING THE P[OX]

TROTH, Tom, I must confess I much admire
Thy water should find passage through the fire;
For fire and water never could agree:
These now by nature have some sympathy.
Sure then his way he forces, for all know 5
The French ne'er grants a passage to his foe.
If it be so, his valour I must praise,
That being the weaker, yet can force his ways;
And wish that to his valour he had strength,
That he might drive the fire quite out at length; 10
For, troth, as yet the fire gets the day,
For evermore the water runs away.

UPON THE FIRST SIGHT OF MY LADY SEYMOUR

WONDER not much, if thus amaz'd I look;
Since I saw you, I have been planet-strook:
A beauty, and so rare, I did descry,
As, should I set her forth, you all, as I,

Would lose your hearts; for he that can   5
Know her and live, he must be more than man—
An apparition of so sweet a creature,
That, credit me, she had not any feature
That did not speak her angel.   But no more
Such heavenly things as these we must adore,   10
Nor prattle of; lest, when we do but touch,
Or strive to know, we wrong her too too much.

UPON L. M. WEEPING

WHOEVER was the cause your tears were shed,
May these my curses light upon his head:
May he be first in love, and let it be
With a most known and black deformity,
Nay, far surpass all witches that have bin   5
Since our first parents taught us how to sin!
Then let this hag be coy, and he run mad
For that which no man else would e'er have had;
And in this fit may he commit the thing
May him impenitent to th' gallows bring!   10
Then might he for one tear his pardon have,
But want that single grief his life to save!
And being dead, may he at heaven venter,
But for the guilt of this one fact ne'er enter.

THE DEFORMED MISTRESS

I KNOW there are some fools that care
Not for the body, so the face be fair;
Some others, too, that in a female creature
Respect not beauty, but a comely feature;
And others, too, that for those parts in sight   5
Care not so much, so that the rest be right.
Each man his humour hath, and, faith, 'tis mine
To love that woman which I now define.
First I would have her wainscot foot and hand
More wrinkled far than any pleated band,   10
That in those furrows, if I' d take the pains,
I might both sow and reap all sorts of grains:
Her nose I 'd have a foot long, not above,
With pimples embroider'd, for those I love;

And at the end a comely pearl of snot,   15
Considering whether it should fall or not:
Provided, next, that half her teeth be out,
Nor do I care much if her pretty snout
Meet with her furrow'd chin, and both together
Hem in her lips, as dry as good whit-leather: 20
One wall-eye she shall have, for that 's a sign
In other beasts the best: why not in mine?
Her neck I 'll have to be pure jet at least,
With yellow spots enamell'd; and her breast,
Like a grasshopper's wing, both thin and lean,   25
Not to be touch'd for dirt, unless swept clean:
As for her belly, 'tis no matter, so
There be a belly, and——
Yet if you will, let it be something high,
And always let there be a tympany.   30
But soft! where am I now? here I should stride,
Lest I fall in, the place must be so wide,
And pass unto her thighs, which shall be just
Like to an ant's that 's scraping in the dust.
Into her legs I 'd have love's issues fall,   35
And all her calf into a gouty small:
Her feet both thick and eagle-like display'd,
The symptoms of a comely, handsome maid.
As for her parts behind, I ask no more:
If they but answer those that are before,   40
I have my utmost wish; and, having so,
Judge whether I am happy, yea or no.

NON EST MORTALE QUOD OPTO

UPON MRS. A. L.

THOU think'st I flatter, when thy praise I tell,
But thou dost all hyperboles excel;
For I am sure thou art no mortal creature,
But a divine one, thron'd in human feature.
Thy piety is such, that heaven by merit,   5
If ever any did, thou shouldst inherit;
Thy modesty is such, that hadst thou bin
Tempted as Eve, thou wouldst have shunn'd her sin:
So lovely fair thou art, that sure Dame Nature

Meant thee the pattern of the female creature.　　10
Besides all this, thy flowing wit is such,
That were it not in thee, 't had been too much
For womankind: should envy look thee o'er,
It would confess thus much, if not much more.
I love thee well, yet wish some bad in thee;　　15
For sure I am thou art too good for me.

HIS DREAM

On a still, silent night, scarce could I number
One of the clock, but that a golden slumber
Had lock'd my senses fast, and carri'd me
Into a world of blest felicity,
I know not how: first to a garden, where　　5
The apricock, the cherry, and the pear,
The strawberry and plum, were fairer far
Than that eye-pleasing fruit that caus'd the jar
Betwixt the goddesses, and tempted more
Than fair Atlanta's ball, though gilded o'er.　　10
I gaz'd awhile on these, and presently
A silver stream ran softly gliding by,
Upon whose banks, lilies more white than snow
New fall'n from heaven, with violets mix'd, did grow;
Whose scent so chaf'd the neighbour air, that you　　15
Would surely swear Arabic spices grew
Not far from thence, or that the place had been
With musk prepar'd to entertain Love's Queen.
Whilst I admir'd, the river pass'd away,
And up a grove did spring, green as in May　　20
When April had been moist; upon whose bushes
The pretty robins, nightingales, and thrushes
Warbled their notes so sweetly, that my ears
Did judge at least the music of the spheres.
But here my gentle dream conveyed me　　25
Into the place where I most long'd to see,
My mistress' bed; who, some few blushes past
And smiling frowns, contented was at last
To let me touch her neck; I, not content
With that, slipp'd to her breast, thence lower went,　　30
And then——— I awak'd.

UPON A. M.

YIELD all, my love; but be withal as coy
As if thou knew'st not how to sport and toy:
The fort resign'd with ease, men cowards prove
And lazy grow.   Let me besiege my love;
Let me despair at least three times a day,   5
And take repulses upon each essay:
If I but ask a kiss, straight blush as red
As if I tempted for thy maidenhead;
Contract thy smiles, if that they go too far,
And let thy frowns be such as threaten war: 10
That face which Nature sure never intended
Should e'er be marr'd, because 't could ne'er be mended.
Take no corruption from thy grandame Eve;
Rather want faith to save thee, than believe
Too soon; for, credit me 'tis true,   15
Men most of all enjoy, when least they do.

A CANDLE

THERE is a thing which in the light
Is seldom us'd; but in the night
It serves the maiden female crew,
The ladies, and the good-wives too:
They use to take it in their hand,   5
And then it will uprightly stand;
And to a hole they it apply,
Where by its goodwill it would die;
It spends, goes out, and still within
It leaves its moisture thick and thin.   10

THE METAMORPHOSIS

THE little boy, to show his might and power,
Turn'd Io to a cow, Narcissus to a flower;
Transform'd Apollo to a homely swain,
And Jove himself into a golden rain.
These shapes were tolerable, but by th' mass!   5
H'as metamorphos'd me into an ass.

TO B. C.

WHEN first, fair mistress, I did see your face,
I brought, but carri'd no eyes from the place;
And since that time god Cupid hath me led
In hope that once I shall enjoy your bed.
      But I despair; for now, alas! I find,   5
      Too late for me, the blind does lead the blind.

UPON SIR JOHN LAURENCE'S BRINGING WATER OVER THE HILLS TO MY LORD MIDDLESEX HIS HOUSE AT WHITTON

AND is the water come? sure 't cannot be;
It runs too much against philosophy:
For heavy bodies to the centre bend,
Light bodies only naturally ascend.
How comes this then to pass? The good knight's skill 5
Could nothing do without the water's will:
      Then 'twas the water's love that made it flow,
      For love will creep where well it cannot go.

A BARBER

I AM a barber, and, I 'd have you know,
A shaver too, sometimes no mad one though;
The reason why you see me now thus bare
Is 'cause I always trade against the hair.
But yet I keep a state; who comes to me,   5
Whos'e'er he is, he must uncover'd be.
When I 'm at work, I 'm bound to find discourse,
To no great purpose, of great Sweden's force,
Of Witel, and the Bourse, and what 'twill cost
To get that back which was this Summer lost: 10
So fall to praising of his Lordship's hair;
Ne'er so deform'd, I swear 'tis *sans* compare:
I tell him that the King's doth sit no fuller,
And yet his is not half so good a colour;
Then reach a pleasing glass, that 's made to lie,   15
Like to its master, most notoriously;
And if he must his mistress see that day,
I with a powder send him straight away.

A SOLDIER

I am a man of war and might,
And know thus much, that I can fight,
Whether I am i' th' wrong or right,
            Devoutly.

No woman under heaven I fear,   5
New oaths I can exactly swear,
And forty healths my brain will bear
            Most stoutly.

I cannot speak, but I can do
As much as any of our crew;   10
And if you doubt it, some of you
            May prove me.

I dare be bold thus much to say:
If that my bullets do but play,
You would be hurt so night and day,   15
            Yet love me.

TO MY LADY E. C. AT HER GOING OUT OF ENGLAND

I must confess, when I did part from you,
I could not force an artificial dew
Upon my cheeks, nor with a gilded phrase
Express how many hundred several ways
My heart was tortur'd, nor, with arms across,   5
In discontented garbs set forth my loss:
Such loud expressions many times do come
From lightest hearts: great griefs are always dumb.
The shallow rivers roar, the deep are still;
Numbers of painted words may show much skill: 10
But little anguish and a cloudy face
Is oft put on, to serve both time and place:
The blazing wood may to the eye seem great,
But 'tis the fire rak'd up that has the heat,
And keeps it long.   True sorrow 's like to wine: 15
That which is good does never need a sign.
My eyes were channels far too small to be
Conveyers of such floods of misery:

And so pray think; or if you 'd entertain
A thought more charitable, suppose some strain   20
Of sad repentance had, not long before,
Quite empti'd for my sins that wat'ry store:
So shall you him oblige that still will be
Your servant to his best ability.

A PEDLAR OF SMALL-WARES

A PEDLAR I am, that take great care
And mickle pains for to sell small-ware:
I had need do so, when women do buy,
That in small-wares trade so unwillingly.

L. W.

A looking-glass will 't please you, madam, buy?   5
A rare one 'tis indeed, for in it I
Can show what all the world besides can't do,
A face like to your own, so fair, so true.

L. E.

For you a girdle, madam; but I doubt me
Nature hath order'd there 's no waist about ye: 10
Pray, therefore, be but pleas'd to search my pack,
There 's no ware that I have that you shall lack.

L. E. L. M.

You, ladies, want you pins? if that you do,
I have those will enter, and that stiffly too:
It 's time you choose, in troth; you will bemoan   15
Too late your tarrying, when my pack 's once gone.

L. B. L. A.

As for you, ladies, there are those behind
Whose ware perchance may better take your mind:
One cannot please ye all; the pedlar will draw back,   19
And wish, against himself, that you may have the knack.

AN ANSWER TO SOME VERSES MADE IN HIS PRAISE

THE ancient poets and their learned rhymes
We still admire in these our later times,
And celebrate their fames.   Thus, though they die,
Their names can never taste mortality:
Blind Homer's muse and Virgil's stately verse,   5
While any live, shall never need a hearse.
Since then to these such praise was justly due
For what they did, what shall be said to you?
These had their helps: they writ of gods and kings,
Of temples, battles, and such gallant things;   10
But you of nothing: how could you have writ,
Had you but chose a subject to your wit?
To praise Achilles or the Trojan crew,
Show'd little art, for praise was but their due.
To say she 's fair that 's fair, this is no pains: 15
He shows himself most poet, that most feigns.
To find out virtues strangely hid in me—
Ay, there 's the art and learned poetry!
To make one striding of a barbed steed,
Prancing a stately round—I use indeed   20
To ride Bat Jewel's jade—this is the skill,
This shows the poet wants not wit at will.
     I must admire aloof, and for my part
     Be well contented, since you do 't with art.

LOVE'S BURNING-GLASS

WONDERING long how I could harmless see
Men gazing on those beams that fired me,
At last I found it was the crystal, love,
Before my heart that did the heat improve:
Which, by contracting of those scatter'd rays   5
Into itself, did so produce my blaze.
Now, lighted by my love, I see the same
Beams dazzle those, that me are wont t' inflame;
And now I bless my love, when I do think
By how much I had rather burn than wink.   10
But how much happier were it thus to burn,
If I had liberty to choose my urn!
But since those beams do promise only fire,
This flame shall purge me of the dross, desire.

THE MIRACLE

If thou be'st ice, I do admire
How thou couldst set my heart on fire;
Or how thy fire could kindle me,
Thou being ice, and not melt thee;
But even my flames, lit at thy own,   5
Have hard'ned thee into a stone!
Wonder of love, that canst fulfil,
Inverting nature thus, thy will;
Making ice one another burn,
Whilst itself doth harder turn!   10

A TRANSLATION

Εἰ μὲν ἦν μαθεῖν

If man might know
  The ill he must undergo,
And shun it so,
  Then it were good to know:
But if he undergo it,   5
  Though he know it,
What boots him know it?
  He must undergo it.

THE EXPOSTULATION

Tell me, ye juster deities,
That pity lovers' miseries,
Why should my own unworthiness
Fright me to seek my happiness?
It is as natural as just   5
Him for to love, whom needs I must:
All men confess that love 's a fire,
Then who denies it to aspire?

Tell me, if thou wert Fortune's thrall,
Wouldst thou not raise thee from the fall,   10
Seek only to o'erlook thy state
Whereto thou art condemn'd by fate?

Then let me love my Coridon,
And by love's leave, him love alone:
For I have read of stories oft,   15
That love hath wings and soars aloft.

Then let me grow in my desire,
Though I be martyr'd in that fire;
For grace it is enough for me,
But only to love such as he: 20
For never shall my thoughts be base,
Though luckless, yet without disgrace:
Then let him that my love shall blame
Or clip love's wings, or quench love's flame.

DETRACTION EXECRATED

THOU vermin slander, bred in abject minds
Of thoughts impure, by vile tongues animate,
Canker of conversation! couldst thou find
Naught but our love whereon to show thy hate?
Thou never wert when we two were alone;   5
What canst thou witness then? thy base dull aid
Was useless in our conversation,
Where each meant more than could by both be said.
Whence hadst thou thy intelligence; from earth?
That part of us ne'er knew that we did love.   10
Or from the air? Our gentle sighs had birth
From such sweet raptures as to joy did move.
Our thoughts, as pure as the chaste morning's breath,
When from the night's cold arms it creeps away,
Were cloth'd in words and maiden's blush that hath 15
More purity, more innocence than they.
Nor from the water couldst thou have this tale:
No briny tear hath furrow'd her smooth cheek;
And I was pleas'd: I pray what should he ail
That had her love, for what else could he seek?   20
We short'ned days to moments by love's art,
Whilst our two souls in amorous ecstasy
Perceiv'd no passing time, as if a part
Our love had been of still eternity.
Much less could have it from the purer fire: 25
Our heat exhales no vapour from coarse sense,

Such as are hopes, or fears, or fond desires;
Our mutual love itself did recompense.
Thou hast no correspondency in heaven,
And th' elemental world thou seest is free: 30
Whence hadst thou then this talking, monster? even
From hell, a harbour fit for it and thee.
Curs'd be th' officious tongue that did address
Thee to her ears, to ruin my content:
May it one minute taste such happiness,   35
Deserving loos'd, unpiti'd it lament!
I must forbear her sight, and so repay
In grief those hours joy short'ned to a dram:
Each minute I will lengthen to a day,
And in one year outlive Methusalem.   40

SONG

UNJUST decrees, that do at once exact
From such a love as worthy hearts should own,
        So wild a passion,
        And yet so tame a presence,
            As, holding no proportion,   5
    Changes into impossible obedience.

Let it suffice, that neither I do love
In such a calm observance as to weigh
        Each word I say,
        And each examin'd look t' approve   10
            That towards her doth move,
            Without so much of fire
    As might in time kindle into desire.

Or give me leave to burst into a flame,
And at the scope of my unbounded will   15
        Love her my fill—
        No superscriptions of fame,
            Of honour, or good name;
            No thought but to improve
    The gentle and quick approaches of my love.   20

But thus to throng and overlade a soul
With love, and then to leave a room for fear,

That shall all that control,
What is it but to rear
Our passions and our hopes on high,   25
That thence they may descry
The noblest way how to despair and die?

A PROLOGUE OF THE AUTHOR'S TO A MASQUE AT WHITTON

EXPECT not here a curious river fine:
Our wits are short of that—alas the time!
The neat refined language of the Court
We know not; if we did, our country sport
Must not be too ambitious; 'tis for kings,   5
Not for their subjects, to have such rare things.
Besides, though, I confess, Parnassus hardly,
Yet Helicon this summer-time is dry:
Our wits were at an ebb, or very low,
And, to say troth, I think they cannot flow.   10
But yet a gracious influence from you
May alter nature in our brow-sick crew.
Have patience then, we pray, and sit a while,
And, if a laugh be too much, lend a smile.

SONGS FROM THE PLAYS

FROM "THE GOBLINS"

I

SOME drink! what, boy, some drink!
Fill it up, fill it up to the brink.
When the pots cry clink,
And the pockets chink,
  Then 'tis a merry world.   5
To the best, to the best, have at her;
And a pox take the woman-hater!

II

A HEALTH to the nut-brown lass,
With the hazel eyes: let it pass.
  She that has good eyes
  Has good thighs.
Let it pass, let it pass!   5

As much to the lively grey,
'Tis as good i' th' night as the day:
  She that has good eyes
    Has good thighs.
Drink away, drink away!   10

I pledge, I pledge: what ho! some wine!
  Here 's to mine and to thine!
The colours are divine.

But O the black, the black!
(Give me as much again, and let 't be sack.)   15
  She that has good eyes
    Has good thighs,
And it may be a better knack.

From "Brennoralt"

I

She 's pretty to walk with,
  And witty to talk with,
And pleasant too to think on:
  But the best use of all
  Is, her health is a stall,   5
And helps us to make us drink on.

II

A hall, a hall
To welcome our friend!
  For some liquor call;
  A new or fresh face
  Must not alter our pace,   5
But make us still drink the quicker:
  Wine, wine! O 'tis divine!
Come, fill it unto our brother:
  What 's at the tongue's end
  It forth does send,   10
And will not a syllable smother.
            Then
  It unlocks the breast,
  And throws out the rest,
And learns us to know each other.   15
    Wine! wine!

III

COME, let the State stay,
    And drink away,
There is no business above it:
    It warms the cold brain,
    Makes us speak in high strain;   5
He 's a fool that does not approve it.
    The Macedon youth
    Left behind him this truth,
That nothing is done with much thinking:
    He drank and he fought,   10
    Till he had what he sought;
The world was his own by good drinking.

FROM "THE SAD ONE"

COME, come away to the tavern, I say;
For now at home is washing-day.
Leave your prittle-prattle, let 's have a pottle:
We are not so wise as Aristotle.

VERSES

[Printed in Henry Lawes' *Musical Airs and Dialogues*, 1653; attributed to Suckling by A. D. in *Notes and Queries*, 1st series, i, 72.]

I AM confirm'd a woman can
Love this, or that, or any other man:
    This day she 's melting hot,
    To-morrow swears she knows you not;
    If she but a new object find,   5
    Then straight she 's of another mind.
      Then hang me, ladies, at your door,
      If e'er I dote upon you more!

Yet still I 'll love the fairsome (why?
For nothing but to please my eye);   10
And so the fat and soft-skinn'd dame
I 'll flatter to appease my flame;
    For she that 's musical I 'll long,
    When I am sad, to sing a song;
      Then hang me, ladies, at your door,   15
      If e'er I dote upon you more!

I 'll give my fancy leave to range
Through everywhere to find out change:
The black, the brown, the fair shall be
But objects of variety;   20
I 'll court you all to serve my turn,
But with such flames as shall not burn.
   Then hang me, ladies, at your door,
   If e'er I dote upon you more!

TO CELIA

[From *The Grove*, 1721; discovered by Norman Ault.]

YOUTH and beauty now are thine,
O let pleasure, Celia, join:
   Be divine.

Shun the folly of disdain,
Pride affords a short-lived reign   5
   Full of pain.

All the graces court the kind,
Beauty by a tender mind
   Is refined.

UPON SIR JOHN SUCKLING'S HUNDRED HORSE

[From manuscripts in the Bodleian Library and the British Museum.
The author is unknown.   Suckling's *Answer* follows in these manuscripts.]

I TELL thee, Jack, thou 'st given the King
So rare a present as nothing
   Would welcomer have been.
A hundred horse!   Beshrew my heart,
It was a noble gallant part,   5
   The like will scarce be seen.

For every horse shall have on 's back
A man as valiant as Sir Jack,
   Although not half so witty;
Yet I did hear, the other day   10
Two tailors made seven run away—
   Good faith, the more 's the pity!

Nay, more than that, thyself dost go
In person to confront thy foe,
   And kill the Lord knows whom;   15

But faith, I hope you are of my mind,
And rather for to stay behind—
   It 's safer being at home.

But yet, methinks I see thee charge,
Thyself with freedom to enlarge,   20
   'Gainst foes that make a sally.
Courage, brave heart! Courage, brave John!
I wish thou now go bravelier on
   Than in Blackfriars Alley.

I would advise thee take a course   25
That thou mayst mount the swiftest horse
   Of all the troops thou givest,
That when the battle is begun,
Thou swiftly then away mayst run,
   And show us that thou livest.   30

Thou shalt be entertained here
By ladies that do hold thee dear
   By day and eke by night;
They 'll make thee do what love commands,
Pull off Mars' gauntlets from those hands   35
   Were never made to fight.

Since under Mars thou wert not born,
To Venus fly, think thou no scorn,
   Let it be my advice:
Leave wars, and thankful be to fate,   40
Recovered th 'ast thy lost estate,
   By carding and by dice.

SIR JOHN SUCKLING'S ANSWER

I TELL thee, fellow, whoe'er thou be,
That made this fine sing-song of me,
   Thou art a rhyming sot;
These very lines do thee bewray,
This barren wit makes all men say,   5
   'Twas some rebellious Scot.

But it 's no wonder that you sing
Such songs of me, who am no king,
   When every Blue Cap swears
He 'll not obey King James his barne,   10
That hugs a bishop under his arm,
   And hangs them in his ears.

Had I been of your covenant,
You would have call'd me John of Gaunt,
   And given me great renown;   15
But now I am John for the King,
You say I am but a poor Suckling,
   And thus you cry me down.

Well, it 's no matter what you say
Of me or mine, that run away:　　　　　　　20
　　　I hold it no good fashion
A loyal subject's blood to spill,
When we have knaves enough to kill
　　　By force of proclamation.

Commend me unto Leslie stout,　　　　　25
And all his pedlars him about:
　　　Tell them without remorse
That I will plunder all their packs,
And ride myself upon their backs,
　　　With these my hundred horse.　　　30

This holy war, this zealous firk
Against the bishops and the kirk,
　　　Is a pretended bravery:
Religion, all the world can tell,
Amongst Highlanders ne'er did dwell—　　35
　　　It 's but to cloak your knavery.

Such desperate gamesters as you be
I cannot blame for tutoring me,
　　　Since all you have is down;
And every boor forgets the plough,　　　40
And swears that he 'll turn gamester now,
　　　To venture for a crown.

ON KING RICHARD THE THIRD SUPPOSED TO BE BURIED UNDER THE BRIDGE AT LEICESTER

[From manuscripts in the British Museum. Not previously included among Suckling's poems.]

WHAT means this wat'ry canopy 'bout thy bed,
These streaming vapours o'er thy sinful head?
Are they thy tears? Alas, in vain they 're spilt,
'Tis now too late to wash away thy guilt.
Thou still art bloody Richard, and 'tis much　　　5
The water should not from thy very touch
Turn quite Egyptian, and the scaly fry
Fear to be kill'd, and so thy carcase fly.
Bathe, bathe thy fill, and take thy pleasure now
In this cold bed; yet, guilty Richard, know,　　　10
Judgment must come, and water then would be
A heaven to thee midst hellish misery.

RICHARD LOVELACE (1618–57)

THE DEDICATION

TO THE RIGHT HONOURABLE MY LADY ANNE LOVELACE

To the richest treasury
That e'er fill'd ambitious eye;
To the fair bright magazine
Hath impoverish'd Love's Queen;
To th' exchequer of all honour   5
(All take pensions but from her);
To the taper of the thore,
Which the god himself but bore;
To the sea of chaste delight,
Let me cast the drop I write.   10
   And as at Loretto's shrine
Cæsar shovels in his mine,
Th' empress spreads her carcanets,
The lords submit their coronets,
Knights their chased arms hang by,   15
Maids diamond-ruby fancies tie;
Whilst from the pilgrim she wears
One poor false pearl, but ten true tears:
So, among the orient prize
(Sapphire-onyx eulogies)   20
Offer'd up unto your fame,
Take my garnet-dublet name,
And vouchsafe 'midst those rich joys
(With devotion) these toys.

SONG

TO LUCASTA, GOING BEYOND THE SEAS

IF to be absent were to be
   Away from thee;
Or that when I am gone
   You or I were alone;

Then, my Lucasta, might I crave 5
Pity from blust'ring wind, or swallowing wave.

But I 'll not sigh one blast or gale
 To swell my sail,
  Or pay a tear to swage
   The foaming blue god's rage; 10
For whether he will let me pass
Or no, I 'm still as happy as I was.

Though seas and land betwixt us both,
 Our faith and troth,
  Like separated souls, 15
   All time and space controls:
Above the highest sphere we meet
Unseen, unknown, and greet as angels greet.

So then we do anticipate
 Our after-fate,
  And are alive i' th' skies, 20
   If thus our lips and eyes
Can speak like spirits unconfin'd
In heav'n, their earthy bodies left behind.

SONG

TO LUCASTA, GOING TO THE WARS

TELL me not, sweet, I am unkind,
 That from the nunnery
Of thy chaste breast and quiet mind,
 To war and arms I fly.

True, a new mistress now I chase, 5
 The first foe in the field;
And with a stronger faith embrace
 A sword, a horse, a shield.

Yet this inconstancy is such
 As you too shall adore; 10
I could not love thee, dear, so much,
 Lov'd I not Honour more.

A PARADOX

'Tis true the beauteous star
  To which I first did bow
Burnt quicker, brighter far
  Than that which leads me now;
    Which shines with more delight;   5
    For gazing on that light
    So long near lost my sight.

Through foul we follow fair,
  For had the world one face,
And earth been bright as air,   10
  We had known neither place:
    Indians smell not their nest;
    A Swiss or Finn tastes best
    The spices of the East.

So from the glorious sun,   15
  Who to his height hath got,
With what delight we run
  To some black cave or grot!
    And heav'nly Sidney you
    Twice read, had rather view   20
    Some odd romance so new.

The god that constant keeps
  Unto his deities
Is poor in joys, and sleeps
  Imprison'd in the skies: 25
    This knew the wisest, who
    From Juno stole, below
    To love a bear or cow.

SONG

TO AMARANTHA, THAT SHE WOULD DISHEVEL HER HAIR

Amarantha sweet and fair,
Ah braid no more that shining hair!
  As my curious hand or eye,
Hovering round thee let it fly.

Let it fly as unconfin'd   5
As its calm ravisher, the wind,
    Who hath left his darling, th' East,
To wanton o'er that spicy nest.

Ev'ry tress must be confess'd
But neatly tangled at the best;   10
    Like a clew of golden thread
Most excellently ravelled.

Do not then wind up that light
In ribbands, and o'ercloud in night;
    Like the sun in 's early ray,   15
But shake your head and scatter day.

See, 'tis broke!   Within this grove,
The bower and the walks of love,
    Weary lie we down and rest,
And fan each other's panting breast.   20

Here we 'll strip and cool our fire
In cream below, in milk-baths higher;
    And when all wells are drawn dry,
I 'll drink a tear out of thine eye,

Which our very joys shall leave,   25
That sorrows thus we can deceive;
    Or our very sorrows weep,
That joys so ripe so little keep.

TO CHLOE,

COURTING HER FOR HIS FRIEND

Chloe, behold! again I bow,
Again possess'd, again I woo;
    From my heat hath taken fire
        Damas, noble youth, and fries:
        Gazing with one of mine eyes,   5
    Damas, half of me, expires.
Chloe, behold!   Our fate 's the same,
Or make me cinders too, or quench his flame.

I 'd not be king, unless there sate
Less lords that shar'd with me in state; 10
 Who by their cheaper coronets know
 What glories from my diadem flow:
 Its use and rate values the gem,
 Pearls in their shells have no esteem; 15
And I being sun within thy sphere, 15
'Tis my chief beauty thinner lights shine there.

The us'rer heaps unto his store
By seeing others praise it more;
 Who not for gain or want doth covet,
 But 'cause another loves doth love it: 20
 Thus gluttons, cloy'd, afresh invite
 Their gusts from some new appetite,
And after cloth remov'd and meat,
Fall to again by seeing others eat.

SONNET

Depose your finger of that ring,
 And crown mine with 't awhile.
Now I restore 't—Pray does it bring
 Back with it more of soil?
Or shines it not as innocent, 5
 As honest, as before 'twas lent?

So then enrich me with that treasure
 Will but increase your store,
And please me, fair one, with that pleasure
 Must please you still the more: 10
Not to save others is a curse
The blackest, when y' are ne'er the worse.

ODE

TO LUCASTA. THE ROSE

Sweet, serene, sky-like flower,
Haste to adorn her bower:
 From thy long cloudy bed
 Shoot forth thy damask head.

New-startled blush of Flora!   5
The grief of pale Aurora,
   Who will contest no more,
   Haste, haste, to strow her floor.

Vermilion ball that's given
From lip to lip in heaven;   10
   Love's couch's coverled,
   Haste, haste, to make her bed.

Dear offspring of pleas'd Venus
And jolly plump Silenus,
   Haste, haste, to deck the hair   15
   Of th' only sweetly fair.

See! rosy is her bower,
Her floor is all this flower,
   Her bed a rosy nest
   By a bed of roses press'd.   20

But early as she dresses,
Why fly you her bright tresses?
   Ah! I have found I fear:
   Because her cheeks are near.

GRATIANA DANCING AND SINGING

SEE! with what constant motion,
Even and glorious as the sun,
   Gratiana steers that noble frame,
Soft as her breast, sweet as her voice
That gave each winding law and poise,   5
   And swifter than the wings of Fame.

She beat the happy pavëment
By such a star made firmament,
   Which now no more the roof envies,
But swells up high with Atlas ev'n,   10
Bearing the brighter, nobler heav'n,
   And, in her, all the deities.

Each step trod out a lover's thought
And the ambitious hopes he brought,

    Chain'd to her brave feet with such arts,   **15**
Such sweet command and gentle awe,
As when she ceas'd, we sighing saw
    The floor lay pav'd with broken hearts.

So did she move; so did she sing
Like the harmonious spheres that bring   **20**
    Unto their rounds their music's aid;
Which she performed such a way,
As all th' enamour'd world will say
    The Graces danced, and Apollo play'd.

THE SCRUTINY

SONG

WHY should you swear I am forsworn,
    Since thine I vow'd to be?
Lady, it is already morn,
    And 'twas last night I swore to thee
That fond impossibility.   **5**

Have I not lov'd thee much and long,
    A tedious twelve hours' space?
I must all other beauties wrong,
    And rob thee of a new embrace,
Could I still dote upon thy face.   **10**

Not but all joy in thy brown hair
    By others may be found;
But I must search the black and fair,
    Like skilful mineralists that sound
For treasure in unplough'd-up ground.   **15**

Then if, when I have lov'd my round,
    Thou prov'st the pleasant she,
With spoils of meaner beauties crown'd,
    I laden will return to thee,
Ev'n sated with variety.   **20**

PRINCESS LOUISA DRAWING

I saw a little deity,
Minerva in epitome,
Whom Venus, at first blush, surpris'd,
Took for her winged wag disguis'd;
But viewing then whereas she made   5
Not a distress'd, but lively shade
Of Echo, whom he had betray'd,
Now wanton, and i' th' cool o' th' sun
With her delight a-hunting gone;
And thousands more, whom he had slain,   10
To live, and love, belov'd again:
Ah, this is true divinity!
I will ungod that toy! cri'd she;
Then mark'd the Syrinx running fast
To Pan's embraces, with the haste   15
She fled him once, whose reed-pipe rent,
He finds now a new instrument.
Theseus, return'd, invokes the air
And winds, then wafts his fair;
Whilst Ariadne ravish'd stood   20
Half in his arms, half in the flood.

Proud Anaxarete doth fall
At Iphis' feet, who smiles of all;
And he, whilst she his curls doth deck,
Hangs nowhere now but on her neck.   25

Here Phœbus with a beam untombs
Long-hid Leucothoë, and dooms
Her father there; Daphne the fair
Knows now no bays but round her hair;
And to Apollo and his sons   30
Who pay him their due orisons,
Bequeaths her laurel-robe, that flame
Contemns, thunder and evil fame.

There kneel'd Adonis fresh as Spring,
Gay as his youth, now offering   35
Herself those joys with voice and hand,
Which first he could not understand.

Transfixed Venus stood amaz'd,
Full of the boy and love she gaz'd;
And in embraces seemed more   40
Senseless and cold than he before.
Useless child! In vain, said she,
You bear that fond artillery:
See here a pow'r above the slow
Weak execution of thy bow.   45

So said, she riv'd the wood in two,
Unedged all his arrows too,
And with the string their feathers bound
To that part whence we have our wound.

See, see! the darts by which we burn'd   50
Are bright Louisa's pencils turn'd;
With which she now enliveth more
Beauties than they destroy'd before.

AN ELEGY

PRINCESS KATHERINE BORN, CHRISTENED, BURIED IN ONE DAY

You that can aptly mix your joys with cries,
And weave white Ios with black elegies,
Can carol out a dirge, and in one breath
Sing to the tune either of life or death;
You that can weep the gladness of the spheres,   5
And pen a hymn, instead of ink, with tears:
Here, here your unproportion'd wit let fall
To celebrate this new-born funeral,
And greet that little greatness, which from th' womb
Dropp'd both a load to th' cradle and the tomb.   10

Bright soul, teach us to warble with what feet
Thy swathing linen and thy winding sheet
Mourn or shout forth that font's solemnity,
Which at once buried and christ'ned thee;
And change our shriller passions with that sound,   15
First toll'd thee into th' air, then the ground.

Ah, wert thou born for this, only to call
The King and Queen guests to your burial?
To bid good night, your day not yet begun,
And show 's a setting ere a rising sun?   20

Or wouldst thou have thy life a martyrdom,
Die in the act of thy religion,
Fit, excellently, innocently good,
First sealing it with water, then thy blood?
As when on blazing wings a blest man soars,   25
And having pass'd to God through fiery doors
Straight 's rob'd with flames, when the same element
Which was his shame proves now his ornament;
Oh, how he hast'ned death, burnt to be fried,
Kill'd twice with each delay, till deified: 30
So swift hath been thy race, so full of flight,
Like him condemn'd, ev'n aged with a night,
Cutting all lets with clouds, as if th' hadst been
Like angels plum'd, and born a cherubin.

Or in your journey towards heav'n, say,   35
Took you the world a little in your way,
Saw'st and dislik'st its vain pomp, then didst fly
Up for eternal glories to the sky?
Like a religious ambitious one,
Aspiredst for the everlasting crown?   40

Ah, holy traitor to your brother prince,
Robb'd of his birthright and pre-eminence!
Could you ascend yon' chair of state ere him,
And snatch from th' heir the starry diadem,
Making your honours now as much uneven   45
As gods on earth are less than saints in heav'n?

Triumph! sing triumphs then! Oh put on all
Your richest looks dress'd for this festival;
Thoughts full of ravish'd reverence, with eyes
So fix'd as when a saint we canonize;   50
Clap wings with seraphins before the Throne,
At this eternal coronation,
And teach your souls new mirth, such as may be
Worthy this birthday to divinity.

But ah! these blast your feasts, the jubilees   55
We send you up are sad, as were our cries,
And of true joy we can express no more,
Thus crown'd, than when we buri'd thee before.

Princess in heav'n, forgiveness! whilst we
Resign our office to the Hierarchy.   60

LOVE CONQUER'D

A SONG

THE childish God of Love did swear
    Thus: "By my awful bow and quiver,
Yon' weeping, kissing, smiling pair,
I 'll scatter all their vows i' th' air,
    And their knit embraces shiver."   5

Up then to th' head with his best art,
    Full of spite and envy blown,
At her constant marble heart
He draws his swiftest surest dart,
    Which bounded back, and hit his own.   10

Now the prince of fires burns!
    Flames in the lustre of her eyes;
Triumphant she refuses, scorns;
He submits, adores, and mourns,
    And is his vot'ress' sacrifice.   15

Foolish boy!   Resolve me now
    What 'tis to sigh and not be heard.
He, weeping, kneel'd, and made a vow,
"The world shall love as yon' fast two";
    So on his sing'd wings up he steer'd.   20

A LOOSE SARABAND

AH me! the little tyrant thief!
    As once my heart was playing,
He snatch'd it up and flew away,
    Laughing at all my praying.

Proud of his purchase, he surveys   5
    And curiously sounds it,
And though he sees it full of wounds,
    Cruel still on he wounds it.

And now this heart is all his sport,
    Which as a ball he boundeth   10
From hand to breast, from breast to lip,
    And all its rest confoundeth.

Then as a top he sets it up,
    And pitifully whips it;
Sometimes he clothes it gay and fine,   15
    Then straight again he strips it.

He cover'd it with false belief,
    Which gloriously show'd it;
And for a morning-cushionet,
    On 's mother he bestow'd it.   20

Each day, with her small brazen stings,
    A thousand times she rac'd it;
But then at night, bright with her gems,
    Once near her breast she plac'd it.

There warm it gan to throb and bleed;   25
    She knew that smart and grieved;
At length this poor condemned heart
    With these rich drugs reprieved.

She wash'd the wound with a fresh tear,
    Which my Lucasta dropped,
And in the sleave-silk of her hair   30
    'Twas hard bound up and wrapped.

She prob'd it with her constancy,
    And found no rancour nigh it;
Only the anger of her eye
    Had wrought some proud flesh by it.   35

Then press'd she nard in ev'ry vein,
    Which from her kisses trilled;
And with the balm heal'd all its pain,
    That from her hand distilled.   40

But yet this heart avoids me still,
    Will not by me be owned;
But 's fled to its physician's breast,
    There proudly sits enthroned.

A FORSAKEN LADY TO HER FALSE SERVANT THAT
IS DISDAINED BY HIS NEW MISTRESS

WERE it that you so shun me 'cause you wish,
Cruel'st, a fellow in your wretchedness,
Or that you take some small ease in your own
Torments, to hear another sadly groan,
I were most happy in my pains, to be   5
So truly blest to be so curs'd by thee;
But oh! my cries to that do rather add,
Of which too much already thou hast had,
And thou art gladly sad to hear my moan,
Yet sadly hear'st me with derision.   10

Thou most unjust, that really dost know,
And feel'st thyself the flames I burn in, oh!
How can you beg to be set loose from that
Consuming stake you bind another at?

Uncharitablest both ways, to deny   15
That pity me, for which yourself must die,
To love not her loves you, yet know the pain
What 'tis to love and not be lov'd again.

Fly on, fly on, swift racer, until she
Whom thou of all ador'st shall learn of thee   20
The pace t' outfly thee, and shall teach thee groan
What terror 'tis t' outgo and be outgone.

Not yet look back, nor yet; must we
Run then like spokes in wheels eternally,
And never overtake? be dragg'd on still   25
By the weak cordage of your untwin'd will,
Round without hope of rest? No, I will turn,
And with my goodness boldly meet your scorn;
My goodness which Heav'n pardon, and that fate
Made you hate love, and fall in love with hate.   30

But I am chang'd! Bright reason, that did give
My soul a noble quickness, made me live
One breath yet longer, and to will and see,
Hath reach'd me pow'r to scorn as well as thee:
That thou, which proudly tramplest on my grave,   35
Thyself mightst fall, conquer'd my double slave;

That thou mightst sinking in thy triumphs moan,
And I triumph in my destruction.

    Hail, holy cold! chaste temper, hail! the fire
Rav'd o'er my purer thoughts I feel t' expire,   40
And I am candi'd ice. Ye pow'rs, if e'er
I shall be forc'd unto my sepulchre,
Or violently hurl'd into my urn,
Oh, make me choose rather to freeze than burn.

ORPHEUS TO BEASTS

SONG

Here, here, oh here Eurydice,
    Here was she slain;
Her soul 'still'd through a vein.
    The gods knew less,
That time, divinity,   5
    Than ev'n, ev'n these
    Of brutishness.

Oh, could you view the melody
    Of ev'ry grace,
And music of her face,   10
    You 'd drop a tear,
Seeing more harmony
    In her bright eye,
    Than now you hear.

ORPHEUS TO WOODS

SONG

Hark! O hark! you guilty trees,
In whose gloomy galleries
Was the cruel'st murder done
That e'er yet eclips'd the sun.
Be then henceforth in your twigs   5
Blasted, ere you sprout to sprigs;
Feel no season of the year,
But what shaves off all your hair;
Nor carve any from your wombs
Aught but coffins and their tombs.   10

THE GRASSHOPPER

TO MY NOBLE FRIEND MR. CHARLES COTTON.   ODE

O THOU that swing'st upon the waving hair
    Of some well-filled oaten beard,
Drunk ev'ry night with a delicious tear
    Dropt thee from heav'n, where now th' art rear'd:

The joys of earth and air are thine entire,   5
    That with thy feet and wings dost hop and fly;
And when thy poppy works thou dost retire
    To thy carv'd acorn-bed to lie.

Up with the day, the sun thou welcom'st then,
    Sport'st in the gilt plats of his beams,   10
And all these merry days mak'st merry men,
    Thyself, and melancholy streams.

But ah the sickle! golden ears are cropt;
    Ceres and Bacchus bid good night;
Sharp frosty fingers all your flow'rs have topt,   15
    And what scythes spar'd, winds shave off quite.

Poor verdant fool, and now green ice! thy joys,
    Large and as lasting as thy perch of grass,
Bid us lay in 'gainst winter rain, and poise
    Their floods with an o'erflowing glass.   20

Thou best of men and friends! we will create
    A genuine Summer in each other's breast;
And spite of this cold Time and frozen Fate,
    Thaw us a warm seat to our rest.

Our sacred hearths shall burn eternally   25
    As vestal flames; the North-wind, he
Shall strike his frost-stretch'd wings, dissolve, and fly
    This Etna in epitome.

Dropping December shall come weeping in,
    Bewail th' usurping of his reign;   30
But when in show'rs of old Greek we begin,
    Shall cry he hath his crown again.

Night as clear Hesper shall our tapers whip
  From the light casements where we play,
And the dark hag from her black mantle strip,   35
  And stick there everlasting day.

Thus richer than untempted kings are we,
  That asking nothing, nothing need:
Though lord of all what seas embrace, yet he
  That wants himself is poor indeed.   40

DIALOGUE

LUCASTA. ALEXIS.

Lucasta. TELL me, Alexis, what this parting is,
  That so like dying is, but is not it.
Alexis. It is a swounding for a while from bliss,
  Till kind "How do you?" calls us from the fit.
  If then the spirits only stray, let mine   5
  Fly to thy bosom. *Lucasta.* And my soul to thine.

Chorus

Thus in our native seat we gladly give
Our right for one where we can better live.

Lucasta. But ah this ling'ring, murd'ring farewell!
  Death quickly wounds, and wounding cures the ill.   10
Alexis. It is the glory of a valiant lover
  Still to be dying, still for to recover.

Chorus

Soldiers suspected of their courage go,
That ensigns and their breasts untorn show:
Love near his standard when his host he sets,   15
Creates alone fresh-bleeding bannerets.

Alexis. But part we when thy figure I retain
  Still in my heart, still strongly in mine eye?
Lucasta. Shadows no longer than the sun remain,
  But when his beams, that made 'em, fly, they fly.   20

Chorus

Vain dreams of love! that only so much bliss
Allow us, as to know our wretchedness;
And deal a larger measure in our pain,
By showing joy, then hiding it again.

Alexis.	No, whilst light reigns, Lucasta still rules here,	25
	And all the night shines wholly in this sphere.	
Lucasta.	I know no morn but my Alexis' ray,	
	To my dark thoughts the breaking of the day.	

Chorus

Alexis.	So in each other if the pitying sun	
	Thus keep us fix'd, ne'er may his course be run!	30
Lucasta.	And oh! if night us undivided make,	
	Let us sleep still, and sleeping, never wake!	

The Close

Cruel adieus may well adjourn awhile
The sessions of a look, a kiss, or smile,
And leave behind an angry grieving blush;   35
But time nor fate can part us joined thus.

TO ELLINDA,

THAT LATELY I HAVE NOT WRITTEN

If in me anger, or disdain
In you, or both, made me refrain
From th' noble intercourse of verse,
That only virtuous thoughts rehearse;
    Then, chaste Ellinda, might you fear   5
    The sacred vows that I did swear.

But if alone some pious thought
Me to an inward sadness brought;
Thinking to breathe your soul too well,
My tongue was charmed with that spell,   10
    And left it (since there was no room
    To voice your worth enough) strook dumb.

So then this silence doth reveal
No thought of negligence, but zeal;
For, as in adoration,   15
This is love's true devotion:
    Children and fools the words repeat,
    But anch'rites pray in tears and sweat.

SONNET

WHEN I by thy fair shape did swear,
And mingled with each vow a tear,
    I lov'd, I lov'd thee best,
    I swore as I profess'd;
For all the while you lasted warm and pure,   5
    My oaths too did endure;
But once turn'd faithless to thyself, and old,
They then with thee incessantly grew cold.

I swore myself thy sacrifice
By th' ebon bows that guard thine eyes,   10
    Which now are alter'd white;
    And by the glorious light
Of both those stars, of which, their spheres bereft,
    Only the jelly 's left.
Then, changed thus, no more I 'm bound to you,   15
Than swearing to a saint that proves untrue.

LUCASTA WEEPING

SONG

LUCASTA wept, and still the bright
    Enamour'd God of Day,
With his soft handkercher of light,
    Kiss'd the wet pearls away.

But when her tears his heat o'ercame,
    In clouds he quench'd his beams,   5
And griev'd, wept out his eye of flame,
    So drowned her sad streams.

At this she smil'd, when straight the sun
   Clear'd with her kind desires,   10
And by her eyes' reflection
   Kindled again his fires.

THE VINTAGE TO THE DUNGEON

A SONG

Sing out, pent souls, sing cheerfully!
Care shackles you in liberty,
Mirth frees you in captivity:
    Would you double fetters add?
     Else why so sad?   5

Chorus

Besides your pinion'd arms you 'll find
Grief too can manacle the mind.

Live then pris'ners uncontroll'd;
Drink o' th' strong, the rich, the old,
Till wine too hath your wits in hold;   10
    Then if still your jollity
     And throats are free—

Chorus

Triumph in your bonds and pains,
And dance to th' music of your chains.

ON THE DEATH OF MISTRESS ELIZABETH FILMER

AN ELEGIACAL EPITAPH

You that shall live awhile before
Old Time tires, and is no more;
When that this ambitious stone
Stoops low as what it tramples on;
Know that in that age when sin   5
Gave the world law, and govern'd queen,
A virgin liv'd, that still put on
White thoughts, though out of fashion;
That trac'd the stars spite of report,
And durst be good though chidden for 't: 10

Of such a soul that infant Heav'n
Repented what it thus had giv'n;
For finding equal happy man,
Th' impatient pow'rs snatch'd it agen.
Thus, chaste as th' air whither she 's fled,   15
She, making her celestial bed
In her warm alabaster, lay
As cold as in this house of clay;
Nor were the rooms unfit to feast
Or circumscribe this angel guest;   20
The radiant gem was brightly set
In as divine a carcanet;
For which the clearer was not known,
Her mind or her complexion:
Such an everlasting grace,   25
Such a beatific face
Encloisters here this narrow floor
That possess'd all hearts before.
    Blest and bewail'd in death and birth!
The smiles and tears of heav'n and earth!   30
Virgins at each step are afear'd,
Filmer is shot by which they steer'd,
Their star extinct, their beauty dead
That the young world to honour led.
But see! the rapid spheres stand still,   35
And tune themselves unto her will.
    Thus, although this marble must,
As all things, crumble into dust,
And though you find this fair-built tomb
Ashes, as what lies in its womb;   40
Yet her saint-like name shall shine
A living glory to this shrine,
And her eternal fame be read.
When all but very Virtue 's dead.

TO LUCASTA

FROM PRISON.   AN EPODE

Long in thy shackles, liberty
I ask, not from these walls but thee
(Left for awhile another's bride),
To fancy all the world beside.

Yet ere I do begin to love,   5
See! how I all my objects prove;
Then my free soul to that confine
'Twere possible I might call mine.

First I would be in love with Peace,
And her rich swelling breasts' increase;   10
But how, alas! how may that be,
Despising earth, she will love me?

Fain would I be in love with War,
As my dear just avenging star;
But War is lov'd so ev'rywhere,   15
Ev'n he disdains a lodging here.

Thee and thy wounds I would bemoan,
Fair thorough-shot Religion;
But he lives only that kills thee,
And whoso binds thy hands is free.   20

I would love a Parliament
As a main prop from heav'n sent;
But ah! who's he that would be wedded
To th' fairest body that's beheaded?

Next would I court my Liberty,   25
And then my birthright, Property;
But can that be, when it is known
There's nothing you can call your own?

A Reformation I would have,
As for our griefs a sov'reign salve;   30
That is, a cleansing of each wheel
Of state, that yet some rust doth feel;

But not a Reformation so
As to reform were to o'erthrow;
Like watches by unskilful men   35
Disjointed, and set ill again.

The Public Faith I would adore,
But she is bankrupt of her store;
Nor how to trust her can I see,
For she that cozens all, must me.   40

Since then none of these can be
Fit objects for my love and me,
What then remains but th' only spring
Of all our loves and joys, the King?

He who, being the whole ball   45
Of day on earth, lends it to all;
When seeking to eclipse his right,
Blinded, we stand in our own light.

And now an universal mist
Of error is spread o'er each breast,   50
With such a fury edg'd as is
Not found in th' inwards of th' Abyss.

Oh, from thy glorious starry wain,
Dispense on me one sacred beam,
To light me where I soon may see   55
How to serve you, and you trust me.

LUCASTA'S FAN,

WITH A LOOKING-GLASS IN IT

ESTRICH, thou feather'd fool and easy prey,
    That larger sails to thy broad vessel need'st;
Snakes through thy guttur-neck hiss all the day,
    Then on thy iron mess at supper feed'st.

Oh what a glorious transmigration   5
    From this to so divine an edifice
Hast thou straight made! near from a winged stone
    Transform'd into a bird of paradise.

Now do thy plumes for hue and lustre vie
    With th' arch of heav'n that triumphs o'er past wet, 10
And in a rich enamell'd pinion lie,
    With sapphires, amethysts and opals set.

Sometime they wing her side, then strive to drown
    The day's eye's piercing beams, whose am'rous heat
Solicits still, till, with this shield of down,   15
    From her brave face his glowing fires are beat.

But whilst a plumy curtain she doth draw,
    A crystal mirror sparkles in thy breast,
In which her fresh aspect whenas she saw,
    And then her foe retired to the west,   20

"Dear engine that o' th' sun got'st me the day,
    Spite of his hot assaults mad'st him retreat,
No wind," said she, "dare with thee henceforth play
    But mine own breath to cool the tyrant's heat.

"My lively shade thou ever shalt retain   25
    In thy enclosed feather-framed glass,
And, but unto ourselves, to all remain
    Invisible, thou feature of this face!"

So said, her sad swain overheard, and cried,
    "Ye gods! for faith unstain'd this a reward!   30
Feathers and glass t' outweigh my virtue tried!
    Ah, show their empty strength!"   The gods accord.

Now fall'n the brittle favourite lies, and burst.
    Amaz'd Lucasta weeps, repents, and flies
To her Alexis, vows herself accurs'd   35
    If hence she dress herself but in his eyes.

LUCASTA TAKING THE WATERS AT TUNBRIDGE

ODE

YE happy floods! that now must pass
    The sacred conduits of her womb,
Smooth and transparent as your face,
    When you are deaf, and winds are dumb

Be proud! and if your waters be   5
    Foul'd with a counterfeited tear,
Or some false sigh hath stained ye,
    Haste, and be purified there.

And when her rosy gates y' have trac'd,
    Continue yet some orient wet,   10
Till, turn'd into a gem, y' are plac'd
    Like diamonds with rubies set.

Ye drops that dew th' Arabian bowers,
  Tell me, did you e'er smell or view
On any leaf of all your flowers   15
  So sweet a scent, so rich a hue?

But as through th' organs of her breath
  You trickle wantonly, beware:
Ambitious seas in their just death
  As well as lovers must have share.   20

And see! you boil, as well as I,
  You that to cool her did aspire
Now troubled and neglected lie,
  Nor can yourselves quench your own fire.

Yet still be happy in the thought   25
  That in so small a time as this,
Through all the heavens you were brought
  Of Virtue, Honour, Love and Bliss.

TO LUCASTA

ODE LYRIC

Ah, Lucasta, why so bright,
Spread with early streaked light!
If still veiled from our sight,
What is 't but eternal night?

Ah, Lucasta, why so chaste!   5
With that vigour, ripeness grac'd!
Not to be by man embrac'd
Makes that royal coin embas'd,
And this golden orchard waste.

Ah, Lucasta, why so great   10
That thy crammed coffers sweat!
Yet not owner of a seat
May shelter you from Nature's heat,
And your earthly joys complete.

Ah, Lucasta, why so good,   15
Blest with an unstained flood

Flowing both through soul and blood!
If it be not understood,
'Tis a diamond in mud.

Lucasta, stay! why dost thou fly? 20
Thou art not bright, but to the eye,
Nor chaste, but in the marriage-tie,
Nor great, but in this treasury,
Nor good, but in that sanctity.

Harder than the orient stone, 25
Like an apparition,
Or as a pale shadow gone,
Dumb and deaf she hence is flown.

Then receive this equal doom:
Virgins strow no tear or bloom, 30
No one dig the Parian womb;
Raise her marble heart i' th' room,
And 'tis both her corse and tomb.

TO MY WORTHY FRIEND MR. PETER LELY, ON THAT EXCELLENT PICTURE OF HIS MAJESTY AND THE DUKE OF YORK, DRAWN BY HIM AT HAMPTON COURT

SEE! what a clouded majesty, and eyes
Whose glory through their mist doth brighter rise!
See! what an humble bravery doth shine,
And grief triumphant breaking through each line!
How it commands the face! so sweet a scorn 5
Never did happy misery adorn!
So sacred a contempt, that others show,
To this, o' th' height of all the wheel, below;
That mightiest monarchs by this shaded book
May copy out their proudest, richest look. 10
 Whilst the true eaglet this quick lustre spies,
And by his sun's enlightens his own eyes;
He cares his cares, his burthen feels, then straight
Joys that so lightly he can bear such weight;
Whilst either either's passion doth borrow, 15
And both do grieve the same victorious sorrow.

These, my best Lely, with so bold a spirit
And soft a grace as if thou didst inherit
For that time all their greatness, and didst draw
With those brave eyes your royal sitters saw,—   20
Not as of old, when a rough hand did speak
A strong aspect, and a fair face a weak;
When only a black beard cri'd villain, and
By hieroglyphics we could understand;
When crystal typifi'd in a white spot,   25
And the bright ruby was but one red blot;—
Thou dost the things orientally the same,
Not only paint'st its colour, but its flame:
Thou sorrow canst design without a tear,
And with the man his very hope or fear;   30
So that th' amazed world shall henceforth find
None but my Lely ever drew a mind.

ELLINDA'S GLOVE

SONNET

THOU snowy farm with thy five tenements!
    Tell thy white mistress here was one
    That call'd to pay his daily rents;
But she a-gathering flow'rs and hearts is gone,
And thou left void to rude possession.   5

But grieve not, pretty ermine cabinet,
    Thy alabaster lady will come home;
    If not, what tenant can there fit
The slender turnings of thy narrow room,
But must ejected be by his own doom?   10

Then give me leave to leave my rent with thee:
    Five kisses, one unto a place;
    For though the lute's too high for me,
Yet servants knowing minikin nor base
Are still allow'd to fiddle with the case.   15

TO FLETCHER REVIV'D

How have I been religious? what strange good
Has scap'd me that I never understood?
Have I hell-guarded heresy o'erthrown?
Heal'd wounded states? made kings and kingdoms one?
That fate should be so merciful to me,   5
To let me live t' have said I have read thee?

Fair star, ascend! the joy, the life, the light
Of this tempestuous age, this dark world's sight!
Oh, from thy crown of glory dart one flame
May strike a sacred reverence, whilst thy name,   10
Like holy flamens to their God of Day,
We bowing sing; and whilst we praise, we pray.

Bright spirit! whose eternal motion
Of wit, like Time, still in itself did run,
Binding all others in it, and did give   15
Commission how far this or that shall live;
Like Destiny of poems, who, as she
Signs death to all, herself can never die.

And now thy purple-robed Tragedy,
In her embroider'd buskins, calls mine eye,   20
Where brave Aëtius we see betray'd
T' obey his death whom thousand lives obey'd;
Whilst that the mighty fool his sceptre breaks,
And through his gen'ral's wounds his own doom speaks:
Weaving thus richly *Valentinian*   25
The costliest monarch with the cheapest man.

Soldiers may here to their old glories add,
The Lover love, and be with reason Mad:
Not, as of old, Alcides furious,
Who wilder than his bull did tear the house,   30
(Hurling his language with the canvas stone):
'Twas thought the monster roar'd the sob'rer tone.

But ah! when thou thy sorrow didst inspire
With passions black as is her dark attire,
Virgins as sufferers have wept to see   35
So white a soul, so red a cruelty;

That thou hast griev'd, and with unthought redress,
Dri'd their wet eyes who now thy mercy bless;
Yet, loth to lose thy wat'ry jewel, when
Joy wip'd it off, Laughter straight sprung 't agen.   40

Now ruddy-cheeked Mirth with rosy wings
Fans ev'ry brow with gladness, whilst she sings
Delight to all, and the whole theatre
A festival in heaven doth appear:
Nothing but pleasure, love, and, like the morn,   45
Each face a gen'ral smiling doth adorn.

Hear, ye foul speakers that pronounce the air
Of stews and shores, I will inform you where
And how to clothe aright your wanton wit,
Without her nasty bawd attending it: 50
View here a loose thought said with such a grace,
Minerva might have spoke in Venus' face;
So well disguis'd, that 'twas conceiv'd by none
But Cupid had Diana's linen on,
And all his naked parts so veil'd, th' express   55
The shape with clouding the uncomeliness;
That if this reformation which we
Receiv'd had not been buried with thee,
The Stage, as this work, might have liv'd and lov'd
Her lines, the austere scarlet had approv'd,   60
And th' actors wisely been from that offence
As clear as they are now from audience.

Thus with thy genius did the Scene expire,
Wanting thy active and correcting fire,
That now—to spread a darkness over all—   65
Nothing remains but Poesy to fall;
And though from these thy embers we receive
Some warmth, so much as may be said we live,
That we dare praise thee, blushless, in the head
Of the best piece Hermes to Love e'er read,   70
That we rejoice and glory in thy wit,
And feast each other with rememb'ring it,
That we dare speak thy thought, thy acts recite;
Yet all men henceforth be afraid to write.

THE LADY A[NNE] L[OVELACE?],

MY ASYLUM IN A GREAT EXTREMITY

WITH that delight the royal captive 's brought
Before the throne, to breathe his farewell thought,
To tell his last tale, and so end with it,
Which gladly he esteems a benefit;
When the brave victor, at his great soul dumb,   5
Finds something there fate cannot overcome,
Calls the chain'd prince, and by his glory led,
First reaches him his crown, and then his head;
Who ne'er till now thinks himself slave and poor;
For though naught else, he had himself before;   10
He weeps at this fair chance, nor will allow
But that the diadem doth brand his brow,
And underrates himself below mankind,
Who first had lost his body, now his mind;—

With such a joy came I to hear my doom,   15
And haste the preparation of my tomb,
When, like good angels who have heav'nly charge
To steer and guide man's sudden-giddy barge,
She snatch'd me from the rock I was upon,
And landed me at life's pavilion: 20
Where I, thus wound out of th' immense abyss,
Was straight set on a pinnacle of bliss.

Let me leap in again! and by that fall
Bring me to my first woe, so cancel all.
Ah, 's this a quitting of the debt you owe,   25
To crush her and her goodness at one blow?
Defend me from so foul impiety,
Would make fiends grieve and furies weep to see.

Now ye sage spirits which infuse in men
That are oblig'd, twice to oblige agen,   30
Inform my tongue in labour, what to say,
And in what coin or language to repay.
But you are silent as the ev'ning's air,
When winds unto their hollow grots repair:
Oh then accept the all that left me is,   40
Devout oblations of a sacred wish!

When she walks forth, ye perfum'd wings o' th' East,
Fan her, till with the sun she hastes to th' West,
And when her heav'nly course calls up the day,
And breaks as bright, descend some glistering ray   40
To circle her and her as glistering hair,
That all may say a living saint shines there.
Slow Time, with woollen feet make thy soft pace,
And leave no tracks i' th' snow of her pure face.
But when this virtue must needs fall, to rise   45
The brightest constellation in the skies,
When we in characters of fire shall read
How clear she was alive, how spotless dead,
All you that are akin to piety
(For only you can her close mourners be),   50
Draw near, and make of hallow'd tears a dearth,
Goodness and Justice both are fled the earth.

If this be to be thankful, I 've a heart
Broken with vows, eaten with grateful smart,
And beside this, the vile world nothing hath   55
Worth anything but her provoked wrath:
So then, who thinks to satisfy in time,
Must give a satisfaction for that crime;
Since she alone knows the gift's value, she
Can only to herself requital be,   60
And worthily to th' life paint her own story
In its true colours and full native glory;
Which when perhaps she shall be heard to tell,
Buffoons and thieves, ceasing to do ill,
Shall blush into a virgin-innocence,   65
And then woo others from the same offence:
The robber and the murderer, in spite
Of his red spots, shall startle into white;
All good (rewards laid by) shall still increase
For love of her, and villainy decease;   70
Naught be ignote, not so much out of fear
Of being punish'd, as offending her.

So that, whenas my future daring bays
Shall bow itself in laurels to her praise,
To crown her conqu'ring goodness, and proclaim   75
The due renown and glories of her name;
My wit shall be so wretched and so poor,
That, 'stead of praising, I shall scandal her,

And leave, when with my purest art I 've done,
Scarce the design of what she is begun;   80
Yet men shall send me home admir'd, exact,
Proud that I could from her so well detract.

Where then, thou bold instinct, shall I begin
My endless task? To thank her were a sin
Great as not speak, and not to speak a blame   85
Beyond what 's worst, such as doth want a name;
So thou my all, poor gratitude, ev'n thou
In this wilt an unthankful office do.
Or will I fling all at her feet I have,
My life, my love, my very soul a slave?   90
Tie my free spirit only unto her,
And yield up my affection prisoner?
Fond thought, in this thou teachest me to give
What first was hers, since by her breath I live;
And hast but show'd me how I may resign   95
Possession of those things are none of mine.

A PROLOGUE TO "THE SCHOLARS,"

A COMEDY PRESENTED AT THE WHITEFRIARS

A GENTLEMAN, to give us somewhat new,
Hath brought up Oxford with him to show you—
Pray, be not frighted, though the scene and gown 's
The University's, the wit 's the Town's;
The lines each honest Englishman may speak,   5
Yet not mistake his mother-tongue for Greek,
For still 'twas part of his vow'd liturgy:
From learned comedies deliver me!
Wishing all those that lov'd 'em here asleep,
Promising Scholars, but no scholarship.   10

You 'd smile to see how he does vex and shake,
Speaks naught; but if the Prologue does but take,
Or the first act were past the pikes once, then—
Then hopes and joys, then frowns and fears agen,
Then blushes like a virgin now to be   15
Robb'd of his comical virginity
In presence of you all—in short, you 'd say
More hopes of mirth are in his looks than play.

These fears are for the noble and the wise;
But if 'mongst you there are such foul dead eyes　　20
As can damn unarraign'd, call law their pow'rs,
Judging it sin enough that it is ours,
And with the house shift their decreed desires,
Fair still to th' black, Black- still to the White-friars,
He does protest he will sit down and weep　　25
Castles and pyramids————
———————— No, he will on,
Proud to be rais'd by such destruction
So far from quarr'lling with himself and wit,
That he will thank them for the benefit,　　30
Since, finding nothing worthy of their hate,
They reach him that themselves must envy at.

THE EPILOGUE

THE stubborn author of the trifle crime,
That just now cheated you of two hours' time,
Presumptuous it lik'd him, began to grow
Careless whether it pleas'd you or no.

But we who ground th' excellence of a play　　5
On what the women at the doors will say,
Who judge it by the benches, and afford
To take your money ere his oath or word,
His Scholars school'd, said if he had been wise
He should have wove in one two comedies:　　10
The first for th' gallery, in which the throne,
To their amazement, should descend alone,
The rosin lightning flash, and monster spire
Squibs and words hotter than his fire.

Th' other for the gentlemen o' th' pit,　　15
Like to themselves all spirit, fancy, wit,
In which plots should be subtle as a flame,
Disguises would make Proteus still the same,
Humours so rarely humour'd and express'd,
That ev'n they should think 'em so, not dress'd;　　20
Vices acted and applauded too, times
Tickled, and th' actors acted, not their crimes:
So he might equally applause have gain'd
Of th' hard'ned, sooty, and the snowy hand.

Where now one "So, so" spatters, t' other, "No;   25
'Tis his first play, 'twere solecism 't should go";
The next, "'T show'd prettily, but search'd within,
It appears bare and bald"—as is his chin;
The town-wit sentences: "A scholar's play!
Pish! I know not why, but th' ave not the way."   30

We, whose gain is all our pleasure, ev'n these
Are bound by justice and religion to please;
Which he, whose pleasure 's all his gain, goes by
As slightly as they do his comedy.

Cull 's out the few, the worthy, at whose feet   35
He sacrifices both himself and it
His fancy's first fruits. Profit he knows none,
Unless that of your approbation,
Which if your thoughts at going out will pay,
He 'll not look farther for a second day.   40

CLITOPHON AND LEUCIPPE TRANSLATED

TO THE LADIES

PRAY ladies, breathe, awhile lay by
Celestial Sidney's *Arcady*;
Here 's a story that doth claim
A little respite from his flame:
Then with a quick dissolving look   5
Unfold the smoothness of this book,
To which no art, except your sight,
Can reach a worthy epithite;
'Tis an abstract of all volumes,
A pilaster of all columns   10
Fancy e'er rear'd to Wit, to be
The smallest god's epitome,
And so compactedly express
All lovers' pleasing wretchedness.

Gallant Pamela's majesty,   15
And her sweet sister's modesty
Are fix'd in each of you; you are,
Distinct, what these together were;
Divinest that are really
What Chariclea 's feign'd to be;   20

That are ev'ry one the Nine,
And brighter here Astræas shine;
View our Leucippe, and remain
In her these beauties o'er again.

Amazement! Noble Clitophon   25
Ev'n now look'd somewhat colder on
His cooler mistress, and she too
Smil'd not as she us'd to do.
See! the individual pair
Are at sad odds, and parted are;   30
They quarrel, emulate, and stand
At strife who first shall kiss your hand.

A new dispute there lately rose
Betwixt the Greeks and Latins, whose
Temples should be bound with glory   35
In best languaging this story.
Ye heirs of love, that with one smile
A ten-years' war can reconcile,
Peaceful Helens, virtuous, see!
The jarring languages agree,   40
And here all arms laid by, they do
In English meet to wait on you.

TO MY TRULY VALIANT, LEARNED FRIEND, WHO IN HIS BOOK RESOLV'D THE ART GLADIATORY INTO THE MATHEMATICS

HARK, Reader! wilt be learn'd i' th' wars?
A gen'ral in a gown?
Strike a league with arts and scars,
And snatch from each a crown?

Wouldst be a wonder? Such a one   5
As should win with a look?
A bishop in a garrison,
And conquer by the book?

Take then this mathematic shield,
And henceforth by its rules   10
Be able to dispute i' th' field,
And combat in the schools.

Whilst peaceful Learning once again
  And the soldier so concord,
As that he fights now with her pen,   15
  And she writes with his sword.

AMYNTOR'S GROVE, HIS CHLORIS, ARIGO, AND GRATIANA

AN ELOGY

It was Amyntor's grove, that Chloris
For ever echoes and her glories;
Chloris, the gentlest shepherdess
That ever lawns and lambs did bless;
Her breath, like to the whispering wind,   5
Was calm as thought, sweet as her mind;
Her lips like coral gates kept in
The perfume and the pearl within;
Her eyes a double-flaming torch
That always shine, and never scorch: 10
Herself the heav'n in which did meet
The all of bright, of fair and sweet.

  Here was I brought with that delight
That separated souls take flight;
And when my reason call'd my sense   15
Back somewhat from this excellence,
That I could see, I did begin
T' observe the curious ordering
Of every room, where 't 's hard to know
Which most excels in scent or show: 20
Arabian gums do breathe here forth,
And th' East 's come over to the North;
The winds have brought their hire of sweet,
To see Amyntor Chloris greet;
Balm and nard, and each perfume   25
To bless this pair chafe and consume;
And th' phœnix, see! already fries,
Her nest a fire in Chloris' eyes!

  Next the great and powerful hand
Beckons my thoughts unto a stand   30

Of Titian, Raphael, Giorgione,
Whose art ev'n Nature hath outdone;
For if weak Nature only can
Intend, not perfect, what is man,
These certainly we must prefer,   35
Who mended what she wrought and her;
And sure the shadows of those rare
And kind incomparable fair
Are livelier, nobler company
Than if they could or speak or see: 40
For these I ask, without a tush
Can kiss or touch, without a blush,
And we are taught that substance is,
If unenjoy'd, but th' shade of bliss.

Now every saint clearly divine   45
Is clos'd so in her several shrine;
The gems so rarely, richly set,
For them we love the cabinet;
So intricately plac'd withal,
As if th' embroidered the wall,   50
So that the pictures seem'd to be
But one continu'd tapestry.

After this travel of mine eyes,
We sate, and piti'd deities;
We bound our loose hair with the vine,   55
The poppy and the eglantine;
One swell'd an oriental bowl
Full, as a grateful, loyal soul
To Chloris. Chloris! Hear, oh hear!
'Tis pledg'd above in ev'ry sphere.   60

Now straight the Indians' richest prize
Is kindled a glad sacrifice;
Clouds are sent up on wings of thyme,
Amber, pom'granates, jessamine,
And through our earthen conduits soar   65
Higher than altars fum'd before.

So drench'd we our oppressing cares,
And chok'd the wide jaws of our fears;
Whilst ravish'd thus we did devise
If this were not a paradise   70

In all except these harmless sins,
Behold! flew in two cherubins,
Clear as the sky from whence they came,
And brighter than the sacred flame:
The boy adorn'd with modesty,   75
Yet armed so with majesty,
That if the Thunderer again
His eagle sends, she stoops in vain.
Besides his innocence he took
A sword and casket, and did look   80
Like Love in arms; he wrote but five,
Yet spake eighteen; each Grace did strive,
And twenty Cupids thronged forth,
Who first should show his prettier worth.

But oh the nymph! did you e'er know   85
Carnation mingled with snow?
Or have you seen the lightning shroud,
And straight break through th' opposing cloud?
So ran her blood, such was its hue,
So through her veil her bright hair flew,   90
And yet its glory did appear
But thin, because her eyes were near.

Blooming boy and blossoming maid,
May your fair sprigs be ne'er betray'd
To eating worm or fouler storm;   95
No serpent lurk to do them harm;
No sharp frost cut, no north-wind tear
The verdure of that fragrant hair;
But may the sun and gentle weather,
When you are both grown ripe together,   100
Load you with fruit, such as your father
From you with all the joys doth gather:
And may you, when one branch is dead,
Graft such another in its stead,
Lasting thus ever in your prime,   105
Till th' scythe is snatch'd away from Time.

AGAINST THE LOVE OF GREAT ONES

UNHAPPY youth, betray'd by fate
To such a love hath sainted hate,
And damned those celestial bands
Are only knit with equal hands,
The love of great ones. 'Tis a love   5
Gods are incapable to prove;
For where there is a joy uneven,
There never, never can be heav'n.
'Tis such a love as is not sent
To fiends as yet for punishment;   10
Ixion willingly doth feel
The gyre of his eternal wheel,
Nor would he now exchange his pain
For clouds and goddesses again.

    Wouldst thou with tempests lie? Then bow   15
To th' rougher furrows of her brow.
Or make a thunderbolt thy choice?
Then catch at her more fatal voice.
Or 'gender with the lightning? Try
The subtler flashes of her eye: 20
Poor Semele well knew the same,
Who both embrac'd her god and flame,
And not alone in soul did burn,
But in this love did ashes turn.

    How ill doth majesty enjoy   25
The bow and gaiety o' th' boy,
As if the purple robe should sit
And sentence give i' th' chair of wit.

    Say, ever-dying wretch to whom
Each answer is a certain doom,   30
What is it that you would possess,
The countess, or the naked Bess?
Would you her gown or title do,
Her box, or gem, her thing or show?
If you mean her, the very her   35
Abstracted from her character,
Unhappy boy! you may as soon
With fawning wanton with the moon,

Or with an amorous complaint
Get prostitute your very saint.   40
Not that we are not mortal, or
Fly Venus' altars, or abhor
The selfsame knack for which you pine;
But we (defend us!) are divine,
Female, but madam born, and come   45
From a right-honourable womb:
Shall we then mingle with the base,
And bring a silver-tinsel race?
Whilst th' issue noble will not pass,
The gold allay'd (almost half brass),   50
And th' blood in each vein doth appear
Part thick boorinn, part lady clear:
Like to the sordid insects sprung
From father Sun and mother Dung.
Yet lose we not the hold we have,   55
But faster grasp the trembling slave;
Play at balloon with 's heart, and wind
The strings like skeins, steal into his mind
Ten thousand hells, and feigned joys
Far worse than they, whilst like whipp'd boys,   60
After this scourge he 's hush with toys.

This heard, sir, play still in her eyes,
And be a-dying lives, like flies
Caught by their angle-legs, and whom
The torch laughs piecemeal to consume.   65

LUCASTA PAYING HER OBSEQUIES TO THE CHASTE MEMORY OF MY DEAREST COUSIN, MISTRESS BOWES BARNE

SEE! what an undisturbed tear
    She weeps for her last sleep;
But viewing her straight wak'd a star,
    She weeps that she did weep.

Grief ne'er before did tyrannize   5
    On th' honour of that brow,
And at the wheels of her brave eyes
    Was captive led till now.

Thus for a saint's apostacy,
  The unimagin'd woes
And sorrows of the Hierarchy
  None but an angel knows.

10

Thus for lost souls' recovery,
  The clapping of all wings,
And triumphs of this victory,
  None but an angel sings.

15

So none but she knows to bemoan
  This equal virgin's fate,
None but Lucasta can her crown
  Of glory celebrate.

20

Then dart on me, chaste light, one ray
  By which I may descry
Thy joy clear through this cloudy day,
  To dress my sorrow by.

TO ALTHEA, FROM PRISON

SONG

WHEN Love with unconfined wings
  Hovers within my gates,
And my divine Althea brings
  To whisper at the grates;
When I lie tangled in her hair,
  And fetter'd to her eye,
The gods, that wanton in the air,
  Know no such liberty.

5

When flowing cups run swiftly round
  With no allaying Thames,
Our careless heads with roses bound,
  Our hearts with loyal flames;
When thirsty grief in wine we steep,
  When healths and draughts go free,
Fishes, that tipple in the deep,
  Know no such liberty.

10

15

When, like committed linnets, I
    With shriller throat shall sing
The sweetness, mercy, majesty,
    And glories of my king;   20
When I shall voice aloud how good
    He is, how great should be,
Enlarged winds, that curl the flood,
    Know no such liberty.

Stone walls do not a prison make,   25
    Nor iron bars a cage;
Minds innocent and quiet take
    That for an hermitage;
If I have freedom in my love,
    And in my soul am free,   30
Angels alone, that soar above,
    Enjoy such liberty.

BEING TREATED

TO ELLINDA

FOR cherries plenty, and for corans
Enough for fifty, were there more on 's;
For ells of beer, flutes of canary
That well did wash down pasties-mary;
For peason, chickens, sauces high,   5
Pig, and the widow ven'son-pie,
With certain promise, to your brother,
Of the virginity of another,
Where it is thought I too may peep in
With knuckles far as any deep in;   10
For glasses, heads, hands, bellies full
Of wine and loin right-worshipful;
Whether all of, or more behind-a:
Thanks, freest, freshest, fair Ellinda.
Thanks for my visit not disdaining,   15
Or, at the least, thanks for your feigning;
For if your mercy door were lock'd well,
I should be justly soundly knock'd well,
'Cause that in dogg'rel I did mutter
Not one rhyme to you from dam-Rotter.   20

Next beg I to present my duty
To pregnant sister in prime beauty,
Whom well I deem, ere few months elder,
Will take out Hans from pretty kelder;
And to the sweetly fair Mabella,   25
A match that vies with Arabella;
In each respect but the misfortune,
Fortune, Fate, I thee importune.

Nor must I pass the lovely Alice,
Whose health I 'd quaff in golden chalice;   30
But since that fate hath made me neuter,
I only can in beaker pewter.
But who 'd forget, or yet left unsung,
The doughty acts of George the young son,
Who yesterday, to save his sister,   35
Had slain the snake, had he not miss'd her?
But I shall leave him till a nag on
He gets to prosecute the dragon;
And then with help of sun and taper,
Fill with his deeds twelve reams of paper,   40
That Amadis, Sir Guy and Topaz
With his fleet neigher shall keep no pace.
      But now to close all I must switch hard,
        Servant ever,
                              Lovelace Richard.

SONNET

TO GENERAL GORING, AFTER THE PACIFICATION AT BERWICK

A la Chabot

Now the peace is made at the foe's rate,
Whilst men of arms to kettles their old helms translate,
And drink in casks of honourable plate:
      In ev'ry hand a cup be found,
        That from all hearts a health may sound   5
To Goring! to Goring! see 't go round.

He whose glories shine so brave and high,
That captive they in triumph lead each ear and eye,
      Claiming uncombated the victory,

And from the earth to heav'n rebound,　　　　　　10
　Fix'd there eternal as this round,
To Goring! to Goring! see him crown'd.

To his lovely bride in love with scars,
Whose eyes wound deep in peace, as doth his sword in wars;
　They shortly must depose the Queen of Stars:　　　15
　　Her cheeks the morning blushes give,
　　And the benighted world reprieve:
To Lettice! to Lettice! let her live.

Give me scorching heat, thy heat, dry sun,
That to this pair I may drink off an ocean,　　　　　20
　Yet leave my grateful thirst unquench'd, undone;
　　Or a full bowl of heav'nly wine,
　　In which dissolved stars should shine:
To the couple! to the couple! th' are divine.

SIR THOMAS WORTLEY'S SONNET ANSWERED

The Sonnet

No more
Thou little winged Archer, now no more
　　As heretofore,
Thou mayst pretend within my breast to bide,
　　No more;　　　　5
Since cruel death of dearest Lindamore
　　Hath me depriv'd,
I bid adieu to love, and all the world beside.

[.　　.　　.　　.]

　　Go, go;　　　　10
Lay by thy quiver and unbend thy bow,
　　Poor silly foe,
Thou spend'st thy shafts but at my breast in vain;
　　Since Death
My heart hath with a fatal icy dart　　　　15
　　Already slain,
Thou canst not ever hope to warm her wound,
　　Or wound it o'er again.

THE ANSWER

AGAIN,
Thou witty cruel wanton, now again,
    Through ev'ry vein
Hurl all your lightning, and strike ev'ry dart,
    Again;   5
Before I feel this pleasing, pleasing pain
    I have no heart,
Nor can I live but sweetly murder'd with
    So dear, so dear a smart.

        Then fly,   10
And kindle all your torches at her eye,
    To make me die
Her martyr, and put on my robe of flame:
    So I,
Advanced on my blazing wings on high,   15
    In death became
Enthron'd a star, and ornament unto
    Her glorious, glorious name.

A GUILTLESS LADY IMPRISONED; AFTER, PENANCED

SONG

HARK, fair one, how whate'er here is
    Doth laugh and sing at thy distress;
Not out of hate to thy relief,
    But joy t' enjoy thee, though in grief.

See! that which chains you you chain here;   5
    The prison is thy prisoner;
How much thy jailor's keeper art!
    He binds your hands, but you his heart.

The gyves to rase so smooth a skin
    Are so unto themselves within;   10
But blest to kiss so fair an arm,
    Haste to be happy with that harm,

And play about thy wanton wrist
    As if in them thou so wert dress'd;
But if too rough, too hard they press,   15
    Oh they but closely, closely kiss.

And as thy bare feet bless the way,
  The people do not mock, but pray,
And call thee, as amaz'd they run,
  Instead of prostitute, a nun.   20

The merry torch burns with desire
  To kindle the eternal fire,
And lightly dances in thine eyes
  To tunes of epithalamies.

The sheet 's ti'd ever to thy waist,   25
  How thankful to be so embrac'd!
And see! thy very very bands
  Are bound to thee, to bind such hands.

UPON THE CURTAIN OF LUCASTA'S PICTURE IT WAS THUS WROUGHT

Oh stay that covetous hand; first turn all eye,
All depth and mind; then mystically spy
Her soul's fair picture, her fair soul's, in all
So truly copi'd from th' original,
That you will swear her body by this law   5
Is but its shadow, as this its;—now draw.

TO HIS DEAR BROTHER COLONEL F[RANCIS] L[OVELACE] IMMODERATELY MOURNING MY BROTHER'S UNTIMELY DEATH AT CARMARTHEN

If tears could wash the ill away,
A pearl for each wet bead I 'd pay;
But as dew'd corn the fuller grows,
So water'd eyes but swell our woes.

One drop another calls, which still   5
(Grief adding fuel) doth distil;
Too fruitful of herself is anguish,
We need no cherishing to languish.

Coward Fate degen'rate man
Like little children uses when   10
He whips us first until we weep,
Then 'cause we still a-weeping keep.

Then from thy firm self never swerve;
Tears fat the grief that they should sterve;
Iron decrees of Destiny   15
Are ne'er wip'd out with a wet eye.

But this way you may gain the field,
Oppose but sorrow, and 'twill yield;
One gallant thorough-made resolve
Doth starry influence dissolve.   20

AN ELEGY

ON THE DEATH OF MISTRESS CASSANDRA COTTON, ONLY SISTER TO MR. C[HARLES] COTTON

HITHER with hallow'd steps as is the ground
That must enshrine this saint, with looks profound,
And sad aspects as the dark veils you wear,
Virgins oppress'd, draw gently, gently near;
Enter the dismal chancel of this room,   5
Where each pale guest stands fix'd a living tomb,
With trembling hands help to remove this earth
To its last death and first victorious birth:
Let gums and incense fume who are at strife
To enter th' hearse and breathe in it new life;   10
Mingle your steps with flowers as you go,
Which as they haste to fade will speak your woe.

And when y' have plac'd your tapers on her urn,
How poor a tribute 'tis to weep and mourn!
That flood the channel of your eyelids fills,   15
When you lose trifles, or what 's less, your wills.
If you 'll be worthy of these obsequies,
Be blind unto the world, and drop your eyes;
Waste and consume, burn downward as this fire
That 's fed no more, so willingly expire;   20
Pass through the cold and obscure narrow way,
Then light your torches at the spring of day,
There with her triumph in your victory.
Such joy alone and such solemnity
Becomes this funeral of virginity.   25

   Or, if you faint to be so blest, oh hear!
If not to die, dare but to live like her:
Dare to live virgins till the honour'd age
Of thrice fifteen calls matrons on the stage,
Whilst not a blemish or least stain is seen   30
On your white robe 'twixt fifty and fifteen;
But as it in your swathing-bands was given,
Bring 't in your winding-sheet unsoil'd to heav'n.
Dare to do purely, without compact good,
Or herald, [though] by no one understood   35
But him who now in thanks bows either knee
For th' early benefit and secrecy.
Dare to affect a serious holy sorrow,
To which delights of palaces are narrow,
And lasting as their smiles, dig you a room   40
Where practise the probation of your tomb,
With ever-bended knees and piercing pray'r
Smooth the rough pass through craggy earth to air;
Flame there as lights, that shipwrack'd mariners
May put in safely, and secure their fears,   45
Who, adding to your joys, now owe you theirs.

   Virgins, if thus you dare but courage take
To follow her in life, else through this lake
Of Nature wade, and break her earthly bars,
Y' are fix'd with her upon a throne of stars   50
Arched with a pure heav'n crystalline,
Where round you Love and Joy for ever shine.

   But you are dumb, as what you do lament,
More senseless than her very monument
Which at your weakness weeps—spare that vain tear,   55
Enough to burst the rev'rend sepulchre:
Rise and walk home; there groaning prostrate fall,
And celebrate your own sad funeral;
For howsoe'er you move, may hear or see,
You are more dead and buried than she.   60

LUCASTA'S WORLD

EPODE

Cold as the breath of winds that blow
To silver shot descending snow,
    Lucasta sigh'd; when she did close
      The world in frosty chains!
    And then a frown to rubies froze   5
      The blood boil'd in our veins,
Yet cooled not the heat her sphere
Of beauties first had kindled there.

Then mov'd, and with a sudden flame
Impatient to melt all again,   10
    Straight from her eyes she lightning hurl'd,
      And earth in ashes mourns;
    The sun his blaze denies the world,
      And in her lustre burns,
Yet warmed not the hearts her nice   15
Disdain had first congeal'd to ice.

And now her tears nor griev'd desire
Can quench this raging, pleasing fire;
    Fate but one way allows: behold
      Her smiles' divinity!   20
    They fann'd this heat, and thaw'd that cold,
      So fram'd up a new sky.
Thus earth, from flames and ice repriev'd,
E'er since hath in her sunshine liv'd.

TO A LADY THAT DESIRED ME I WOULD BEAR MY PART WITH HER IN A SONG

MADAM A. L.

This is the prettiest motion:
Madam, th' alarums of a drum
That calls your lord, set to your cries,
To mine are sacred symphonies.

    What though 'tis said I have a voice;   5
I know 'tis but that hollow noise
Which, as it through my pipe doth speed,
Bitterns do carol through a reed;

In the same key with monkeys' jigs,
Or dirges of proscribed pigs, 10
Or the soft serenades above
In calm of night, when cats make love.

Was ever such a consort seen!
Fourscore and fourteen with fourteen!
Yet sooner they 'll agree, one pair, 15
Than we in our Spring-Winter air;
They may embrace, sigh, kiss the rest:
Our breath knows naught but east and west.
Thus have I heard to children's cries
The fair nurse 'stil such lullabies 20
That well all said, for what there lay,
The pleasure did the sorrow pay.

Sure there 's another way to save
Your fancy, madam; that 's to have
('Tis but petitioning kind Fate) 25
The organs sent to Billingsgate;
Where they to that soft murm'ring choir
Shall reach you all you can admire!
Or do but hear how love-bang Kate
In pantry dark, for fridge of meat, 30
With edge of steel the square wood shapes,
And *Dido* to it chants or scrapes.
The merry Phaëton o' th' car
You 'll vow makes a melodious jar;
Sweeter and sweeter whistleth he 35
To unanointed axletree;
Such swift notes he and 's wheels do run;
For me, I yield him Phœbus' son.

Say, fair commandress, can it be
You should ordain a mutiny? 40
For where I howl, all accents fall
As kings' harangues to one and all.

Ulysses' art is now withstood,
You ravish both with sweet and good;
Saint siren, sing, for I dare hear, 45
But when I ope, oh stop your ear!

Far less be 't emulation
To pass me or in trill or tone,
Like the thin throat of Philomel,
And the smart lute, who should excel,   50
As if her soft chords should begin,
And strive for sweetness with the pin.

Yet can I music too; but such
As is beyond all voice or touch;
My mind can in fair order chime,   55
Whilst my true heart still beats the time;
My soul so full of harmony,
That it with all parts can agree:
If you wind up to the highest fret,
It shall descend an eight from it,   60
And when you shall vouchsafe to fall,
Sixteen above you it shall call,
And yet so disassenting one,
They both shall meet an unison.

Come then, bright cherubin, begin!   65
My loudest music is within:
Take all notes with your skilful eyes,
Hark if mine do not sympathize!
Sound all my thoughts, and see express'd
The tablature of my large breast,   70
Then you 'll admit that I too can
Music above dead sounds of man;
Such as alone doth bless the spheres,
Not to be reach'd with human ears.

VALIANT LOVE

Now fie upon that everlasting life I die!
    She hates! Ah me! It makes me mad;
As if Love fir'd his torch at a moist eye,
    Or with his joys e'er crown'd the sad!
Oh let me live and shout, when I fall on!   5
    Let me ev'n triumph in the first attempt!
Love's duellist from conquest 's not exempt,
When his fair murd'ress shall not gain one groan,
And he expire ev'n in ovation.

Let me make my approach, when I lie down   10
    With counter-wrought and traverse eyes;
With peals of confidence batter the town:
    Had ever beggar yet the keys?
No, I will vary storms with sun and wind;
    Be rough, and offer calm condition,   15
    March in, and pray 't, or starve the garrison.
Let her make sallies hourly, yet I 'll find,
Though all beat off, she 's to be undermin'd.

Then may it please Your Little Excellence
    Of Hearts t' ordain, by sound of lips,   20
That henceforth none in tears dare love commence
    (Her thoughts i' th' full, his in th' eclipse),
On pain of having 's lance broke on her bed,
    That he be branded all free beauties' slave,
    And his own hollow eyes be doom'd his grave: 25
Since in your host that coward ne'er was fed,
Who to his prostrate e'er was prostrated.

THE APOSTACY OF ONE AND BUT ONE LADY

THAT frantic error I adore,
    And am confirm'd the earth turns round;
Now satisfied o'er and o'er,
    As rolling waves so flows the ground,
And as her neighbour reels the shore: 5
    Find such a woman says she loves,
    She 's that fix'd heav'n which never moves.

In marble, steel, or porphyry
    Who carves or stamps his arms or face,
Looks it by rust or storm must die: 10
    This woman's love no time can rase,
Hard'ned like ice in the sun's eye,
    Or your reflection in a glass,
    Which keeps possession though you pass.

We not behold a watch's hand   15
    To stir, nor plants or flowers to grow:
Must we infer that this doth stand,
    And therefore that those do not blow?

This she acts calmer; like heav'n's brand
  The steadfast lightning, slow love's dart,   20
She kills but ere we feel the smart.

Oh, she is constant as the wind
  That revels in an ev'ning's air!
Certain, as ways unto the blind,
  More real than her flatt'ries are;   25
Gentle, as chains that honour bind,
  More faithful than an Hebrew Jew,
But as the Devil not half so true.

TO MY LADY H.

ODE

TELL me, ye subtle judges in love's treasury,
Inform me which hath most enrich'd mine eye,
This diamond's greatness, or its clarity?

Ye cloudy spark-lights, whose vast multitude
Of fires are harder to be found than view'd,   5
Wait on this star in her first magnitude.

Calmly or roughly, ah! she shines too much!
That now I lie (her influence is such)
Crush'd with too strong a hand, or soft a touch.

Lovers, beware! a certain, double harm   10
Waits your proud hopes, her looks' all-killing charm,
Guarded by her as true victorious arm.

Thus with her eyes brave Tamyris spake dread,
Which when the king's dull breast not entered,
Finding she could not look, she strook him dead.   15

LA BELLA BONA-ROBA

I CANNOT tell who loves the skeleton
Of a poor marmoset, naught but bone, bone:
Give me a nakedness with her clothes on.

Such whose white-satin upper coat of skin,
Cut upon velvet rich incarnadin,   5
Has yet a body (and of flesh) within.

Sure it is meant good husbandry in men,
Who do incorporate with aëry lean,
T' repair their sides, and get their rib again.

Hard hap unto that huntsman that decrees   10
Fat joys for all his sweat, whenas he sees,
After his 'say, naught but his keeper's fees.

Then Love, I beg, when next thou tak'st thy bow,
Thy angry shafts, and dost heart-chasing go,
Pass rascal deer, strike me the largest doe.   15

A LA BOURBON

*Done moy plus de pitiè ou plus de cruaulté, car sans ce Je ne
puis pas vivre, ne morir*

DIVINE destroyer, pity me no more,
  Or else more pity me;
Give me more love, ah quickly give me more,
  Or else more cruelty!
    For left thus as I am,   5
    My heart is ice and flame;
  And languishing thus I
  Can neither live nor die!

Your glories are eclips'd, and hidden in the grave
  Of this indifferency;   10
And, Celia, you can neither altars have,
  Nor I a deity:
    They are aspects divine
    That still or smile or shine,
  Or, like th' offended sky,   15
  Frown death immediately.

THE FAIR BEGGAR

COMMANDING asker, if it be
  Pity that you fain would have,
Then I turn beggar unto thee,
  And ask the thing that thou dost crave;
I will suffice thy hungry need,   5
So thou wilt but my fancy feed.

In all ill years was 't ever known
  On so much beauty such a dearth,
Which, in that thrice-bequeathed gown,
  Looks like the sun eclips'd with earth,　　10
Like gold in canvas, or with dirt
Unsoiled ermines close begirt?

Yet happy he, that can but taste
  This whiter skin, who thirsty is;
Fools dote on satin motions lac'd,　　15
  The gods go naked in their bliss;
At th' barrel's head there shines the vine,
There only relishes the wine.

There quench my heat, and thou shalt sup
  Worthy the lips that it must touch;　　20
Nectar from out the starry cup,
  I beg thy breath not half so much:
So both our wants suppli'd shall be,
You 'll give for love, I charity.

Cheap then are pearl-embroideries,　　25
  That not adorn, but clouds thy waist;
Thou shalt be cloth'd above all price,
  If thou wilt promise me embrac'd;
We 'll ransack neither chest or shelf,
I 'll cover thee with mine own self.　　30

But, cruel, if thou dost deny
  This necessary alms to me,
What soft-soul'd man but with his eye
  And hand will hence be shut to thee?
Since all must judge you more unkind:　　35
I starve your body you my mind.

TO ELLINDA

UPON HIS LATE RECOVERY. A PARADOX

How I grieve that I am well!
  All my health was in my sickness;
Go then, Destiny, and tell
  Very death is in this quickness.

Such a fate rules over me,   5
    That I glory when I languish,
And do bless the remedy
    That doth feed, not quench my anguish.

'Twas a gentle warmth that ceas'd
    In the vizard of a fever;   10
But I fear, now I am eas'd,
    All the flames, since I must leave her.

Joys, though wither'd, circled me,
    When unto her voice inured,
Like those who by harmony   15
    Only can be throughly cured.

Sweet, sure, was that malady,
    Whilst the pleasant angel hover'd,
Which ceasing, they are all, as I,
    Angry that they are recover'd.   20

And as men in hospitals,
    That are maim'd, are lodg'd and dined;
But when once their danger falls,
    Ah, th' are healed to be pined!

Fainting so, I might before   25
    Sometime have the leave to hand her,
But lusty, am beat out of door,
    And for love compell'd to wander.

AMYNTOR, FROM BEYOND THE SEA, TO ALEXIS

A DIALOGUE

Amyntor.   ALEXIS! ah Alexis! can it be,
                  Though so much wet and dry
                      Doth drown our eye,
              Thou keep'st thy winged voice from me?

Alexis.   Amyntor, a profounder sea, I fear,   5
                  Hath swallow'd me; where now
                      My arms do row,
              I float i' th' ocean of a tear.

Lucasta weeps lest I look back and tread
　　Your wat'ry land again.   10
Amyntor.　　　　I 'd through the rain;
Such show'rs are quickly overspread.

Conceive how joy, after this short divorce,
　　Will circle her with beams,
　　　　When, like your streams,   15
You shall roll back with kinder force,

And call the helping winds to vent your thought.
Alexis.　　　Amyntor!　Chloris! where,
　　　　Or in what sphere
Say, may that glorious fair be sought?   20

Amyntor. She 's now the centre of these arms e'er blest,
　　Whence may she never move,
　　　　Till Time and Love
Haste to their everlasting rest.

Alexis.　Ah subtle swain! doth not my flame rise high   25
　　As yours, and burn as hot?
　　　　Am not I shot
With the selfsame artillery?

And can I breathe without her air? *Amynt.* Why then,
　　From thy tempestuous earth,   30
　　　　Where blood and dearth
Reign 'stead of kings, agen

Waft thyself over, and lest storms from far
　　Arise, bring in our sight
　　　　The sea's delight,   35
Lucasta, that bright Northern star.

Alexis.　But as we cut the rugged deep, I fear
　　The green god stops his fell
　　　　Chariot of shell,
And smoothes the main to ravish her.   40

Amyntor. Oh no, the Prince of Waters' fires are done;
　　He as his empire old,
　　　　And rivers, cold;
His queen now runs abed to th' sun;

But all his treasure he shall ope that day: 45
    Tritons shall sound, his fleet
        In silver meet,
And to her their rich off'rings pay.

Alexis.   We fly, Amyntor, not amaz'd how sent
        By water, earth, or air;   50
            Or if with her
            By fire, ev'n there
I move in mine own element.

A LADY WITH A FALCON ON HER FIST

TO THE HONOURABLE MY COUSIN A[NNE] L[OVELACE]

THIS queen of prey (now prey to you),
    Fast to that perch of ivory
In silver chains and silken clew,
    Hath now made full thy victory:

The swelling admiral of the dread   5
    Cold deep burnt in thy flames, O fair!
Was 't not enough, but thou must lead
    Bound too the princess of the air?

Unarm'd of wings and scaly oar,
    Unhappy crawler on the land,   10
To what heav'n fli'st? div'st to what shore,
    That her brave eyes do not command?

Ascend the chariot of the Sun,
    From her bright pow'r to shelter thee:
Her captive, fool, outgazes him;   15
    Ah what lost wretches then are we!

Now, proud usurpers on the right
    Of sacred beauty, hear your doom;
Recant your sex, your mast'ry, might;
    Lower you cannot be o'ercome: 20

Repent ye e'er nam'd he or head,
    For y' are in falcons' monarchy,
And in that just dominion bred,
    In which the nobler is the she.

CALLING LUCASTA FROM HER RETIREMENT

ODE

FROM the dire monument of thy black room,
Where now that vestal flame thou dost entomb,
As in the inmost cell of all earth's womb,

Sacred Lucasta, like the pow'rful ray
Of heavenly truth, pass this Cimmerian way,   5
Whilst all the standards of your beams display.

Arise, and climb our whitest, highest hill;
There your sad thoughts with joy and wonder fill,
And see seas calm as earth, earth as your will.

Behold how lightning like a taper flies,   10
And gilds your chari't, but ashamed dies,
Seeing itself outglori'd by your eyes.

Threat'ning and boist'rous tempests gently bow,
And to your steps part in soft paths, when now
There nowhere hangs a cloud, but on your brow;   15

No show'rs but 'twixt your lids, nor gelid snow,
But what your whiter, chaster breast doth owe,
Whilst winds in chains colder your sorrow blow.

Shrill trumpets now do only sound to eat,
Artillery hath loaden ev'ry dish with meat,   20
And drums at ev'ry health alarums beat.

All things, Lucasta! but, Lucasta! call;
Trees borrow tongues, waters in accents fall,
The air doth sing, and fire 's musical.

Awake from the dead vault in which you dwell,   25
All 's loyal here, except your thoughts rebel,
Which, so let loose, often their gen'ral quell.

See! she obeys! by all obeyed thus;
No storms, heats, colds, no souls contentious,
Nor civil war is found—I mean, to us.   30

Lovers and angels, though in heav'n they show
And see the woes and discords here below,
What they not feel must not be said to know.

ARAMANTHA
A PASTORAL

Up with the jolly bird of light,
Who sounds his third retreat to night,
Fair Aramantha from her bed
Ashamed starts, and rises red
As the carnation-mantled morn,   5
Who now the blushing robe doth spurn,
And puts on angry grey, whilst she,
The envy of a deity,
Arrays her limbs, too rich indeed
To be enshrin'd in such a weed;   10
Yet lovely 'twas, and strait, but fit,
Not made for her, but she to it:
By nature it sate close and free,
As the just bark unto the tree:
Unlike love's martyrs of the town,   15
All day imprison'd in a gown,
Who, rack'd in silk 'stead of a dress,
Are clothed in a frame or press,
And with that liberty and room
The dead expatiate in a tomb.   20
    No cabinets with curious washes,
Bladders, and perfumed plashes,
No venom-temper'd water 's here,
Mercury is banished this sphere:
Her pail 's all this, in which wet glass   25
She both doth cleanse and view her face.
    Far hence all Iberian smells,
Hot amulets, pomander spells;
Fragrant gales, cool air, the fresh
And natural odour of her flesh   30
Proclaim her sweet from th' womb as morn.
Those colour'd things were made not born,
Which, fix'd within their narrow straits,
Do look like their own counterfeits.
So like the Provence rose she walk'd,   35
Flower'd with blush, with verdure stalk'd;
Th' officious wind her loose hair curls,
The dew her happy linen purls,
But wets a tress, which instantly
Sol with a crisping beam doth dry.   40

Into the garden is she come,
Love and delight's Elysium;
If ever earth show'd all her store,
View her discolour'd budding floor;
Here her glad eye she largely feeds,   45
And stands, 'mongst them, as they 'mong weeds;
The flowers, in their best array,
As to their queen their tribute pay,
And freely to her lap proscribe
A daughter out of ev'ry tribe: 50
Thus as she moves, they all bequeath
At once the incense of their breath.

The noble heliotropion
Now turns to her, and knows no sun;
And as her glorious face doth vary,   55
So opens loyal golden Mary;
Who, if but glanced from her sight,
Straight shuts again as it were night.

The violet (else lost i' th' heap)
Doth spread fresh purple for each step;   60
With whose humility possess'd,
Sh' enthrones the poor girl in her breast.
The July-flow'r that hereto thriv'd,
Knowing herself no longer liv'd,
But for one look of her upheaves,   65
Then 'stead of tears straight sheds her leaves.

Now the rich-robed tulip, who
Clad all in tissue close doth woo
Her, (sweet to th' eye but smelling sour),
She gathers to adorn her bower.   70
But the proud honeysuckle spreads
Like a pavilion her heads,
Contemns the wanting commonalty,
That but to two ends useful be,
And to her lips thus aptly plac'd,   75
With smell and hue presents her taste.

So all their due obedience pay,
Each thronging to be in her way:
Fair Aramantha with her eye
Thanks those that live, which else would die;   80
The rest, in silken fetters bound,
By crowning her are crown and crown'd.

And now the sun doth higher rise,

Our Flora to the meadow hies;
The poor distressed heifers low,   85
And as sh' approacheth gently bow,
Begging her charitable leisure
To strip them of their milky treasure.

Out of the yeomanry o' th' herd,
With grave aspect, and feet prepar'd,   90
A rev'rend lady cow draws near,
Bids Aramantha welcome here;
And from her privy purse lets fall
A pearl or two, which seem to call
This adorn'd, adored fairy   95
To the banquet of her dairy.

Soft Aramantha weeps to see
'Mongst men such inhumanity,
That those who do receive in hay,
And pay in silver twice a day,   100
Should, by their cruel barb'rous theft,
Be both of that and life bereft.

But 'tis decreed, whene'er this dies,
That she shall fall a sacrifice
Unto the gods, since those that trace   105
Her stem show 'tis a godlike race,
Descending in an even line
From heifers and from steers divine,
Making the honour'd extract full
In Iö and Europa's bull.   110
She was the largest, goodliest beast
That ever mead or altar blest;
Round as her udder, and more white
Than is the Milky Way in night;
Her full broad eye did sparkle fire,   115
Her breath was sweet as kind desire,
And in her beauteous crescent shone,
Bright as the argent-horned moon.

But see! this whiteness is obscure,
Cynthia spotted, she impure;   120
Her body writhell'd, and her eyes
Departing lights at obsequies;
Her lowing hot to the fresh gale
Her breath perfumes the field withal;
To those two suns that ever shine,   125
To those plump parts she doth enshrine,

To th' hovering snow of either hand,
That love and cruelty command.

After the breakfast on her teat,
She takes her leave o' th' mournful neat,   130
Who, by her touch'd, now prize their life,
Worthy alone the hallow'd knife.

Into the neighb'ring wood she 's gone,
Whose roof defies the telltale sun,
And locks out ev'ry prying beam;   135
Close by the lips of a clear stream
She sits and entertains her eye
With the moist crystal, and the fry
With burnish'd silver mail'd, whose oars
Amazed still make to the shores.   140
What need she other bait or charm
But look? or angle, but her arm?
The happy captive, gladly ta'en,
Sues ever to be slave in vain,
Who instantly, confirm'd in 's fears,   145
Hastes to his element of tears.

From hence her various windings rove
To a well order'd stately grove;
This is the palace of the wood,
And court o' th' royal oak, where stood   150
The whole nobility, the pine,
Straight ash, tall fir, and wanton vine,
The proper cedar, and the rest:
Here she her deeper senses bless'd;
Admires great Nature in this pile   155
Floor'd with green-velvet camomile,
Garnish'd with gems of unset fruit,
Suppli'd still with a self-recruit;
Her bosom wrought with pretty eyes
Of never-planted strawberries;   160
Where th' winged music of the air
Do richly feast, and for their fare,
Each evening in a silent shade,
Bestow a grateful serenade.

Thus, ev'n tired with delight,   165
Sated in soul and appetite;
Full of the purple plum and pear,
The golden apple with the fair
Grape, that mirth fain would have taught her,

And nuts which squirrels cracking brought her; 170
She softly lays her weary limbs,
Whilst gentle slumber now begins
To draw the curtains of her eye;
When straight awaken'd with a cry
And bitter groan, again reposes, 175
Again a deep sigh interposes.
And now she hears a trembling voice:
"Ah, can there aught on earth rejoice!
Why wears she this gay livery,
Not black as her dark entrails be? 180
Can trees be green, and to the air
Thus prostitute their flowing hair?
Why do they sprout, not wither'd die?
Must each thing live save wretched I?
Can days triumph in blue and red, 185
When both their light and life is fled?
Fly, joy, on wings of popinjays,
To courts of fools; there, as your plays,
Die, laugh'd at and forgot; whilst all
That 's good mourns at this funeral. 190
Weep, all ye Graces, and you sweet
Choir, that at the Hill inspir'd meet;
Love, put thy tapers out, that we
And th' world may seem as blind as thee;
And be, since she is lost (ah wound!) 195
Not heav'n itself by any found."
   Now, as a prisoner new cast,
Who sleeps in chains that night his last,
Next morn is wak'd with a reprieve,
And from his trance not dream bid live, 200
Wonders (his sense not having scope)
Who speaks, his friend or his false hope:
   So Aramantha heard, but fear
Dares not yet trust her tempting ear;
And as again her arms o' th' ground 205
Spread pillows for her head, a sound
More dismal makes a swift divorce,
And starts her thus: "Rage, Rapine, Force!
Ye blue-flam'd daughters o' th' Abyss,
Bring all your snakes, here let them hiss; 210
Let not a leaf its freshness keep;
Blast all their roots, and as you creep

And leave behind your deadly slime,
Poison the budding branch in 's prime;
Waste the proud bowers of this grove,   215
That fiends may dwell in it, and move
As in their proper hell, whilst she,
Above, laments this tragedy;
Yet pities not our fate.   O fair
Vow-breaker, now betroth'd to th' air,   220
Why by those laws did we not die,
As live but one, Lucasta! why——"
As he Lucasta nam'd, a groan
Strangles the fainting passing tone;
But as she heard, Lucasta smiles,   225
Posses her round; she 's slipp'd meanwhiles
Behind the blind of a thick bush,
When, each word temp'ring with a blush,
She gently thus bespake: "Sad swain,
If mates in woe do ease our pain,   230
Here 's one full of that antic grief
Which, stifled, would for ever live,
But told, expires; pray then, reveal
(To show our wound is half to heal)
What mortal nymph or deity   235
Bewail you thus?"   "Whoe'er you be,"
The shepherd sigh'd, "my woes I crave
Smother'd in me, I in my grave;
Yet be in show or truth a saint,
Or, fiend, breathe anthems, hear my plaint   240
For her and her breath's symphony,
Which now makes full the harmony
Above, and to whose voice the spheres
Listen, and call her music theirs.
This was I blest on earth with, so   245
As Druids amorous did grow
Jealous of both, for as one day
This star, as yet but set in clay,
By an embracing river lay,
They steep'd her in the hollow'd brook,   250
Which from her human nature took,
And straight to heaven with winged fear,
Thus ravish'd with her, ravish her."
     The nymph repli'd, "This holy rape
Became the gods, whose obscure shape   255

They cloth'd with light, whilst ill you grieve
Your better life should ever live,
And weep that she to whom you wish
What heav'n could give, has all its bliss;
Calling her angel here, yet be   260
Sad at this true divinity:
She 's for the altar not the skies,
Whom first you crown, then sacrifice.

"Fond man thus to a precipice
Aspires, till at the top his eyes   265
Have lost the safety of the plain,
Then begs of Fate the vales again."

The now confounded shepherd cries,
"Ye all-confounding Destinies!
How did you make that voice so sweet   270
Without that glorious form to it?
Thou sacred spirit of my dear,
Where'er thou hover'st o'er us, hear!
Imbark thee in the laurel tree,
And a new Phœbus follows thee,   275
Who, 'stead of all his burning rays,
Will strive to catch thee with his lays;
Or if within the orient vine,
Thou art both deity and wine;
But if thou takest the myrtle grove,   280
That Paphos is, thou Queen of Love,
And I thy swain who else must die
By no beasts, but thy cruelty.
But you are rougher than the wind:
Are souls on earth than heav'n more kind?   285
Imprison'd in mortality,
Lucasta would have answer'd me."

"Lucasta!" Aramantha said.
"Is she that virgin-star a maid,
Except her prouder livery,   290
In beauty poor, and cheap as I?
Whose glory like a meteor shone,
Or aëry apparition,
Admir'd a while but slighted known."

Fierce, as the chafed lion hies,   295
He rouses him, and to her flies,
Thinking to answer with his spear.
Now, as in war intestine, where,

I' th' mist of a black battle, each
Lays at his next, then makes a breach   300
Through th' entrails of another, whom
He sees nor knows when he did come,
Guided alone by rage and th' drum,
But stripping and impatient wild,
He finds too soon his only child: 305
    So our expiring desp'rate lover
Far'd, when amaz'd he did discover
Lucasta in this nymph; his sin
Darts the accursed javelin
'Gainst his own breast, which she puts by,   310
With a soft lip and gentle eye,
Then closes with him on the ground;
And now her smiles have heal'd his wound,
Alexis too again is found;
But not until those heavy crimes   315
She hath kiss'd off a thousand times,
Who, not contented with this pain,
Doth threaten to offend again.
    And now they gaze, and sigh, and weep,
Whilst each cheek doth the other's steep,   320
Whilst tongues as exorcis'd are calm;
Only the rhet'ric of the palm
Prevailing pleads, until at last,
They chain'd in one another fast,
Lucasta to him doth relate   325
Her various chance and diff'ring fate:
How chas'd by Hydraphil, and track'd,
The num'rous foe to Philanact,
Who, whilst they for the same things fight,
As bards' decrees and druids' rite,   330
For safeguard of their proper joys
And shepherd's freedom, each destroys
The glory of this Sicily;
Since, seeking thus the remedy,
They fancy (building on false ground)   335
The means must them and it confound,
Yet are resolv'd to stand or fall,
And win a little or lose all.
    From this sad storm of fire and blood
She fled to this yet living wood;   340
Where she 'mongst savage beasts doth find

Herself more safe than humankind.
Then she relates how Cælia,
The Lady here, strips her array,
And girdles her in homespun bays,   345
Then makes her conversant in lays
Of birds, and swains more innocent,
That ken not guile or courtshipment.

Now walks she to her bow'r to dine
Under a shade of eglantine,   350
Upon a dish of Nature's cheer,
Which both grew dress'd and serv'd up there;
That done, she feasts her smell with posies
Pluck'd from the damask cloth of roses,
Which there continually doth stay,   355
And only frost can take away;
Then wagers which hath most content,
Her eye, ear, hand, her gust or scent.

Entranc'd Alexis sees and hears,
As walking above all the spheres;   360
Knows and adores this, and is wild
Until with her he live thus mild.
So that which to his thoughts he meant
For loss of her a punishment,
His arms hung up and his sword broke,   365
His ensigns folded, he betook
Himself unto the humble crook;
And for a full reward of all,
She now doth him her shepherd call,
And in a see of flow'rs instal;   370
Then gives her faith immediately,
Which he returns religiously;
Both vowing in her peaceful cave
To make their bridal-bed and grave.

But the true joy this pair conceiv'd,   375
Each from the other first bereav'd,
And then found, after such alarms
Fast pinion'd in each other's arms,
Ye panting virgins, that do meet
Your loves within their winding-sheet,   380
Breathing and constant still ev'n there;
Or souls their bodies in yon' sphere,
Or angels men return'd from hell,
And separated minds can tell.

TO LUCASTA: HER RESERVED LOOKS

Lucasta, frown and let me die,
    But smile and see I live;
The sad indifference of your eye
    Both kills and doth reprieve.
You hide our fate within its screen,   5
    We feel our judgment ere we hear:
So in one picture I have seen
    An angel here, the Devil there.

LUCASTA LAUGHING

Hark how she laughs aloud,
    Although the world put on its shroud;
Wept at by the fantastic crowd,
    Who cry, One drop let fall
From her might save the universal ball.   5
        She laughs again
        At our ridiculous pain;
    And at our merry misery
        She laughs until she cry.
            Sages, forbear   10
            That ill-contrived tear,
            Although your fear
Doth barricado hope from your soft ear.
That which still makes her mirth to flow
    Is our sinister-handed woe,   15
Which downwards on its head doth go;
    And ere that it is sown, doth grow.
        This makes her spleen contract,
            And her just pleasure feast;
        For the unjustest act   20
            Is still the pleasant'st jest.

SONG

Strive not, vain lover, to be fine,
    Thy silk 's the silkworm's, and not thine;
You lessen to a fly your mistress' thought,
To think it may be in a cobweb caught.

What though her thin transparent lawn   5
Thy heart in a strong net hath drawn:
Not all the arms the God of Fire e'er made
Can the soft bulwarks of nak'd Love invade.

Be truly fine, then, and yourself dress
In her fair soul's immac'late glass: 10
Then by reflection you may have the bliss
Perhaps to see what a true fineness is,
    When all your gawderies will fit
    Those only that are poor in wit:
She that a clinquant outside doth adore,   15
Dotes on a gilded statue, and no more.

IN ALLUSION TO THE FRENCH SONG, N'ENTENDEZ VOUS PAS CE LANGUAGE

Chorus.   Then understand you not, fair choice,
          This language without tongue or voice ?

        How often have my tears
        Invaded your soft ears,
        And dropp'd their silent chimes
        A thousand thousand times,   5
        Whilst Echo did your eyes,
        And sweetly sympathize;
        But that the wary lid
        Their sluices did forbid!   10

Chorus.   Then understand you not, fair choice,
          This language without tongue or voice ?

        My arms did plead my wound,
        Each in the other bound;
        Volleys of sighs did crowd,   15
        And ring my griefs aloud;
        Groans, like a cannon ball,
        Batter'd the marble wall,
        That the kind neighb'ring grove
        Did mutiny for love.   20

Chorus.   Then understand you not, fair choice,
          This language without tongue or voice ?

The rhet'ric of my hand
Woo'd you to understand;
Nay, in our silent walk   25
My very feet would talk,
My knees were eloquent,
And spake the love I meant;
But deaf unto that air,
They, bent, would fall in prayer.   30

Chorus.   *Yet understand you not, fair choice;*
This language without tongue or voice ?

No?   Know then, I would melt
On every limb I felt,
And on each naked part   35
Spread my expanded heart,
That not a vein of thee
But should be fill'd with me;
Whilst on thine own down I
Would tumble, pant, and die.   40

Chorus.   *You understand not this, fair choice ;*
This language wants both tongue and voice.

NIGHT

TO LUCASTA

NIGHT! loathed jailor of the lock'd-up sun,
    And tyrant-turnkey on committed day,
Bright eyes lie fetter'd in thy dungeon,
    And heaven itself doth thy dark wards obey:
        Thou dost arise our living hell,   5
        With thee groans, terrors, furies dwell,
        Until Lucasta doth awake,
And with her beams these heavy chains off shake.

Behold, with opening her almighty lid,
Bright eyes break rolling and with lustre spread,   10
    And captive Day his chariot mounted is;
        Night to her proper hell is beat,
        And screwed to her ebon seat;
        Till th' earth with play oppressed lies,
And draws again the curtains of her eyes.   15

But bondslave I know neither day nor night,
    Whether she murth'ring sleep or saving wake;
Now broil'd i' th' zone of her reflected light,
    Then froze, my icicles not sinews shake.
        Smile then, new Nature, your soft blast   20
        Doth melt our ice, and fires waste;
Whilst the scorch'd shiv'ring world new-born
Now feels it all the day one rising morn.

LOVE ENTHRON'D

ODE

In troth, I do myself persuade
    That the wild boy is grown a man;
And, all his childishness off laid,
    E'er since Lucasta did his fires fan.
        H' has left his apish jigs,   5
        And whipping hearts like gigs;
For t' other day I heard him swear
That Beauty should be crown'd in Honour's chair.

With what a true and heavenly state
    He doth his glorious darts dispense,   10
Now cleans'd from falsehood, blood, and hate,
    And newly tipp'd with innocence;
        Love Justice is become,
        And doth the cruel doom:
        Reversed is the old decree: 15
Behold! he sits enthron'd with majesty.

Enthroned in Lucasta's eye,
    He doth our faith and hearts survey;
Then measures them by sympathy,
    And each to th' other's breast convey;   20
        Whilst to his altars now
        The frozen Vestals bow,
    And strict Diana, too, doth go
A-hunting with his fear'd, exchanged bow.

Th' embracing seas and ambient air   25
    Now in his holy fires burn;
Fish couple, birds and beasts in pair
    Do their own sacrifices turn.

This is a miracle
That might religion swell: 30
But she, that these and their god awes,
Her crowned self submits to her own laws.

HER MUFF

'Twas not for some calm blessing to receive,
Thou didst thy polish'd hands in shagg'd furs weave;
   It were no blessing thus obtain'd;
   Thou rather wouldst a curse have gain'd,
Than let thy warm driven snow be ever stain'd. 5

Not that you feared the discolouring cold
Might alchemize their silver into gold;
   Nor could your ten white nuns so sin
   That you should thus penance them in,
Each in her coarse hair smock of discipline. 10

Nor hero-like, who on their crest still wore
A lion, panther, leopard, or a boar,
   To look their enemies in their hearse;
   Thou wouldst thy hand should deeper pierce,
And, in its softness rough, appear more fierce. 15

No, no, Lucasta, destiny decreed
That beasts to thee a sacrifice should bleed,
   And strip themselves to make you gay;
   For ne'er yet herald did display
A coat where sables upon ermine lay. 20

This for lay-lovers, that must stand at door,
Salute the threshold, and admire no more:
   But I, in my invention tough,
   Rate not this outward bliss enough,
But still contemplate must the hidden muff. 25

A BLACK PATCH ON LUCASTA'S FACE

DULL as I was, to think that a court fly
    Presum'd so near her eye,
      When 'twas th' industrious bee
Mistook her glorious face for Paradise,
To sum up all his chemistry of spice;   5
   With a brave pride and honour led,
    Near both her suns he makes his bed;
And, though a spark, struggles to rise as red;
        Then emulates the gay
        Daughter of day,   10
   Acts the romantic phœnix' fate:
When now, with all his sweets laid out in state,
   Lucasta scatters but one heat,
And all the aromatic pills do sweat,
And gums, calcin'd, themselves to powder beat,   15
        Which a fresh gale of air
        Conveys into her hair;
        Then chaf'd he 's set on fire,
And in these holy flames doth glad expire;
   And that black marble tablet there,   20
    So near her either sphere,
  Was plac'd: nor foil, nor ornament,
But the sweet little bee's large monument.

ANOTHER

As I beheld a winter's evening air,
Curl'd in her court false locks of living hair,
Butter'd with jessamine the sun left there,

Galliard and clinquant she appear'd to give,
A serenade or ball to us that grieve,   5
And teach us *à la mode* more gently live.

But as a Moor, who to her cheeks prefers
White spots t' allure her black idolaters,
Methought she look'd all o'er bepatch'd with stars;

Like the dark front of some Ethiopian queen   10
Veiled all o'er with gems of red, blue, green,
Whose ugly night seem'd masked with day's screen;

Whilst the fond people offer'd sacrifice
To sapphires 'stead of veins and arteries,
And bow'd unto the diamonds, not her eyes.   15

Behold Lucasta's face, how 't glows like noon!
A sun entire is her complexion,
And form'd of one whole constellation.

So gently shining, so serene, so clear,
Her look doth universal Nature cheer;   20
Only a cloud or two hangs here and there.

TO LUCASTA

I LAUGH and sing, but cannot tell
Whether the folly on 't sounds well;
          But then I groan,
          Methinks in tune,
Whilst Grief, Despair and Fear dance to the air   5
          Of my despised prayer.

A pretty antic Love does this,
Then strikes a galliard with a kiss;
          As in the end
          The chords they rend: 10
So you but with a touch from your fair hand
          Turn all to saraband.

TO LUCASTA

LIKE to the sent'nel stars, I watch all night;
For still the grand round of your light,
          And glorious breast,
          Awakes in me an east,
Nor will my rolling eyes e'er know a west.   5

Now on my down I 'm toss'd as on a wave,
  And my repose is made my grave;
      Fluttering I lie,
     Do beat myself and die,
But for a resurrection from your eye.   10

Ah, my fair murd'ress! dost thou cruelly heal,
  With various pains to make me well?
      Then let me be
     Thy cut anatomy,
And in each mangled part my heart you 'll see.   15

LUCASTA AT THE BATH

I' TH' autumn of a summer's day,
When all the winds got leave to play,
Lucasta, that fair ship, is launch'd,
And from its crust this almond blanch'd.

Blow then, unruly North-wind, blow,   5
Till in their holds your eyes you stow;
And swell your cheeks, bequeath chill death:
See! she hath smil'd thee out of breath!

Court, gentle Zephyr, court and fan
Her softer breast's carnation'd wan;   10
Your charming rhetoric of down
Flies scatter'd from before her frown.

Say, my white water-lily, say,
How is 't those warm streams break away,
Cut by thy chaste cold breast which dwells   15
Amidst them arm'd in icicles?

And the hot floods, more raging grown
In flames of thee than in their own,
In their distempers wildly glow,
And kiss thy pillar of fix'd snow.   20

No sulphur, through whose each blue vein
The thick and lazy currents strain,
Can cure the smarting, nor the fell
Blisters of love wherewith they swell.

These great physicians of the blind,   25
The lame, and fatal blains of Ind,
In every drop themselves now see
Speckled with a new leprosy.

As sick drinks are with old wine dash'd,
Foul waters too with spirits wash'd,   30
Thou griev'd, perchance, one tear let'st fall,
Which straight did purify them all.

And now is cleans'd enough the flood,
Which since runs clear, as doth thy blood;
Of the wet pearls uncrown thy hair,   35
And mantle thee with ermine air.

Lucasta, hail! fair conqueress
Of fire, air, earth, and seas;
Thou whom all kneel to, yet even thou
Wilt unto Love, thy captive, bow.   40

THE ANT

FORBEAR, thou great good husband, little ant;
  A little respite from thy flood of sweat!
Thou, thine own horse and cart, under this plant
  Thy spacious tent, fan thy prodigious heat;
Down with thy double load of that one grain!   5
It is a granary for all thy train.

Cease, large example of wise thrift, a while,
  (For thy example is become our law),
And teach thy frowns a seasonable smile:
  So Cato sometimes the nak'd Florals saw.   10
And, thou almighty foe, lay by thy sting,
Whilst thy unpaid musicians, crickets, sing.

Lucasta, she that holy makes the day,
  And 'stils new life in fields of feuillemorte,
Hath back restor'd their verdure with one ray,   15
  And with her eye bid all to play and sport.
Ant, to work still: age will thee truant call;
And to save now, th' art worse than prodigal.

Austere and cynic! not one hour t' allow,
   To lose with pleasure what thou got'st with pain,   20
But drive on sacred festivals thy plough,
   Tearing highways with thy o'ercharged wain.
Not all thy lifetime one poor minute live,
And thy o'erlabour'd bulk with mirth relieve?

Look up, then, miserable ant, and spy   25
   Thy fatal foes, for breaking of her law,
Hov'ring above thee: Madam—Margaret Pie,
   And her fierce servant, Meagre—Sir John Daw;
Thyself and storehouse now they do store up,
And thy whole harvest too within their crop.   30

Thus we unthrifty thrive within earth's tomb
   For some more rav'nous and ambitious jaw:
The grain in th' ant's, the ant's in the pie's womb.
   The pie in th' hawk's, the hawk's i' th' eagle's maw:
So scattering to hoard 'gainst a long day,   35
Thinking to save all, we cast all away.

THE SNAIL

WISE emblem of our politic world,
Sage snail, within thine own self curl'd,
Instruct me softly to make haste,
Whilst these my feet go slowly fast.
   Compendious snail! thou seem'st to me   5
Large Euclid's strict epitome;
And, in each diagram, dost fling
Thee from the point unto the ring.
A figure now triangular,
An oval now, and now a square;   10
And then a serpentine dost crawl,
Now a straight line, now crook'd, now all.
   Preventing rival of the day,
Th' art up and openest thy ray,
And ere the morn cradles the moon,   15
Th' art broke into a beauteous noon.
Then, when the sun sups in the deep,
Thy silver horns ere Cynthia's peep,
And thou, from thine own liquid bed,

New Phœbus, heav'st thy pleasant head.　　20
　Who shall a name for thee create,
Deep riddle of mysterious state?
Bold Nature, that gives common birth
To all products of seas and earth,
Of thee, as earthquakes, is afraid,　　25
Nor will thy dire deliv'ry aid.
　Thou thine own daughter, then, and sire,
That son and mother art entire,
That big still with thyself dost go,
And liv'st an aged embryo;　　30
That, like the cubs of India,
Thou from thyself a while dost play;
But frighted with a dog or gun,
In thine own belly thou dost run,
And as thy house was thine own womb,　　35
So thine own womb concludes thy tomb.
　But now I must, analys'd king,
Thy economic virtues sing;
Thou great staid husband still within,
Thou thee, that 's thine, dost discipline;　　40
And when thou art to progress bent,
Thou mov'st thyself and tenement,
As warlike Scythians travell'd, you
Remove your men and city too;
Then, after a sad dearth and rain,　　45
Thou scatterest thy silver train;
And when the trees grow nak'd and old,
Thou clothest them with cloth of gold,
Which from thy bowels thou dost spin,
And draw from the rich mines within.　　50
　Now hast thou chang'd thee saint, and made
Thyself a fane that 's cupola'd;
And in thy wreathed cloister thou
Walkest thine own grey friar too;
Strict, and lock'd up, th' art hood all o'er,　　55
And ne'er eliminat'st thy door.
On salads thou dost feed severe,
And 'stead of beads thou dropp'st a tear,
And when to rest each calls the bell,
Thou sleep'st within thy marble cell;　　60
Where, in dark contemplation plac'd,
The sweets of Nature thou dost taste;

Who now with Time thy days resolve,
And in a jelly thee dissolve:
Like a shot star, which doth repair 65
Upward, and rarefy the air.

ANOTHER

THE centaur, siren, I forgo,
Those have been sung, and loudly too;
Nor of the mixed sphinx I 'll write,
Nor the renown'd hermaphrodite:
Behold, this huddle doth appear 5
Of horses, coach, and charioteer;
That moveth him by traverse law,
And doth himself both drive and draw;
Then, when the sun the south doth win,
He baits him hot in his own inn. 10
I heard a grave and austere clerk
Resolv'd him pilot both and bark,
That, like the fam'd ship of Trevere,
Did on the shore himself lavere:
Yet the authentic do believe, 15
Who keep their judgment in their sleeve,
That he is his own double man,
And, sick, still carries his sedan:
Or that like dames i' th' land of Luyck,
He wears his everlasting huke. 20
But, banish'd, I admire his fate,
Since neither ostracism of state,
Nor a perpetual exile
Can force this virtue change his soil:
For wheresoever he doth go, 25
He wanders with his country too.

COURANTE MONSIEUR

THAT frown, Aminta, now hath drown'd
Thy bright front's power, and crown'd
Me that was bound.
No, no, deceived cruel, no;
Love's fiery darts, 5
Till tipp'd with kisses, never kindle hearts.

Adieu, weak beauteous tyrant, see!
Thy angry flames meant me
          Retort on thee:
For know, it is decreed, proud fair,   10
          I ne'er must die
By any scorching, but a melting eye.

A LOOSE SARABAND

Nay, prithee dear, draw nigher,
   Yet closer, nigher yet;
Here is a double fire,
   A dry one and a wet.
True lasting heavenly fuel   5
Puts out the vestal jewel,
When once we twining marry
Mad love with wild canary.

Off with that crowned Venice,
   Till all the house doth flame,   10
We 'll quench it straight in Rhenish,
   Or what we must not name.
Milk lightning still assuageth,
So when our fury rageth,
As th' only means to cross it,   15
We 'll drown it in love's posset.

Love never was well-willer
   Unto my nag or me,
Ne'er water'd us i' th' cellar,
   But the cheap buttery: 20
At th' head of his own barrels,
Where broach'd are all his quarrels,
Should a true noble master
Still make his guest his taster.

See all the world, how 't staggers,   25
   More ugly drunk than we,
As if far gone in daggers
   And blood it seem'd to be:
We drink our glass of roses,
Which naught but sweets discloses,   30
Then, in our loyal chamber,
Refresh us with love's amber.

Now tell me, thou fair cripple,
    That dumb canst scarcely see
Th' almightiness of tipple,   35
    And th' odds 'twixt thee and thee:
What of Elysium 's missing?
Still drinking and still kissing;
Adoring plump October:
Lord! what is man and sober?   40

Now is there such a trifle
    As honour, the fool's giant?
What is there left to rifle,
    When wine makes all parts pliant?
Let others glory follow,   45
In their false riches wallow,
And with their grief be merry:
Leave me but love and sherry.

THE FALCON

FAIR princess of the spacious air,
That hast vouchsaf'd acquaintance here,
With us are quarter'd below stairs,
That can reach heav'n with naught but pray'rs;
Who, when our activ'st wings we try,   5
Advance a foot into the sky;

    Bright heir t' th' bird imperial,
From whose avenging pennons fall
Thunder and lightning twisted spun;
Brave cousin-german to the sun,   10
That didst forsake thy throne and sphere,
To be an humble pris'ner here;
And, for a perch of her soft hand,
Resign the royal wood's command:

    How often wouldst thou shoot heav'n's arc,   15
Then mount thyself into a lark;
And after our short faint eyes call,
When now a fly, now naught at all;
Then stoop so swift unto our sense,
As thou wert sent intelligence!   20

Free beauteous slave, thy happy feet
In silver fetters varvels meet,
And trample on that noble wrist
The gods have kneel'd in vain t' have kiss'd.
But gaze not, bold deceived spy,   25
Too much o' th' lustre of her eye;
The sun thou dost outstare, alas!
Winks at the glory of her face.

Be safe then in thy velvet helm,
Her looks are calms that do o'erwhelm,   30
Than the Arabian bird more blest,
Chafe in the spicery of her breast,
And loose you in her breath, a wind
Sours the delicious gales of Ind.

But now a quill from thine own wing   35
I pluck, thy lofty fate to sing;
Whilst we behold the various fight
With mingled pleasure and affright,
The humbler hinds do fall to pray'r,
As when an army 's seen i' th' air,   40
And the prophetic spaniels run,
And howl thy epicedium.

The heron mounted doth appear
On his own Peg'sus a lancier,
And seems on earth, when he doth hut,   45
A proper halberdier on foot;
Secure i' th' moor, about to sup,
The dogs have beat his quarters up.

And now he takes the open air,
Draws up his wings with tactic care,   50
Whilst th' expert falcon swift doth climb
In subtle mazes serpentine;
And to advantage closely twin'd
She gets the upper sky and wind,
Where she dissembles to invade,   55
And lies a pol'tic ambuscade.

The hedg'd-in heron, whom the foe
Awaits above, and dogs below,
In his fortification lies,
And makes him ready for surprise;   60

When roused with a shrill alarm,
Was shouted from beneath, they arm.

    The falcon charges at first view
With her brigade of talons, through
Whose shoots the wary heron beat,   65
With a well counterwheel'd retreat.
But the bold gen'ral, never lost,
Hath won again her airy post;
Who, wild in this affront, now fries,
Then gives a volley of her eyes.   70

    The desp'rate heron now contracts
In one design all former facts;
Noble he is resolv'd to fall
His and his en'my's funeral,
And, to be rid of her, to die   75
A public martyr of the sky.

    When now he turns his last to wreak
The palisadoes of his beak,
The raging foe impatient,
Rack'd with revenge, and fury rent,   80
Swift as the thunderbolt he strikes
Too sure upon the stand of pikes;
There she his naked breast doth hit,
And on the case of rapiers 's split.

    But ev'n in her expiring pangs,   85
The heron 's pounc'd within her fangs,
And so above she stoops to rise
A trophy and a sacrifice;
Whilst her own bells in the sad fall
Ring out the double funeral.   90

    Ah victory unhapp'ly won!
Weeping and red is set the sun,
Whilst the whole field floats in one tear,
And all the air doth mourning wear:
Close-hooded all thy kindred come   95
To pay their vows upon thy tomb;
The hobby and the musket too
Do march to take their last adieu.

The lanner and the lanneret
Thy colours bear as banneret;　　　　　100
The goshawk and her tercel, rous'd,
With tears attend thee as new bows'd,
All these are in their dark array
Led by the various herald-jay.

But thy eternal name shall live　　　　105
Whilst quills from ashes fame reprieve,
Whilst open stands renown's wide door,
And wings are left on which to soar:
Doctor Robin, the prelate Pie,
And the poetic Swan shall die,　　　　110
Only to sing thy elegy.

LOVE MADE IN THE FIRST AGE

TO CHLORIS

In the nativity of time,
Chloris! it was not thought a crime
　　In direct Hebrew for to woo.
Now we make love as all on fire,
Ring retrograde our loud desire,　　　　5
　　And court in English backward too.

Thrice happy was that golden age,
When compliment was constru'd rage,
　　And fine words in the centre hid;
When cursed No stain'd no maid's bliss,　　10
And all discourse was summ'd in Yes,
　　And naught forbade, but to forbid.

Love, then unstinted, love did sip,
And cherries pluck'd fresh from the lip,
　　On cheeks and roses free he fed;　　　15
Lasses like Autumn plums did drop,
And lads indifferently did crop
　　A flower and a maidenhead.

Then unconfined each did tipple
Wine from the bunch, milk from the nipple,　　20
　　Paps tractable as udders were;

Then equally the wholesome jellies
Were squeez'd from olive-trees and bellies,
   Nor suits of trespass did they fear.

A fragrant bank of strawberries,   25
Diaper'd with violets' eyes,
   Was table, tablecloth, and fare;
No palace to the clouds did swell,
Each humble princess then did dwell
   In the piazza of her hair.   30

Both broken faith and th' cause of it,
All-damning gold, was damn'd to th' Pit;
   Their troth, seal'd with a clasp and kiss,
Lasted until that extreme day
In which they smil'd their souls away,   35
   And in each other breath'd new bliss.

Because no fault, there was no tear;
No groan did grate the granting ear;
   No false foul breath their del'cat smell:
No serpent kiss poison'd the taste,   40
Each touch was naturally chaste,
   And their mere sense a miracle.

Naked as their own innocence,
And unembroider'd from offence
   They went, above poor riches, gay;   45
On softer than the cygnet's down
In beds they tumbled of their own:
   For each within the other lay.

Thus did they live; thus did they love,
Repeating only joys above,   50
   And angels were, but with clothes on,
Which they would put off cheerfully
To bathe them in the Galaxy,
   Then gird them with the heavenly zone.

Now, Chloris! miserably crave   55
The offer'd bliss you would not have,
   Which evermore I must deny;
Whilst, ravish'd with these noble dreams,
And crowned with mine own soft beams,
   Enjoying of myself I lie.   60

TO A LADY WITH CHILD, THAT ASK'D AN OLD SHIRT

AND why an honour'd ragged shirt, that shows,
Like tatter'd ensigns, all its body's blows?
Should it be swathed in a vest so dire,
It were enough to set the child on fire;
Dishevell'd queens should strip them of their hair,   5
And in it mantle the new rising heir:
Nor do I know aught worth to wrap it in,
Except my parchment upper-coat of skin:
And then expect no end of its chaste tears,
That first was roll'd in down, now furs of bears.   10
    But since to ladies 't hath a custom been
Linen to send, that travail and lie in;
To the nine sempstresses, my former friends,
I su'd, but they had naught but shreds and ends.
At last, the jolli'st of the three times three   15
Rent th' apron from her smock, and gave it me;
'Twas soft and gentle, subtly spun, no doubt:
Pardon my boldness, madam: *here's the clout.*

SONG

IN mine own monument I lie,
    And in myself am buried;
Sure the quick lightning of her eye
    Melted my soul i' th' scabbard dead;
And now like some pale ghost I walk,   5
And with another's spirit talk.

Nor can her beams a heat convey
    That may my frozen bosom warm,
Unless her smiles have pow'r, as they
    That a cross charm can countercharm;   10
But this is such a pleasing pain,
I 'm loth to be alive again.

ANOTHER

I DID believe I was in heav'n,
When first the heav'n herself was giv'n,
That in my heart her beams did pass
As some the sun keep in a glass.

So that her beauties thorough me
Did hurt my rival-enemy.
But fate, alas! decreed it so,
That I was engine to my woe;
For as a corner'd crystal spot
My heart diaphanous was not,   10
But solid stuff, where her eye flings
Quick fire upon the catching strings:
Yet, as at triumphs in the night,
You see the prince's arms in light,
So when I once was set on flame,   15
I burnt all o'er the letters of her name.

ODE

You are deceiv'd: I sooner may, dull fair,
Seat a dark Moor in Cassiopeia's Chair,
    Or on the glow-worm's useless light
    Bestow the watching flames of night,
      Or give the rose's breath   5
      To executed death,
        Ere the bright hue
        Of verse to you;
It is just Heaven on beauty stamps a fame,
And we, alas! its triumphs but proclaim.   10

What chains but are too light for me, should I
Say that Lucasta in strange arms could lie?
    Or that Castara were impure,
    Or Saccharissa's faith unsure;
      That Chloris' love, as hair,   15
      Embrac'd each en'my's air:
        That all their good
        Ran in their blood?
'Tis the same wrong th' unworthy to enthrone,
As from her proper sphere t' have Virtue thrown. 20

That strange force on the ignoble hath renown,
As *aurum fulminans* it blows Vice down;
    'Twere better, heavy one, to crawl
    Forgot, than, raised, trod on fall:

All your defections now 25
Are not writ on your brow.
Odes to faults give
A shame must live.
When a fat mist we view, we coughing run;
But that once meteor drawn, all cry, Undone! 30

How bright the fair Paulina did appear,
When hid in jewels she did seem a star!
But who could soberly behold
A wicked owl in cloth of gold?
Or the ridiculous ape 35
In sacred Vesta's shape?
So doth agree
Just praise with thee;
For since thy birth gave thee no beauty, know
No poet's pencil must or can do so. 40

THE DUEL

Love, drunk the other day, knock'd at my breast,
  But I, alas! was not within:
My man, my ear, told me he came t' attest
  That without cause h' had boxed him,
And battered the windows of mine eyes, 5
And took my heart for one of 's nunneries.

I wond'red at the outrage safe return'd,
  And stormed at the base affront;
And by a friend of mine, bold Faith, that burn'd,
  I call'd him to a strict accompt. 10
He said that, by the law, the challeng'd might
Take the advantage both of arms and fight.

Two darts of equal length and points he sent,
  And nobly gave the choice to me;
Which I not weigh'd, young and indifferent, 15
  Now full of naught but victory.
So we both met in one of 's mother's groves,
The time, at the first murm'ring of her doves.

I stripp'd myself naked all o'er, as he,
    For so I was best arm'd, when bare;   20
His first pass did my liver rase, yet I
    Made home a falsify too near,
For when my arm to its true distance came,
I nothing touch'd but a fantastic flame.

This, this is Love we daily quarrel so,   25
    An idle Don-Quixotery:
We whip ourselves with our own twisted woe,
    And wound the air for a fly.
The only way t' undo this enemy
Is to laugh at the boy, and he will cry.   30

CUPID FAR GONE

WHAT so beyond all madness is the elf,
    Now he hath got out of himself!
    His fatal enemy the bee,
    Nor his deceiv'd artillery,
    His shackles, nor the rose's bough   5
Ne'er half so nettled him as he is now.

See! at 's own mother he is offering,
    His finger now fits any ring:
    Old Cybele he would enjoy,
    And now the girl, and now the boy.   10
    He proffers Jove a back caress,
And all his love in the Antipodes.

Jealous of his chaste Psyche, raging he
    Quarrels the student Mercury;
    And with a proud submissive breath   15
    Offers to change his darts with Death.
    He strikes at the bright eye of day,
And Juno tumbles in her Milky Way.

The dear sweet secrets of the gods he tells,
    And with loath'd hate lov'd heaven he swells;   20
    Now like a fury he belies
    Myriads of pure virginities;
    And swears, with this false frenzy hurl'd,
There 's not a virtuous she in all the world.

Olympus he renounces, then descends, 25
  And makes a friendship with the fiends;
    Bids Charon be no more a slave,
    He Argos rigg'd with stars shall have;
    And triple Cerberus from below
Must leash'd t' himself with him a-hunting go. 30

A MOCK SONG

  Now Whitehall 's in the grave,
  And our head is our slave,
The bright pearl in his close shell of oyster;
  Now the mitre is lost,
  The proud prelates, too, cross'd, 5
And all Rome 's confin'd to a cloister;
  He that Tarquin was styl'd
  Our white land 's exil'd,
    Yea undefil'd;
Not a court ape 's left to confute us: 10
  Then let your voices rise high,
  As your colours did fly,
    And flour'shing cry,
Long live the brave Oliver-Brutus!

  Now the sun is unarm'd, 15
  And the moon by us charm'd,
All the stars dissolv'd to a jelly;
  Now the thighs of the crown
  And the arms are lopp'd down,
And the body is all but a belly: 20
  Let the Commons go on,
  The town is our own,
    We 'll rule alone;
For the knights have yielded their spent gorge;
  And an order is ta'en, 25
  With Honi Soit profane,
    Shout forth amain,
For our Dragon hath vanquish'd the St. George.

A FLY CAUGHT IN A COBWEB

SMALL type of great ones, that do hum
Within this whole world's narrow room,
That with a busy hollow noise
Catch at the people's vainer voice,
And with spread sails play with their breath,   5
Whose very hails new christen death.
Poor fly caught in an airy net,
Thy wings have fetter'd now thy feet;
Where, like a lion in a toil,
Howe'er, thou keep'st a noble coil,   10
And beat'st thy gen'rous breast, that o'er
The plains thy fatal buzzes roar,
Till thy all-belli'd foe, round elf,
Hath quarter'd thee within himself.
      Was it not better once to play   15
I' th' light of a majestic ray?
Where, though too near and bold, the fire
Might singe thy upper down attire,
And thou i' th' storm to lose an eye,
A wing, or a self-trapping thigh;   20
Yet hadst thou fall'n like him, whose coil
Made fishes in the sea to broil;
When now th' 'ast scap'd the noble flame,
Trapp'd basely in a slimy frame,
And free of air, thou art become   25
Slave to the spawn of mud and loam.
      Nor is 't enough thyself dost dress
To thy swoln lord a num'rous mess,
And by degrees thy thin veins bleed,
And piecemeal dost his poison feed;   30
But now devour'd, art like to be
A net spun for thy family,
And, straight expanded in the air,
Hang'st for thy issue too a snare.
Strange witty death, and cruel ill,   35
That killing thee, thou thine dost kill!
Like pies in whose entombed ark,
All fowl crowd downward to a lark,
Thou art thine en'my's sepulchre,
And in thee buriest too thine heir.   40

Yet Fates a glory have reserv'd
For one so highly hath deserv'd;
As the rhinoceros doth die
Under his castle-enemy,
As through the crane's trunk throat doth speed   45
The asp doth on his feeder feed;
Fall yet triumphant in thy woe,
Bound with the entrails of thy foe.

A FLY ABOUT A GLASS OF BURNT CLARET

FORBEAR this liquid fire, fly,
It is more fatal than the dry,
That singly, but embracing, wounds,
And this at once both burns and drowns.

The salamander, that in heat   5
And flames doth cool his monstrous sweat,
Whose fan a glowing cake, 'tis said,
Of this red furnace is afraid.

Viewing the ruby crystal shine,
Thou tak'st it for heaven crystalline;   10
Anon thou wilt be taught to groan,
'Tis an ascended Acheron.

A snowball heart in it let fall,
And take it out a fire-ball:
An icy breast in it betray'd   15
Breaks a destructive wild grenade.

'Tis this makes Venus' altars shine,
This kindles frosty Hymen's pine;
When the Boy grows old in his desires,
This flambeau doth new light his fires.   20

Though the cold hermit ever wail,
Whose sighs do freeze, and tears drop hail,
Once having passed this, will ne'er
Another flaming purging fear.

The Vestal drinking this doth burn   25
Now more than in her fun'ral urn;
Her fires, that with the sun kept race,
Are now extinguish'd by her face.

The chemist, that himself doth still,
Let him but taste this limbeck's bill, 30
And prove this sublimated bowl,
He 'll swear it will calcine a soul.

Noble and brave! now thou dost know
The false prepared decks below,
Dost thou the fatal liquor sup, 35
One drop, alas! thy bark blows up.

What airy country hast to save,
Whose plagues thou 'lt bury in thy grave?
For even now thou seem'st to us
On this gulf's brink a Curtius. 40

And now th' art fall'n, magnanimous fly,
In, where thine ocean doth fry,
Like the Sun's son who blush'd the flood
To a complexion of blood.

Yet see! my glad auricular 45
Redeems thee (though dissolv'd) a star;
Flaggy thy wings, and scorch'd thy thighs,
Thou li'st a double sacrifice.

And now my warming, cooling breath
Shall a new life afford in death: 50
See! in the hospital of my hand
Already cur'd, thou fierce dost stand.

Burnt insect! dost thou reaspire
The moist-hot glass and liquid fire?
I see! 'tis such a pleasing pain, 55
Thou wouldst be scorch'd and drown'd again.

FEMALE GLORY

'MONGST the world's wonders, there doth yet remain
One greater than the rest, that 's all those o'er again,
And her own self beside: a lady whose soft breast
Is with vast honour's soul and virtue's life possess'd.
Fair, as original light first from the chaos shot, 5
When day in virgin-beams triumph'd, and night was not.
And as that breath infus'd in the new-breather good,
When ill unknown was dumb, and bad not understood;

Cheerful, as that aspect at this world's finishing,
When Cherubims clapp'd wings, and th' Sons of Heav'n did sing;
Chaste as th' Arabian bird, who all the air denies,   11
And ev'n in flames expires, when with herself she lies.
Oh! she 's as kind as drops of new fall'n April showers,
That on each gentle breast spring fresh perfuming flowers;
She 's constant, gen'rous, fix'd, she 's calm, she is the all   15
We can of virtue, honour, faith, or glory call,
And she is (whom I thus transmit to endless fame)
Mistress o' th' world and me, and LAURA is her name.

A DIALOGUE

LUTE AND VOICE

Lute. Sing, Laura, sing, whilst silent are the spheres,
    And all the eyes of heaven are turn'd to ears.
Voice. Touch thy dead wood, and make each living tree
    Unchain its feet, take arms, and follow thee.

Chorus

Lute. Sing. *Voice.* Touch. O touch. *Lute.* O sing: 5
Both. It is the soul's, soul's sole offering.

Voice. Touch the divinity of thy chords, and make
    Each heartstring tremble, and each sinew shake.
Lute. Whilst with your voice you rarefy the air,
    None but an host of angels hover here.   10

Chorus

Lute. Sing. *Voice.* Touch, etc.

Voice. Touch thy soft lute, and in each gentle thread
    The lion and the panther captive lead.
Lute. Sing, and in heav'n enthrone deposed Love,
    Whilst angels dance, and fiends in order move.   15

Double Chorus

What sacred charm may this then be
    In harmony,
That thus can make the angels wild,
    The devils mild,
And teach low hell to heav'n to swell,   20
And the high heav'n to stoop to hell?

A MOCK CHARON

Dialogue

CHARON. W[HARTON?]

W. Charon! Thou slave! Thou fool! Thou Cavalier!
Char. A slave, a fool—what traitor's voice I hear?
W. Come, bring thy boat. *Char.* No sir. *W.* No, sirrah! why?
Char. The blest will disagree, and fiends will mutiny
    At thy, at thy unnumb'red treachery. 5
W. Villain, I have a pass, which who disdains,
    I will sequester the Elysian plains.
Char. Woe 's me! Ye gentle shades! where shall I dwell?
    He 's come! It is not safe to be in hell.

Chorus

Thus man, his honour lost, falls on these shelves; 10
Furies and fiends are still true to themselves.

Char. You must, lost fool, come in. *W.* Oh let me in!
    But now I fear thy boat will sink with my o'er-weighty sin.
    Where, courteous Charon, am I now? *Char.* Vile rant!
    At th' gates of thy supreme judge, Rhadamant. 15

Double Chorus of Devils

Welcome to rape, to theft, to perjury,
To all the ills thou wert, we cannot hope to be.
Oh pity us condemn'd! Oh cease to woo,
And softly, softly breathe, lest you infect us too.

THE TOAD AND SPIDER

A DUEL

Upon a day when the dog-star
Unto the world proclaim'd a war,
And poison bark'd from his black throat,
And from his jaws infection shot,
Under a deadly henbane shade 5
With slime infernal mists are made,
Met the two dreaded enemies,
Having their weapons in their eyes.

First from his den rolls forth that load
Of spite and hate, the speckl'd toad,   10
And from his chaps a foam doth spawn,
Such as the loathed three heads yawn;
Defies his foe, with a fell spit,
To wade through death to meet with it;
Then in his self the limbeck turns,   15
And his elixir'd poison urns.
Arachne, once the fear o' th' maid
Celestial, thus unto her pray'd:
"Heaven's blue-ey'd daughter, thine own mother!
The python-killing Sun 's thy brother;   20
O thou from gods that didst descend,
With a poor virgin to contend,
Shall seed of Earth and Hell e'er be
A rival in thy victory?"
Pallas assents: for now long time   25
And pity had clean rins'd her crime;
When straight she doth with active fire
Her many-legged foe inspire.
Have you not seen a carrack lie
A great cathedral in the sea,   30
Under whose Babylonian walls
A small thin frigate-almshouse stalls?
So in his slime the toad doth float,
And th' spider by but seems his boat.
And now the naumachy begins.   35
Close to the surface herself spins
Arachne, when her foe lets fly
A broadside of his breath too high,
That 's overshot, the wisely stout
Advised maid doth tack about,   40
And now her pitchy barque doth sweat,
Chaf'd in her own black fury wet;
Lazy and cold before, she brings
New fires to her contracted stings,
And with discolour'd spumes doth blast   45
The herbs that to their centre haste.
Now to the neighb'ring henbane top
Arachne hath herself wound up,
And thence, from its dilated leaves,
By her own cordage downwards weaves,   50
And doth her town of foe attack,

And storms the rampires of his back;
Which taken in, her colours spread
March to th' citadel of 's head.
Now as in witty torturing Spain   55
The brain is vex'd, to vex the brain,
Where heretics' bare heads are arm'd
In a close helm, and in it charm'd
An overgrown and meagre rat,
That piecemeal nibbles himself fat: 60
So on the toad's blue-chequer'd skull
The spider gluttons herself full,
And vomiting her Stygian seeds,
Her poison, on his poison feeds.
Thus the envenom'd toad, now grown   65
Big with more poison than his own,
Doth gather all his pow'rs, and shakes
His stormer in 's disgorged lakes;
And wounded now, apace crawls on
To his next plantain surgeon;   70
With whose rich balm no sooner dress'd,
But purged is his sick swoln breast;
And as a glorious combatant
That only rests a while to pant,
Then with repeated strength, and scars   75
That, smarting, fire him to new wars,
Deals blows that thick themselves prevent,
As they would gain the time he spent:
   So the disdaining angry toad
That calls but a thin useless load;   80
His fatal feared self comes back
With unknown venom fill'd to crack.
Th' amazed spider, now untwin'd,
Hath crept up, and herself new lin'd
With fresh salt foams, and mists that blast   85
The ambient air as they pass'd.
And now methinks a sphinx's wing
I pluck, and do not write but sting;
With their black blood my pale ink 's blent,
Gall 's but a faint ingredient.   90
The pol'tic toad doth now withdraw,
Warn'd, higher *in Campania.*
There wisely doth, entrenched deep,
His body in a body keep,

And leaves a wide and open pass   95
T' invite the foe up to his jaws;
Which there within a foggy blind
With fourscore fire-arms were lin'd.
The gen'rous active spider doubts
More ambuscadoes than redoubts;   100
So within shot she doth pickeer,
Now galls the flank, and now the rear;
As that the toad in 's own despite
Must change the manner of his fight,
Who, like a glorious general,   105
With one home charge lets fly at all.
Chaf'd with a fourfold ven'mous foam
Of scorn, revenge, his foe's and 's own,
He seats him in his loathed chair,
New-made him by each morning's air;   110
With glowing eyes he doth survey
Th' undaunted host he calls his prey;
Then his dark spume he greed'ly laps,
And shows the foe his grave, his chaps.

Whilst the quick wary Amazon   115
Of 'vantage takes occasion,
And with her troop of legs careers
In a full speed with all her spears;
Down, as some mountain on a mouse,
On her small cot he flings his house;   120
Without the poison of the elf,
The toad had like t' have burst himself,
For sage Arachne with good heed
Had stopp'd herself upon full speed;
And 's body now disorder'd, on   125
She falls to execution.
The passive toad now only can
Contemn, and suffer.   Here began
The wronged maid's ingenious rage,
Which his heart venom must assuage.   130
One eye she hath spit out—strange smother!
When one flame doth put out another;
And one eye wittily spar'd, that he
Might but behold his misery.
She on each spot a wound doth print,   135
And each speck hath a sting within 't;
Till he but one new blister is,

And swells his own periphrasis;
Then fainting sick, and yellow-pale,
She baths him with her sulph'rous stale;   140
Thus slacked is her Stygian fire,
And she vouchsafes now to retire.
Anon the toad begins to pant,
Bethinks him of th' almighty plant,
And, lest he piecemeal should be sped,   145
Wisely doth finish himself dead.
Whilst the gay girl, as was her fate,
Doth wanton and luxuriate,
And crowns her conqu'ring head all o'er
With fatal leaves of hellebore,   150
Not guessing at the precious aid
Was lent her by the heavenly maid.
The near-expiring toad now rolls
Himself in lazy bloody scrolls,
To th' sov'reign salve of all his ills,   155
That only life and health distils.
But lo! a terror above all
That ever yet did him befal!
    Pallas, still mindful of her foe,
(Whilst they did with each fires glow)   160
Had to the place the spiders' lar
Despatch'd before the ev'ning's star;
He learned was in Nature's laws,
Of all her foliage knew the cause,
And 'mongst the rest in his choice want   165
Unplanted had this plantain plant.
    The all-confounded toad doth see
His life fled with his remedy,
And in a glorious despair
First burst himself, and next the air;   170
Then with a dismal horrid yell,
Beats down his loathsome breath to hell.
    But what inestimable bliss
This to the sated virgin is,
Who as before of her fiend foe,   175
Now full is of her goddess too;
She from her fertile womb hath spun
Her stateliest pavilion,
Whilst all her silken flags display,
And her triumphant banners play;   180

Where Pallas she i' th' midst doth praise,
And counterfeits her brother's rays;
Nor will she her dear lar forget,
Victorious by his benefit,
Whose roof enchanted she doth free   185
From haunting gnat and goblin bee,
Who, trapp'd in her prepared toil,
To their destruction keep a coil.
   Then she unlocks the toad's dire head,
Within whose cell is treasured   190
That precious stone, which she doth call
A noble recompense for all,
And to her lar doth it present,
Of his fair aid a monument.

THE TRIUMPHS OF PHILAMORE AND AMORET

TO THE NOBLEST OF OUR YOUTH AND BEST OF FRIENDS,

CHARLES COTTON, ESQUIRE,

BEING AT BERESFORD, AT HIS HOUSE IN STAFFORDSHIRE.

FROM LONDON

A POEM

SIR, your sad absence I complain, as earth
Her long-hid Spring, that gave her verdures birth,
Who now her cheerful aromatic head
Shrinks in her cold and dismal widow'd bed;
Whilst the false sun, her lover, doth him move   5
Below, and to th' Antipodes make love.
   What fate was mine, when in mine obscure cave
(Shut up almost close prisoner in a grave)
Your beams could reach me through this vault of night,
And canton the dark dungeon with light!   10
Whence me, as gen'rous spahis, you unbound,
Whilst I now know myself both free and crown'd.
   But as, at Mecca's tomb, the devout blind
Pilgrim, great husband of his sight and mind,
Pays to no other object this chaste price,   15
Then with hot earth anoints out both his eyes:
So, having seen your dazzling glories' store,
Is it enough, and sin for to see more?

Or do you thus those precious rays withdraw
To whet my dull beams, keep my bold in awe?   20
Or are you gentle and compassionate,
You will not reach me Regulus his fate?
Brave prince who, eagle-ey'd of eagle kind,
Wert blindly damn'd to look thine own self blind!

But oh, return those fires, too cruel nice!   25
For whilst you fear me cinders, see! I 'm ice;
A numbed speaking clod, and mine own show,
Myself congeal'd, a man cut out in snow.
Return those living fires, thou who that vast
Double advantage from one-ey'd heav'n hast;   30
Look with one sun, though 't but obliquely be,
And if not shine, vouchsafe to wink on me.

Perceive you not a gentle, gliding heat,
And quick'ning warmth that makes the statua sweat?
As rev'rend Deucalion's back-flung stone,   35
Whose rough outside softens to skin, anon
Each crusty vein with wet red is suppli'd,
Whilst naught of stone but in its heart doth bide:
So from the rugged North, where your soft stay
Hath stamp'd them a meridian, and kind day;   40
Where now each *à la mode* inhabitant
Himself and 's manners both do pay you rent,
And 'bout your house (your palace) doth resort,
And 'spite of fate and war creates a court:

So from the taught North when you shall return   45
To glad those looks that ever since did mourn,
When men unclothed of themselves you 'll see,
Then start new made, fit, what they ought to be;
Haste! haste! you that your eyes on rare sights feed,
For thus the golden triumph is decreed.   50

The twice-born god, still gay and ever young,
With ivy crown'd, first leads the glorious throng:
He Ariadne's starry coronet
Designs for th' brighter beams of Amoret;
Then doth he broach his throne, and singing quaff   55
Unto her health his pipe of godhead off.

Him follow the recanting, vexing Nine,
Who, wise, now sing thy lasting fame in wine;
Whilst Phœbus not from th' East, your feast t' adorn,
But from th' inspir'd Canaries rose this morn.   60

Now you are come, winds in their caverns sit,

And nothing breathes but new-enlarged wit.
Hark! one proclaims it piacle to be sad,
And th' people call 't religion to be mad.

But now, as at a coronation,   65
When noise, the guard, and trumpets are o'erblown,
The silent commons mark their prince's way,
And with still reverence both look and pray;
So they, amaz'd, expecting do adore,
And count the rest but pageantry before.   70

Behold! an host of virgins, pure as th' air,
In her first face, ere mists durst veil her hair,
Their snowy vests white as their whiter skin,
Or their far chaster whiter thoughts within.
Roses they breath'd and strew'd, as if the fine   75
Heaven did to Earth his wreath of sweets resign;
They sang aloud, *Thrice, oh thrice happy, they*
That can, like these, in love both yield and sway!

Next Herald Fame (a purple cloud her bears)
In an embroider'd coat of eyes and ears,   80
Proclaims the triumph, and these lovers' glory;
Then in a book of steel records the story.

And now a youth of more than godlike form
Did th' inward minds of the dumb throng alarm;
All nak'd, each part betray'd unto the eye,   85
Chastely, for neither sex ow'd he or she.
And this was Heav'nly Love. By his bright hand,
A boy of worse than earthly stuff did stand,
His bow broke, his fires out, and his wings clipp'd,
And the black slave from all his false flames stripp'd;   90
Whose eyes were new restor'd but to confess
This day's bright bliss and his own wretchedness;
Who, swell'd with envy, bursting with disdain,
Did cry to cry, and weep them out again.

And now what heav'n must I invade, what sphere   95
Rifle of all her stars t' enthrone her there?
No, Phœbus, by thy boy's fate we beware
Th' unruly flames o' th' firebrand, thy car;
Although, she there once plac'd, thou, Sun, shouldst see
Thy day both nobler governed and thee.   100
Drive on, Boötes, thy cold heavy wain,
Then grease thy wheels with amber in the main;
And, Neptune, thou to thy false Thetis gallop,
Apollo 's set within thy bed of scallop;

Whilst Amoret, on the reconciled winds   105
Mounted, is drawn by six celestial minds;
She armed was with innocence, and fire
That did not burn, for it was chaste desire;
Whilst a new light doth gild the standers by:
Behold! it was a day shot from her eye!   110
Chafing perfumes o' th' East did throng and sweat,
But by her breath they melting back were beat.
A crown of yet ne'er lighted stars she wore,
In her soft hand a bleeding heart she bore,
And round her lay millions of broken more;   115
Then a wing'd crier thrice aloud did call,
"Let Fame proclaim this one great prize for all."
   By her a lady that might be call'd fair—
And justly, but that Amoret was there—
Was pris'ner led; th' unvalu'd robe she wore   120
Made infinite lay-lovers to adore,
Who vainly tempt her rescue (madly bold),
Chained in sixteen thousand links of gold;
Chrysetta thus, loaden with treasures, slave,
Did strow the pass with pearls, and her way pave.   125
   But lo! the glorious cause of all this high
True heav'nly state, brave Philamore draws nigh!
Who, not himself, more seems himself to be,
And with a sacred ecstasy doth see.
Fix'd and unmov'd on 's pillars he doth stay,   130
And joy transforms him his own statua;
Nor hath he pow'r to breathe, or strength to greet
The gentle offers of his Amoret,
Who now amaz'd at 's noble breast doth knock,
And with a kiss his gen'rous heart unlock;   135
Whilst she and the whole pomp doth enter there,
Whence her nor Time nor Fate shall ever tear.
But whither am I hurl'd? Ho! Back! Awake
From thy glad trance; to thine old sorrow take!
Thus, after view of all the Indies' store,   140
The slave returns unto his chain and oar;
Thus poets, who all night in blest heav'ns dwell,
Are call'd next morn to their true living hell;
So I unthrifty, to myself untrue,
Rise cloth'd with real wants, 'cause wanting you,   145
And what substantial riches I possess
I must to these unvalu'd dreams confess.

But all our clouds shall be o'erblown, when thee
In our horizon, bright, once more we see;
When thy dear presence shall our souls new dress, 150
And spring an universal cheerfulness;
When we shall be o'erwhelm'd in joy, like they
That change their night for a vast half-year's day.

   Then shall the wretched few that do repine
See; and recant their blasphemies in wine; 155
Then shall they grieve that thought I 've sung too free,
High and aloud, of thy true worth and thee,
And their foul heresies and lips submit
To th' all-forgiving breath of Amoret,
And me alone their anger's object call, 160
That from my height so miserably did fall;
And cry out my invention thin and poor,
Who have said naught, since I could say no more.

ADVICE TO MY BEST BROTHER,
COLONEL FRANCIS LOVELACE

FRANK, wilt live handsomely? trust not too far
Thyself to waving seas; for what thy star,
Calculated by sure event, must be,
Look in the glassy epithet and see.

   Yet settle here your rest, and take your state, 5
And in calm halcyon's nest ev'n build your fate;
Prithee lie down securely, Frank, and keep
With as much no noise the inconstant deep
As its inhabitants; nay, steadfast stand,
As if discover'd were a New-found-land 10
Fit for plantation here; dream, dream still,
Lull'd in Dione's cradle, dream, until
Horror awake your sense, and you now find
Yourself a bubbled pastime for the wind,
And in loose Thetis' blankets torn and toss'd: 15
Frank, to undo thyself why art at cost?

   Nor be too confident, fix'd on the shore,
For even that too borrows from the store
Of her rich neighbour, since now wisest know
(And this to Galileo's judgment owe) 20

The palsy earth itself is every jot
As frail, inconstant, waving as that blot
We lay upon the deep; that sometimes lies
Chang'd, you would think, with 's bottom's properties,
But this eternal strange Ixion's wheel   25
Of giddy earth, ne'er whirling leaves to reel,
Till all things are inverted, till they are
Turn'd to that antique confus'd state they were.

Who loves the golden mean doth safely want
A cobwebb'd cot, and wrongs entail'd upon 't;   30
He richly needs a palace for to breed
Vipers and moths, that on their feeder feed;
The toy that we, too true, a mistress call,
Whose looking-glass and feather weighs up all;
And cloths which larks would play with in the sun,   35
That mock him in the night when 's course is run.

To rear an edifice by art so high
That envy should not reach it with her eye,
Nay, with a thought come near it—wouldst thou know
How such a structure should be rais'd? build low.   40
The blust'ring wind's invisible rough stroke
More often shakes the stubborn'st, prop'rest oak,
And in proud turrets we behold withal,
'Tis the imperial top declines to fall.
Nor does Heav'n's lightning strike the humble vales,   45
But high aspiring mounts batters and scales.

A breast of proof defies all shocks of fate,
Fears in the best, hopes in the worser state;
Heaven forbid that, as of old, Time ever
Flourish'd in Spring so contrary, now never: 50
That mighty breath which blew foul Winter hither
Can eas'ly puff it to a fairer weather.
Why dost despair then, Frank? Æolus has
A Zephyrus as well as Boreas.

'Tis a false sequel, solecism, 'gainst those   55
Precepts by fortune giv'n us, to suppose
That, 'cause it is now ill, 'twill e'er be so;
Apollo doth not always bend his bow;
But oft uncrowned of his beams divine,
With his soft harp awakes the sleeping Nine.   60

In strictest things magnanimous appear,
Greater in hope, howe'er thy fate, than fear:
Draw all your sails in quickly, though no storm
Threaten your ruin with a sad alarm;
For tell me how they differ, tell me pray,   65
A cloudy tempest, and a too fair day.

AN ANNIVERSARY ON THE HYMENEALS OF MY NOBLE KINSMAN THOMAS STANLEY, ESQUIRE

THE day is curl'd about agen
To view the splendour she was in,
        When first with hallow'd hands
The holy man knit the mysterious bands;
When you two your contracted souls did move,   5
        Like cherubims above,
            And did make love;
As your un-understanding issue now
In a glad sigh, a smile, a tear, a vow.

Tell me, O self-reviving Sun,   10
In thy peregrination
        Hast thou beheld a pair
Twist their soft beams like these in their chaste air?
As from bright numberless embracing rays
        Are sprung th' industrious days,   15
            So when they gaze,
And change their fertile eyes with the new morn,
A beauteous offspring is shot forth, not born.

Be witness then, all-seeing Sun,
Old spy, thou that thy race hast run   20
        In full five thousand rings;
To thee were ever purer offerings
Sent on the wings of faiths? And thou, O Night!
        Curtain of their delight,
            By these made bright,   25
Have you not marked their celestial play,
And no more peek'd the gaieties of day?

Come then, pale virgins, roses strow,
Mingled with Ios, as you go;

The snowy ox is kill'd,   30
The fane with pros'lyte lads and lasses fill'd,
You too may hope the same seraphic joy
        Old Time cannot destroy,
            Nor fulness cloy,
When, like these, you shall stamp by sympathies   35
Thousands of new-born loves with your chaste eyes.

PARIS'S SECOND JUDGMENT, UPON THE THREE DAUGHTERS OF MY DEAR BROTHER MR. R[OBERT] CÆSAR

BEHOLD! three sister-wonders, in whom met,
Distinct and chaste, the splendours counterfeit
Of Juno, Venus, and the warlike Maid,
Each in their three divinities array'd!
The majesty and state of heav'n's great queen,   5
And when she treats the gods, her noble mien;
The sweet victorious beauties and desires
O' th' sea-born princess, empress too of fires;
The sacred arts and glorious laurels torn
From the fair brow o' th' goddess father-born: 10
All these were quarter'd in each snowy coat,
With canton'd honours of their own to boot.
Paris, by fate new-wak'd from his dead cell,
Is charg'd to give his doom impossible.
He views in each the brav'ry of all Ide,   15
Whilst one, as once three, doth his soul divide.
Then sighs, so equally they 're glorious all,
"What pity the whole world is but one ball!"

PAINTURE

A PANEGYRIC TO THE BEST PICTURE OF FRIENDSHIP, MR. PETER LELY

IF Pliny, Lord High Treasurer of all
Nature's exchequer shuffled in this our ball,
Painture, her richer rival, did admire,
And cri'd she wrought with more almighty fire,
That judg'd the unnumber'd issue of her scroll,   5
Infinite and various as her mother soul,

That contemplation into matter brought,
Bodi'd ideas, and could form a thought:
Why do I pause to couch the cataract,
And the gross pearls from our dull eyes abstract?   10
That, pow'rful Lely, now awaken'd, we
This new Creation may behold by thee.
    To thy victorious pencil all that eyes
And minds can reach do bow; the deities
Bold poets first but feign'd you do, and make,   15
And from your awe they our devotion take.
Your beauteous palette first design'd Love's Queen,
And made her in her heav'nly colours seen;
You strung the bow of the bandit her son,
And tipp'd his arrows with religion.   20
Neptune as unknown as his fish might dwell,
But that you seat him in his throne of shell.
The Thunderer's artillery and brand,
You fanci'd Rome in his fantastic hand.
And the pale frights, the pains and fears of hell,   25
First from your sullen melancholy fell.
Who cleft th' infernal dog's loath'd head in three,
And spun out Hydra's fifty necks?   By thee
As prepossess'd w' enjoy th' Elysian plain,
Which but before was flatter'd in our brain.   30
Whoe'er yet view'd air's child invisible,
A hollow voice, but in thy subtle skill?
Faint stamm'ring Echo you so draw that we
The very repercussion do see.
    Cheat hocus-pocus Nature an essay   35
O' th' Spring affords us, presto! and away:
You all the year do chain her and her fruits,
Roots to their beds, and flowers to their roots.
Have not mine eyes feasted i' th' frozen zone
Upon a fresh new-grown collation   40
Of apples, unknown sweets, that seem'd to me
Hanging to tempt as on the fatal tree,
So delicately limn'd I vow'd to try
My appetite impos'd upon my eye?
    You, sir, alone, Fame and all-conqu'ring rhyme   45
Files the set teeth of all-devouring Time.
When Beauty once thy virtuous paint hath on,
Age needs not call her to vermilion;
Her beams ne'er shed or change like th' hair of day,

She scatters fresh her everlasting ray; 50
Nay, from her ashes her fair virgin fire
Ascends, that doth new massacres conspire,
Whilst we wipe off the num'rous score of years,
And do behold our grandsires as our peers;
With the first father of our house compare 55
We do the features of our new-born heir;
For though each copied a son, they all
Meet in thy first and true original.
    Sacred luxurious! what princess not
But comes to you to have herself begot? 60
As when first man was kneaded, from his side
Is born to 's hand a ready-made-up bride.
He husband to his issue then doth play,
And for more wives remove the obstructed way:
So by your art you spring up in two moons 65
What could not else be form'd by fifteen suns;
Thy skill doth an'mate the prolific flood,
And thy red oil assimilates to blood.
    Where then, when all the world pays its respect,
Lies our transalpine barbarous neglect? 70
When the chaste hands of pow'rful Titian
Had drawn the scourges of our God and man,
And now the top of th' altar did ascend,
To crown the heav'nly piece with a bright end,
Whilst he who to seven languages gave law, 75
And always like the sun his subjects saw,
Did, in his robes imperial and gold,
The basis of the doubtful ladder hold:
O Charles! a nobler monument than that
Which thou thine own executor wert at! 80
When to our huffling Henry there complain'd
A grieved earl, that thought his honour stain'd,
"Away!" frown'd he, "for your own safeties, haste!
In one cheap hour ten coronets I 'll cast;
But Holbein's noble and prodigious worth 85
Only the pangs of an whole age brings forth."
Henry! a word so princely saving said,
It might new raise the ruins thou hast made.
    O sacred painture! that dost fairly draw
What but in mists deep inward poets saw; 90
'Twixt thee and an Intelligence no odds,
That art of privy counsel to the gods;

By thee unto our eyes they do prefer
A stamp of their abstracted character;
Thou that in frames eternity dost bind,   95
And art a written and a bodi'd mind;
To thee is ope the junto o' th' Abyss,
And its conspiracy detected is,
Whilst their cabal thou to our sense dost show,
And in thy square paint'st what they threat below. 100
   Now, my best Lely, let 's walk hand in hand,
And smile at this un-understanding land;
Let them their own dull counterfeits adore,
Their rainbow-cloths admire, and no more;
Within one shade of thine more substance is   105
Than all their varnish'd idol-mistresses:
Whilst great Vasari and Vermander shall
Interpret the deep mystery of all,
And I unto our modern Picts shall show
What due renown to thy fair art they owe,   110
In the delineated lives of those
By whom this everlasting laurel grows.
Then if they will not gently apprehend,
Let one great blot give to their fame an end;
Whilst no poetic flower their hearse doth dress,   115
But perish they and their effigies.

TO MY DEAR FRIEND MR. E[LDRED] R[EVETT], ON HIS POEMS MORAL AND DIVINE

CLEFT, as the top of the inspired Hill,
Struggles the soul of my divided quill,
Whilst this foot doth the wat'ry mount aspire,
That Sinai's living and enlivening fire.
Behold my pow'rs storm'd by a twisted light   5
O' th' sun and his first kindled his sight,
And my left thoughts invoke the Prince of Day,
My right to th' spring of it and him do pray.
   Say, happy youth, crown'd with a heav'nly ray
Of the first flame, and interwreathed bay,   10
Inform my soul in labour to begin
Ios or anthems, pæans or a hymn.
Shall I a hecatomb on thy tripod slay,
Or my devotions at thy altar pay?

While which t' adore th' amaz'd world cannot tell,   15
The sublime Urim or deep oracle.

Hark how the moving chords temper our brain,
As, when Apollo serenades the main,
Old Ocean smoothes his sullen furrow'd front,
And nereids do glide soft measures on 't;   20
Whilst th' air puts on its sleekest, smoothest face,
And each doth turn the other's looking-glass:
So by the sinewy lyre now strook we see
Into soft calms all storms of poesy,
And former thundering and lightning lines,   25
And verse now in its native lustre shines.

How wert thou hid within thyself! how shut!
Thy precious Iliads lock'd up in a nut!
Not hearing of thee thou dost break out strong,
Invading forty thousand men in song;   30
And we, secure in our thin empty heat,
Now find ourselves at once surpris'd and beat;
Whilst the most valiant of our wits now sue,
Fling down their arms, ask quarter too of you.

So cabin'd up in its disguis'd coarse rust,   35
And scurf'd all o'er with its unseemly crust,
The diamond, from midst the humbler stones
Sparkling, shoots forth the price of nations.

Ye sage unriddlers of the stars, pray tell,
By what name shall I stamp my miracle?   40
Thou strange inverted Æson, that leap'st o'er
From thy first infancy into fourscore,
That to thine own self hast the midwife play'd,
And from thy brain spring'st forth the heav'nly maid!
Thou staff of him bore him, that bore our sins,   45
Which, but set down, to bloom and bear begins!
Thou rod of Aaron, with one motion hurl'd,
Budd'st a perfume of flowers through the world!
Thou strange calcined seeds within a glass,
Each species' idea spring'st as 'twas;   50
Bright vestal flame, that, kindled but ev'n now,
For ever dost thy sacred fires throw!

Thus the repeated acts of Nestor's age,
That now had three times o'er outliv'd the stage,
And all those beams contracted into one,   55
Alcides in his cradle hath outdone.

But all these flour'shing hues, with which I dye

Thy virgin paper, now are vain as I;
For 'bove the poet's heav'n th' art taught to shine,
And move, as in thy proper crystalline;   60
Whence that molehill, Parnassus, thou dost view,
And us small ants there dabbling in its dew;
Whence thy seraphic soul such hymns doth play,
As those to which first danced the first day;
Where, with a thorn from the world-ransoming wreath,   65
Thou, stung, dost antiphons and anthems breathe;
Where, with an angel's quill dipp'd i' th' Lamb's blood,
Thou sing'st our pelican's all-saving flood,
And bath'st thy thoughts in everliving streams
Rench'd from earth's tainted, fat, and heavy steams.   70
There move, translated youth! enroll'd i' th' choir
That only doth with holy lays inspire;
To whom his burning coach Eliah sent,
And th' royal prophet-priest his harp hath lent,
Which thou dost tune in consort unto those   75
Clap wings for ever at each hallow'd close;
Whilst we, now weak and fainting in our praise,
Sick, echo o'er thy Halleluiahs.

TO MY NOBLE KINSMAN T[HOMAS] S[TANLEY], ESQUIRE, ON HIS LYRIC POEMS COMPOSED BY MR. J[OHN] G[AMBLE]

WHAT means this stately tablature,
    The balance of thy strains,
Which seems, instead of sifting pure,
    T' extend and rack thy veins?
Thy odes first their own harmony did break,   5
For singing troth is but in tune to speak.

Nor thus thy golden feet and wings,
    May it be thought false melody
T' ascend to heav'n by silver strings,
    This is Urania's heraldry: 10
Thy royal poem now we may extol,
And truly Luna blazon'd upon Sol.

As when Amphion first did call
    Each list'ning stone from 's den,
And with the lute did form his wall,   15
    But with his words the men;
So, in your twisted numbers now, you thus
Not only stocks persuade, but ravish us.

Thus do your airs echo o'er
    The notes and anthems of the spheres,
And their whole consort back restore,   20
    As if Earth too would bless Heav'n's ears:
But yet the spokes, by which they scal'd so high,
Gamble hath wisely laid of *ut re mi*.

ON THE BEST, LAST, AND ONLY REMAINING COMEDY OF MR. FLETCHER, "THE WILD GOOSE CHASE"

I 'M un-o'erclouded too! free from the mist!
The blind and late heaven's eye's great oculist,
Obscured, with the false fires of his scheme,
Not half those souls are light'ned by this theme.
    Unhappy murmurers, that still repine,   5
(After th' eclipse our sun doth brighter shine)
Recant your false grief and your true joys know,
Your bliss is endless, as you fear'd your woe!
What fort'nate flood is this? what storm of wit?
Oh, who would live and not o'erwhelm'd in it?   10
No more a fatal deluge shall be hurl'd,
This inundation hath sav'd the world.
Once more the mighty Fletcher doth arise,
Rob'd in a vest studded with stars and eyes
Of all his former glories, his last worth   15
Embroider'd with what yet light e'er brought forth.
See! in this glad farewell he doth appear
Stuck with the constellations of his sphere,
Hearing we, numb'd, fear'd no flagration,
Hath curled all his fires in this one *one*;   20
Which, as they guard his hallowed chaste urn,
The dull approaching heretics do burn.
    Fletcher at his adieu carouses thus
To the luxurious ingenious,

As Cleopatra did of old outvie   25
Th' unnumb'red dishes of her Antony,
When (he at th' empty board a wonderer)
Smiling she calls for pearl and vinegar,
First pledges him in 's breath, then at one draught
Swallows three kingdoms off "To his best thought."   30
    Hear, O ye valiant writers, and subscribe;
(His force set by) y' are conquer'd by this bribe.
Though you hold out yourselves, he doth commit
In this a sacred treason on your wit;
Although in poems desperately stout,   35
Give up: this overture must buy you out.
    Thus with some prodigal us'rer 't doth fare,
That keeps his gold still veil'd, his steel breast bare;
That doth exclude his coffers all but 's eye,
And his eye's idol the wing'd deity;   40
That cannot lock his mines with half the art
As some rich beauty doth his wretched heart:
Wild at his real poverty, and so wise
To win her, turns himself into a prize.
First startles her with th' emerald *Mad Lover*,   45
The ruby Arcas; lest she should recover
Her dazzled thought, a diamond he throws,
Splendid in all the bright Aspatia's woes;
Then, to sum up the abstract of his store,
He flings a rope of pearl of forty more.   50
Ah see! the stagg'ring virtue faints! which he
Beholding, darts his wealth's epitome;
And now, to consummate her wished fall,
Shows this one carbuncle, that darkens all.

TO DR. F. B. ON HIS BOOK OF CHESS

Sir, now unravell'd is the Golden Fleece:
Men that could only fool at fox-and-geese
Are new-made politicians by thy book,
And both can judge and conquer with a look.
The hidden fate of princes you unfold,   5
Court, clergy, commons by your law controll'd.
    Strange serious wantoning: all that they
    Bluster'd and clutter'd for, you *play*.

TO THE GENIUS OF MR. JOHN HALL

ON HIS EXACT TRANSLATION OF HIEROCLES HIS COMMENT UPON
THE "GOLDEN VERSES" OF PYTHAGORAS

'TIS not from cheap thanks thinly to repay
Th' immortal grove of thy fair order'd bay
Thou plantedst round my humble fane, that I
Stick on thy hearse this sprig of elegy;
Nor that your soul so fast was link'd in me,   5
That now I 've both, since 't has forsaken thee:
That thus I stand a Swiss before thy gate,
And dare for such another time and fate.
Alas! our faiths made different essays,
Our minds and merits brake two several ways;   10
Justice commands I wake thy learned dust,
And truth, in whom all causes centre must.

    Behold! when but a youth thou fierce didst whip
Upright the crooked age, and gilt Vice strip;
A senator prætextat, that knew'st to sway   15
The fasces, yet under the ferula;
Rank'd with the sage ere blossom did thy chin,
Sleeked without, and hair all o'er within;
Who in the school couldst argue as in schools,
Thy lessons were ev'n academy rules.   20
So that fair Cam saw thee matriculate
At once a tyro and a graduate.

    At nineteen, what essays have we beheld!
That well might have the book of dogmas swell'd;
Tough paradoxes, such as Tully's, thou   25
Didst heat thee with, when snowy was thy brow,
When thy undown'd face mov'd the Nine to shake,
And of the Muses did a decade make.
What shall I say? by what allusion bold?
None but the sun was e'er so young and old.   30
    Young reverend shade, ascend a while! whilst we
Now celebrate this posthume victory,
This victory that doth contract in death
Ev'n all the pow'rs and labours of thy breath:
Like the Judæan hero, in thy fall   35
Thou pull'st the house of Learning on us all,
And as that soldier conquest doubted not,
Who but one splinter had of Castriot,

But would assault ev'n death so strongly charm'd,
And naked oppose rocks, with this bone arm'd;　　40
So we, secure in this fair relic, stand
The slings and darts shot by each profane hand;
These sovereign leaves thou left'st us are become
Cereclothes against all time's infection.

　　Sacred Hierocles! whose heav'nly thought　　45
First acted o'er this comment ere it wrought,
Thou hast so spirited, elixir'd, we
Conceive there is a noble alchemy,
That 's turning of this gold to something more
Precious than gold we never knew before.　　50
Who now shall doubt the metempsychosis
Of the great author, that shall peruse this?
Let others dream thy shadow wandering strays
In th' Elysian mazes, hid with bays;
Or that, snatch'd up in th' upper region,　　55
'Tis kindled there a constellation:
I have inform'd me, and declare with ease,
Thy soul is fled into Hierocles.

ON SANNAZAR'S BEING HONOURED WITH SIX
HUNDRED DUCATS BY THE CLARISSIMI OF
VENICE, FOR COMPOSING AN ELEGIAC HEXASTICH
OF THE CITY

A SATIRE

'Twas a blithe prince exchang'd five hundred crowns
For a fair turnip—dig, dig on, O clowns!—
But how this comes about, Fates, can you tell,
This more than Maid of Meurs, this miracle?
Let me not live, if I think not St. Mark　　5
Has all the ore, as well as beasts, in 's ark!
No wonder 'tis he marries the rich Sea;
But to betroth him to nak'd Poesy,
And with a bankrupt Muse to merchandize—
His treasure's beams, sure, have put out his eyes.　　10
　　His conquest at Lepanto I 'll let pass,
When the sick sea with turbans night-capp'd was;
And now at Candy his full courage shown,
That wan'd to a wan line the half-half-moon;

This is a wreath, this is a victory   15
Cæsar himself would have look'd pale to see,
And, in the height of all his triumphs, feel
Himself but chain'd to such a mighty wheel.
    And now methinks we ape Augustus' state,
So ugly we his high worth imitate,   20
Monkey his godlike glories; so that we
Keep light and form with such deformity
As I have seen an arrogant baboon
With a small piece of glass zany the sun.
    Rome to her bard, who did her battles sing,   25
Indifferent gave to poet and to king;
With the same laurels were his temples fraught,
Who best had written, and who best had fought;
The selfsame fame they equally did feel,
One's style ador'd as much as th' other's steel.   30
A chain or fasces she could then afford
The sons of Phœbus, we, an axe or cord;
Sometimes a coronet was her renown,
And ours the dear prerogative of a crown.
In marble-statu'd walks great Lucan lay,   35
And now we walk our own pale statua.
They the whole year with roses crown'd would dine,
And we in all December know no wine;
Disciplin'd, dieted, sure there hath bin
Odds 'twixt a poet and a Capuchin.   40
    Of princes, women, wine to sing I see
Is no apocrypha; for, to rise high,
Commend this olio of this lord, 'tis fit,
Nay, ten to one but you have part of it;
There is that justice left, since you maintain   45
His table, he should counterfeed your brain.
Then write how well he in his sack hath droll'd,
Straight there 's a bottle to your chamber roll'd;
Or with embroider'd words praise his French suit,
Month hence 'tis yours, with his man's curse to boot;   50
Or but applaud his boss'd legs, two to none
But he most nobly doth give you one;
Or spin an elegy on his false hair,
"'Tis well," he cries, "but living hair is dear";
Yet say that out of order there 's one curl,   55
And all the hopes of your reward you furl.
    Write a deep epic poem, and you may

As soon delight them as the opera,
Where they Diogenes thought in his tub
Never so sour did look, so sweet a club.　　　　60
　　You that do suck for thirst your black quill's blood,
And chaw your labour'd papers for your food,
I will inform you how and what to praise,
Then skin y' in satin as young Loveless plays.
Beware, as you would your fierce guests, your lice,　　65
To strip the cloth of gold from cherish'd Vice:
Rather stand off with awe and reverend fear,
Hang a poetic pendant in her ear.
Court her as her adorers do their glass,
Though that as much of a true substance has,　　　70
Whilst all the gall from your wild ink you drain,
The beauteous sweets of Virtue's cheeks to stain;
And in your livery let her be known
As poor and tattered as in her own.
Nor write, nor speak you more of sacred writ,　　　75
But what shall force up your arrested wit.
Be chaste Religion and her priests your scorn,
Whilst the vain fanes of idiots you adorn.
It is a mortal error, you must know,
Of any to speak good, if he be so,　　　　　80
Rail till your edged breath flay your raw throat,
And burn all marks on all of gen'rous note;
Each verse be an indictment, be not free
Sanctity 'tself from thy scurrility.
Libel your father, and your dam buffoon,　　　85
The noblest matrons of the isle lampoon,
Whilst Aretine and 's bodies you dispute,
And in your sheets your sister prostitute.
　　Yet there belongs a sweetness, softness too,
Which you must pay, but first pray know to who.　　90
There is a creature (if I may so call
That unto which they do all prostrate fall)
Term'd mistress, when they 're angry, but pleas'd high,
It is a princess, saint, divinity.
To this they sacrifice the whole day's light,　　　95
Then lie with their devotion all night:
For this you are to dive to the Abyss,
And rob for pearl the closet of some fish.
Arabia and Sabæa you must strip
Of all their sweets, for to supply her lip;　　　　100

And steal new fire from heav'n to repair
Her unfledg'd scalp with Berenice's hair;
Then seat her in Cassiopeia's Chair,
As now you 're in your coach. Save you, bright sir,
(Oh, spare your thanks) is not this finer far   105
Than walk unhided, when that every stone
Has knock'd acquaintance with your ankle-bone?
When your wing'd papers, like the last dove, ne'er
Return'd to quit you of your hope or fear,
But left you to the mercy of your host,   110
And your day's fare, a fortified toast.

How many battles, sung in epic strain,
Would have procur'd your head thatch from the rain?
Not all the arms of Thebes and Troy would get
One knife but to anatomize your meat;   115
A funeral elegy, with a sad boon,
Might make you (*heil*) sip wine like macaroon;
But if perchance there did a ribband come,
Not the train-band so fierce with all its drum;
Yet with your torch you homeward would retire,   120
And heart'ly wish your bed your fun'ral pyre.

With what a fury have I known you feed
Upon a contract, and the hopes 't might speed!
Not the fair bride, impatient of delay,
Doth wish like you the beauties of that day;   125
Hotter than all the roasted cooks you sat
To dress the fricasse of your alphabet,
Which sometimes would be drawn dough anagram,
Sometimes acrostic parched in the flame;
Then posies stew'd with sippets, mottoes by,   130
Of minced verse a miserable pie.
How many knots slipp'd ere you twist their name,
With th' old device, as both their hearts the same!
Whilst, like to drills, the feast in your false jaw
You would transmit at leisure to your maw;   135
Then after all your fooling, fat, and wine,
Glutton'd at last, return at home to pine.

Tell me, O Sun, since first your beams did play
To night, and did awake the sleeping day;
Since first your steeds of light their race did start,   140
Did you e'er blush as now? O thou that art
The common father to the base pismire,
As well as great Alcides, did the fire

From thine own altar which the gods adore
Kindle the souls of gnats and wasps before?   145
  Who would delight in his chaste eyes to see
Dormice to strike at lights of poesy?
Faction and envy now is downright rage.
Once a five-knotted whip there was, the Stage,
The beadle and the executioner,   150
To whip small errors, and the great ones tear.
Now, as ere Nimrod the first king, he writes
That 's strongest, th' ablest deepest bites.
The Muses weeping fly their Hill, to see
Their noblest sons of peace in mutiny.   155
Could there naught else this civil war complete,
But poets raging with poetic heat,
Tearing themselves and th' endless wreath, as though,
Immortal they, their wrath should be so too?
And doubly fir'd Apollo burns to see   160
In silent Helicon a naumachy.
Parnassus hears these as his first alarms;
Never till now Minerva was in arms.
  O more than conqu'ror of the world, great Rome!
Thy heroes did with gentleness o'ercome   165
Thy foes themselves, but one another first,
Whilst Envy, stripp'd, alone was left, and burst.
The learn'd Decemviri, 'tis true, did strive
But to add flames to keep their fame alive;
Whilst the eternal laurel hung i' th' air;   170
Nor of these ten sons was there found one heir,
Like to the golden tripod it did pass
From this to this, till 't came to him whose 'twas:
Cæsar to Gallus trundled it, and he
To Maro; Maro, Naso, unto thee;   175
Naso to his Tibullus flung the wreath,
He to Catullus; thus did each bequeath
This glorious circle to another round;
At last the temples of their god it bound.
  I might believe, at least, that each might have   180
A quiet fame contented in his grave,
Envy the living, not the dead, doth bite,
For after death all men receive their right.[1]
If it be sacrilege for to profane
Their holy ashes, what is 't then their flame?   185

[1] Ovid, _Elegy_ 15.

He does that wrong unwitting or in ire,
As if one should put out the vestal fire.
   Let earth's four quarters speak, and thou, Sun, bear
Now witness for thy fellow-traveller;
I was alli'd, dear uncle, unto thee   190
In blood, but thou, alas, not unto me:
Your virtues, pow'rs, and mine differ'd at best
As they whose springs you saw, the east and west:
Let me a while be twisted in thy shine,
And pay my due devotions at thy shrine.   195
   Might learned Wenman rise, who went with thee
In thy heav'n's work beside divinity,
I should sit still; or mighty Falkland stand,
To justify with breath his pow'rful hand;
The glory that doth circle your pale urn   200
Might hallow'd still and undefiled burn.
But I forbear; flames that are wildly thrown
At sacred heads curl back upon their own.
Sleep, heav'nly Sandys, whilst what they do or write
Is to give God himself and you your right.   205
   There is not in my mind one sullen fate
Of old, but is concentred in our state.
Vandal o'errunners, Goths in literature,
Ploughmen that would Parnassus new manure,
Ringers of verse that all-in all-in chime,   210
And toll the changes upon every rhyme.
A mercer now by th' yard does measure o'er
An ode which was but by the foot before;
Deals you an ell of epigram, and swears
It is the strongest, and the finest wears.   215
No wonder if a drawer verses rack,
If 'tis not his 't may be the spir't of sack;
Whilst the fair barmaid strokes the Muse's teat,
For milk to make the posset up complete.
   Arise, thou rev'rend shade, great Jonson, rise!   220
Break through thy marble natural disguise!
Behold a mist of insects, whose mere breath
Will melt thy hallow'd leaden house of death.
What was Crispinus that you should defy
The age for him? He durst not look so high   225
As your immortal rod, he still did stand
Honour'd, and held his forehead to thy brand.
These scorpions with which we have to do

Are fiends, not only small but deadly too.
Well mightst thou rive thy quill up to the back,   230
And screw thy lyre's grave chords until they crack.
For though once hell resented music, these
Devils will not, but are in worse disease.
How would thy masc'line spirit, Father Ben,
Sweat to behold basely deposed men   235
Justled from the prerog'tive of their bed,
Whilst wives are per'wigg'd with their husband's head!
Each snatches the male quill from his faint hand,
And must both nobler write and understand,
He to her fury the soft plume doth bow: 240
O pen! ne'er truly justly slit till now!
Now as herself a poem she doth dress,
And curls a line as she would do a tress;
Powders a sonnet as she does her hair,
Then prostitutes them both to public air.   245
Nor is 't enough that they their faces blind
With a false dye, but they must paint their mind;
In metre scold, and in scann'd order brawl:
Yet there 's one Sappho left may save them all.

But now let me recall my passion.   250
O (from a noble father, nobler son!)
You that alone are the Clarissimi,
And the whole gen'rous state of Venice be,
It shall not be recorded Sannazar
Shall boast enthron'd alone this new-made star;   255
You whose correcting sweetness hath forbade
Shame to the good, and glory to the bad,
Whose honour hath ev'n into virtue tam'd
These swarms that now so angerly I nam'd;
Forgive what thus distemper'd I indite,   260
For it is hard a satire not to write.
Yet as a virgin that heats all her blood
At the first motion of bad understood,
Then at mere thought of fair chastity,
Straight cools again the tempests of her sea: 265
   So, when to you I my devotions raise,
   All wrath and storms do end in calms and praise.

TRANSLATIONS

SANNAZAR'S HEXASTICH

In Adriatic waves when Neptune saw
The City stand, and give the seas a law,
"Now i' th' Tarpeian tow'rs Jove rival me,
And Mars his walls impregnable," said he;
"Let seas to Tiber yield, view both their odds,   5
You 'll grant that built by men, but this by gods.'

PENTADIUS: ON VIRGIL

A swain, hind, knight, I fed, till'd, did command
Goats, fields, my foes, with leaves, a spade, my hand.

OF SCÆVOLA

The hand by which no king but sergeant dies
Mutius in fire doth freely sacrifice;
The prince admires the hero, quits his pains,
And, victor from the siege, peace entertains:
Rome 's more oblig'd to flames than arms or pow'r,   5
When one burnt hand shall the whole war devour.

[SENECA:] OF CATO

The world o'ercome, victorious Cæsar, he
That conquer'd all, great Cato, could not thee.

[SENECA:] ANOTHER

One stab could not fierce Cato's life untie;
Only his hand of all that wound did die.
Deeper his fingers tear to make a way
Open, through which his mighty soul might stray.
Fortune made this delay to let us know   5
That Cato's hand more than his sword could do.

[Seneca:] Another

The hand of sacred Cato, bade to tear
His breast, did start, and the made wound forbear;
Then to the gash he said, with angry brow,
"And is there aught great Cato cannot do?"

Another

What doubt'st thou, hand? sad Cato 'tis to kill;
But he 'll be free: sure, hand, thou doubt'st not still!
Cato alive, 'tis just all men be free,
Nor conquers he himself, now if he die.

Pentadius

It is not, y' are deceiv'd, it is not bliss,
What you conceive a happy living is:
To have your hands with rubies bright to glow,
Then on your tortoise bed your body throw,
And sink yourself in down; to drink in gold,   5
And have your looser self in purple roll'd;
With royal fare to make the tables groan,
Or else with what from Libyc fields is mown;
Nor in one vault hoard all your magazine:
But at no coward's fate t' have frighted bin,   10
Nor with the people's breath to be swoll'n great,
Nor at a drawn stiletto basely sweat.
He that dares this, nothing to him 's unfit,
But proud o' th' top of Fortune's wheel may sit.

Catullus: To Marcus T. Cicero

Tully, to thee, Rome's eloquent sole heir,
The best of all that are, shall be, and were,
I the worst poet send my best thanks and pray'r:
Ev'n by how much the worst of poets I,
By so much you the best of patrons be.   5

Catullus: To Juvencius

Juvencius, thy fair sweet eyes
If to my fill that I may kiss,
Three hundred thousand times I 'd kiss,
Nor future age should cloy this bliss;
No, not if thicker than ripe ears   5
The harvest of our kisses bears.

CATULLUS: OF THE BOY AND THE CRIER

WITH a fair boy a crier we behold.
What should we think, but he would not be sold?

PORTIUS LICINIUS

IF you are Phœbus' sister Delia, pray
This my request unto the Sun convey:
O Delphic god, I built thy marble fane,
And sung thy praises with a gentle cane;
Now, if thou art divine Apollo, tell   5
Where he whose purse is empty may go fill.

THE VERSES OF SENECA FROM CLEANTHES

PARENT and Prince of Heav'n, O lead, I pray,
Where'er you please; I follow and obey.
Active I go, sighing if you gainsay,
And suffer bad what to the good was law.
Fates lead the willing, but unwilling draw.   5

QUINTUS CATULUS

As once I bade good morning to the day,
O' th' sudden Roscius breaks in a bright ray:
Gods, with your favour, I 've presum'd to see
A mortal fairer than a deity.

"BLANDITUR PUERO SATYRUS"

WITH looks and hands a satyr courts the boy,
Who draws back his unwilling cheek as coy.
Although of marble hewn, whom move not they?
The boy ev'n seems to weep, the satyr pray.

FLORIDUS: OF A DRUNKARD

PHŒBUS asleep forbade me wine to take:
I yield; and now am only drunk awake.

THE ASS EATING THE ÆNEIDS

A WRETCHED ass the Æneids did destroy:
A horse or ass is still the fate of Troy.

AUSONIUS: EPIGRAM

ON the Sicilian strand a hare well wrought
Before the hounds was by a dogfish caught;
Quoth she, "All rape of sea and earth 's on me,
Perhaps of heav'n, if there a dog-star be."

AUSONIUS: EPIGRAM

THE Cynic's narrow household stuff of crutch,
A stool and dish, was lumber thought too much:
For whilst a hind drinks out on 's palms, o' th' strand
He flings his dish, cries, "I 've one in my hand."

AUSONIUS: EPIGRAM

A TREASURE found one ent'ring at death's gate;
Triumphing, leaves that cord was meant his fate;
But he the gold missing, which he did hide,
The halter, which he found, he knit; so di'd.

A LA CHABOT

OBJECT adorable of charms,
My sighs and tears may testify my harms,
But my respect forbids me to reveal.
Ah what a pain 'tis to conceal,
And how I suffer worse than hell,   5
To love, and not to dare to tell!

THÉOPHILE, BEING DENI'D HIS ADDRESSES TO KING JAMES, TURNED THE AFFRONT TO HIS OWN GLORY, IN THIS EPIGRAM

IF James the king of wit
To see me thought not fit,
    Sure this the cause hath been,
That, ravish'd with my merit,
He thought I was all spirit,   5
    And so not to be seen.

AUSONIUS: EPIGRAM

VAIN painter, why dost strive my face to draw.
With busy hands, a goddess' eyes ne'er saw?
Daughter of air and wind, I do rejoice

In empty shouts, without a mind a voice.
Within your ears, shrill echo, I rebound,   5
And if you 'll paint me like, then paint a sound.

AUSONIUS: EPIGRAM

HER jealous husband an adultress gave
Cold poisons, which too weak she thought for 's grave.
A fatal dose of quicksilver then she
Mingles, to haste his double destiny.
Now whilst within themselves they are at strife,   5
The deadly potion yields to that of life,
And straight from th' hollow stomach both retreat
To th' slipp'ry pipes known to digested meat.
Strange care o' th' gods! the murth'ress doth avail;
So when fates please, ev'n double poisons heal.   10

AUSONIUS: EPIGRAM

BECAUSE with bought books, sir, your study 's fraught,
A learned grammarian you would fain be thought.
Nay, then, buy lutes and strings; so you may play
The merchant now, the fiddler the next day.

AVIENUS: TO HIS FRIENDS

ASK'D in the country what I did, I said:
I view my men and meads, first having pray'd;
Then each of mine hath his just task outlaid.
I read, Apollo court, I rouse my Muse.
Then I anoint me, and stripp'd willing loose   5
Myself on a soft plat; from us'ry blest,
I dine, drink, sing, play, bath, I sup, I rest.

CATULLUS: TO FABULLUS

FABULLUS, I will treat you handsomely
Shortly, if the kind gods will favour thee.
If thou dost bring with thee a del'cate mess,
An olio or so, a pretty lass,
Brisk wine, sharp tales, all sorts of drollery.   5
These if thou bring'st, I say, along with thee,

You shall feed highly, friend; for know, the ebbs
Of my lank purse are full of spiders' webs.
But then again you shall receive clear love,
Or what more grateful or more sweet may prove: 10
For with an ointment I will favour thee,
My Venuses and Cupids gave to me,
Of which once smelt, the gods thou wilt implore,
Fabullus, that they 'd make thee nose all o'er.

MARTIAL: EPIGRAM

WHEN brave chaste Arria to her Pætus gave
The sword from her own breast did bleeding wave,
"If there be faith, this wound smarts not," said she;
"But what you 'll make—ah, that will murder me!"

MARTIAL: EPIGRAM

WHEN Portia her dear lord's sad fate did hear,
And noble grief sought arms were hid from her,
"Know you not yet no hinderance of death is?
Cato, I thought, enough had taught you this."
So said, her thirsty lips drink flaming coals.   5
"Go now, deny me steel, officious fools!"

MARTIAL: EPIGRAM

WHILST in an amber-shade the ant doth feast,
A gummy drop ensnares the small wild beast,
A full reward for all her toils hath she:
'Tis to be thought she would herself so die.

MARTIAL: EPIGRAM

BOTH lurks and shines, hid in an amber tear,
The bee in her own nectar prisoner;
So she, who in her lifetime was contemn'd,
Ev'n in her very funerals is gemm'd.

MARTIAL: EPIGRAM

CINNA seems poor in show,
And he is so.

Out of the [Greek] Anthology

A fool, much bit by fleas, put out the light;
You shall not see me now (quoth he); good night.

Catullus: To Rufus

That no fair woman will, wonder not why,
Clap, Rufus, under thine her tender thigh;
Not a silk gown shall once melt one of them,
Nor the delights of a transparent gem.
A scurvy story kills thee, which doth tell   5
That in thine armpits a fierce goat doth dwell.
Him they all fear full of an ugly stench,
Nor 's 't fit he should lie with a handsome wench.
Wherefore this noses' cursed plague first crush,
Or cease to wonder why they fly you thus.   10

Catullus: Female Inconstancy

My mistress says she 'll marry none but me,
No, not if Jove himself a suitor be.
She says so; but what women say to kind
Lovers we write in rapid streams and wind.

Catullus: To Lesbia

That me alone you lov'd you once did say,
Nor should I to the King of Gods give way.
Then I lov'd thee not as a common dear,
But as a father doth his children cheer.
Now thee I know, more bitterly I smart,   5
Yet thou to me more light and cheaper art.
What pow'r is this, that such a wrong should press
Me to love more, yet wish thee well much less?

Catullus: Of his Love

I hate and love: wouldst thou the reason know?
I know not; but I burn, and feel it so.

Catullus: To Lesbia

By thy fault is my mind brought to that pass
That it its office quite forgotten has:
For beest thou best, I cannot wish thee well,
And beest thou worst, yet must I love thee still.

Catullus: To Quintius

Quintius, if you 'll endear Catullus' eyes,
Or what he dearer than his eyes doth prize,
Ravish not what is dearer than his eyes,
Or what he dearer than his eyes doth prize.

Catullus: Of Quintia and Lesbia

Quintia is handsome, fair, tall, straight, all these
Very particulars I grant with ease:
But she all o'er 's not handsome; here 's her fault:
In all that bulk there 's not one corn of salt;
Whilst Lesbia, fair, and handsome too all o'er,   5
All graces and all wit from all hath bore.

Catullus: Of his Love for Lesbia

No one can boast herself so much belov'd,
Truly, as Lesbia my affections prov'd;
No faith was e'er with such a firm knot bound,
As in my love on my part I have found.

Catullus: To Sylo

Sylo, pray pay me my ten sesterces,
Then rant and roar as much as you shall please;
Or if that money takes [you], pray give o'er
To be a pimp, or else to rant and roar.

VOITURE

Prefixed to John Davies's translation of Voiture's *Letters*, 1657.]

VOITURE! whose gentle paper 's so refin'd,
As he comes out not characters but mind;
Whose Letters so abstract he doth dispense,
That he 's not writer but intelligence,
All air, fire, spirit.   Reader, be blest   5
To be calcin'd thus nobly, and possess'd,
Whilst your first thoughts now break as prim'tive wit,
And what you speak not tastes on 't, but is it.

INDEX OF FIRST LINES

PAGE